a darker
shade of
magic

Also by V.E. SCHWAB and available from TITAN BOOKS

Vicious

V. E. SCHWAB

a darker shade of magic

TITAN BOOKS

A DARKER SHADE OF MAGIC

Print edition ISBN: 9781783295401
E-book edition ISBN: 9781783295418

Published by Titan Books
A division of Titan Publishing Group Ltd
144 Southwark Street, London SE1 0UP

First Titan edition: February 2015
10 9 8 7 6 5

A CIP catalogue record for this title is available from the British Library.

Printed and bound in Great Britain by CPI Group (UK) Ltd, Croydon, CR0 4YY.

What did you think of this book?
We love to hear from our readers. Please email us at readerfeedback@titanmail.com
or write to us at the above address.

To receive advance information, news, competitions, and exclusive offers online,
please sign up for the Titan newsletter on our website:
www.titanbooks.com

For the ones who dream of stranger worlds

Such is the quandary when it comes to magic, that it is not an issue of strength but of balance. For too little power, and we become weak. Too much, and we become something else entirely.

TIEREN SERENSE,
head priest of the London Sanctuary

I
THE
TRAVELER

Kell wore a very peculiar coat.

It had neither one side, which would be conventional, nor two, which would be unexpected, but *several*, which was, of course, impossible.

The first thing he did whenever he stepped out of one London and into another was take off the coat and turn it inside out once or twice (or even three times) until he found the side he needed. Not *all* of them were fashionable, but they each served a purpose. There were ones that blended in and ones that stood out, and one that served no purpose but of which he was just particularly fond.

So when Kell passed through the palace wall and into the anteroom, he took a moment to steady himself—it took its toll, moving between worlds—and then shrugged out of his red, high-collared coat and turned it inside out from right to left so that it became a simple black jacket. Well, a simple black jacket elegantly lined with silver thread and adorned with two gleaming columns of silver buttons. Just because he adopted a more modest palette when he was abroad (wishing neither to offend the local royalty nor to draw attention) didn't mean he had to sacrifice style.

Oh, kings, thought Kell as he fastened the buttons on the

coat. He was starting to think like Rhy.

On the wall behind him, he could just make out the ghosted symbol made by his passage. Like a footprint in sand, already fading.

He'd never bothered to mark the door from *this* side, simply because he never went back this way. Windsor's distance from London was terribly inconvenient considering the fact that, when traveling between worlds, Kell could only move between a place in one and the same *exact* place in another. Which was a problem because there was no Windsor Castle a day's journey from *Red* London. In fact, Kell had just come through the stone wall of a courtyard belonging to a wealthy gentleman in a town called Disan. Disan was, on the whole, a very pleasant place.

Windsor was not.

Impressive, to be sure. But not pleasant.

A marble counter ran against the wall, and on it a basin of water waited for him, as it always did. He rinsed his bloody hand, as well as the silver crown he'd used for passage, then slipped the cord it hung on over his head, and tucked the coin back beneath his collar. In the hall beyond, he could hear the shuffle of feet, the low murmur of servants and guards. He'd chosen the anteroom specifically to avoid them. He knew very well how little the Prince Regent liked him being here, and the last thing Kell wanted was an audience, a cluster of ears and eyes and mouths reporting the details of his visit back to the throne.

Above the counter and the basin hung a mirror in a gilded frame, and Kell checked his reflection quickly—his hair, a reddish brown, swept down across one eye, and he did not fix it, though he did take a moment to smooth the shoulders of his coat—before passing through a set of doors to meet his host.

The room was stiflingly warm—the windows latched despite what looked like a lovely October day—and a fire raged oppressively in the hearth.

George III sat beside it, a robe dwarfing his withered frame

12

and a tea tray untouched before his knees. When Kell came in, the king gripped the edges of his chair.

"Who's there?" he called out without turning. "Robbers? Ghosts?"

"I don't believe ghosts would answer, Your Majesty," said Kell, announcing himself.

The ailing king broke into a rotting grin. "Master Kell," he said. "You've kept me waiting."

"No more than a month," he said, stepping forward.

King George squinted his blind eyes. "It's been longer, I'm sure."

"I promise, it hasn't."

"Maybe not for *you*," said the king. "But time isn't the same for the mad and the blind."

Kell smiled. The king was in good form today. It wasn't always so. He was never sure what state he'd find his majesty in. Perhaps it had seemed like more than a month because the last time Kell visited, the king had been in one of his moods, and Kell had barely been able to calm his fraying nerves long enough to deliver his message.

"Maybe it's the year that has changed," continued the king, "and not the month."

"Ah, but the year is the same."

"And what year is that?"

Kell's brow furrowed. "Eighteen nineteen," he said.

A cloud passed across King George's face, and then he simply shook his head and said, "Time," as if that one word could be to blame for everything. "Sit, sit," he added, gesturing at the room. "There must be another chair here somewhere."

There wasn't. The room was shockingly sparse, and Kell was certain the doors in the hall were locked and unlocked from without, not within.

The king held out a gnarled hand. They'd taken away his rings, to keep him from hurting himself, and his nails were cut to nothing.

"My letter," he said, and for an instant Kell saw a glimmer of George as he once was. Regal.

Kell patted the pockets of his coat and realized he'd forgotten to take the notes out before changing. He shrugged out of the jacket and returned it for a moment to its red self, digging through its folds until he found the envelope. When he pressed it into the king's hand, the latter fondled it and caressed the wax seal—the red throne's emblem, a chalice with a rising sun—then brought the paper to his nose and inhaled.

"Roses," he said wistfully.

He meant the magic. Kell never noticed the faint aromatic scent of Red London clinging to his clothes, but whenever he traveled, someone invariably told him that he smelled like freshly cut flowers. Some said tulips. Others stargazers. Chrysanthemums. Peonies. To the king of England, it was always roses. Kell was glad to know it was a pleasant scent, even if he couldn't smell it. He could smell Grey London (smoke) and White London (blood), but to him, Red London simply smelled like home.

"Open it for me," instructed the king. "But don't mar the seal."

Kell did as he was told, and withdrew the contents. For once, he was grateful the king could no longer see, so he could not know how brief the letter was. Three short lines. A courtesy paid to an ailing figurehead, but nothing more.

"It's from my queen," explained Kell.

The king nodded. "Go on," he commanded, affecting a stately countenance that warred with his fragile form and his faltering voice. "Go on."

Kell swallowed. "'Greetings to his majesty, King George III,'" he read, "'from a neighboring throne.'"

The queen did not refer to it as the *red* throne, or send greetings from *Red* London (even though the city was in fact quite crimson, thanks to the rich, pervasive light of the river), because she did not think of it that way. To her, and to everyone else who inhabited only one London, there was

14

little need to differentiate among them. When the rulers of one conversed with those of another, they simply called them *others*, or *neighbors*, or on occasion (and particularly in regard to White London) less flattering terms.

Only those few who could move among the Londons needed a way to keep them straight. And so Kell—inspired by the lost city known to all as Black London—had given each remaining capital a color.

Grey for the magic-less city.

Red, for the healthy empire.

White, for the starving world.

In truth, the cities themselves bore little resemblance to one another (and the countries around and beyond bore even less). The fact they were all called *London* was its own mystery, though the prevailing theory was that one of the cities had taken the name long ago, before the doors were all sealed and the only things allowed through were letters between kings and queens. As to which city had first laid claim to the name, none could agree.

"'We hope to learn that you are well,'" continued the queen's letter, "'and that the season is as fair in your city as it is in ours.'"

Kell paused. There was nothing more, save a signature. King George wrung his hands.

"Is that all it says?" he asked.

Kell hesitated. "No," he said, folding the letter. "That's only the beginning."

He cleared his throat and began to pace as he pulled his thoughts together and put them into the queen's voice. "Thank you for asking after our family, she says. The King and I are well. Prince Rhy, on the other hand, continues to impress and infuriate in equal measure, but has at least gone the month without breaking his neck or taking an unsuitable bride. Thanks be to Kell alone for keeping him from doing either, or both."

Kell had every intention of letting the queen linger on his own merits, but just then the clock on the wall chimed five, and Kell swore under his breath. He was running late.

"Until my next letter," he finished hurriedly, "stay happy and stay well. With fondness. Her Highness Emira, Queen of Arnes."

Kell waited for the king to say something, but his blind eyes had a steady, faraway look, and Kell feared he had lost him. He set the folded note on the tea tray and was halfway to the wall when the king spoke up.

"I don't have a letter for her," he murmured.

"That's all right," said Kell softly. The king hadn't been able to write one for years. Some months he tried, dragging the quill haphazardly across the parchment, and some months he insisted on having Kell transcribe, but most months he simply told Kell the message and Kell promised to remember.

"You see, I didn't have the time," added the king, trying to salvage a vestige of his dignity. Kell let him have it.

"I understand," he said. "I'll give the royal family your regards."

Kell turned again to go, and again the old king called out to stop him.

"Wait, wait," he said. "Come back."

Kell paused. His eyes went to the clock. Late, and getting later. He pictured the Prince Regent sitting at his table in St. James, gripping his chair and quietly stewing. The thought made Kell smile, so he turned back toward the king as the latter pulled something from his robe with fumbling fingers.

It was a coin.

"It's fading," said the king, cupping the metal in his weathered hands as if it were precious and fragile. "I can't feel the magic anymore. Can't smell it."

"A coin is a coin, Your Majesty."

"Not so and you know it," grumbled the old king. "Turn out your pockets."

Kell sighed. "You'll get me in trouble."

"Come, come," said the king. "Our little secret."

Kell dug his hand into his pocket. The first time he had visited the king of England, he'd given him a coin as proof of who he was and where he came from. The story of the other Londons was entrusted to the crown and handed down heir to heir, but it had been years since a traveler had come. King George had taken one look at the sliver of a boy and squinted and held out his meaty hand, and Kell had set the coin in his palm. It was a simple lin, much like a grey shilling, only marked with a red star instead of a royal face. The king closed his fist over the coin and brought it to his nose, inhaling its scent. And then he'd smiled, and tucked the coin into his coat, and welcomed Kell inside.

From that day on, every time Kell paid his visit, the king would insist the magic had worn off the coin, and make him trade it for another, one new and pocket-warm. Every time Kell would say it was forbidden (it was, expressly), and every time the king would insist that it could be their little secret, and Kell would sigh and fetch a fresh bit of metal from his coat.

Now he plucked the old lin out of the king's palm and replaced it with a new one, folding George's gnarled fingers gently over it.

"Yes, yes," cooed the ailing king to the coin in his palm.

"Take care," said Kell as he turned to go.

"Yes, yes," said the king, his focus fading until he was lost to the world, and to his guest.

Curtains gathered in the corner of the room, and Kell pulled the heavy material aside to reveal a mark on the patterned wallpaper. A simple circle, bisected by a line, drawn in blood a month ago. On another wall in another room in another palace, the same mark stood. They were as handles on opposite sides of the same door.

Kell's blood, when paired with the token, allowed him to move *between* the worlds. He needn't specify a place because wherever he was, that's where he'd be. But to make a door *within* a world, both sides had to be marked by the same exact symbol. Close wasn't close enough. Kell had learned that the hard way.

The symbol on the wall was still clear from his last visit, the edges only slightly smeared, but it didn't matter. It had to be redone.

He rolled up his sleeve and freed the knife he kept strapped to the inside of his forearm. It was a lovely thing, that knife, a work of art, silver from tip to hilt and monogrammed with the letters *K* and *L*.

The only relic from another life.

A life he didn't know. Or at least, didn't remember.

Kell brought the blade to the back of his forearm. He'd already carved one line today, for the door that brought him this far. Now he carved a second. His blood, a rich ruby red, welled up and over, and he returned the knife to its sheath and touched his fingers to the cut and then to the wall, redrawing the circle and the line that ran through it. Kell guided his sleeve down over the wound—he'd treat all the cuts once he was home—and cast a last glance back at the babbling king before pressing his palm flat to the mark on the wall.

It hummed with magic.

"*As Tascen,*" he said. *Transfer.*

The patterned paper rippled and softened and gave way under his touch, and Kell stepped forward and through.

✑ II ✑

Between one stride and the next, dreary Windsor became elegant St. James. The stuffy cell of a room gave way to bright tapestries and polished silver, and the mad king's mumblings were replaced by a heavy quiet and a man sitting at the head of an ornate table, gripping a goblet of wine and looking thoroughly put out.

"You're late," observed the Prince Regent.

"Apologies," said Kell with a too-short bow. "I had an errand."

The Prince Regent set down his cup. "I thought *I* was your errand, Master Kell."

Kell straightened. "My orders, Your Highness, are to see to the *king* first."

"I wish you wouldn't indulge him," said the Prince Regent, whose name was also George (Kell found the Grey London habit of sons taking father's names both redundant and confusing) with a dismissive wave of his hand. "It gets his spirits up."

"Is that a bad thing?" asked Kell.

"For him, yes. He'll be in a frenzy later. Dancing on the tables talking of magic and other Londons. What trick did you do for him this time? Convince him he could fly?"

Kell had only made that mistake once. He learned on his next visit that the King of England had nearly walked out a window. On the third floor. "I assure you I gave no demonstrations."

Prince George pinched the bridge of his nose. "He cannot hold his tongue the way he used to. It's why he is confined to quarters."

"Imprisoned, then?"

Prince George ran his hand along the table's gilded edge. "Windsor is a perfectly respectable place to be kept."

A respectable prison is still a prison, thought Kell, withdrawing a second letter from his coat pocket. "Your correspondence."

The prince forced him to stand there as he read the note (he never commented on the way it smelled of flowers), and then as he withdrew a half-finished reply from the inside pocket of his coat and completed it. He was clearly taking his time in an effort to spite Kell, but Kell didn't mind. He occupied himself by drumming his fingers on the edge of the gilded table. Each time he made it from pinky to forefinger, one of the room's many candles went out.

"Must be a draft," he said absently while the Prince Regent's grip tightened on his quill. By the time he finished the note, he'd broken two and was in a bad mood, while Kell found his own disposition greatly improved.

He held out his hand for the letter, but the Prince Regent did not give it to him. Instead, he pushed up from his table. "I'm stiff from sitting. Walk with me."

Kell wasn't a fan of the idea, but since he couldn't very well leave empty-handed, he was forced to oblige. But not before pocketing the prince's latest unbroken quill from the table.

"Will you go straight back?" asked the prince as he led Kell down a hall to a discreet door half concealed by a curtain.

"Soon," said Kell, trailing by a stride. Two members of the royal guard had joined them in the hall and now slunk behind like shadows. Kell could feel their eyes on him, and he wondered how much they'd been told about their guest. The royals were always expected to know, but the understanding of those in their service was left to their discretion.

"I thought your only business was with me," said the prince.

"I'm a fan of your city," responded Kell lightly. "And what I do is draining. I'll go for a walk and get some air, then make my way back."

The prince's mouth was a thin grim line. "I fear the air is not as replenishing here in the city as in the countryside. What is it you call us . . . *Grey* London? These days that is far too apt a name. Stay for dinner." The prince ended nearly every sentence with a period. Even the questions. Rhy was the same way, and Kell thought it must simply be a by-product of never being told *no*.

"You'll fare better here," pressed the prince. "Let me revive you with wine and company."

It seemed a kind enough offer, but the Prince Regent didn't do things out of kindness.

"I cannot stay," said Kell.

"I insist. The table is set."

And who is coming? wondered Kell. What did the prince want? To put him on display? Kell often suspected that he would like to do as much, if for no other reason than that the younger George found secrets cumbersome, preferring spectacle. But for all his faults, the prince wasn't a fool, and only a fool would give someone like Kell a chance to stand out. Grey London had forgotten magic long ago. Kell wouldn't be the one to remind them of it.

"A lavish kindness, your highness, but I am better left a specter than made a show." Kell tipped his head so that his copper hair tumbled out of his eyes, revealing not only the crisp blue of the left one but the solid black of the right. A black that ran edge to edge, filling white and iris both. There was nothing human about that eye. It was pure magic. The mark of a blood magician. Of an *Antari*.

Kell relished what he saw in the Prince Regent's eyes when

they tried to hold Kell's gaze. Caution, discomfort . . . and fear.

"Do you know why our worlds are kept separate, Your Highness?" He didn't wait for the prince to answer. "It is to keep yours safe. You see, there was a time, ages ago, when they were not so separate. When doors ran between your world and mine, and others, and anyone with a bit of power could pass through. Magic itself could pass through. But the thing about magic," added Kell, "is that it preys on the strong-minded and the weak-willed, and one of the worlds couldn't stop itself. The people fed on the magic and the magic fed on them until it ate their bodies and their minds and then their souls."

"Black London," whispered the Prince Regent.

Kell nodded. He hadn't given that city its color mark. Everyone—at least everyone in Red London and White, and those few in Grey who knew anything at all—knew the legend of Black London. It was a bedtime story. A fairy tale. A *warning*. Of the city—and the world—that wasn't, anymore.

"Do you know what Black London and yours have in common, Your Highness?" The Prince Regent's eyes narrowed, but he didn't interrupt. "Both lack temperance," said Kell. "Both hunger for power. The only reason your London still exists is because it was cut off. It learned to forget. You do not want it to remember." What Kell didn't say was that Black London had a wealth of magic in its veins, and Grey London hardly any; he wanted to make a point. And by the looks of it, he had. This time, when he held out his hand for the letter, the prince didn't refuse, or even resist. Kell tucked the parchment into his pocket along with the stolen quill.

"Thank you, as ever, for your hospitality," he said, offering an exaggerated bow.

The Prince Regent summoned a guard with a single snap of his fingers. "See that Master Kell gets where he is going." And then, without another word, he turned and strode away.

The royal guards left Kell at the edge of the park. St. James Palace loomed behind him. Grey London lay ahead. He took a deep breath and tasted smoke on the air. As eager as he was to get back home, he had some business to attend to, and after dealing with the king's ailments and the prince's attitude, Kell could use a drink. He brushed off his sleeves, straightened his collar, and set out toward the heart of the city.

His feet carried him through St. James Park, down an ambling dirt path that ran beside the river. The sun was setting, and the air was crisp if not clean, a fall breeze fluttering the edges of his black coat. He came upon a wooden footbridge that spanned the stream, and his boots sounded softly as he crossed it. Kell paused at the arc of the bridge, Buckingham House lantern-lit behind him and the Thames ahead. Water sloshed gently under the wooden slats, and he rested his elbows on the rail and stared down at it. When he flexed his fingers absently, the current stopped, the water stilling, smooth as glass, beneath him.

He considered his reflection.

"You're not *that* handsome," Rhy would say whenever he caught Kell gazing into a mirror.

"I can't get enough of myself," Kell would answer, even though he was never looking at himself—not *all* of himself anyway—only his eye. His right one. Even in Red London, where magic flourished, the eye set him apart. Marked him always as *other*.

A tinkling laugh sounded off to Kell's right, followed by a grunt, and a few other, less distinct noises, and the tension went out of his hand, the stream surging back into motion beneath him. He continued on until the park gave way to the streets of London, and then the looming form of Westminster. Kell had a fondness for the abbey, and he nodded to it, as if to an old friend. Despite the city's soot and dirt, its clutter and its poor, it had something Red London lacked: a resistance to change. An appreciation for the enduring, and the effort it took to make something so.

How many years had it taken to construct the abbey? How

many more would it stand? In Red London, tastes turned as often as seasons, and with them, buildings went up and came down and went up again in different forms. Magic made things simple. *Sometimes,* thought Kell, *it made things* too *simple.*

There had been nights back home when he felt like he went to bed in one place and woke up in another.

But here, Westminster Abbey always stood, waiting to greet him.

He made his way past the towering stone structure, through the streets, crowded with carriages, and down a narrow road that hugged the dean's yard, walled by mossy stone. The narrow road grew narrower still before it finally stopped in front of a tavern.

And here Kell stopped, too, and shrugged out of his coat. He turned it once more from right to left, exchanging the black affair with silver buttons for a more modest, street-worn look: a brown high-collared jacket with fraying hems and scuffed elbows. He patted the pockets and, satisfied that he was ready, went inside.

❦ III ❧

The Stone's Throw was an odd little tavern.

Its walls were dingy and its floors were stained, and Kell knew for a fact that its owner, Barron, watered down the drinks, but despite it all, he kept coming back.

It fascinated him, this place, because despite its grungy appearance and grungier customers, the fact was that, by luck or design, the Stone's Throw was *always there*. The name changed, of course, and so did the drinks it served, but at this very spot in Grey, Red, and White London alike, stood a tavern. It wasn't a *source*, per se, not like the Thames, or Stonehenge, or the dozens of lesser-known beacons of magic in the world, but it was *something*. A phenomenon. A fixed point.

And since Kell conducted his affairs in the tavern (whether the sign read the Stone's Throw, or the Setting Sun, or the Scorched Bone), it made Kell himself a kind of fixed point, too.

Few people would appreciate the poetry. Holland might. If Holland appreciated anything.

But poetry aside, the tavern was a perfect place to do business. Grey London's rare believers—those whimsical few who clung to the idea of magic, who caught hold of a whisper or a whiff—gravitated here, drawn by the sense of something else, something more. Kell was drawn to it, too. The difference was that *he* knew what was tugging at them.

Of course, the magically inclined patrons of the Stone's Throw weren't drawn only by the subtle, bone-deep pull of power, or the promise of something different, something more. They were also drawn by *him*. Or at least, the rumor of him. Word of mouth was its own kind of magic, and here, in the Stone's Throw, word of *the magician* passed men's lips as often as the diluted ale.

He studied the amber liquid in his own cup.

"Evening, Kell," said Barron, pausing to top off his drink.

"Evening, Barron," said Kell.

It was as much as they ever said to each other.

The owner of the Stone's Throw was built like a brick wall—if a brick wall decided to grow a beard—tall and wide and impressively steady. No doubt Barron had seen his share of strange, but it never seemed to faze him.

Or if it did, he knew how to keep it to himself.

A clock on the wall behind the counter struck seven, and Kell pulled a trinket from his now-worn brown coat. It was a wooden box, roughly the size of his palm and fastened with a simple metal clasp. When he undid the clasp and slid the lid off with his thumb, the box unfolded into a game board with five grooves, each of which held an element.

In the first groove, a lump of earth.

In the second, a spoon's worth of water.

In the third, in place of air, sat a thimble of loose sand.

In the fourth, a drop of oil, highly flammable.

And in the fifth, final groove, a bit of bone.

Back in Kell's world, the box and its contents served not only as a toy, but as a test, a way for children to discover which elements they were drawn to, and which were drawn to them. Most quickly outgrew the game, moving on to either spellwork or larger, more complicated versions as they honed their skills. Because of both its prevalence and its limitations, the element set could be found in almost every household in

Red London, and most likely in the villages beyond, (though Kell could not be certain). But here, in a city without magic, it was truly rare, and Kell was certain his client would approve. After all, the man was a Collector.

In Grey London, only two kinds of people came to find Kell. Collectors and Enthusiasts.

Collectors were wealthy and bored and usually had no interest in magic itself—they wouldn't know the difference between a healing rune and a binding spell—and Kell enjoyed their patronage immensely.

Enthusiasts were more troublesome. They fancied themselves true magicians, and wanted to purchase trinkets, not for the sake of owning them or for the luxury of putting them on display, but for *use*. Kell did not like Enthusiasts—in part because he found their aspirations wasted, and in part because serving them felt so much closer to treason—which is why, when a young man came to sit beside him, and Kell looked up, expecting his Collector client and finding instead an unknown Enthusiast, his mood soured considerably.

"Seat taken?" asked the Enthusiast, even though he was already sitting.

"Go away," said Kell evenly.

But the Enthusiast did not leave.

Kell knew the man was an Enthusiast—he was gangly and awkward, his jacket a fraction too short for his build, and when he brought his long arms to rest on the counter and the fabric inched up, Kell could make out the end of a tattoo. A poorly drawn power rune meant to bind magic to one's body.

"Is it true?" the Enthusiast persisted. "What they say?"

"Depends on who's talking," said Kell, closing the box, sliding the lid and clasp back into place, "and what's being said." He had done this dance a hundred times. Out of the corner of his blue eye he watched the man's lips choreograph his next move. If he'd been a Collector, Kell might have cut him some slack, but men who waded into waters claiming they could swim should not need a raft.

"That you bring *things*," said the Enthusiast, eyes darting around the tavern. "*Things* from other places."

Kell took a sip of his drink, and the Enthusiast took his silence for assent.

"I suppose I should introduce myself," the man went on. "Edward Archibald Tuttle, the third. But I go by Ned." Kell raised a brow. The young Enthusiast was obviously waiting for him to respond with an introduction of his own, but as the man clearly already had a notion of who he was, Kell bypassed the formalities and said, "What do you want?"

Edward Archibald—*Ned*—twisted in his seat, and leaned in conspiratorially. "I'm looking for a bit of earth."

Kell tipped his glass toward the door. "Check the park."

The young man managed a low, uncomfortable laugh. Kell finished his drink. *A bit of earth.* It seemed like a small request. It wasn't. Most Enthusiasts knew that their own world held little power, but many believed that possessing a piece of *another* world would allow them to tap into its magic.

And there was a time when they would have been right. A time when the doors stood open at the sources, and power flowed between the worlds, and anyone with a bit of magic in their veins and a token from another world could not only tap into that power, but could also move with it, step from one London to another.

But that time was gone.

The doors were gone. Destroyed centuries ago, after Black London fell and took the rest of its world with it, leaving nothing but stories in its wake. Now only the *Antari* possessed enough power to make new doors, and even then only they could pass through them. *Antari* had always been rare, but none knew *how* rare until the doors were closed, and their numbers began to wane. The source of *Antari* power had always been a mystery (it followed no bloodline) but one thing was certain: the longer the worlds were kept apart, the fewer *Antari* emerged.

Now, Kell and Holland seemed to be the last of a rapidly dying breed.

"Well?" pressed Ned. "Will you bring me the earth or not?"

Kell's eyes went to the tattoo on the Enthusiast's wrist. What so many Grey-worlders didn't seem to grasp was that a spell was only as strong as the person casting it. How strong was this one?

A smiled tugged at the corner of Kell's lips as he nudged the game box in the man's direction. "Know what that is?"

Ned lifted the child's game gingerly, as if it might burst into flames at any moment (Kell briefly considered igniting it, but restrained himself). He fiddled with the box until his fingers found the clasp and the board fell open on the counter. The elements glittered in the flickering pub light.

"Tell you what," said Kell. "Choose one element. Move it from its notch—without touching it, of course—and I'll bring you your dirt."

Ned's brow furrowed. He considered the options, then jabbed a finger at the water. "That one."

At least he wasn't fool enough to try for the bone, thought Kell. Air, earth, and water were the easiest to will—even Rhy, who showed no affinity whatsoever, could manage to rouse those. Fire was a bit trickier, but by far, the hardest piece to move was the bit of bone. And for good reason. Those who could move bones could move bodies. It was strong magic, even in Red London.

Kell watched as Ned's hand hovered over the game board. He began to whisper to the water under his breath in a language that might have been Latin, or gibberish, but surely wasn't the King's English. Kell's mouth quirked. Elements had no tongue, or rather, they could be spoken to in any. The words themselves were less important than the focus they brought to the speaker's mind, the connection they helped to form, the *power* they tapped into. In short, the language did not matter, only the *intention* did. The Enthusiast could have spoken to the water in plain English (for all the good it would do him) and yet he muttered on in his invented language. And as he did, he moved his hand clockwise over the small board.

Kell sighed, and propped his elbow on the counter and rested his head on his hand while Ned struggled, face turning red from the effort.

After several long moments, the water gave a single ripple (it could have been caused by Kell yawning or the man gripping the counter) and then went still.

Ned stared down at the board, veins bulging. His hand closed into a fist, and for a moment Kell worried he'd smash the little game, but his knuckles came down beside it, hard.

"Oh well," said Kell.

"It's rigged," growled Ned.

Kell lifted his head from his hand. "Is it?" he asked. He flexed his fingers a fraction, and the clod of earth rose from its groove and drifted casually into his palm. "Are you certain?" he added as a small gust caught up the sand and swirled it into the air, circling his wrist. "Maybe it is"—the water drew itself up into a drop and then turned to ice in his palm—"or maybe it's not. . . ." he added as the oil caught fire in its groove.

"*Maybe . . .*" said Kell as the piece of bone rose into the air, ". . . you simply lack any semblance of power."

Ned gaped at him as the five elements each performed their own small dance around Kell's fingers. He could hear Rhy's chiding: *Show-off.* And then, as casually as he'd willed the pieces up, he let them fall. The earth and ice hit their grooves with a thud and a clink while the sand settled soundlessly in its bowl and the flame dancing on the oil died. Only the bone was left, hovering in the air between them. Kell considered it, all the while feeling the weight of the Enthusiast's hungry gaze.

"How much for it?" he demanded.

"Not for sale," answered Kell, then corrected himself, "Not for you."

Ned shoved up from his stool and turned to go, but Kell wasn't done with him yet.

"If I brought you your dirt," he said, "what would you give me for it?"

He watched the Enthusiast freeze in his steps. "Name your price."

"My price?" Kell didn't smuggle trinkets between worlds for the *money*. Money changed. What would he do with shillings in Red London? And pounds? He'd have better luck burning them than trying to buy anything with them in the White alleys. He supposed he could spend the money here, but what ever would he spend it *on*? No, Kell was playing a different game. "I don't want your money," he said. "I want something that matters. Something you don't want to lose."

Ned nodded hastily. "Fine. Stay here and I'll—"

"Not tonight," said Kell.

"Then when?"

Kell shrugged. "Within the month."

"You expect me to sit here and *wait*?"

"I don't *expect* you to do anything," said Kell with a shrug. It was cruel, he knew, but he wanted to see how far the Enthusiast was willing to go. And if his resolve held firm and he were here next month, decided Kell, he would bring the man his bag of earth. "Run along now."

Ned's mouth opened and closed, and then he huffed, and trudged off, nearly knocking into a small, bespectacled man on his way out.

Kell plucked the bit of bone out of the air and returned it to its box as the bespectacled man approached the now-vacant stool.

"What was that about?" he asked, taking the seat.

"Nothing of bother," said Kell.

"Is that for me?" asked the man, nodding at the game box.

Kell nodded and offered it to the Collector, who lifted it gingerly from his hand. He let the gentleman fiddle with it, then proceeded to show him how it worked. The Collector's eyes widened. "Splendid, splendid."

And then the man dug into his pocket and withdrew a folded kerchief. It made a thud when he set it on the counter. Kell reached out and unwrapped the parcel to find a glimmering silver box with a miniature crank on the side.

A *music* box. Kell smiled to himself.

They had music in Red London, and music boxes, too, but most of theirs played by enchantment, not cog, and Kell was rather taken by the effort that went into the little machines. So much of the Grey world was clunky, but now and then its lack of magic led to ingenuity. Take its music boxes. A complex but elegant design. So many parts, so much work, all to create a little tune.

"Do you need me to explain it to you?" asked the Collector.

Kell shook his head. "No," he said softly. "I have several."

The man's brow knit. "Will it still do?"

Kell nodded and began to fold the kerchief over the trinket to keep it safe.

"Don't you want to hear it?"

Kell did, but not here in the dingy little tavern, where the sound could not be savored. Besides, it was time to go home.

He left the Collector at the counter, tinkering with the child's game—marveling at the way that neither the melted ice nor the sand spilled out of their grooves, no matter how he shook the box—and stepped out into the night. Kell made his way toward the Thames, listening to the sounds of the city around him, the nearby carriages and faraway cries, some in pleasure, some in pain (though they were still nothing compared to the screams that carried through White London). The river soon came into sight, a streak of black in the night as church bells rang out in the distance, eight of them in all.

Time to go.

He reached the brick wall of a shop that faced the water, and stopped in its shadow, pushing up his sleeve. His arm had started to ache from the first two cuts, but he drew out his knife and carved a third, touching his fingers first to the blood and then to the wall.

One of the cords around his throat held a red lin, like the one King George had returned to him that afternoon, and he took hold of the coin and pressed it to the blood on the bricks.

"Well, then," he said. "Let's go home." He often found himself speaking to the magic. Not commanding, simply conversing. Magic was a living thing—that, everyone knew—but to Kell it felt like more, like a friend, like family. It was, after all, a part of him (much more than it was a part of most) and he couldn't help feeling like it knew what he was saying, what he was feeling, not only when he summoned it, but always, in every heartbeat and every breath.

He was, after all, *Antari*.

And *Antari* could speak to blood. To life. To magic itself. The first and final element, the one that lived in all and was of none.

He could feel the magic stir against his palm, the brick wall warming and cooling at the same time with it, and Kell hesitated, waiting to see if it would answer without being asked. But it held, waiting for him to give voice to his command. Elemental magic may speak any tongue, but *Antari* magic—true magic, blood magic—spoke one, and only one. Kell flexed his fingers on the wall.

"*As Travars,*" he said. *Travel.*

This time, the magic listened, and obeyed. The world rippled, and Kell stepped forward through the door and into darkness, shrugging off Grey London like a coat.

II

RED
ROYAL

❡ I ❡

"Sanct!" announced Gen, throwing a card down onto the pile, faceup. On its front, a hooded figure with a bowed head held up a rune like a chalice, and in his chair, Gen grinned triumphantly.

Parrish grimaced and threw his remaining cards facedown on the table. He could accuse Gen of cheating, but there was no point. Parrish himself had been cheating for the better part of an hour and still hadn't won a single hand. He grumbled as he shoved his coins across the narrow table to the other guard's towering pile. Gen gathered up the winnings and began to shuffle the deck. "Shall we go again?" he asked.

"I'll pass," answered Parrish, shoving to his feet. A cloak— heavy panels of red and gold fanning like rays of sun—spilled over his armored shoulders as he stood, the layered metal plates of his chest piece and leg guards clanking as they slid into place.

"*Ir chas era*," said Gen, sliding from Royal into Arnesian. The common tongue.

"I'm not bitter," grumbled Parrish back. "I'm broke."

"Come on," goaded Gen. "Third time's the charm."

"I have to piss," said Parrish, readjusting his short sword.

"Then go piss."

Parrish hesitated, surveying the hall for signs of trouble. The hall was devoid of trouble—or any other forms of activity—but full of pretty things: royal portraits, trophies, tables (like the one they'd been playing on), and, at the hall's end, a pair of ornate doors. Made of cherrywood, the doors were carved with the royal emblem of Arnes, the chalice and rising sun, the grooves filled with melted gold, and above the emblem, the threads of metallic light traced an *R* across the polished wood.

The doors led to Prince Rhy's private chambers, and Gen and Parrish, as part of Prince Rhy's private guard, had been stationed outside of them.

Parrish was fond of the prince. He was spoiled, of course, but so was every royal—or so Parrish assumed, having served only the one—but he was also good-natured and exceedingly lenient when it came to his guard (hell, he'd given Parrish the deck of cards himself, beautiful, gilded-edge things) and sometimes, after a night of drinking, would shed his Royal and its pretentions and converse with them in the common tongue (his Arnesian was flawless). If anything, Rhy seemed to feel guilty for the persistent presence of the guards, as if surely they had something better to do with their time than stand outside his door and be vigilant (and in truth, most nights it was more a matter of discretion than vigilance).

The best nights were the ones when Prince Rhy and Master Kell set out into the city, and he and Gen were allowed to follow at a distance or relieved of their duties entirely and allowed to stay for company rather than protection (everyone knew that Kell could keep the prince safer than any of his guard). But Kell was still away—a fact that had put the ever-restless Rhy in a mood—and so the prince had withdrawn early to his chambers, and Parrish and Gen had taken up their watch, and Gen had robbed Parrish of most of his pocket money.

Parrish scooped up his helmet from the table, and went to relieve himself; the sound of Gen counting his coins followed him out. Parrish took his time, feeling he was owed as much after losing so many lin, and when he finally ambled back to the prince's hall, he was distressed to find it empty. Gen was nowhere to be seen. Parrish frowned; leniency went only so far. Gambling was one thing, but if the prince's chambers were caught unguarded, their captain would be furious.

The cards were still on the table, and Parrish began to clean them up when he heard a male voice in the prince's chamber and stopped. It was not a strange thing to hear, in and of itself—Rhy was prone to entertaining and made little secret of his varied tastes, and it was hardly Parrish's place to question his proclivities.

But Parrish recognized the voice at once; it did not belong to one of Rhy's pursuits. The words were English, but accented, the edges rougher than an Arnesian tongue.

It was a voice like a shadow in the woods at night. Quiet and dark and cold.

And it belonged to Holland. The *Antari* from afar.

Parrish paled a little. He worshipped Master Kell—a fact Gen gave him grief for daily—but Holland terrified him. He didn't know if it was the evenness in the man's tone or his strangely faded appearance or his haunted eyes—one black, of course, the other a milky green. Or perhaps it was the way he seemed to be made more of water and stone than flesh and blood and soul. Whatever it was, the foreign *Antari* had always given Parrish the shivers.

Some of the guards called him Hollow behind his back, but Parrish never dared.

"What?" Gen would tease. "Not like he can hear you through the wall between worlds."

"You don't know," Parrish would whisper back. "Maybe he can."

And now Holland was in Rhy's room. Was he supposed to be there? Who had let him in?

Where was *Gen?* wondered Parrish as he took up his spot in front of the door. He didn't mean to eavesdrop, but there was a narrow gap between the left side of the door and the right, and when he turned his head slightly, the conversation reached him through the crack.

"Pardon my intrusion," came Holland's voice, steady and low.

"It's none at all," answered Rhy casually. "But what business brings you to me instead of to my father?"

"I have been to your father for business already," said Holland. "I come to you for something else."

Parrish's cheeks reddened at the seductiveness in Holland's tone. Perhaps it would be better to abandon his post than listen in, but he held his ground, and heard Rhy slump back onto a cushioned seat.

"And what's that?" asked the prince, mirroring the flirtation.

"It is nearly your birthday, is it not?"

"It is nearly," answered Rhy. "You should attend the celebrations, if your king and queen will spare you."

"They will not, I fear," replied Holland. "But my king and queen are the reason I've come. They've bid me deliver a gift."

Parrish could hear Rhy hesitate. "Holland," he said, the sound of cushions shifting as he sat forward, "you know the laws. I cannot take—"

"I know the laws, young prince," soothed Holland. "As to the gift, I picked it out here, in your own city, on my masters' behalf."

There was a long pause, followed by the sound of Rhy standing. "Very well," he said.

Parrish heard the shuffle of a parcel being passed and opened.

"What is it for?" asked the prince after another stretch of quiet.

Holland made a sound, something between a smile and a laugh, neither of which Parrish had borne witness to before. "For strength," he said.

Rhy began to say something else, but at the same instant, a set of clocks went off through the palace, marking the hour and masking whatever else was said between the *Antari* and the prince. The bells were still echoing through the hall when the door opened and Holland stepped out, his two-toned eyes landing instantly on Parrish.

Holland guided the door shut and considered the royal guard with a resigned sigh. He ran a hand through his charcoal hair.

"Send away one guard," he said, half to himself, "and another takes his place."

Before Parrish could think of a response, the *Antari* dug a coin from his pocket and flicked it into the air toward him.

"I wasn't here," said Holland as the coin rose and fell. And by the time it hit Parrish's palm, he was alone in the hall, staring down at the disk, wondering how it got there, and certain he was forgetting something. He clutched the coin as if he could catch the slipping memory, and hold on.

But it was already gone.

ᯓ II ᯓ

Even at night, the river shone red.

As Kell stepped from the bank of one London onto the bank of another, the black slick of the Thames was replaced by the warm, steady glow of the Isle. It glittered like a jewel, lit from within, a ribbon of constant light unraveling through Red London. A source.

A vein of power. An artery.

Some thought magic came from the mind, others the soul, or the heart, or the will.

But Kell knew it came from the blood.

Blood was magic made manifest. There it thrived. And there it poisoned. Kell had seen what happened when power warred with the body, watched it darken in the veins of corrupted men, turning their blood from crimson to black. If red was the color of magic in balance—of harmony between power and humanity—then black was the color of magic without balance, without order, without restraint.

As an *Antari*, Kell was made of both, balance and chaos; the blood in his veins, like the Isle of Red London, ran a shimmering, healthy crimson, while his right eye was the color of spilled ink, a glistening black.

He wanted to believe that his strength came from his blood

alone, but he could not ignore the signature of dark magic that marred his face. It gazed back at him from every looking glass and every pair of ordinary eyes as they widened in awe or fear. It hummed in his skull whenever he summoned power.

But his blood never darkened. It ran true and red. Just as the Isle did.

Arcing over the river, in a bridge of glass and bronze and stone, stretched the royal palace. It was known as the Soner Rast. The "Beating Heart" of the city. Its curved spires glittered like beads of light.

People flocked to the river palace day and night, some to bring cases to the king or queen, but many simply to be near the Isle that ran beneath. Scholars came to the river's edge to study the source, and magicians came hoping to tap into its strength, while visitors from the Arnesian countryside only wanted to gaze upon the palace and river alike, and to lay flowers—from lilies to shooting stars, azaleas to moondrops— all along the bank.

Kell lingered in the shadow of a shop across the road from the riverside and looked up at the palace, like a sun caught in constant rise over the city, and for a moment, he saw it the way visitors must. With wonder.

And then a flicker of pain ran through his arm, and he came back to his senses. He winced, slipped the traveling coin back around his neck, and made his way toward the Isle, the banks of the river teeming with life.

The Night Market was in full swing.

Vendors in colored tents sold wares by the light of river and lantern and moon, some food and others trinkets, the magic and mundane alike, to locals and to pilgrims. A young woman held a bushel of starflowers for visitors to set on the palace steps. An old man displayed dozens of necklaces on a raised arm, each adorned with a burnished pebble, tokens said to amplify control over an element.

The subtle scent of flowers was lost beneath the aroma of

cooking meat and freshly cut fruit, heavy spices and mulled wine. A man in dark robes offered candied plums beside a woman selling scrying stones. A vendor poured steaming tea into short glass goblets across from another vibrant stall displaying masks and a third offering tiny vials of water drawn from the Isle, the contents still glowing faintly with its light. Every night of the year, the market lived and breathed and thrived. The stalls were always changing, but the energy remained, as much a part of the city as the river it fed on. Kell traced the edge of the bank, weaving through the evening fair, savoring the taste and smell of the air, the sound of laughter and music, the thrum of magic.

A street mage was doing fire tricks for a cluster of children, and when the flames burst up from his cupped hands into the shape of a dragon, a small boy stumbled back in surprise and fell right into Kell's path. He caught the boy's sleeve before he hit the street stones, and hoisted him to his feet.

The boy was halfway through mumbling a *thankyousirsorry* when he looked up and caught sight of Kell's black eye beneath his hair, and the boy's own eyes—both light brown—went wide.

"Mathieu," scolded a woman as the boy tore free of Kell's hand and fled behind her cloak.

"Sorry, sir," she said in Arnesian, shaking her head. "I don't know what's gotten—"

And then she saw Kell's face, and the words died. She had the decency not to turn and flee like her son, but what she did was much worse. The woman bowed in the street so deeply that Kell thought she would fall over.

"*Aven*, Kell," she said, breathless.

His stomach twisted, and he reached for her arm, hoping to make her straighten before anyone else could see the gesture, but he was only halfway to her, and already too late.

"He was . . . not l-looking," she stammered, struggling to find the words in English, the royal tongue. It only made Kell cringe more.

"It was my fault," he said gently in Arnesian, taking her elbow and urging her up out of the bow.

"He just . . . he just . . . he did not recognize you," she said, clearly grateful to be speaking the common tongue. "Dressed as you are."

Kell looked down at himself. He was still wearing the brown and fraying coat from the Stone's Throw, as opposed to his uniform. He hadn't forgotten; he'd simply wanted to enjoy the fair, just for a few minutes, as one of the pilgrims or locals. But the ruse was at an end. He could feel the news ripple through the crowd, the mood shifting like a tide as the patrons of the Night Market realized who was among them.

By the time he let go of the woman's arm, the crowd was parting for him, the laughter and shouting reduced to reverent whispers. Rhy knew how to deal with these moments, how to twist them, how to own them.

Kell wanted only to disappear.

He tried to smile, but knew it must look like a grimace, so he bid the woman and her son good night, and made his way quickly down the river's edge, the murmurings of the vendors and patrons trailing him as he went. He didn't look back, but the voices followed all the way to the flower-strewn steps of the royal palace.

The guards did not move from their posts, acknowledging him with only a slight tilt of their heads as he ascended the stairs. He was grateful that most of them did not bow—only Rhy's guard Parrish seemed unable to resist, but at least he had the decency to be discreet. As Kell climbed the steps, he shrugged off his coat and turned it inside out from right to left. When he slid his arms into the sleeves again, they were no longer tattered and soot-stained. Instead, they were lovely, polished, the same shimmering red as the Isle running beneath the palace.

A red reserved for royalty.

Kell paused at the top step, fastened the gleaming gold buttons, and went in.

❧ III ❧

He found them in the courtyard, taking a late tea under the cloudless night and the fall canopy of trees.

The king and queen were sitting at a table, while Rhy was stretched on a sofa, rambling on again about his birthday and the slew of festivities intended to surround it.

"It's called a birth*day*," chided King Maxim—a towering man with broad shoulders and bright eyes and a black beard—without looking up from a stack of papers he was reading. "Not a birth*days* and certainly not a birth*week*."

"Twenty years!" countered Rhy, waving his empty teacup. "Twenty! A few days of celebration hardly seems excessive." His amber eyes glittered mischievously. "And besides, half of them are for the people, anyway. Who am I to deny them?"

"And the other half?" asked Queen Emira, her long dark hair threaded with gold ribbon and gathered in a heavy braid behind her.

Rhy flashed his winning smile. "You're the one determined to find me a match, Mother."

"Yes," she said, absently straightening the teaware, "but I'd rather not turn the palace into a brothel to do it."

"Not a brothel!" said Rhy, running his fingers through his rich black hair and upsetting the circle of gold that rested there.

"Merely an efficient way of assessing the many necessary attributes of— Ah, Kell! Kell will support my thinking."

"I think it's a horrible idea," said Kell, striding toward them.

"Traitor!" said Rhy with mock affront.

"But," he added, approaching the table, "he'll do it anyway. You might as well throw the party here at the palace, where we can all keep him out of trouble. Or at least minimize it."

Rhy beamed. "Sound logic, sound logic," he said, mimicking his father's deep voice.

The king set aside the paper he was holding and considered Kell. "How was your trip?"

"Longer than I would have liked," said Kell, sorting through his coats and pockets until he found the Prince Regent's letter.

"We were beginning to worry," said Queen Emira.

"The king was not well and the prince was worse," said Kell, offering the note. King Maxim took it and set it aside, unread.

"Sit," urged the queen. "You look pale."

"Are you well?" asked the king.

"Quite, sir," said Kell, sinking gratefully into a chair at the table. "Only tired." The queen reached out and brought her hand to Kell's cheek. Her complexion was darker than his— the royal family bore a rich tan that, when paired with their honey eyes and black hair, made them look like polished wood. With fair skin and reddish hair, Kell felt perpetually out of place. The queen brushed a handful of copper strands off his forehead. She always went looking for the truth in his right eye, as if it were a scrying board, something to be gazed into, seen past. But what she saw, she never shared. Kell took her hand and kissed it. "I'm fine, Your Majesty." She gave him a weary look, and he corrected himself. "Mother."

A servant appeared bearing tea, sweet and laced with mint, and Kell took a long drink and let his family talk, his mind wandering in the comfort of their noise.

When he could barely keep his eyes open, he excused himself. Rhy pushed up from the sofa with him. Kell wasn't surprised. He had felt the prince's gaze on him since he'd first taken his seat. Now, as the two bid their parents good night, Rhy trailed Kell into the hall, fiddling with the circle of gold nested in his black curls.

"What did I miss?" asked Kell.

"Not much," said Rhy. "Holland paid a visit. He only just left."

Kell frowned. Red London and White kept in much closer contact than Red and Grey, but their communication still held a kind of routine. Holland was off schedule by nearly a week.

"What have you come back with tonight?" asked Rhy.

"A headache," said Kell, rubbing his eyes.

"You know what I mean," countered the prince. "What did you bring through that door?"

"Nothing but a few lins." Kell spread his arms wide. "Search me if you like," he added with a smirk. Rhy had never been able to figure out Kell's coat and its many sides, and Kell was already turning back down the hall, considering the matter done, when Rhy surprised him by reaching not for his pockets but for his shoulders, and pushing him back against the wall. Hard. A nearby painting of the king and queen shuddered, but did not fall. The guards dotting the hall looked up but did not move from their posts.

Kell was a year older than Rhy but built like an afternoon shadow, tall and slim, while Rhy was built like a statue, and nearly as strong.

"Do not lie," warned Rhy. "Not to me."

Kell's mouth became a hard line. Rhy had caught him, two years before. Not caught in the *act*, of course, but snagged him in another, more devious way. Trust. The two had been drinking on one of the palace's many balconies one summer night, the glow of the Isle beneath them and the stretch of sky above, and the truth had stumbled out. Kell had told his brother about the deals he struck in Grey London, and in White, and even on occasion in Red, about the various things he'd smuggled, and Rhy had stared at him, and listened, and when he spoke, it wasn't to lecture Kell on all the ways it was wrong, or illegal. It was to ask *why*.

"I don't know," said Kell, and it had been the truth.

Rhy had sat up, eyes bleary from drink. "Have we not provided?" he'd asked, visibly upset. "Is there anything you want for?"

"No," Kell had answered, and that had been a truth and a lie at the same time.

"Are you not loved?" whispered Rhy. "Are you not welcomed as family?"

"But I'm *not* family, Rhy," Kell had said. "I'm not truly a Maresh, for all that the king and queen have offered me that name. I feel more like a possession than a prince."

At that, Rhy had punched him in the face.

For a week after, Kell had two black eyes instead of one, and he'd never spoken like that again, but the damage was done. He'd hoped Rhy would prove too drunk to remember the conversation, but he'd remembered everything. He hadn't told the king or queen, and Kell supposed he owed Rhy that, but now, every time he traveled, he had to endure Rhy's questioning and with it, the reminder that what he was doing was foolish and wrong.

Rhy let go of Kell's shoulders. "Why do you insist on keeping up these pursuits?"

"They amuse me," said Kell, brushing himself off.

Rhy shook his head. "Look, I've turned a blind eye to your childish rebellion for quite a while now, but those doors were shut for a reason," he warned. "Transference is *treason*."

"They're only trinkets," said Kell, continuing down the hall. "There's no real danger in it."

"There's plenty," said Rhy, matching his stride. "Like the danger that awaits you if our parents ever learn—"

"Would you tell them?" asked Kell.

Rhy sighed. Kell watched him try to answer several ways

49

before he finally said, "There is nothing I would not give you."

Kell's chest ached. "I know."

"You are my brother. My closest friend."

"I know."

"Then put an end to this foolishness, before I do."

Kell managed a small, tired smile. "Careful, Rhy," he said. "You're beginning to sound like a king."

Rhy's mouth quirked. "One day I will be. And I need you there beside me."

Kell smiled back. "Believe me. There's no place I'd rather be." It was the truth.

Rhy patted his shoulder and went to bed. Kell shoved his hands into his pockets and watched him go. The people of London—and of the country beyond—loved their prince. And why shouldn't they? He was young and handsome and kind. Perhaps he played the part of rake too often and too well, but behind the charismatic smile and the flirtatious air was a sharp mind and a good intent, the desire to make everyone around him happy. He had little gift for magic—and even less focus for it—but what he lacked in power he more than made up for in charm. Besides, if Kell had learned anything from his trips to White London, it was that magic made rulers worse, not better.

He continued down the hall to his own rooms, where a dark set of oak doors led onto a sprawling chamber. The Isle's red glow poured through the open doors of a private balcony, tapestry billowed and dipped in fabric clouds from the high ceiling, and a luxurious canopied bed, filled with feather and lined with silk, stood waiting. Beckoning. It took all of Kell's will not to collapse into it. Instead, he crossed through the chamber and into a second smaller room lined with books—a variety of tomes on magic, including what little he could find on *Antari* and their blood commands, the majority destroyed out of fear in the Black London purge—and closed the door behind him. He snapped his fingers absently and a candle perching on the edge of a shelf sparked to life. In its light he could make out a series of marks on the back of the door. An inverted triangle, a set of lines, a circle—simple marks, easy enough to re-create, but specific enough to differentiate. Doors to different places in Red London. His eyes went to the one in the middle. It was made up of two crossed lines. X *marks the spot*, he thought to himself, pressing his fingers to the most recent cut on his arm—the blood still wet—then tracing the mark.

"*As Tascen*," he said tiredly.

The wall gave way beneath his touch, and his private library became a cramped little room, the lush quiet of his royal chambers replaced by the din of the tavern below and the city beyond, much nearer than it had been a mere moment before.

Is Kir Ayes—the Ruby Fields—was the name that swung above the tavern's door. The place was run by an old woman named Fauna; she had the body of a gran, the mouth of a sailor, and the temper of a drunk. Kell had cut a deal with her when he was young (she was still old then, always old), and the room at the top of the stairs became his.

The room itself was rough and worn and several strides too small, but it belonged entirely to him. Spellwork—and not strictly legal at that—marked the window and the door, so that no one else could find the room, or perceive that it was there. At first glance, the chamber looked fairly empty, but a closer inspection would reveal that the space under the cot and the drawers in the dresser were filled with boxes and in those boxes were treasures from every London.

Kell supposed that *he* was a Collector, too.

The only items on display were a book of poems, a glass ball filled with black sand, and a set of maps. The poems were by a man named Blake, and had been given to Kell by a Collector in Grey London the year before, the spine already worn to nothing. The glass ball was a trinket from White London, said to show one's dreams in the sands, but Kell had yet to try it.

The maps were a reminder.

The three canvases were tacked side by side, the sole decoration on the walls. From a distance, they could have passed for the *same* map—the same outline of the same island country—but up close, only the word *London* could be found on all three. Grey London. Red London. White London. The map on the left was of Great Britain, from the English Channel up through the tips of Scotland, every facet rendered in detail. By contrast, the map on the right held almost none. Makt, the country called itself, the capital city held by the ruthless Dane twins, but the territory beyond was in constant flux. The map in the middle Kell knew best, for it was home. Arnes. The country's name was written in elegant script down the length of the island, though in truth, the land on which London stood was only the tip of the royal empire.

Three very different Londons, in three very different countries, and Kell was one of the only living souls to have seen them all. The great irony, he supposed, was that he had never seen the worlds *beyond* the cities. Bound to the service of his king and crown, and constantly kept within reach, he had never been more than a day's journey from one London or another.

Fatigue ate at Kell's body as he stretched and shrugged off his coat. He dug through the pockets until he found the Collector's parcel, which he set carefully on the bed, gingerly undoing the wrapping to reveal the tiny silver music box inside. The room's lanterns grew brighter as he held up the trinket to the light, admiring it. The ache in his arm drew him back, and he set the music box aside and turned his attention to the dresser.

A basin of water and a set of jars waited there, and Kell rolled up the sleeve of his black tunic and set to work on his forearm. He moved with expert hands, and in minutes he'd rinsed the skin and applied a salve. There was a blood command for healing—*As Hasari*—but it wasn't meant for *Antari* to use on themselves, especially not for minor wounds, as it took more energy than it afforded health. As it was, the cuts on his arm were already beginning to mend. *Antari* healed quickly, thanks to the amount of magic in their veins, and by morning the shallow marks would be gone, the skin smooth. He was about to pull down his sleeve when the small shiny scar captured his attention. It always did. Just below the crook of his elbow, the lines were so blurred that the symbol was almost unreadable.

Almost.

Kell had lived in the palace since he was five. He first noticed the mark when he was twelve. He had spent weeks searching for the rune in the palace libraries. *Memory.*

He ran his thumb over the scar. Contrary to its name, the symbol wasn't meant to help one remember. It was meant to make one forget.

Forget a moment. A day. A life. But magic that bound a person's body or mind was not only forbidden—it was a capital offense. Those accused and convicted were stripped of their power, a fate some found worse than death in a world ruled by magic. And yet, Kell bore the mark of such a spell. Worse, he suspected that the king and queen themselves had sanctioned it.

K.L.

The initials on his knife. There were so many things he didn't understand—would never understand—about the weapon, its monogram, and the life that went with it. (Were the letters English? Or Arnesian? The letters could be found in both alphabets. What did the *L* stand for? Or even the *K*, for that matter? He knew nothing of the letters that had formed his name—*K.L.* had become *Kay-Ell* and *Kay-Ell* had become *Kell.*) He was only a child when he was brought to the palace. Had the knife always been his? Or had it been his father's? A token, something to take with him, something to help him remember who he'd been? Who *had* he been? The absence of memory ate at him. He often caught himself staring at the center map on the wall, wondering where he'd come from. *Who* he'd come from.

Whoever they were, they hadn't been *Antari*. Magic might live in the blood, but not in the bloodline. It wasn't passed from parent to child. It chose its own way. Chose its shape. The strong sometimes gave birth to the weak, or the other way around. Fire wielders were often born from water mages, earth movers from healers. Power could not be cultivated like a crop, distilled through generations. If it could, *Antari* would be sewn and reaped. They were ideal vessels, capable of controlling any element, of drawing any spell, of using their own blood to command the world around them. They were tools, and in the wrong hands, weapons. Perhaps the lack of inheritance was nature's way of balancing the scales, of maintaining order.

In truth, none knew what led to the birth of an *Antari*. Some believed that it was random, a lucky throw of dice. Others claimed that *Antari* were divine, destined for greatness. Some scholars, like Tieren, believed that *Antari* were the result of transference between the worlds, magic of different kinds intertwining, and that that was why they were dying out. But no matter the theory on how they came to be, most believed that *Antari* were sacred. Chosen by magic or blessed by it, perhaps. But certainly *marked* by it.

Kell brought his fingers absently to his right eye.

Whatever one chose to believe, the fact remained that *Antari* had grown even more rare, and therefore more precious. Their talent had always made them something to be coveted, but now their scarcity made them something to be gathered and guarded and kept. Possessed. And whether or not Rhy wanted to admit it, Kell belonged to the royal collection.

He took up the silver music box, winding the tiny metal crank.

A valuable trinket, he thought, *but a trinket all the same.* The song started, tickling his palm like a bird, but he didn't set down the box. Instead, he held it tight, the notes whispering out as he fell back onto the stiff cot and considered the small beautiful contraption.

How had he ended up on this shelf? What had happened when his eye turned black? Was he born that way and hidden, or did the mark of magic manifest? Five years. Five years he'd been someone else's son. Had they been sad to let him go? Or had they gratefully offered him up to the crown?

The king and queen refused to tell him of his past, and he'd learned to stop voicing his questions, but fatigue wore away his walls, and let them through.

What life had he forgotten?

Kell's hand fell away from his face as he chided himself. How much could a child of five really have to remember? Whoever he'd been before he was brought to the palace, that person didn't matter anymore.

That person didn't exist.

The music box's song faltered and came to a stop, and Kell rewound it again, and closed his eyes, letting the Grey London melody and the Red London air drag him down to sleep.

III

GREY
THIEF

❦ I ❧

Lila Bard lived by a simple rule: if a thing was worth having, it was worth taking.

She held the silver pocket watch up to the faint glow of the streetlamp, admiring the metal's polished shine, wondering what the engraved initials—*L.L.E.*—on the back might stand for. She'd nicked the watch off a gentleman, a clumsy collision on a too-crowded curb that had led to a swift apology, a hand on the shoulder to distract from a hand on the coat. Lila's fingers weren't just fast; they were light. A tip of the top hat and a pleasant good night, and she was the proud new owner of a timepiece, and he was on his way and none the wiser.

She didn't care about the object itself, but she cared a great deal for what it bought her: freedom. A poor excuse for it, to be sure, but better than a prison or a poorhouse. She ran a gloved thumb over the crystal watch face.

"Do you have the time?" asked a man at her shoulder.

Lila's eyes flicked up. It was a constable.

Her hand went to the brim of her top hat—stolen from a dozing chauffeur the week before—and she hoped the gesture passed for a greeting and not a nervous slip, an attempt to hide her face.

"Half past nine," she murmured deeply, tucking the watch

into the vest pocket under her cloak, careful not to let the constable catch sight of the various weapons glittering beneath it. Lila was tall and thin, with a boyish frame that helped her pass for a young man, but only from a distance. Too close an inspection, and the illusion would crumble.

Lila knew she should turn and go while she could, but when the constable searched for something to light his pipe and came up empty, she found herself fetching up a sliver of wood from the street. She put one boot up on the base of the lamppost and stepped lithely up to light the stick in the flame. Lantern light glanced off her jawline, lips, cheekbones, the edges of her face exposed beneath the top hat. A delicious thrill ran through her chest, spurned on by the closeness of danger, and Lila wondered, not for the first time, if something was wrong with her. Barron used to say so, but Barron was a bore.

Looking for trouble, he'd say. *You're gonna look till you find it.*

Trouble is the looker, she'd answer. *It keeps looking till it finds you. Might as well find it first.*

Why do you want to die?

I don't, she'd say. *I just want to live.*

She stepped down from the lamppost, her face plunging back into her hat's shadow as she handed the constable the burning sliver of wood. He offered a muttered thanks and lit the pipe, gave a few puffs, and seemed about to go, but then he paused. Lila's heart gave a nervous flutter as he considered her again, this time more carefully. "You ought to be mindful, sir," he said at last. "Out alone at night. Likely to get your pocket picked."

"Robbers?" asked Lila, struggling to keep her voice low. "Surely not in Eaton."

"Aye." The constable nodded and pulled a folded sheet of paper from his coat. Lila reached out and took it, even though she knew at first glance what it was. A WANTED poster. She stared down at a sketch that was little more than a shadowy outline wearing a mask—a haphazard swatch of fabric over the eyes—

and a broad brim hat. "Been picking pockets, even robbed a few gentlemen and a lady outright. Expect that mess, of course, but not 'round here. A right audacious crook, this one."

Lila fought back a smile. It was true. Nicking spare change in South Bank was one thing, stealing silver and gold from the carriage-bound in Mayfair quite another, but thieves were fools to stay in slums. The poor kept up their guards. The rich strutted around, assuming they'd be safe, so long as they stayed in the good parts of town. But Lila knew there were no good parts. Only smart parts and stupid parts, and she was quick enough to know which one to play.

She handed back the paper and tipped the stolen top hat to the constable. "I'll mind my pockets, then."

"Do," urged the constable. "Not like it used to be. Nothing is . . ." He ambled away, sucking on his pipe and muttering about the way the world was falling apart or some such—Lila couldn't hear the rest over the thudding pulse in her ears.

The moment he was out of sight, Lila sighed and slumped back against the lamppost, dizzy with relief. She dragged the top hat from her head and considered the mask and the broad brim cap stuffed inside. She smiled to herself. And then she put the hat back on, pushed off the post, and made her way to the docks, whistling as she walked.

II

The *Sea King* wasn't nearly as impressive as the name suggested.

The ship leaned heavily against the dock, its paint stripped by salt, its wooden hull half rotted in some places, and fully rotted in others. The whole thing seemed to be sinking very, very slowly into the Thames.

The only thing keeping the boat up appeared to be the dock itself, the state of which wasn't much better, and Lila wondered if one day the side of the ship and the boards of the dock would simply rot together or crumble away into the murky bay.

Powell claimed that the *Sea King* was as sturdy as ever. *Still fit for the high seas,* he swore. Lila thought it was hardly fit for the sway of the London port's swells.

She put a boot up on the ramp, and the boards groaned underfoot, the sound rippling back until it seemed like the whole boat was protesting her arrival. A protest she ignored as she climbed aboard, loosening the cloak's knot at her throat.

Lila's body ached for sleep, but she carried out her nightly ritual, crossing the dock to the ship's bow and curling her fingers around the wheel. The cold wood against her palms, the gentle roll of the deck beneath her feet, it all felt *right*. Lila

Bard knew in her bones that she was meant to be a pirate. All she needed was a working ship. And once she had one . . . A breeze caught up her coat, and for a moment she saw herself far from the London port, far from any land, plowing forward across the high seas. She closed her eyes and tried to imagine the feel of the sea breeze rushing through her threadbare sleeves. The beat of the ocean against the ship's sides. The thrill of freedom—true freedom—and adventure. She tipped her chin up as an imaginary spray of salty water tickled her chin. She drew a deep breath and smiled at the taste of the sea air. By the time she opened her eyes, she was surprised to find the *Sea King* just as it had been. Docked and dead.

Lila pushed off the rail and made her way across the deck, and for the first time all night, as her boots echoed on the wood, she felt something like safe. She knew it *wasn't* safe, knew nowhere in the city was, not a plush carriage in Mayfair and certainly not a half-rotten ship on the dodgy end of the docks, but it felt a little something like it. Familiar . . . was that it? Or maybe simply hidden. That was as close to safe as it got. No eyes watched her cross the deck. None saw her descend the steep set of steps that ran into the ship's bones and bowels. None followed her through the dank little hall, or into the cabin at the end.

The knot at her throat finally came loose, and Lila pulled the cloak from her shoulders and tossed it onto a cot that hugged one of the cabin walls. It fell fluttering to the bed, soon followed by the top hat, which spilled its disguise like jewels onto the dark fabric. A small coal stove sat in the corner, the embers barely enough to warm the room. Lila stirred them up and used the stick to light a couple of tallow candles scattered around the cabin. She then tugged off her gloves and lobbed them onto the cot with the rest. Finally, she slid off her belt, freeing holster and dagger both from the leather strap. They weren't her only weapons, of course, but they were the only ones she bothered to take off. The knife was nothing special, just wickedly sharp—she tossed it onto the bed with the rest of the discarded things—but the pistol was a gem, a flintlock revolver that had fallen out of a wealthy dead man's hand and into hers the year before. Caster—for all good weapons deserved a name—was a beauty of a gun, and she slipped him gently, almost reverently, into the drawer of her desk.

The thrill of the night had gone cold with the walk to the docks, excitement burned to ash, and Lila found herself slouching into a chair. It protested as much as everything else on the ship, groaning roundly as she kicked her boots up onto the desk, the worn wooden surface of which was piled with maps, most rolled, but one spread and pinned in place by stones or stolen trinkets. It was her favorite one, that map, because none of the places on it were labeled. Surely, someone knew what kind of map it was, and where it led, but Lila didn't. To her, it was a map to anywhere.

A large slab of mirror sat propped on the desk, leaning back against the hull wall, its edges fogged and silvering. Lila found her gaze in the glass and cringed a little. She ran her fingers through her hair. It was ragged and dark and scraped against her jaw.

Lila was nineteen.

Nineteen, and every one of the years felt carved into her. She poked at the skin under her eyes, tugged at her cheeks, ran a finger along her lips. It had been a long time since anyone had called her pretty.

Not that Lila wanted to be pretty. Pretty wouldn't serve her well. And lord knew she didn't envy the *ladies* with their cinched corsets and abundant skirts, their falsetto laughs and the ridiculous way they used them. The way they swooned and leaned on men, feigning weakness to savor their strength.

Why anyone would ever *pretend* to be weak was beyond her.

Lila tried to picture herself as one of the ladies she'd stolen from that night—so easy to get tangled up in all that fabric, so easy to stumble and be caught—and smiled. How many ladies had flirted with *her*? Swooned and leaned and pretended to marvel at *her* strength?

She felt the weight of the night's take in her pocket.

Enough.

It served them right, for playing weak. Maybe they wouldn't be so quick to swoon at every top hat and take hold of every offered hand.

Lila tipped her head back against the back of the chair. She could hear Powell in his quarters, acting out his own nightly routine of drinking and cursing and muttering stories to the bowed walls of the rotting ship. Stories of lands he'd never visited. Maidens he'd never wooed. Treasures he'd never plundered. He was a liar and a drunkard and a fool—she'd seen him be all three on any given night in the Barren Tide—but he had an extra cabin and she had need of one, and they had reached an agreement. She lost a cut of every night's take to his hospitality, and in return he forgot that he was renting the room to a wanted criminal, let alone a girl.

Powell rambled on within his room. He carried on for hours, but Lila was so used to the noise that soon it faded in with the other groans and moans and murmurings of the old *Sea King*.

Her head had just started to slump when someone knocked on her door three times. Well, someone knocked twice, but was clearly too drunk to finish the third, dragging their hand down the wood. Lila's boots slid from the desk and landed heavily on the floor.

"What is it?" she called, getting to her feet as the door swung open. Powell stood there, swaying from drink and the gentle rock of the boat.

"Liiiila," he sang her name. "Liiiiilaaaaaa."

"What?"

A bottle sloshed in one hand. He held out the other, palm up. "My cut."

Lila shoved her hand into her pocket and came out with a handful of coins. Most of them were faded, but a few bits of silver glinted in the mix, and she picked them out and dropped them into Powell's palm. He closed his fist and jingled the money.

"It's not enough," he said as she returned the coppers to her pocket. She felt the silver watch in her vest, warm against her ribs, but didn't pull it out. She wasn't sure why. Maybe she'd taken a liking to the timepiece after all. Or maybe she was afraid that if she started offering such pricey goods, Powell would come to expect them.

"Slow night," she said, crossing her arms. "I'll make up the difference tomorrow."

"You're trouble," slurred Powell.

"Indeed," she said, flashing a grin. Her tone was sweet but her teeth were sharp.

"Maybe more trouble than you're worth," he slurred. "Certainly more than you're worth tonight."

"I'll get you the rest tomorrow," she said, hands slipping back to her side. "You're drunk. Go to bed." She started to turn away, but Powell caught her elbow.

"I'll take it tonight," he said with a sneer.

"I said I don't—"

The bottle tumbled from Powell's other hand as he forced her back into the desk, pinning her with his hips.

"Doesn't have to be coin," he whispered, dragging his eyes down her shirtfront. "Must be a girl's body under there somewhere." His hands began to roam, and Lila drove her knee into his stomach and sent him staggering backward.

"Shouldn't a done that," growled Powell, face red. His fingers fumbled with his buckle. Lila didn't wait. She went for the pistol in the drawer, but Powell's head snapped up and he lunged and caught her wrist, dragging her toward him. He threw her bodily back onto the cot, and she landed on the hat and the gloves and the cloak and the discarded knife.

Lila scrambled for the dagger as Powell charged forward. He grabbed her knee as her fingers wrapped around the leather sheath. He jerked her toward him as she drew the blade free, and when he caught her other hand with his, she used his grip to pull herself to her feet and drive the knife into his gut.

And just like that, all the struggle went out of the cramped little room.

Powell stared down at the blade jutting out of his front, eyes wide with surprise, and for a moment it looked like he might carry on despite it, but Lila knew how to use a knife, knew where to cut to hurt and where to cut to kill.

Powell's grip on her tightened. And then it went slack. He swayed and frowned, and then his knees buckled.

"Shouldn't a done that," she echoed, pulling the knife free before he could collapse forward onto it.

Powell's body hit the floor and stayed there. Lila stared down at it a moment, marveling at the stillness, the quiet broken only by her pulse and the hush of the water against the hull of the ship. She toed the man with her boot.

Dead.

Dead . . . and making a mess.

Blood was spreading across the boards, filling in the cracks and dripping through to lower parts of the ship. Lila needed to do something. *Now.*

She crouched, wiped her blade on Powell's shirt, and recovered the silver from his pocket. And then she stepped over his body, retrieved the revolver from its drawer, and got dressed. When the belt was back around her waist and the cloak around her shoulders, she took up the bottle of whiskey from the floor. It hadn't broken when it fell. Lila pulled the cork free with her teeth and emptied the contents onto Powell, even though there was probably enough alcohol in his blood to burn without it.

She took up a candle and was about to touch it to the floor when she remembered the map. The one to anywhere. She freed it from the desk and tucked it under her cloak, and then, with a last look around the room, she set fire to the dead man and the boat.

Lila stood on the dock and watched the *Sea King* burn.

She stared up at it, face warmed by the fire that danced on her chin and cheeks the way the lamp light had before the constable. *It's a shame,* she thought. She'd rather liked the rotting ship. But it wasn't hers. No, hers would be much better.

The *Sea King* groaned as the flames gnawed its skin and then its bones, and Lila watched the dead ship begin to sink. She stayed until she could hear the far-off cries and the sound of boots, too late, of course, but coming all the same.

And then she sighed and went in search of another place to spend the night.

∽ III ∾

Barron was standing on the steps of the Stone's Throw, staring absently toward the docks when Lila strolled up, the top hat and the map both tucked under her arm. When she followed his gaze, she could see the dregs of the fire over the building tops, the smoke ghosted against the cloudy night.

Barron pretended not to notice her at first. She couldn't blame him. The last time he'd seen her, almost a year before, he'd kicked her out for thieving—not from him, of course, from a patron—and she'd stormed off, damning him and his little tavern inn alike.

"Where you going, then?" he'd rumbled after her like thunder. It was as close as he'd ever come to shouting.

"To find an adventure," she'd called without looking back.

Now she scuffed her boots along the street stones. He sucked on a cigar. "Back so soon?" he said without looking up. She climbed the steps, and slouched against the tavern door. "You find adventure already? Or it find you?"

Lila didn't answer. She could hear the clink of cups inside and the chatter of drunk men getting drunker. She hated that noise, hated most taverns altogether, but not the Stone's Throw. The others all repulsed her, *repelled* her, but this place dragged at her like gravity, a low and constant pull. Even when she didn't mean to, she always seemed to end up here. How many times in the last year had her feet carried her back to these steps? How many times had she almost gone inside? Not that Barron needed to know about that. She watched him tip his head back and stare up at the sky as if he could see something there besides clouds.

"What happened to the *Sea King*?" he asked.

"It burned down." A defiant flutter of pride filled her chest when his eyes widened a fraction in surprise. She liked surprising Barron. It wasn't an easy thing to do.

"Did it now?" he asked lightly.

"You know how it is," said Lila with a shrug. "Old wood goes up so easy."

Barron gave her a long look, then exhaled a smoke-filled breath. "Powell should've been more careful with his brig."

"Yeah," said Lila. She fiddled with the brim of the top hat.

"You smell like smoke."

"I need to rent a room." The words stuck in her throat.

"Funny," said Barron, taking another puff. "I distinctly remember you suggesting that I take my tavern and all its many—albeit modest—rooms and shove each and every one of them up my—"

"Things change," she said as she plucked the cigar from his mouth and took a drag.

He studied her in the lamplight. "You okay?"

Lila studied the smoke as it poured through her lips. "I'm always okay."

She handed back the cigar and dug the silver watch out of her vest pocket. It was warm and smooth, and she didn't know why she liked it so much, but she did. Maybe because it was a choice. Taking it had been a choice. Keeping it had been one, too. And maybe the choice started as a random one, but there was something to it. Maybe she'd kept it for a reason. Or maybe she'd only kept it for this. She held it out to Barron. "Will this buy me a few nights?"

The owner of the Stone's Throw considered the watch. And then he reached out and curled Lila's fingers over it.

"Keep it," he said casually. "I know you're good for the coin."

Lila slid the trinket back into her pocket, thankful for its weight as she realized she was back to nothing. Well, almost nothing. A top hat, a map to anywhere—or nowhere—a handful of knives, a flintlock, a few coins, and a silver watch.

Barron pushed the door open, but when she turned to go inside, he barred her path. "No one here's a mark. You got that?"

Lila nodded stiffly. "I'm not staying long," she said. "Just till the smoke clears."

The sound of glass breaking reached them beyond the doorway, and Barron sighed and went inside, calling over his shoulder, "Welcome back."

Lila sighed and looked up, not at the sky but at the upper windows of the dingy little tavern. It was hardly a pirate ship, a place for freedom and adventure.

Just till the smoke clears, she echoed to herself.

Maybe it wasn't so bad. After all, she hadn't come back to the Stone's Throw with her tail tucked between her legs. She was in hiding. A wanted man. She smiled at the irony of the term.

A piece of paper flapped on a post beside the door. It was the same notice the constable had showed her, and she smiled at the figure in the broad-brimmed hat and mask staring out at her beneath the word WANTED. The Shadow Thief, they called her. They'd drawn her even taller and thinner than she actually was, stretched her into a wraith, black-clad and fearsome. The stuff of fairy tales. And legends.

Lila winked at the shadow before going in.

IV

WHITE
THRONE

℃ I ℈

"Perhaps it should be a masquerade instead."

"Focus."

"Or maybe a costume ball. Something with a bit of flare."

"Come on, Rhy. Pay attention."

The prince sat in a high-backed chair, gold-buckled boots kicked up on the table, rolling a glass ball between his hands. The orb was part of a larger, more intricate version of the game Kell had pawned off in the Stone's Throw. In place of pebbles or puddles or piles of sand nesting on the little board, there were five glass balls, each containing an element. Four still sat in the dark wood chest on the table, its inside lined with silk and its edges capped in gold. The one in Rhy's hands held a handful of earth, and it tipped side to side with the motion of his fingers. "Costumes with layers, ones that can be taken off . . ." he went on.

Kell sighed.

"We can all start the night in full-dress and end in—"

"You're not even trying."

Rhy groaned. His boots hit the floor with a thud as he straightened and held the glass ball up between them. "Fine," he said. "Observe my magical prowess." Rhy squinted at the dirt trapped inside the glass and, attempting to focus, spoke to the earth under his breath in low murmuring English. But the earth did not move. Kell watched a crease appear between Rhy's eyes as he focused and whispered and waited and grew increasingly irritated. At last, the dirt shifted (albeit half-heartedly) within the glass.

"I did it!" exclaimed Rhy.

"You shook it," said Kell.

"I wouldn't dare!"

"Try again."

Rhy made a sound of dismay as he slumped in his chair. "Sanct, Kell. What's wrong with me?"

"Nothing is wrong," insisted Kell.

"I speak eleven languages," said Rhy. "Some for countries I have never seen, nor am likely to set foot in, yet I cannot coax a clod of dirt to move, or a drop of water to rise from its pool." His temper flared. "It's maddening!" he growled. "Why is the language of magic so hard for my tongue to master?"

"Because you cannot win the elements over with your charm or your smile or your status," said Kell.

"They disrespect me," said Rhy with a dry smile.

"The earth beneath your feet does not care you will be king. Nor the water in your cup. Nor the air you breathe. You must speak to them as equal, or even better, as supplicant."

Rhy sighed and rubbed his eyes. "I know. I know. I only wish . . ." he trailed off.

Kell frowned. Rhy looked genuinely upset. "Wish what?"

Rhy's gaze lifted to meet Kell's, the pale gold glittering even as a wall went up behind them. "I wish I had a drink," he said, burying the matter. He shoved up from his chair and crossed the chamber to pour himself one from a sideboard against the wall. "I do try, Kell. I want to be good, or at least better. But we can't all be . . ." Rhy took a sip and waved his hand at Kell.

The word he assumed Rhy was looking for was *Antari*. The word he used was *"You."*

"What can I say?" said Kell, running his hand through his hair. "I'm one of a kind."

"Two of a kind," corrected Rhy.

Kell's brow creased. "I've been meaning to ask; what was Holland doing here?"

Rhy shrugged and wandered back toward the chest of elements. "The same thing he always is. Delivering mail." Kell considered the prince. Something was off. Rhy was a notorious fidgeter whenever he was lying, and Kell watched him shift his weight from foot to foot and tap his fingers against the open lid of the chest. But rather than press the issue, Kell let it drop and, instead, reached down and plucked another of the glass balls from the chest, this one filled with water. He balanced it in his palm, fingers splayed.

"You're trying too hard." Kell bid the water in the glass to move, and it moved, swirling first loosely within the orb and then faster and tighter, creating a small, contained cyclone.

"That's because it *is* hard," said Rhy. "Just because *you* make it look easy doesn't mean it is."

Kell wouldn't tell Rhy that he didn't even need to speak in order to move the water. That he could simply think the words, feel them, and the element listened, and answered. Whatever flowed through the water—and the sand, and the earth, and the rest—flowed through him, too, and he could will it, as he would a limb, to move for him. The only exception was blood. Though it flowed as readily as the rest, blood itself did not obey the laws of elements—it could not be manipulated, told to move, or forced to still. Blood had a will of its own, and had to be addressed not as an object, but as an equal, an adversary. Which was why *Antari* stood apart. For they alone held dominion not only over elements, but also over blood. Where elemental invocation was designed simply to help the mind focus, to find a personal synchronicity with the magic—it was meditative, a chant as much as a summoning—the *Antari* blood commands were, as the term suggested, *commands*. The words Kell spoke to open doors or heal wounds with his blood were *orders*. And they had to be given in order to be obeyed.

"What's it like?" asked Rhy out of nowhere.

Kell dragged his attention away from the glass, but the water kept spinning inside it. "What's what like?"

"Being able to travel. To see the other Londons. What are *they* like?"

Kell hesitated. A scrying table sat against one wall. Unlike the smooth black panels of slate that broadcast messages throughout the city, the table served a different purpose. Instead of stone, it held a shallow pool of still water, enchanted to project one's ideas, memories, images from their mind onto the surface of the water. It was used for reflection, yes, but also to share one's thoughts with others, to help when words failed to convey, or simply fell short.

With the table, Kell could show him. Let Rhy see the other Londons as he saw them. A selfish part of Kell wanted to share them with his brother, so that he wouldn't feel so alone, so that someone else would see, would know. But the thing about people, Kell had discovered, is that they didn't *really* want to know. They thought they did, but knowing only made them miserable. Why fill up a mind with things you can't use? Why dwell on places you can't go? What good would it do Rhy, who, for all the privileges his royal status might grant him, could never set foot in another London?

"Uneventful," said Kell, returning his glass to the chest. As soon as his fingers left its surface, the cyclone fell apart, the water sloshing and settling to a stop. Before Rhy could ask any more questions, Kell pointed at the glass in the prince's hand and told him to try again.

Rhy tried again—and failed again—to move the earth within the glass. He made a frustrated noise and knocked the sphere away across the table. "I'm rubbish at this, and we both know it."

Kell caught the glass ball as it reached the table's edge and tumbled over. "Practice—" he started.

"Practice won't do a damned thing."

"Your problem, Rhy," chided Kell, "is that you don't want to learn magic to learn magic. You only want to learn it because you think it will help you lure people into your bed."

Rhy's lips twitched. "I don't see how that's a *problem*," he said, "And it would. I've seen the way the girls—and boys— fawn over your pretty black eye, Kell." He shoved to his feet. "Forget the lesson. I'm in no mood for learning. Let's go out."

"Why?" asked Kell. "So you can use *my* magic to lure people into *your* bed?"

"A fine idea," said Rhy. "But no. We must go out, you see, because we're on a mission."

"Oh?" asked Kell.

"Yes. Because unless you plan to wed me yourself—and don't get me wrong, I think we'd make a dashing pair—I must try and find a mate."

"And you think you'll find one traipsing around the city?"

"Goodness, no," said Rhy with a crooked grin. "But who knows what fun I'll find while failing."

Kell rolled his eyes and put the orbs away. "Moving on," he said.

"Let's be done with this," whined Rhy.

"We shall be done," said Kell. "As soon as you can contain a flame."

Of all the elements, fire was the only one Rhy had shown a . . . well, *talent* was too strong a word, but perhaps an *ability* for. Kell cleared the wooden table and set a sloped metal dish before the prince, along with a piece of white chalk, a vial of oil, and an odd little device like a pair of crossed pieces of blackened wood joined by a hinge in the middle. Rhy sighed and drew a binding circle on the table around the dish using the chalk. He then emptied the vial onto the plate, the oil pooling in the center, no bigger than a ten-lin coin. Finally, he lifted the device, which fit easily in his palm. It was a fire starter. When Rhy closed his hand around it and squeezed, the two stems scraped together, and a spark fell from the hinge to the pool of oil, and caught.

A small blue flame danced across the surface of the coin-size pool, and Rhy cracked his knuckles, rolled his neck, and pushed up his sleeves.

"Before the light goes out," urged Kell.

Rhy shot him a look, but brought his hands to either side of the chalk-binding circle, palms in, and began to speak to the fire not in English, but in Arnesian. It was a more fluid, coaxing tongue that leant itself to magic. The words poured out in a whisper, a smooth, unbroken line of sound that seemed to take shape in the room around them.

And to their mutual amazement, it worked. The flame in the dish turned white and grew, enveloping what was left of the oil and continuing to burn without it. It spread, coating the surface of the plate and flaring up into the air before Rhy's face.

"Look!" said Rhy, pointing at the light. "Look, I did it!"

And he had. But even though he'd stopped speaking to the flame, it kept growing.

"Don't lose focus," said Kell as the white fire spread, licking the edges of the chalk circle.

"What?" challenged Rhy as the fire twisted and pressed against the binding ring. "No word of praise?" He looked away from the fire and toward Kell, his fingers brushing along the table as he turned. "Not even a—"

"*Rhy,*" warned Kell, but it was too late. Rhy's hand had skimmed the circle, smudging the line of chalk. The fire tore free.

It flared up across the table, sudden and hot, and Rhy nearly toppled backward in his chair trying to get out of its way.

In a single motion, Kell had freed his knife, drawn it across his palm, and pressed his bloodied hand to the tabletop. "*As Anasae,*" he ordered—*dispel*. The enchanted fire died instantly, vanishing into air. Kell's head spun.

Rhy stood there, breathless. "I'm sorry," he said guiltily. "I'm sorry, I shouldn't have . . ."

Rhy hated it when Kell was forced to use blood magic, because he felt personally responsible—he often was—for the sacrifice that came with it. He had caused Kell a great deal of pain once, and had never quite forgiven himself for it. Now Kell took up a cloth and wiped his wounded hand. "It's fine," he said, tossing aside the rag. "I'm fine. But I think we're done for today."

Rhy nodded shakily. "I could use another drink," he said. "Something strong."

"Agreed," said Kell with a tired smile.

"Hey, we haven't been to the Aven Stras in ages," said Rhy.

"We can't go there," said Kell. What he meant was, *I can't let* you *go there.* Despite its name, the Aven Stras—"Blessed Waters"—had become a haunt for the city's unsavory sorts.

"Come on," said Rhy, already returned to his sporting self. "We'll get Parrish and Gen to dig up some uniforms and we'll all go as—"

Just then a man cleared his throat, and Rhy and Kell both turned to find King Maxim standing in the doorway.

"Sir," they said in unison.

"Boys," he said. "How are your studies going?"

Rhy gave Kell a weighted look, and Kell raised a brow, but said only, "They've come and gone. We just finished."

"Good," said the king, producing a letter.

Kell didn't realize how much he badly he wanted that drink with Rhy until he saw the envelope, and he knew he wouldn't get it. His heart sank, but he didn't let it show.

"I need you to carry a message," said the king. "To our strong neighbor."

Kell's chest tightened with the familiar mixture of fear and excitement that was inextricable when it came to White London.

"Of course, sir," he said.

"Holland delivered a letter yesterday," explained the king.

"But couldn't stay to collect the response. I told him I would send it back with you."

Kell frowned. "All is well, I hope," he said carefully. He rarely knew the contents of the royal messages he carried, but he could usually glean the tone—the correspondences with Grey London had devolved to mere formality, the cities having little in common, while the dialogue with White was constant and involved and left a furrow in the king's brow. Their "strong neighbor" (as the king called the other city) was a place torn by violence and power, the name at the end of the royal letters changing with disturbing frequency. It would have been too easy to discontinue correspondence and leave White London to its decay, but the Red crown couldn't. Wouldn't.

They felt responsible for the dying city.

And they were.

After all, it had been *Red* London's decision to seal itself off, leaving White London—which sat between Red and Black— trapped and forced to fight back the dark plague on its own, to seal itself in, and the corrupted magic out. It was a decision that haunted centuries of kings and queens, but at the time, White London was strong—stronger even than Red—and the Red crown believed (or *claimed* to believe) it was the only way they would all survive. They were right and wrong. Grey London receded into quiet obliviousness. Red not only survived but flourished. But White was forever changed. The city, once glorious, fell to chaos and conquering. Blood and ash.

"All is as well as it can be," said the king as he handed Kell the note and turned back toward the door. Kell moved to follow when Rhy caught his arm.

"Promise," the prince whispered under his breath. "Promise you'll come back empty-handed this time."

Kell hesitated. "I promise," he said, wondering how many times he had said those words, how empty they'd become.

But as he pulled a pale piece of silver from beneath his collar, he hoped that this time they might prove true.

～ II ～

Kell stepped through the door in the world and shivered. Red London had vanished, taking the warmth with it; his boots hit cold stone, and his breath blossomed in the air before his lips, and he pulled his coat—the black one with the silver buttons—tightly around his shoulders.

Priste ir Essen. Essen ir Priste.

"Power in Balance. Balance in Power." Equal parts motto, mantra, and prayer, the words ran beneath the royal emblem in Red London, and could be found in shops and homes alike. People in Kell's world believed that magic was neither an infinite resource nor a base one. It was meant to be used but not abused, wielded with reverence as well as caution.

White London had a very different notion.

Here, magic was not seen as equal. It was seen as something to be *conquered. Enslaved. Controlled.* Black London had let magic in, let it take over, let it consume. In the wake of the city's fall, White London had taken the opposite approach, seeking to bind power in any way they could. *Power in Balance* became *Power in Dominance.*

And when the people fought to control the magic, the magic resisted them. Shrank away into itself, burrowed down into the earth and out of reach. The people clawed the surface of the world, digging up what little magic they could still grasp, but it was thin and only growing thinner, as were those fighting for it. The magic seemed determined to starve its captors out. And slowly, surely, it was succeeding.

This struggle had a side effect, and that effect was the reason Kell had named White London *white*: every inch of the city, day or night, summer or winter, bore the same pall, as though a fine coat of snow—or ash—had settled over everything. And everyone. The magic here was bitter and mean, and it bled the world's life and warmth and color, leaching it out of everything and leaving only the pale and bloated corpse behind.

Kell looped the White London coin—a weighty iron thing—around his neck, and tucked it back beneath his collar. The crisp blackness of his coat made him stand out against the faded backdrop of the city streets, and he shoved his blood-streaked hand into his pocket before the rich red sight of it gave anyone ideas. The pearl-toned surface of the half-frozen river—here called neither the Thames, nor the Isle, but the Sijlt—stretched at his back, and across it, the north side of the city reached to the horizon. In front of him, the south side waited, and several blocks ahead, the castle lunged into the air with knifelike spires, its stone mass dwarfing the buildings on every side.

He didn't waste time, but made his way directly toward it.

Being lanky, Kell had a habit of slouching, but walking through the streets of White London, he pulled himself to his full height and kept his chin up and his shoulders back as his boots echoed on the cobblestones. His posture wasn't the only thing that changed. At home, Kell masked his power. Here he knew better. He let his magic fill the air, and the starving air ate it up, warming against his skin, wicking off in tendrils of fog. It was a fine line to walk. He had to show his strength while still holding fast to it. Too little, and he'd be seen as prey. Too much, and he'd be seen as a prize.

In *theory*, the people of the city knew Kell, or of him, and knew that he was under the protection of the white crown. And in *theory*, no one would be foolish enough to defy the Dane twins. But hunger—for energy, for life—did things to people. Made *them* do things.

And so Kell kept his guard up and watched the sinking sun as he walked, knowing that White London was at its most docile in the light of day. The city changed at night. The quiet—an unnatural, heavy, held-breath kind of silence—broke and gave way to noise, sounds of laughter, of passion—some thought it a way to summon power—but mostly those of fighting, and killing. A city of extremes. Thrilling, maybe, but deadly. The streets would have been stained dark with blood long ago if the cutthroats didn't drink it all.

With the sun still up, the lowly and the lost lingered in doorways, and hung out of windows, and loitered in the gaps between buildings. And all of them watched Kell as he passed, gaunt stares and bony edges. Their clothes had the same faded quality as the rest of the city. So did their hair, their eyes, and their skin, the surface of which was covered in markings. Brands and scars, mutilations meant to bind what magic they could summon to their bodies. The weaker they were, the more scars they made on themselves, ruining their flesh in a frantic attempt to hold on to what little power they had.

In Red London, such markings would be seen as base, tainting not only body but also magic by binding it to them. Here, only the strong could afford to scorn the marks, and even then, they did not see them as defiling—merely desperate. But even those above such brands relied on amulets and charms (Holland alone went without any jewelry, save the broach that marked him as a servant of the throne). Magic did not come willingly here. The language of elements had been abandoned when they ceased to listen (the only element that could be summoned was a perverted kind of energy, a bastard of fire and something darker, corrupted). What magic *could* be had was taken, forced into shape by amulets and spells and bindings. It was never enough, never filling.

But the people did not leave.

The power of the Sijlt—even in its half-frozen state—tethered them to the city, its magic the only remaining flicker of warmth.

And so they stayed, and life went on. Those who had not (yet) fallen victim to the gnawing hunger for magic went about their daily work, and minded their own, and did their best to forget about the slow way their world was dying. Many clung to the belief that the magic would return. That a strong enough ruler would be able to force the power back into the veins of the world and revive it.

And so they waited.

Kell wondered if the people of White London truly believed that Astrid and Athos Dane were strong enough, or if they were simply waiting for the next magician to rise up and overthrow them. Which someone would, eventually. Someone always did.

The quiet got heavier as the castle came into sight. Grey and Red London both had palaces for their rulers.

White London had a *fortress*.

A high wall surrounded the castle, and between the vaulting citadel and its outer wall stood an expansive stone courtyard, running like a moat around the looming structure and brimming with marble forms. The infamous Krös Mejkt, the "Stone Forest," was made up not of trees but of statues, all of them people. It was rumored the figures hadn't always been stone, that the forest was actually a graveyard, kept by the Danes to commemorate those they killed, and remind any who passed through the outer wall of what happened to traitors in the twins' London.

Passing under the entryway and through the courtyard, Kell approached the massive stone steps. Ten guards flanked the stairs of the fortress, still as the statues in the forest. They were nothing but puppets, stripped by King Athos of everything but the breath in their lungs and the blood in their veins and his order in their ears. The sight of them made Kell shiver. In Red London, using magic to control, possess, or bind the body and mind of another person was forbidden. Here, it was yet another sign of Athos and Astrid's strength, their might—and therefore *right*—to rule.

The guards stood motionless; only their empty eyes followed him as he approached and passed through the heavy doors. Beyond, more guards lined the walls of an arching antechamber, still as stone save for their shifting gazes. Kell crossed the room and into a second corridor, this one empty. It wasn't until the doors closed behind him that Kell let himself exhale and lower his guard a fraction.

"I wouldn't do that just yet," said a voice from the shadows. A moment later a shape stepped out of them. Torches lined the walls, burning but never burning out, and in their flickering light Kell saw the man.

Holland.

The *Antari*'s skin was nearly colorless, and charcoal hair swept across his forehead, ending just above his eyes. One of them was a greyish green, but the other was glossy and black. And when that eye met Kell's, it felt like two stones sparking against each other.

"I've come with a letter," said Kell.

"Have you?" Holland said drily. "I thought you'd come for tea."

"Well, I'll take that, too, I suppose, while I'm here."

Holland's mouth quirked in something that wasn't a smile.

"Athos or Astrid?" he asked, as if it were a riddle. But riddles had right answers, and when it came to the Dane twins, there was none. Kell could never decide which one he would rather face. He didn't trust the siblings, not together, and certainly not apart.

"Astrid," he said, wondering if he'd chosen well.

Holland gave no indication, only nodded, and led the way.

The castle was built like a church (and maybe it had been one, once), its skeleton vast and hollow. Wind whistled through the halls, and their steps echoed over the stone. Well, *Kell's* steps did. Holland moved with the terrifying grace of a predator. A white half-cloak draped over one of his shoulders, billowing behind him as he walked. It was held together by a clasp, a silver circular broach, etched with markings that at a distance looked like nothing more than decoration.

But Kell knew the story of Holland and the silver clasp.

He hadn't heard it from the *Antari's* lips, of course, but had bought the truth off a man at the Scorched Bone, traded the full story for a Red London lin several years before. He couldn't understand why Holland—arguably the most powerful person in the city, and perhaps the world—would serve a pair of glorified cutthroats like Astrid and Athos. Kell had himself been to the city a handful of times before the last king fell, and he had seen Holland at the ruler's side, but as an ally, not a servant. He had been different then, younger and more arrogant, yes, but there was also something else, something more, a light in his eyes. A *fire*. And then, between one visit and the next, the fire was gone, and so was the king, replaced by the Danes. Holland was still there, at their side as if nothing had changed. But *he* had changed, gone cold and dark, and Kell wanted to know what had happened—what had *really* happened.

So he went looking for an answer. And he found it, as he found most things—and most found him—in the tavern that never moved.

Here it was called the Scorched Bone.

The storyteller clutched the coin as if for warmth as he hunched on his stool and spun the tale in Maktahn, the guttural native tongue of the harsh city.

"Ön vejr tök . . ." he began under his breath. *The story goes . . .*

"Our throne is not something you're born to. It's not held by blood. But taken by it. Someone cuts their way to the throne and holds it as long as they can—a year, maybe two—until they fall, and someone else rises. Kings come and go. It is a constant cycle. And usually, it is a simple enough matter. The murderer takes the place of the murdered.

"Seven years ago," the man continued, "when the last king was killed, several tried to claim his crown, but in the end, it came down to three. Astrid, Athos, and Holland."

Kell's eyes widened. While he knew Holland had served the prior crown, he had not known of his aspirations to be king. Though it made sense; Holland was *Antari* in a world where power meant everything. He should have been the obvious victor. Still, the Dane twins proved nearly as powerful as they were ruthless and cunning. And together, they defeated him. But they didn't kill him. Instead, they *bound* him.

At first Kell thought he'd misunderstood—his Maktahn wasn't as flawless as his Arnesian—and he made the man repeat the word. *Vöxt.* "Bound."

"It's that clasp," said the man in the Scorched Bone, tapping his chest. "The silver circle."

It was a binding spell, he explained. And a dark one at that. Made by Athos himself. The king had an unnatural gift for controlling others—but the seal didn't make Holland a mindless slave, like the guards that lined the castle halls. It didn't make him think or feel or want. It only made him *do*.

"The pale king is clever," added the man, fiddling with his coin. "*Terrible*, but clever."

Holland stopped abruptly, and Kell forced his mind and his gaze back to the castle hall and the door that now waited in front of them. He watched as the White *Antari* brought his hand to the door, where a circle of symbols was burned into the wood. He drew his fingers deftly across them, touching four in sequence; a lock yielded within, and he led Kell through.

The throne room was just as sprawling and hollow as the rest of the castle, but it was circular and made of brilliant white stone, from the rounded walls and the arching ribs of the ceiling to the glittering floors and the twin thrones on the raised platform in its center. Kell shivered, despite the fact the room wasn't cold. It only *looked* like ice.

He felt Holland slip away, but did not turn his attention from the throne, or the woman sitting on it.

Astrid Dane would have blended right in, if it weren't for her veins.

They stood out like dark threads on her hands and at her temples; the rest of her was a study in white. So many tried to hide the fact they were fading, covering their skin or painting it up to look healthier. The queen of White London did not. Her long colorless hair was woven back into a braid, and her porcelain skin bled straight into the edges of her tunic. Her entire outfit was fitted to her like armor; the collar of her shirt was high and rigid, guarding her throat, and the tunic itself ran from chin to wrist to waist, less out of a sense of modesty, Kell was sure, than protection. Below a gleaming silver belt, she wore fitted pants that tapered into tall boots (rumor had it that a man once spat at her for refusing to wear a dress; she'd cut off his lips). The only bits of color were the pale blue of her eyes and the greens and reds of the talismans that hung from her neck and wrists and were threaded through her hair.

Astrid had draped herself over one of the two thrones, her long thin body like taut wire under her clothes. Sinewy, but far from weak. She fiddled with a pendant at her neck, its surface like frosted glass, its edges as red as freshly drawn blood. *Strange*, thought Kell, *to see something so bright in White London*.

"I smell something sweet," she said. She'd been gazing up at the ceiling. Now her eyes wandered down and landed on Kell. "Hello, flower boy."

The queen spoke in English. Kell knew that she hadn't studied the language, that she—like Athos—relied on spellwork instead. Somewhere under her close-fitting clothes, a translation rune was scarred into her skin. Unlike the desperate tattoos made by the power hungry, the language rune was a soldier's response to a politician's problem. Red

London treated English as a mark of high society, but White London found little use for it. Holland had told Kell once that this was a land of warriors, not diplomats. They valued battle more than ballrooms and saw no value in a tongue that their own people did not understand. Rather than waste years learning the common tongue between kings, those who took the throne simply took the rune as well.

"Your Majesty," said Kell.

The queen drew herself up into a sitting position. The laziness of her motions was a farce. Astrid Dane was a serpent, slow only until she chose to strike. "Come closer," she said. "Let me see how you've grown."

"I've been grown for some time," said Kell.

She drew a nail down the arm of the throne. "Yet you do not fade."

"Not yet," he said, managing a guarded smile.

"Come to me," she said again, holding out her hand. "Or I will come to you."

Kell was not sure if it was a promise or a threat, but he had no choice regardless, and so he stepped forward into the serpent's nest.

~~ III ~~

The whip cracked through the air, the forked end splitting open the skin of the boy's back. He did not scream—Athos wished he would—but a gasp of pain whistled through his clenched teeth.

The boy was pinned against a square metal frame like a moth, his arms spread wide, wrists bound to each of the two vertical bars that formed the square's sides. His head hung forward, sweat and blood trickling down the lines of his face, dripping from his chin.

The boy was sixteen, and he had not bowed.

Athos and Astrid had ridden through the streets of White London on their pale steeds, surrounded by their empty-eyed soldiers, relishing the fear in their people's eyes, and with it, their obedience. Knees hit stone. Heads bowed low.

But one boy—Athos later learned his name was Beloc, the word coughed through bloody lips—stood there, his head barely tipped forward. The eyes of the crowd had gone to him, a visceral ripple rolling through them—shock, yes, but underneath it, amazement bordering on approval. Athos had pulled his horse to a stop and gazed down at the boy, considering his moment of stubborn youthful defiance.

Athos had been a boy once, of course. He had done foolish,

headstrong things. But he had learned many lessons in the struggle for the White crown, and many more since taking it as his own, and he knew above all that defiance was like a weed, something to be ripped out at the roots.

On her steed, his sister watched, amused, as Athos tossed a coin to the boy's mother, who stood beside him.

"Öt vosa rijke," he said. "For your loss."

That night, the empty-eyed soldiers came, broke down the doors of Beloc's small house, and dragged the boy kicking and screaming and hooded into the street, his mother held back by a spell scrawled across the stone walls, unable to do anything but wail.

The soldiers dragged the boy all the way to the palace and delivered him, bloody and beaten, to the glittering white floor in front of Athos's throne.

"Look at this," Athos chided his men. "You've hurt him." The king stood and looked down at the boy. "That's my job."

Now the whip split air and flesh again, and this time, at last, Beloc screamed.

The whip cascaded from Athos's palm like liquid silver, pooling on the ground beside his boot. He began to coil it around his hand.

"Do you know what I see in you?" He wound the silver rope and slid it into a holster at his waist. "A fire."

Beloc spit blood on the floor between them. Athos's lips twisted. He strode across the chamber, caught hold of the boy's face by his jaw, and slammed his head back against the wood of the frame. Beloc groaned in pain, the sound muffled by Athos's hand over his mouth. The king brought his lips to the boy's ear.

"It burns through you," he whispered against the boy's cheek. "I cannot wait to carve it out."

"Nö kijn avost," growled Beloc when the king's hand fell away. *I don't fear death.*

"I believe you," said Athos smoothly. "But I'm not going to

kill you. Though, I'm sure," he added, turning away, "you'll wish I had."

A stone table stood nearby. On it sat a metal chalice filled with ink, and beside it, a very sharp blade. Athos took up both and brought them to Beloc's pinned body. The boy's eyes widened as he realized what was about to happen, and he tried to fight against his binds, but they did not give.

Athos smiled. "You have heard then, about the marks I make."

The whole city knew of Athos's penchant—and his prowess—for binding spells. Marks that stripped away a person's freedom, their identity, their soul. Athos took his time readying the knife, letting the boy's fear fill the room as he swirled the metal through the ink, coating it. The length of the blade was grooved, the ink filling the notch as if it were a pen. When it was ready, the king drew the stained knife out, the gesture seductively slow, cruel. He smiled, and brought the tip to the boy's heaving chest.

"I'm going to let you keep your mind," said Athos. "Do you know why?" The blade's tip bit in, and Beloc gasped. "So I can watch the war play in your eyes every time your body obeys my will instead of yours."

Athos pressed down, and Beloc bit back a scream as the knife carved its way across his flesh, down his collar, over his heart. Athos whispered something low and constant as he drew the lines of the binding spell. Skin broke, and blood welled and spilled into the blade's path, but Athos seemed unbothered, his eyes half closed as he guided the knife.

When it was over, he set the blade aside and stepped back to admire his work.

Beloc was slumped against his binds, chest heaving. Blood and ink ran down his skin.

"Stand up straight," commanded Athos, satisfaction washing over him as he watched Beloc try to resist, his muscles shuddering against the instruction before giving in and dragging his wounded body up into a semblance of posture. Hatred burned through the boy's eyes, bright as ever, but his body now belonged to Athos.

"What is it?" asked the king.

The question wasn't directed at the boy, but at Holland, who had appeared in the doorway. The *Antari's* eyes slid over the scene—the blood, the ink, the tortured commoner—his expression lodged between distant surprise and disinterest. As if the sight meant nothing to him.

Which was a lie.

Holland liked to play at being hollow, but Athos knew it was a ruse. He might have feigned numbness, but he was hardly immune to sensation. To pain.

"*Ös-vo tach?*" asked Holland, nodding at Beloc. *Are you busy?*

"No," answered Athos, wiping his hands on a dark cloth. "I think we're done for now. What is it?"

"He is here."

"I see," said Athos, setting aside the towel. His white cloak hung on a chair, and he took it up and slung it around his shoulders in one fluid motion, fastening the clasp at his throat. "Where is he now?"

"I delivered him to your sister."

"Well then," said Athos, "let's hope we're not too late."

Athos turned toward the door, but as he did, he caught Holland's gaze wandering back to the boy strapped against the metal frame.

"What should I do with him?" he asked.

"Nothing," said Athos. "He'll still be here when I get back."

Holland nodded, but before he could turn to go, Athos brought a hand to his cheek. Holland did not pull away, did not even stiffen under the king's touch. "Jealous?" he asked. Holland's two-toned eyes held Athos's, the green and the black both steady, unblinking. "He suffered," added Athos softly. "But not like you." He brought his mouth closer. "No one suffers as beautifully as you."

There it was, in the corner of Holland's mouth, the crease of his eye. Anger. Pain. Defiance. Athos smiled, victorious.

"We better go," he said, hand falling away. "Before Astrid swallows our young guest whole."

IV

Astrid beckoned.

Kell wished he could set the letter on the narrow table that sat between the thrones and go, keep his distance, but the queen sat there holding out her hand for it, for him.

He drew King Maxim's letter from his pocket and offered it to her, but when she reached to take it, her hand slid past the paper and closed around his wrist. He pulled back on instinct, but her grip only tightened. The rings on her fingers glowed, and the air crackled as she mouthed a word and lightning danced up Kell's arm, followed almost instantly by pain. The letter tumbled from his hand as the magic in his blood surged forward, willing him to act, to *react*, but he fought the urge. It was a game. Astrid's game. She *wanted* him to fight back, so he willed himself not to, even when her power—the closest thing to an element she could summon, something sharp, electric, and unnatural—forced a leg to buckle beneath him.

"I like it when you kneel," she said softly, letting go of his wrist. Kell pressed his hands flat against the cool stone floor and took a shaky breath. Astrid swiped the letter from the ground and set it on the table before sinking back into her throne.

"I should keep you," she added, tapping a finger thoughtfully against the pendant that hung from her throat.

Kell rose slowly to his feet. An aching pain rolled up his arm in the energy's wake. "Why's that?" he asked.

Her hand fell from the charm. "Because I do not like things that don't belong to me," she said. "I do not trust them."

"Do you trust *anything*?" he countered, rubbing his wrist. "Or any*one*, for that matter?"

The queen considered him, her pale lips curling at the edges. "The bodies in my floor all trusted someone. Now I walk on them to tea."

Kell's gaze drifted down to the granite beneath his feet. There were rumors, of course, about the bits of duller white that studded the stone.

Just then the door swung open behind him, and Kell turned to see King Athos striding in, Holland trailing several steps behind. Athos was a reflection of his sister, only faintly distorted by his broader shoulders and shorter hair. But everything else about him, from complexion to wiry muscle to the wanton cruelty they shared, was an exact replica.

"I heard we had company," he said cheerfully.

"Your Highness," said Kell with a nod. "I was just leaving."

"Already?" said the king. "Stay and have a drink."

Kell hesitated. Turning down the Prince Regent's invitation was one thing; turning down Athos Dane's was quite another.

Athos smiled at his indecision. "Look at how he worries, sister."

Kell did not realize she had risen from her seat until he felt her there beside him, running a finger down the silver buttons of his coat. *Antari* or not, the Danes made him feel like a mouse in the company of snakes. He willed himself not to pull away from the queen's touch a second time, lest it provoke her.

"I want to keep him, brother," said Astrid.

"I fear our neighboring crown would not be pleased," said Athos. "But he'll stay for a drink. Won't you, Master Kell?" Kell felt himself nodding slowly, and Athos's smile spread, teeth glinting like knifepoints. "Splendid." He snapped his fingers and a servant appeared, turning his dead eyes up to his master. "A chair," ordered Athos, and the servant fetched one and set it behind Kell's knees before retreating, quiet as a ghost.

"Sit," commanded Athos.

Kell did not. He watched the king ascend the dais and approach the table between the thrones. On it sat a decanter of golden liquid and two empty glass goblets. Athos lifted one of the glasses, but did not pour from the decanter. Instead, he turned toward Holland.

"Come here."

The other *Antari* had retreated to the far wall, fading into it despite the near black of his hair and the true black of his eye. Now he came forward with his slow and silent steps. When he reached Athos, the king held out the empty goblet and said, "Cut yourself."

Kell's stomach turned. Holland's fingers drifted for an instant toward the clasp at his shoulder before making their way to his exposed side of his half-cloak. He rolled up his sleeve, revealing the tracery of his veins, but also a mess of scars. *Antari* healed faster than most. The cuts must have been deep.

He drew a knife from his belt and raised arm and blade both over the goblet.

"Your Majesty," said Kell hastily. "I have no taste for blood. Could I trouble you for something else?"

"Of course," said Athos lightly. "It's no trouble at all."

Kell was halfway through a shaky sigh of relief when Athos turned back to Holland, who'd begun to lower his arm. The king frowned. "I thought I said cut."

Kell cringed as Holland raised his arm over the goblet and drew the knife across his skin. The cut was shallow, a graze, just deep enough to draw blood. It welled and spilled in a thin ribbon into the glass.

Athos smiled and held Holland's gaze. "We haven't got all night," he said. "Press down harder."

Holland's jaw clenched, but he did as he was told. The knife bit into his arm, deep, and the blood flowed, a rich dark red, into the glass. When the goblet was full, Athos passed it to his sister and ran a finger along Holland's cheek.

"Go clean up," he said softly, gently, the way a parent would to a child. Holland withdrew, and Kell realized that he'd not only taken his seat, but was now gripping the arms of his chair with whitening knuckles. He forced his fingers free as Athos plucked the second glass from the table and poured the pale gold liquid into it.

He held it up for Kell to see, then drank to show the glass and contents alike were safe before pouring a new measure and offering it to Kell. The gesture of a man used to sabotage.

Kell took the glass and drank too fast and too deep in an effort to calm his nerves. As soon as the goblet was empty, Athos filled it again. The drink itself was light and sweet and strong, and went down easily. Meanwhile, the Danes shared their cup, Holland's blood turning their lips a vibrant red as they drank. *Power lies in the blood*, thought Kell as his own began to warm.

"It's amazing," he said, forcing himself to drink his second portion slower than his first.

"What is?" asked Athos, sinking into his throne.

Kell nodded at the goblet of Holland's blood. "That you manage to keep your clothes so white." He finished his second glass, and Astrid laughed and poured him a third.

❧ V ❧

Kell should have stopped at one drink.

Or two.

He thought he'd stopped at three, but he couldn't be entirely sure. He hadn't felt the full effects of the drink until he'd gotten to his feet, and the white stone floor had tilted dangerously beneath him. Kell knew that it was foolish, drinking as much as he had, but the sight of Holland's blood had rattled him. He couldn't get the *Antari*'s expression out of his mind, the look that crossed his face just before the knife bit down. Holland's visage was a perpetual mask of menacing calm, but just for an instant it had cracked. And Kell had done nothing. Had not pleaded—or even pressed—for Athos to yield. It wouldn't have done any good, but still. They were both *Antari*. Luck alone cast Holland here in ruthless White and Kell in vibrant Red. What if their fortunes had been reversed?

Kell took a shaky breath, the air fogging before his lips. The cold was doing little to clear his head, but he knew he couldn't go home, not yet, not like this, so he made his wandering way through the streets of White London.

This, too, was foolish. Reckless. He was always being reckless.

Why? he thought, suddenly angry at himself. Why did he

always do this? Step out of safety and into shadow, into risk, into danger? *Why?* he heard Rhy begging on the roof that night.

He didn't know. He wished he did, but he didn't. All he knew was that he wanted to stop. The anger bled away, leaving something warm and steady. Or maybe that was the drink.

It had been a good drink, whatever it was. A strong drink. But not the kind of strong that made you weak. No, no, the kind of strong that made you strong. That made your blood sing. That made . . . Kell tipped his chin to look at the sky, and nearly lost his balance.

He needed to focus.

He was fairly sure he was heading in the general direction of the river. The air was biting against his lips, and it was getting dark—when had the sun gone down?—and in the dregs of light, the city was starting to stir around him. Silence cracking into noise.

"Pretty thing," whispered an old woman from a doorway in Maktahn. "Pretty skin. Pretty bones."

"This way, Master," called another.

"Come inside."

"Rest your feet."

"Rest your bones."

"Pretty bones."

"Pretty blood."

"Drink your magic."

"Eat your life."

"Come inside."

Kell tried to focus, but he couldn't seem to hold his thoughts together. As soon as he managed to gather a few, a breeze would blow through his head and scatter them, leaving him dazed and a little dizzy. Danger prickled at the edge of his senses. He closed his eyes, but every time he did, he saw Holland's blood running into the glass, so he forced them open and looked up.

He hadn't meant to head for the tavern. His feet had set

out on their own. His body had made its way. Now he found himself staring at the sign over the door of the Scorched Bone.

Despite being a fixed point, the tavern in White London didn't *feel* like the others. It still pulled at him, but the air smelled like blood as well as ash, and the street stones were cold beneath his boots. They tugged at his warmth. His power. His feet tried to carry him forward, but he willed them to stay.

Go home, thought Kell.

Rhy was right. Nothing good could come of these deals. Nothing good enough. It wasn't worth it. The baubles he traded for, they brought him no peace. It was just a silly game. And it was time to stop.

He held on to that thought as he drew the knife from its holster and brought it to his forearm.

"It's you," came a voice behind him.

Kell turned, the blade sliding back to his side.

A woman stood there at the mouth of the alley, her face hidden by the hood of a threadbare blue cloak. If they'd been in any other London, the blue might have been the color of sapphires or the sea. Here it was the faintest shade, like the sky through layers and layers of clouds.

"Do I know you?" he asked, squinting into the dark.

She shook her head. "But I know you, *Antari*."

"No, you don't," he said with a fair amount of certainty.

"I know what you *do*. When you're not at the castle."

Kell shook his head. "I am not making deals tonight."

"Please," she said, and he realized that she was clutching an envelope. "I don't want you to bring me anything." She held out the letter. "I only want you *take* it."

Kell's brow crinkled. A letter? The worlds had been sealed off from one another for centuries. Who could she be writing *to*?

"My family," said the woman, reading the question in his eyes. "Ages ago, when Black London fell, and the doors were sealed, we were divided. Over the centuries our families have tried to keep the thread . . . but I'm the only one left. Everyone here is dead but myself, and everyone there is dead but one. Olivar. He's the only family I have and he's on that side of the door and he's dying and I just want . . ." She brought the letter to her chest. "We are all that's left."

Kell's head was still swimming. "How did you even hear," he asked, "that Olivar was ill?"

"The other *Antari*," she explained, glancing around as if she feared someone would hear. "Holland. He brought me a letter."

Kell couldn't picture Holland deigning to smuggle *anything* between Londons, let alone correspondences between commoners.

"He didn't want to," added the woman. "Olivar gave him everything he had to buy the letter's passage and even then"— she brought her hand to her collar as if reaching for a necklace, and finding only skin—"I paid the rest."

Kell frowned. That seemed even less in Holland's nature. Not that he was selfless, but Kell doubted that he was greedy in this way, doubted that he cared about that kind of payment. Then again, everyone had secrets, and Holland wore his so close that Kell was forced to wonder how much he truly knew of the *Antari*'s character.

The woman thrust out the letter again. *"Nijk shöst,"* she said. *"Please,* Master Kell."

He tried to focus, to think. He'd promised Rhy . . . but it was only a letter. And technically, under the laws set out by the crowns of all three Londons, letters were a necessary exemption from the rule of no transference. Sure, they only meant letters between the *crowns* themselves, but still . . .

"I can pay you in advance," she pressed. "You needn't come back to close the deal. This is the last and only letter. Please." She dug in her pocket and retrieved a small parcel wrapped in cloth, and before Kell could say yes or no, she pushed the note and payment both into his hands. A strange feeling shot through him as the fabric of the parcel met his skin. And then the woman was pulling away.

Kell looked down at the letter, an address penned onto the envelope, and then to the parcel. He went to unwrap it, and the woman shot forward and caught his hand.

"Don't be a fool," she whispered, glancing around the alley. "They'll cut you for a coin in these parts." She folded his fingers over the package. "Not here," she warned. "But it's enough, I swear. It must be." Her hands slipped away. "It's all I can give."

Kell frowned down at the object. The mystery of it was tempting, but there were too many questions, too many pieces that didn't make sense, and he looked up and started to refuse. . . .

But there was no one to refuse.

The woman was gone.

Kell stood there, at the mouth of the Scorched Bone, feeling dazed. What had just happened? He'd finally mustered the resolve to make no deals, and the deal had come to him. He stared down at the letter and the payment, whatever it was. And then, in the distance, someone screamed, and the sound jarred Kell back to the darkness and the danger. He shoved the letter and parcel both into the pocket of his coat, and drew his knife across his arm, trying to ignore the dread that welled with his blood as he summoned the door home.

V

BLACK
STONE

❧ I ❧

The silver jingled in Lila's pocket as she made her way back to the Stone's Throw.

The sun had barely set on the city, but she'd already managed a fair take that day. It was risky, picking pockets by anything but night—especially with her particular disguise, which required a blurred eye or low light—but Lila had to shoulder the risk if she was going to rebuild. A map and a silver watch did not a ship buy or a fortune make.

Besides, she liked the weight of coins in her pocket. They sang like a promise. Added swagger to her step. A pirate without a ship, that's what she was, through and through. And one day, she'd have the ship, and then she'd sail away and be done with this wretched city once and for all.

As Lila strolled down the cobblestones, she began making a mental list (as she often did) of all the things she'd need to be a proper privateer. A pair of good leather sea boots, for one. And a sword and scabbard, of course. She had the pistol, Caster— beauty that it was—and her knives, all sharp enough to cut, but every pirate had a sword and scabbard. At least the ones she'd met . . . and the ones she'd read about in books. Lila had never had much time for reading, but she *could* read—it was a good skill for a thief, and she turned out to be a quick study—

and on the occasion that she nicked books, she nicked only the ones about pirates and adventures.

So, a pair of good boots, a sword, and scabbard. Oh, and a hat. Lila had the black, broad-brim one, but it wasn't very flashy. Didn't even have a feather, or a ribbon, or—

Lila passed a boy perched on a stoop a few doors shy of the Stone's Throw, and slowed, her thoughts trailing off. The boy was ragged and thin, half her age and as dirty as a chimney broom. He was holding out his hands, palms skyward, and Lila reached into her pocket. She didn't know what made her do it—good spirits, maybe, or the fact that the night was young—but she dropped a few coppers into the kid's cupped hands as she walked by. She didn't stop, didn't talk, and didn't acknowledge his thanks, but she did it all the same.

"Careful now," said Barron when she reached the tavern steps. She hadn't heard him come out. "Someone might think you've got a heart under all that brass."

"No heart," said Lila, pulling aside her cloak to reveal the holstered pistol and one of her knives. "Just these."

Barron sighed and shook his head, but she caught the edge of a smile, and behind it, something like pride. It made her squirm.

"Got anything to eat?" she asked, toeing the step with her worn-out boot.

He tipped his head toward the door, and she was about to follow him inside for a pint and a bowl of soup—she could spare that much coin, if he'd take it—when she heard a scuffle behind her. She turned to see a cluster of street rats—three of them, no older than she was—hustling the ragged boy. One of the rats was fat and one of them was skinny and one of them was short, and all of them were obviously scum. Lila watched as the short one barred the boy's path. The fat one shoved him up against the wall. The skinny one snatched the copper coins from his fingers. The boy barely fought back. He just looked down at his hands with a kind of grim resignation. They had been empty moments before, and they were empty again.

Lila's fists clenched as the three thugs vanished down a side road.

"Lila," warned Barron.

They weren't worth the work, Lila knew that. She robbed from the rich for a reason: they had more to steal. These boys probably didn't have anything worth taking besides what they'd already picked off of the boy in the street. A few coins Lila obviously hadn't minded parting with. But that wasn't the *point*.

"I don't like that look," said Barron when she didn't come inside.

"Hold my hat." She thrust the top hat into his hands, but reached in as she did and pulled the nested disguise from its depths.

"They're not worth it," he said. "And in case you didn't notice, there were three of them, and one of you."

"So little faith," she said, snapping the soft broad-brim hat into form. "And besides, it's the principle of the thing, Barron."

The tavern owner sighed. "Principle or not, Lila, one of these days, you're going to get yourself killed."

"Would you miss me?" she asked.

"Like an itch," he shot back.

She gave him the edge of a grin and tied the mask over her eyes. "Look after the kid," she said, pulling the brim of the hat down over her face. Barron grunted as she hopped down from the step.

"Hey, you," she heard Barron calling to the boy huddled on the nearby stoop, still staring at his empty hands. "Come over here. . . ."

And then she was off.

ᐤ II ᐤ

7 Naresk Vas.

That was the address written on the envelope.

Kell had sobered considerably, and decided to go straight to the point of delivery and be done with the peculiar business of the letter. Rhy need never know. Kell would even drop the trinket—whatever it was—in his private room at the Ruby Fields before heading back to the palace so that he could, in good conscience, return empty-handed.

It seemed like a good plan, or at least, like the best of several bad ones.

But as he reached the corner of Otrech and Naresk, and the address on the paper came into sight, Kell slowed, and stopped, and then took two steps sideways into the nearest shadow.

Something was wrong.

Not in an obvious way, but under his skin, in his bones.

Naresk Vas looked empty, but it wasn't.

That was the thing about magic. It was everywhere. In everything. In *everyone*. And while it coursed like a low and steady pulse, through the air and the earth, it beat louder in the bodies of living things. And if Kell tried—if he *reached*—he could feel it. It was a sense, not as strong as sight or sound or smell, but there all the same, its presence now drifting toward

112

him from the shadows across the street.

Which meant that Kell was not alone.

He held his breath and hung back in the alley, eyes fixed on the address across the street. And then, sure enough, he saw something *move*. A hooded figure hovered in the dark between 7 and 9 Naresk Vas. Kell couldn't see anything about him except the glint of a weapon at his side.

For a second, Kell—still a little off from his time with the Danes—thought it might be Olivar, the man whose letter he was holding. But it *couldn't* be Olivar. The woman said the man was dying, and even if he were well enough to meet Kell on the street, he couldn't *know* to meet him there, not when Kell himself had only just accepted the task. Which meant it wasn't Olivar. But if it wasn't him, who was it?

Danger prickled at the edges of Kell's skin.

He dragged the letter from his pocket, studying the address, then held his breath as he broke the seal and pulled the letter free. He bit back a curse.

Even in the dark, he could see that the paper was blank.

Nothing but a piece of folded parchment.

Kell's mind reeled. He'd been set up.

If they—whoever they were—weren't after the letter, then . . .

Sanct. Kell's hand went to the parcel still in his pocket. The *payment*. When his fingers curled around the folded cloth, that strange sensation ran up his arm again. What had he taken?

What had he done?

Just then, the shadow across the street looked up.

The paper in Kell's hand had caught the lantern light, just for a moment, but a moment was all it took. The shadow charged forward toward Kell.

And Kell turned, and ran.

113

ᕬ III ᕫ

Lila trailed the group of thugs through the winding London streets, waiting for them to go their separate ways. Barron was right: the odds weren't great against all three, but she had her sights set on one. And as the three broke into two and the two at last diverged, she followed her mark.

It was the thin one she was after, the rat who'd taken the coins off skin-and-bones back on the step. She hugged the shadows as she trailed him through the maze of narrowing roads, the stolen copper rattling in his pocket, a sliver of wood between his teeth. Finally, he turned off down an alley, and Lila slipped after, unheard, unseen, unnoticed.

As soon as they were alone, she closed the gap between them in a single stride and brought her knife up to the skinny rat's throat, pressing down hard enough to draw blood.

"Empty the pockets," she growled in a husky voice.

He didn't move. "Yer making a mistake," he said, shifting the wooden pick in his mouth.

She shifted her grip so the knife bit into his throat. "Am I?"

And then she heard the shuffle of steps rushing up behind her and ducked just in time to dodge a fist. Another one of the rats stood there, the short sod, one meaty hand clenched, the other gripping a metal bar. And then, an instant later, the fat one finally caught up, red-cheeked and breathless.

"It's *you*," he said, and for an instant Lila thought he recognized her. Then she realized he recognized the sketch in the WANTED ad. "The Shadow Thief."

The skinny one spit out his chewing stick and broke into a grin. "Looks like we caught ourselves a prize, gents."

Lila hesitated. She knew she could win against one street rat, and thought she might even be able to win against two, but three? Maybe, if they'd stand still, but they kept shifting so she couldn't see all of them at once. She heard the snick of a switchblade, the tap of the metal bar against the street stones. She had the gun in her holster and the knife in her hand, and another in her boot, but she wouldn't be fast enough to level all three boys.

"Did the poster say dead or alive?" asked the short one.

"You know, I don't think it specified," said the skinny one, wiping the blood from his throat.

"I think it said dead," added the fat one.

"Even if it said alive," reasoned the skinny one, "I don't suppose they'd mind if he were missing pieces." He lunged for her and she lunged away, accidentally stepping into the fat one's reach. He grabbed for her and she slashed, drawing blood before the short one got his hands on her. But when his arms circled her chest, she felt his grip stiffen.

"What's this now?" he hissed. "Our boy's a—"

Lila didn't wait. She slammed her boot into his foot, hard, and he gasped and let go. Only an instant, but it was enough for Lila to do the thing she knew she had to do, the one thing she *hated* to do.

She ran.

Ꮕ IV Ᏼ

Kell could hear the footsteps, first one set and then two and then three—or maybe the third was just the pumping of his heart—as he raced through the alleys and side streets. He didn't stop, didn't breathe, not until he reached the Ruby Fields. Fauna met his gaze as he passed within, her grey brow furrowing—he almost never came by the front door—but she didn't stop him, didn't ask. The footsteps had fallen away a few blocks back, but he still checked the markings on the stairs as he climbed toward the room at the top, and on the room's door—charms bound to the building itself, to wood and stone, designed to keep the room hidden from all eyes but his.

Kell shut the door and sagged back against the wood as candles flickered to life around the narrow room.

He'd been set up, but by who? And for *what*?

He wasn't sure he *wanted* to know, but he needed to, and so he dragged the stolen parcel from his pocket. It was wrapped in a swatch of faded grey fabric, and when he unfolded the cloth, a rough-cut stone tumbled out into his palm.

It was small enough to nest in a closed fist, and as black as Kell's right eye, and it sang in his hand, a low, deep vibration that called on his own power like a tuning fork. Like to like. Resonating. Amplifying. His pulse quickened.

Part of him wanted to drop the stone. The other part wanted to grip it tighter.

When Kell held it up to the candlelight, he saw that one side was jagged, as if broken, but the other was smooth, and on that smooth face a symbol glowed faintly.

Kell's heart lurched when he saw it.

He'd never seen the stone before, but he recognized the mark.

It was written in a language few could speak and fewer still could use. A language that ran through his veins with his blood and pulsed in his black eye.

A language he had come to think of simply as *Antari*.

But the language of magic hadn't always belonged to *Antari* alone. No, there were stories. Of a time when others could speak directly to magic (even if they couldn't command it by blood). Of a world so bonded to power that every man, woman, and child became fluent in its tongue.

Black London. The language of magic had belonged to them.

But after the city fell, every relic had been destroyed, every remnant in every world forcibly erased as part of a cleansing, a purge—a way to ward against the plague of power that had devoured it.

That was the reason there were no books written in *Antari*. What few texts existed now were piecemeal, the spells collected and transcribed phonetically and passed down, the original language eradicated.

It made him shiver now, to see it drawn as it was meant to be, not in letters, but in rune.

The only rune he knew.

Kell possessed a single book on the *Antari* tongue, entrusted to him by his tutor, Tieren. It was a leather journal filled with blood commands—spells that summoned light or darkness, encouraged growth, broke enchantments—all of them sounded out and explained, but on its cover, there was a symbol.

"What does it mean?" he'd asked the tutor.

"It's a word," explained Tieren. "One that belongs to every world and none. It is the word for 'magic.' It refers to its existence, and its creation. . . ." Tieren brought a finger to the rune. "If magic had a name, it would be this," he said, tracing the symbol's lines. *"Vitari."*

Now Kell ran his thumb over the stone's rune, the word echoing in his head.

Vitari.

Just then, footsteps fell on the stairs, and Kell stiffened. No one should be able to see those stairs, let alone use them, but he could hear the boots. How had they followed him here?

And that's when Kell saw the pattern on the swatch of pale fabric that had once been wrapped around the stone and now lay unfolded on his bed. There were symbols scrawled across it. A tracing spell.

Sanct.

Kell shoved the stone in his pocket and lunged for the window as the small door behind him burst open violently. He mounted the sill and jumped out, and down, hitting the street below hard and rolling to his feet as the intruders came crashing into his room.

Someone had set him up. Someone wanted him to bring a forbidden relic out of White London and into *his* city.

A figure leaped through the window in his wake, and Kell spun to face the shadows on his heels. He expected two of them, but found only one. The hooded stranger slowed, and stopped.

"Who are you?" demanded Kell.

The shadow didn't answer him. It strode forward, reaching for the weapon at its hip, and in the low alley light Kell saw an X scarred the back of his hand. The mark of cutthroats and traitors. A knife-for-hire. But when the man drew his weapon, Kell froze. It was no rusted dagger, but a gleaming half-sword, and he knew the sigil on its hilt. The chalice and rising sun. The symbol of the royal family. It was the blade wielded by members of the royal guard. And only by them.

"Where did you get that?" growled Kell, anger rolling through him.

The cutthroat flexed his fingers around his half-sword. It began to glow dully, and Kell tensed. The swords of the royal guards weren't just beautiful or sharp; they were *enchanted*. Kell himself had helped create the spellwork that ran through the metal, spellwork that dampened a magician's power with only one cut. The blades were designed to put a stop to conflicts before they began, to remove the threat of magical retaliation. Because of their potential, and the fear of that potential in the wrong hands, the royal guards were told to keep the blade on them at *all* times. If one of them had lost their sword, they'd likely lost their life as well.

"*Sarenach*," said the cutthroat. *Surrender.* The command caught Kell by surprise. Knives-for-hire took loot and blood, not prisoners.

"Put down that sword," ordered Kell. He tried to will the weapon from the cutthroat's grip, but it was warded. Another fail-safe to keep the blade from falling into the wrong hands. Which it already had. Kell swore and drew his own knife from its holster. It was a good foot shorter than the royal blade.

"Surrender," said the cutthroat again, his voice strangely even. He tilted up his chin and Kell caught a glimmer of magic in the man's eyes. A compulsion spell? Kell had only a moment to note the use of forbidden magic before the man lunged, the glowing weapon slicing through the air toward him. He jerked back, dodging the sword as a second figure appeared at the other end of the alley.

"Surrender," said the second man.

"One at a time," snapped Kell. He threw his hand into the air, and the street stones shuddered and then shot upward in a wall of rock and dirt, barring the second attacker's path.

But the first kept coming, kept slashing, and Kell scrambled backward out of the sword's arc. He almost made it; the blade caught his arm, slicing through fabric but narrowly missing his skin. He lunged away as the weapon cut again, but this time it found flesh, slashing across his ribs. Pain tore through Kell's chest as blood welled and spilled down his stomach. The man pressed forward and Kell retreated a step and tried to will the street stones to rise between them. They shuddered and laid still.

"Surrender," ordered the cutthroat in his too-even tone.

Kell pressed his hand to his shirtfront, trying to stem the blood as he dodged another slice. "No." He spun the dagger in his hand, took it by the tip, and threw as hard as he could. The blade found its mark, and buried itself in the cutthroat's shoulder. But to Kell's horror, the man didn't drop his weapon. He kept coming. Pain didn't even register on his face as he pulled the knife free and cast it aside.

"Surrender the stone," he said, dead-eyed.

Kell's hand closed protectively around the talisman in his pocket. It hummed against his palm, and Kell realized as he held it that even if he could give it away—which he couldn't, he wouldn't, not without knowing what it was for and who was after it—he didn't *want* to let it go. Couldn't bear the thought of parting with it. Which was absurd. And yet, something in him ached to keep it.

The cutthroat came at him again.

Kell tried to take another step back, but his shoulders met the makeshift barricade.

There was nowhere to run.

Darkness glittered in the cutthroat's eyes and his blade sang through the air, and Kell threw out his empty hand and ordered, "*Stop,*" as if that would do a damned thing.

And yet, somehow, it did.

The word echoed through the alley, and between one reverberation and the next, the night changed around him. Time seemed to slow, and so did the cutthroat, and so did Kell, but the stone clutched in his hand surged to life. Kell's own magic had bled out through the wound across his ribs, but the stone sang with power, and thick black smoke poured between his fingers. It shot up Kell's arm and across his chest and down his outstretched hand, and rushed forward through the air toward the cutthroat. When the smoke reached him, it did not strike him, did not force him off his feet. Instead, it twisted and coiled around the cutthroat's body, spreading over his legs, up his arms, around his chest. And everywhere it touched, as soon as it touched, it *froze*, catching the cutthroat between one stride and the next, one breath and the next.

Time snapped back into motion, and Kell gasped, his pulse pounding in his ears and the stone singing in his grip.

The stolen royal blade hung mid-slash, inches from his face. The cutthroat himself stood motionless, his coat caught mid-billow behind him. Through the sheet of shadowy ice or stone or whatever it was, Kell could see the cutthroat's stiff form, eyes open and empty. Not the blank gaze of the compelled, but the vacancy of the dead.

Kell stared down at the stone still thrumming in his hand, at the glowing symbol on its face.

Vitari.

It is the word for magic. It refers to its existence, and its creation.

Could it also mean the *act* of creating?

There was no blood command for *create*. The golden rule of magic said that it couldn't *be* created. The world was made of give and take, and magic could be strengthened and weakened, but it could not be manifested out of nothing. And yet . . . he reached out to touch the frozen man.

Had the power somehow been summoned by his blood? But he hadn't given a blood command, hadn't done anything but say "Stop."

The stone had done the rest.

Which was impossible. Even with the strongest elemental magic, one had to focus on the form they wanted it to take. But Kell hadn't envisioned the frozen shell, which meant the stone didn't simply follow an order. It *interpreted*. It *created*. Was this the way magic had worked in Black London? Without walls, without rules, without anything but want and will?

Kell forced himself to return the talisman to his pocket. His fingers didn't want to relinquish it. It took all his focus to let go, and the moment the stone slipped from his hand back into his coat, a dizzy chill ran through him, and the world rocked. He felt weak as well as wounded. Drained. *It isn't something for nothing after all,* thought Kell. But it was still something. Something powerful. Something dangerous.

He tried to straighten, but pain tore across his stomach, and he groaned, slumping back against the alley wall. Without his power, he couldn't will the wound closed, couldn't even keep his own blood in his veins. He needed to catch his breath, needed to clear his mind, needed to *think*, but just then the stones at his back began to shake, and he pushed off the wall an instant before it crumbled to reveal the second hooded figure.

"Surrender," said the man in the same even tone as his counterpart.

Kell could not.

He didn't trust the stone—even as he itched to take hold of it again—didn't know how to control it, but neither could he surrender it, so Kell lunged forward, recovering his own knife from the ground, and when the man came at him, he buried it in his attacker's chest. For a second, Kell worried the man wouldn't go down, feared the compulsion would keep him on his feet as it had the other one. Kell forced the blade deep and wrenched it up through organ and bone, and at last the man's knees buckled. For one brief moment, the compulsion broke, and the light flooded back into his eyes. And then it was gone.

It wasn't the first time Kell had killed someone, but he still felt ill as he pulled the knife free and the man crumpled, dead, at his feet.

The alley swayed and Kell clutched his stomach, fighting for breath as pain rolled through him. And then he heard another set of steps in the distance and forced himself upright. He stumbled past the bodies, the frozen and the fallen both, and ran.

ꝏ V ꝏ

Kell couldn't stop the blood.

It soaked through his shirtfront, the fabric clinging to him as he ran—stumbled—through the narrow maze of streets that gathered, weblike, in the corners of Red London.

He clutched at his pocket to make sure the stone was safe, and a thrum ran through his fingers as they felt it there. He should have run for the river, should have pitched the talisman into the glittering Isle and let it sink. He should have, but he hadn't, and that left him with a problem.

And the problem was catching up.

Kell cut a corner too sharp and skidded into the wall, biting back a gasp as his wounded side collided with the bricks. He couldn't keep running, but he had to get away. Somewhere he wouldn't be followed.

Somewhere he *couldn't* be followed.

Kell dragged himself to a stop and reached for the Grey London pendant at his neck, ripping the cord over his head.

Footsteps echoed, heavy and too close, but Kell held his ground and pressed his hand to his blood-soaked ribs, wincing. He brought his palm and the coin in it against the alley stones and said, "*As Travars.*"

He felt the word pass his lips and shiver against his hand at the same time.

But nothing happened. The wall stayed where it was, and so did Kell.

Pain tore white-hot through his side from the royal blade, the spellwork cutting him off from his power. *No*, pleaded Kell silently. Blood magic was the strongest kind in the world. It couldn't be disabled, not by a simple piece of spellwork. It was stronger. It *had* to be stronger. Kell closed his eyes.

"As Travars," he said again.

He shouldn't have to say anything else, shouldn't have to force it, but he was tired and bleeding and fighting to focus his eyes, let alone his power, and so he added *"Please."*

He swallowed and brought his forehead to rest against the stones and heard the steps getting closer and closer and said, again, *"Please let me through."*

The stone hummed in his pocket, a whispered promise of power, of aid, and he was about draw it out and call upon its strength, when the wall finally shuddered and gave way beneath his touch.

The world vanished and an instant later reappeared, and Kell collapsed to the cobblestoned street, the subtle, steady light of Red London replaced by the dank, smoke-filled Grey London night. He stayed a moment on his hands and knees, and actually considered losing consciousness right there in the alley, but finally managed to get to his feet. When he did, the city slanted dangerously around him. He took two steps, and promptly collided with a man in a mask and a broad brim hat. Distantly, Kell knew it was strange, to be wearing a disguise, but he was hardly in a position to judge appearances, given his current state.

"Sorry," he mumbled, pulling his coat close around him to hide the blood.

"Where'd you come from?" asked the man, and Kell looked

up and realized that under that disguise it wasn't a man at all. It was a woman. Not even that. A girl. All stretched out like a shadow, like Kell, but one even later in the day. Too long, too thin. But she was *dressed* like a man, boots and britches and a cloak (and under that, a few glinting weapons). And, of course, the mask and the hat. She seemed out of breath, as though she'd been running. *Strange,* thought Kell again.

He swayed a little on his feet.

"You all right there, gent?" asked the girl in disguise.

Footsteps sounded in the street beyond the alley, and Kell tensed, forcing himself to remember that he was safe now, safe here. The girl cast a quick glance back before returning her attention to him. He took a step toward her, and his legs nearly buckled beneath him. She went to catch him, but he caught himself against the wall first.

"I'll be okay," he whispered shakily.

The girl tipped her chin up, and there was something strong and defiant in her eyes and the lines of her jaw. A challenge. And then she smiled. Not with her whole mouth, just the edges, and Kell thought—in a far-off, woozy way—that under different circumstances, they might have been friends.

"There's blood on your face," she said.

Where wasn't *there blood?* Kell brought his hand to his cheek, but his hand was damp with it, too, so it wasn't much help. The girl came closer. She drew a small, dark kerchief from her pocket and reached out, dabbing his jaw with it before pressing the fabric into his hand.

"Keep it," she said. And then she turned and strode away.

Kell watched the strange girl go, then slumped back against the alley wall.

He tipped his head back and stared up at the Grey London sky, starless and bleak over the tops of the buildings. And then he reached into his pocket for the Black London stone, and froze.

It wasn't there.

He dug furiously through his pockets, every one of them, but it was no good. The talisman was gone. Breathless and bleeding and exhausted, Kell looked down at the kerchief clutched in his hand.

He couldn't believe it.

He'd been robbed.

VI

THIEVES
MEET

✧ I ✧

A London away, the city bells struck eight.

The sound came from the sanctuary at the city's edge, but it rang out over the glittering Isle and through the streets, pouring in open windows and out open doors and down alleys until it reached the Ruby Fields and, just beyond, the frozen figure of a man in the dark.

A man with an *X* on the back of his hand and a stolen royal sword still raised above his head. A man trapped in ice, or stone, or something stranger.

As the bells trailed off, a jagged crack formed in the shell over the man's face. And then another, down his arm. And a third, along the blade. Small fissures that deepened quickly, spreading like fingers through the casing.

"*Stop*," the young *Antari* had ordered his attacker, and the attacker had not listened, but the magic had. It had poured out of the black stone in the *Antari*'s hand, coiled around the man, and hardened into a shell.

And now, the shell was breaking.

Not as a shell *should* break, the surface fracturing and the shards crumbling away, raining down upon the street. No, this shell broke apart and yet never let go of the man beneath. Instead, it clung to him as it melted, not down his body, but *into* it. Seeping in through his clothes and his skin until it was gone—or not gone. *Absorbed*.

The once-frozen man shuddered, then took a breath. The royal half-sword slipped from his fingers and clattered to the stones as the last shimmering drops of magic glistened like oil on his skin before sinking in, the veins darkening, tracing over him like ink. The man's head hung forward, eyes open, but empty. And fully black, pupils blown and spreading through irises and into whites.

The compulsion spell already cast on him had stripped the man's resistance and allowed the other magic to slip right in, through vein and brain and muscle, taking hold of everything it touched, the once-red core of life now burning pure and dark.

Slowly, the man—or rather now, the thing inside him— lifted his head. His black eyes shone, slick against the dry dark as he surveyed the alley. The body of the second cutthroat lay nearby, but he was already quite dead, the light snuffed out. Nothing to salvage. Nothing to burn. There wasn't much life left in his own body, either—just enough flame to feed on— but it would do for now.

He rolled his shoulders and began to walk, haltingly at first, as a man unused to his body. And then faster, surer. His posture straightened, and his legs strode toward the lights of the nearest building. The man's mouth drew into a smile. It was late, but the lanterns were lit in the windows, and laughter, high and sweet and promising, filled the air like the sound of bells.

꧁ II ꧂

Lila hummed as she made her way back to the Stone's Throw.

As she walked, she began to divest herself of the disguise; the mask came off first, followed by the broad-brim hat. She'd forgotten she was wearing them when she ran into the drunk fellow back in the alley, but he'd been so deep in his cups that he'd hardly seemed to notice. Just as he'd hardly seemed to notice her hand in his coat as she held up the kerchief, or her fingers curling around the contents of his pocket as she pressed the dark cloth into his palm. An easy mark.

Truth be told, she was still cross with herself for running— or rather, for falling into a trap and *needing* to run—from the trio of street rats. *But,* she thought, closing her hand around the satisfying weight in her cloak pocket, *the outing hadn't been a total waste.*

As the tavern came into sight, she pulled the trinket from her cloak and paused beneath a lamppost to get a closer look at the take. When she did, her heart sank. She'd hoped for metal, something silver, or gold, but the lump was stone. Not a gem or a jewel, either. Not even a bit of crystal. It looked like a river rock—glossy and black—one side smooth and the other jagged, like it had been smashed or chipped off from a larger piece of stone. What kind of gent walked around with rocks in his pocket? And broken ones at that?

And yet, she thought she could feel something, a kind of prickle where her skin met the stone's surface. Lila held it up to the light, and squinted at it a moment before dismissing the sensation and deeming the rock worthless—a sentimental trifle at best. Her mood soured as she shoved it back in her pocket and climbed the steps of the Stone's Throw.

Even though the tavern was bustling, Barron looked up when she came in, eyes going from her face to the disguise tucked under her arm. She thought she saw a flicker of concern, and it made her cringe. She wasn't his family. He wasn't hers. She didn't need his worry, and he didn't need her weight.

"Run into trouble?" he asked as she passed up the counter and went straight for the stairs.

She wasn't about to own up to being snared in the alley or running away from the fight, and her take had been a total bust, so she simply shrugged. "Nothing I couldn't handle."

The scrawny boy from the steps sat on a corner stool, eating a bowl of stew. Lila realized she was hungry—that is to say, hungrier than usual, Lila hadn't felt *full* in years—but she was tired, too, and relieved to find that the call of her bones to bed was louder than that of her stomach to table. Besides, she hadn't retrieved the coins. She had the silver, of course, but she had to save it if she was ever going to get out of this tavern, out of this city. Lila knew too well how the cycle went, thieves stealing only enough to stay thieves.

She had no intention of contenting herself to such meager victories. And now that she'd been made—she cursed the thought of three street rats discovering what three dozen constables hadn't, that their wanted man wasn't a man at all—stealing would only get harder. She needed larger scores, and she needed them soon.

Her stomach growled, and she knew Barron would give her something for nothing if she could bring herself to ask for it, but she couldn't. She *wouldn't*.

Lila Bard might have been a thief but she wasn't a beggar.

And when she left—and she would—she had every intention of leaving behind the coin she owed him, down to the last farthing. She set off up the stairs.

At the top of the narrow steps stood a little landing with a green door. She remembered slamming that same door, shoving past Barron and down the steps, leaving only a tantrum in her wake. She remembered the fight—she'd stolen from a patron, and Barron had put her to task for it. What was worse, he'd wanted rent but barred her from paying him room and board with any "borrowed" coin. He'd wanted only honest money, and she had no way to get it, so he'd offered to pay her to help him run the tavern. She'd shot him down. Saying yes would have meant staying, and staying would have meant settling. In the end it'd been easier to hang the place and run. *Not away*, Lila had told herself. No, Lila had been running toward something. Something better. And even if she hadn't reached it yet, she would.

"This isn't a life!" she'd shouted, the handful of things she owned shoved under her arm. "This isn't anything. It's not enough. It's not fucking enough."

She hadn't adopted the disguise yet, hadn't been bold enough to rob outright.

There has to be more, she'd thought. *I have to be more.*

She'd grabbed the broad-brim hat from a hook near the door as she'd stormed out. It hadn't been hers.

Barron hadn't tried to stop her. He'd only gotten out of her way.

A life worth having is a life worth taking.

It had been almost a year—eleven months, two weeks, and a handful of days—since she'd stormed away from the little room and the Stone's Throw, swearing she was done with both.

And yet here she was again. She reached the top of the stairs—each protesting her arrival as much as she did—and let herself in.

The sight of the room filled her with a mix of revulsion and relief. Bone-tired, she dug the rock from her pocket and dropped it with a thud onto a wooden table by the door.

Barron had set her top hat on the bed, and Lila sank down beside it to unlace her boots. They were worn to nearly nothing, and she cringed at the thought of how much it would cost to buy a decent pair. It wasn't an easy thing to steal. Relieving a man of his pocket watch was one thing. Relieving him of his shoes was quite another.

She was halfway through the strings on the first boot when she heard a sound of strain, like an *oof*, and looked up to find a man standing in her bedroom.

He hadn't come through the door—it was locked—and yet there he was, one bloody hand braced against the wall. Lila's kerchief was balled up between his palm and the wooden boards, and she thought she could make out a mark of some sort ghosted into the paneling beneath.

His hair hung down into his eyes, but she recognized him at once.

It was the fellow from the alley. The drunk one.

"Give it back," he said, breathing heavily. He had a faint accent, one she couldn't place.

"How the bloody hell did you get in?" she asked, rising to her feet.

"You have to give it back." Here, in the light of the close little room, she could see the shirt matted to his chest, the sheen of sweat across his brow. "You shouldn't . . . have taken . . . it. . . ."

Lila's eyes flicked to the stone where it sat on the table, and his gaze followed and stuck. They lunged for it at the same time. Or rather, Lila lunged for it. The stranger pushed off the wall in that general direction, swayed sharply, and then collapsed at her feet. His head bounced a little when it hit the floor.

Great, thought Lila, staring down at his body. She toed his shoulder with her boot, and when he didn't move, she knelt and rolled him over. He looked like he'd had a hell of a night. His black tunic was stuck to his skin; at first she thought it was sweat, but when she touched it, her fingers came away red. She considered searching his pockets and dumping his body out the window, but then she noticed the faint rise and fall of his chest through his stained shirt and realized he was not, in fact, dead.

Yet.

Up close, the stranger wasn't nearly as old as she'd first thought. Beneath a bit of soot and blood, his skin was smooth, and his face still held some boyish angles. He looked to be a year or two older than Lila herself, but not much more. She brushed the coppery hair from his forehead, and his eyelids fluttered and began to drift open.

Lila pulled back sharply. One of his eyes was a lovely blue. The other was pitch black. Not black-irised like some of the men she'd seen from the Far East, but a pure, *unnatural* black, running edge to edge, uninterrupted by color or white.

His gaze began to focus, and Lila reached for the nearest thing—a book—and struck him with it. His head lolled and his body went slack, and when he showed no signs of waking, she set the book aside, and took hold of his wrists.

He smells like flowers, she thought absently as she dragged his body across the floor.

ᴄᴏ III ᴄᴏ

When Kell came to, he was tied to a bed.

Coarse rope wound over his wrists, pinning them to the headboard behind him. His head was pounding, and dull pain spread through his ribs when he tried to move, but at least the bleeding had stopped, and when he reached for his power, he was relieved to feel it rise to meet him. The royal blade's spell had worn off.

After a few moments of self-assessment, Kell realized he wasn't alone in the room. Dragging his head up off the pillow, he found the thief perched in a chair at the foot of the bed, winding up a silver timepiece and watching him over her knees. She'd done away with her disguise, and Kell was surprised by the face beneath. Her dark hair was cut short along her jaw, which ended at a pointed chin. She looked young, but sharp, bony in a starved-bird kind of way. The only roundness came from her eyes, both brown, but not quite the same shade. He opened his mouth, intending to start their conversation with a question, like, *Will you untie me?* or *Where is the stone?* but instead found himself saying, "One of your eyes is lighter than the other."

"And one of your eyes is black," she shot back. She sounded cautious, but not frightened. Or, if she was, she was very good at hiding it. "What are you?" she asked.

"A monster," said Kell hoarsely. "You'd better let me go."

The girl gave a small, mocking laugh. "Monsters don't faint in the presence of ladies."

"Ladies don't dress like men and pick pockets," retorted Kell.

Her smile only sharpened. "What are you really?"

"Tied to your bed," said Kell matter-of-factly.

"And?"

His brow furrowed. "And in trouble."

That, at least, garnered a sliver of surprise. "Aside from the obvious being tied to my bed?"

"Yes," said Kell, struggling to sit up a little despite the binds so he could look her in the eye. "I need you to let me go and give me back the thing you stole." He scanned the room, hoping to catch sight of the stone, but it no longer sat on the table. "I won't turn you in," he added. "We'll pretend this never happened, but I *need* it."

He hoped she would glance, inch, even lean in the direction of the talisman, but she stayed perfectly still, her gaze unwavering. "How did you get in here?" she asked.

Kell chewed his cheek. "You wouldn't believe me," he said dismissively.

She shrugged. "I suppose we'll find out."

He hesitated. She hadn't flinched at the sight of his eye, and she hadn't turned him in or called for help when he marched bloodstained through a wall and into her room. The Grey world knew so little of magic, had forgotten so much, but there was something in the girl's gaze, a challenge that made him wonder if she would prove him wrong. If she *could*.

"What is your name?" he asked.

"Don't change the subject."

"I'm not," he said, twining his fingers around the ropes binding him to the bed. "I want only to know my captor."

She considered him a moment before answering. "Delilah Bard," she said. "But Lila will do." *Lila.* A soft name but she

139

used it like a knife, slashing out on the first syllable, the second barely a whisper of metal through air. "And my captive?"

"Kell," he said. "My name is Kell, and I come from another London, and I got into your room using magic."

Sure enough, her lips quirked. "Magic," she echoed drily.

"Yes," he said. "Magic." This time when he said the word, his grip tightened on the ropes and they caught fire and burned instantly to ash. A bit showy, perhaps, but it had the desired effect. Lila stiffened visibly in her chair as Kell sat fully upright on the bed. A wave of dizziness rolled over him, and he paused there, rubbing his wrists while he waited for the room to right itself.

"Specifically," he said, "I used magic to make a door."

He patted himself down and discovered that his knife was missing. She'd disarmed him. He frowned and swung his legs slowly off the bed, boots coming to rest against the floor. "When you picked my pocket in the alley, you gave me your kerchief. I was able to use it to make a door, one that led from me to you." Which was, incidentally, *much* harder than it sounded. Doors were meant to lead to places, not people. It was only the second time Kell had ever successfully used his magic to find his way to someone. Not to mention, he had been bleeding power with every step. It had been too much. The last dregs of magic had gotten him here, and then . . .

"Another London," said Lila.

"Yes."

"And you made a door."

"Yes."

"Using magic."

"Yes." He met her eyes then, expecting confusion, skepticism, disbelief, and finding something else. She was staring at him blankly—no, *not* blankly. Her gaze was intense. Assessing. Kell hoped she wouldn't ask for another demonstration. His power was only just trickling back, and he needed to save it.

She lifted a finger to the wall, where the ghosted echo of his door still lingered. "I guess that explains the mark."

Kell frowned a little. Most people here couldn't see the echoes of spellwork, or at least, they didn't notice them. The marks, like most magic, passed beneath the spectrum of their senses.

"And the rock?" she asked.

"Magic," he said. *Black magic. Strong magic. Dead magic.* "*Bad* magic."

Finally, Lila slipped. For the briefest moment, her eyes flicked to a chest along the wall. Kell didn't hesitate. He lunged for the top drawer, but before his fingers met the wood, a knife found his throat. It had come out of nowhere. A pocket. A sleeve. A thin blade resting just below his chin. Lila's smile was as sharp as its metal edge.

"Sit down before you fall down, magic boy."

Lila lowered the knife, and Kell sank slowly onto the foot of the bed. And then, she surprised him a second time by producing the talisman, not from the top drawer of the chest as she'd hinted, but out of thin air. One moment her palm was empty, and the next the stone was simply there, her sleight of hand flawless. Kell swallowed, thinking. He could strip the knife from her grip, but she probably had another, and worse, she had the stone. She was human and knew nothing of magic, but if she made a request, the stone might very well answer. Kell thought of the cutthroat, encased in rock.

Lila ran her thumb over the talisman. "What's so bad about it?"

He hesitated, choosing his words. "It should not exist."

"What is it worth?"

"Your life," said Kell, clenching his fists. "Because trust me, whoever's after me will kill you in a blink to take it back."

Lila's gaze went to the window. "Were you followed?"

Kell shook his head. "No," he said slowly. "They can't follow me here."

"Then I have nothing to worry about." Her attention returned to the talisman. Kell could see the curiosity burning through her, and he wondered if the stone pulled at her the way it had at him.

"Lila," he said slowly. "Please put it down."

She squinted at the symbol on its face, as if somehow that would help her read it. "What does it mean?" Kell did not answer. "If you tell me, I will give it back."

Kell did not believe her but answered anyway. "It's the symbol for magic," he said. *"Vitari."*

"A magic stone called 'magic'? Not very original. What does it do?"

"I don't know." It was a kind of truth.

"I don't believe you."

"I don't care."

Lila frowned. "I'm beginning to think you don't want it back."

"I don't," said Kell, and it was mostly true, though a part of him wanted nothing more than to hold it again. "But I need it. And I answered your question."

Lila considered the stone. "A magic stone called magic," she mused, turning it over in her palm. "Which leads me to believe that it, what? *Makes* magic? Or makes things *out of* magic?" She must have seen the answer in Kell's worried face, because she smiled triumphantly. "A source of power, then . . ." She appeared to be having a conversation with herself. "Can it make anything? I wonder how it wor—"

Kell went for the talisman. His hand made it halfway there before Lila's knife slashed through the air and across his palm. He gasped as blood dripped to the floor.

"I warned you," she said, wagging the knife like a finger.

"Lila," he said wearily, cradling his hand to his chest. "Please. Give it back."

But Kell knew she wouldn't. There was a glint of mischief in her eye—a look, he knew, he had worn himself—as her fingers curled around the stone. What would she summon? What *could* she summon, this gangly little human? She held both hands ceremoniously out before her, and Kell watched, half in curiosity and half in concern, as smoke plumed out between her fingers. It wrapped around her free hand, twisting and hardening until she was holding a beautiful sword in a polished scabbard.

Her eyes widened with shock and pleasure.

"It worked," she whispered, half to herself.

The hilt shone the same glossy black of Kell's eye and the stolen stone, and when she pulled the sword free of its sheath, the metal glinted—black as well—in the candlelight, and solid as any hammered steel. Lila let out a delighted sound. Kell let out a breath of relief at the sight of the sword—it could have been worse—and watched as she set it against the wall.

"So you see," said Kell carefully. "Now hand it over." She didn't realize—couldn't realize—that this kind of magic was *wrong*, or that the stone was feeding on her energy. "Please. Before you hurt yourself."

Lila gave him a derisive glare and fondled the stone. "Oh no," she said. "I'm just getting started."

"Lila . . . ," began Kell, but it was too late. Black smoke was already pouring between her knuckles, much more of it than before, and taking shape in the room between them. This time, instead of a weapon, it pulled itself into the form of a young man. Not just any young man, Kell realized as the features smoothed from smoke into flesh.

It was *Kell*.

The resemblance was nearly flawless, from the coat with its fraying hem to the reddish hair that fell across his face, obscuring his black eye. Only this Kell had no blue eye. Both glistened as hard and black as the rock in Lila's hand. The apparition didn't move, not at first, only stood there waiting.

The Kell that *was* Kell glared at the Kell that wasn't. "What do you think you're doing?" The question was directed at Lila.

"Just having a bit of fun," she said.

"You can't go around *making people*."

"Obviously I can," she said.

And then, the black-eyed Kell began to *move*. He shrugged off his coat and tossed it onto the nearest chair. And then, Kell watched with horror as his echo began to unfasten his tunic, one button at a time.

Kell gave a small, strangled laugh. "You've got to be kidding me." Lila only smiled and rolled the stone in her palm as the Kell that wasn't Kell slid slowly, teasingly, out of his tunic and stood there, bare chested. His fingers began to undo the belt at his waist.

"Okay, enough," said Kell. "Dispel it."

She sighed. "You're no fun."

"This *isn't* fun."

"Maybe not for you," she said with a smirk as the other Kell continued his striptease, sliding the belt from its loops.

But Lila didn't see what he saw: the once-blank face of the echo was beginning to *change*. It was a subtle shift in the magic, a hollow thing starting to fill.

"Lila," insisted Kell. "Listen to me. Dispel it *now*."

"Fine, fine," she said, meeting the black-eyed Kell's gaze. "Um . . . how do I do that?"

"You willed him into being," said Kell, getting to his feet. "Now will him *away*."

Lila's brow creased, and the phantom stopped divesting himself of clothes but did not disappear.

"*Lila.*"

"I'm trying," she said, tightening her grip on the stone.

At that, the phantom Kell's face contorted, shifting rapidly from vacant to aware to *angry*. It was as if he *knew* what was happening. His eyes flicked from Lila's face to her hand and back to her face. And then he *lunged*. He moved so fast, an instant, a blink, and he was upon her. The stone tumbled from Lila's grip as the Kell that wasn't Kell slammed her back against the wall. His mouth opened to speak, but before he could, his hands dissolved—*he* dissolved—suddenly back into smoke, and then into nothing, and Lila found herself face-to-face with the Kell that *was* Kell, his bloody hand raised to the place where the illusion had been, his command—*As Anasae*—still echoing through the room.

Lila swayed on her feet and caught herself on the chest of drawers, her brief possession of the stone clearly taking its toll, the way it had on Kell. She managed to drag in a single shaky breath before he closed his bleeding hand around her throat.

"Where is my knife?" he growled.

"Top drawer," she said, gasping.

Kell nodded but didn't let her go. Instead, he grabbed her wrist and pinned it back to the wall beside her head.

"What are you doing?" she snapped, but Kell didn't answer. He focused on the wood, and it began to crack and warp, peeling away and growing up around her wrist. Lila struggled, but in an instant it was done. When Kell let go, the wall did not. He retrieved the stone from the floor as Lila twisted and fought against the makeshift bind.

"What the bloody hell . . . ?" She tried to pull free of the wooden cuff as Kell forced himself to pocket the stone. "You've ruined the wall. How am I supposed to pay for this? How am I supposed to *explain* this?"

Kell went to the drawer. There he found most of the contents of his pockets—thankfully she'd only raided the black coat he'd been wearing—and his knife.

"You can't leave me here like this," she muttered.

Kell refilled his pockets and ran a thumb over the familiar letters on his blade before returning it to the holster against his forearm. And then he heard the sound of metal sliding free of leather behind him as Lila fetched another dagger from a sheath at her back.

"I wouldn't throw that if I were you," he said, crossing to the window.

"Why's that?" she growled.

"Because," he said, sliding up the glass. "You're going to need it to saw yourself free."

And with that Kell stepped up onto the sill, and through.

It was a longer drop than he had hoped for, but he landed in a crouch, the air in the alley rushing up to ease his fall. The window had seemed the safest route, since Kell wasn't actually sure where in Grey London he was, or even what kind of house he'd been kept in. From the street, he realized it was not a house at all, but a tavern, and when he rounded the corner, he saw the sign swaying in the evening air. It swung from shadow into lamplight and then back to shadow, but Kell knew at a glimpse what it said.

THE STONE'S THROW.

He shouldn't have been surprised to see it—all roads seemed to lead here—but it still threw him. *What are the odds?* he thought, even though he knew that the thing about magic was that it bent the odds. But still.

Kell had a strange feeling about the girl, but he pushed it aside.

She didn't matter. He had the stone.

Now he just had to figure out what to do about it.

⤳ IV ⤳

It took Lila the better part of an hour to hack, slash, and saw herself free. By the time the wood finally gave way under her knife, the blade's edge was irreparably dulled, a portion of the wall was destroyed, and she was desperately in need of a stiff drink. Her coins had not multiplied, but savings be damned: tonight she needed the drink.

She rubbed the pain out of her wrist, tossed the dulled knife onto the bed, and fetched her second, still-sharp dagger from the floor, where she had dropped it. A steady stream of oaths crossed her lips as she wiped Kell's blood from the blade, and a steady stream of questions filled her head as she sheathed it, but she pushed them all down and dug her revolver out of the drawer, slotting it into its holster—if she'd had it on her at the time, she'd have blown a hole in Kell's head.

She was still quietly cursing and pulling her cloak about her shoulders when something caught her eye. The sword, the one she'd summoned, was still propped up against the wall. The bastard hadn't stopped to dispense of *that* on his way out. Now she lifted it carefully, beautiful thing that it was, and admired the glittering black hilt. It was everything she'd imagined it would be. Down to the details carved into the grip. The scabbard hummed beneath her fingers, just as the rock had when she'd held it. She *wanted* to keep the blade, wanted to keep *holding* it, with a strange, bone-deep sense of longing that she didn't trust. Lila knew what it felt like to want something, knew the way it whispered and sang and screamed in your bones. And this felt like that, but wasn't. An impostor of longing.

She remembered the way she had felt when she lost the rock, the sudden, gutting dizziness that followed, like all the energy had gone out of her limbs. Stolen when she wasn't looking. In a strange way, it reminded Lila of a pickpocket, a sly piece of sleight of hand. That was the way it worked. A proper trick took *two* hands, one you paid attention to, the other you failed to notice. Lila had been so focused on the one in front of her face, waving something shiny, that she hadn't noticed the other stealing from her pocket.

Bad magic, Kell had called it.

No, thought Lila now. *Clever magic*.

And *clever* was more dangerous than *bad* any day of the week. Lila knew that much. And so, much as it pained her to do it, she went to the open window and cast the sword out. *Good riddance*, she thought as she watched it tumble to the alley stones below.

Her gaze drifted up to the rooftops and the chimneystacks, and she wondered where Kell had gone. She wondered, but the question spawned a dozen others, and knowing she would never learn the answers to any of them, she slammed the window shut and went to find that drink.

A man stumbled through the front door of the Stone's Throw and nearly fell down the front stairs. *Tricky buggers*, he thought groggily. Surely, they hadn't been there when he entered the tavern only a few hours earlier. Or if they had, they'd gone and changed, rearranged somehow. Maybe there were more of them now. Or fewer. He tried to count them, but his vision blurred and he gave up, swaying on his feet.

The man's name was Booth, and he had to piss.

The thought rose up out of the fog and there it was, bright as a light. Booth scuffed his boots along the cobblestones to the nearest alley (he had the decency not to relieve himself on the steps, even if they *had* come out of nowhere).

He half walked, half tumbled into the narrow gap between the buildings, realizing only then how dark it was—he couldn't see his own hand, even if he'd been sober enough to look for it—but his eyes kept drifting shut anyway, so it didn't really matter.

Booth leaned his forehead against the cool stones of the tavern wall as he pissed, humming softly to himself, a shanty about women and wine and . . . something else that probably began with *w*, though he couldn't remember now. He let the melody wander off as he refastened his pants, but as he turned back toward the mouth of the alley, his boot caught something on the ground. It skidded away with a scrape before fetching up against the wall, and he might have left it there had a gust of wind not blown the nearest lantern on its hook, sending a flash of brightness into the darkened alley.

The shard of light glinted off metal, and Booth's eyes widened. He might have been several pints along, but greed was a sobering thing, and as the light vanished again, he found himself on his hands and knees on the damp alley floor, grasping in the shadows until his fingers finally curled around the prize.

Booth struggled to his feet and toddled a few steps nearer to the lantern light, and there realized that he was holding the casing of a sword, the weapon still safe within. The hilt glittered, not silver or gold or steel, but black. Black as oil, and smooth as rock. He wrapped his fingers around the grip and drew the weapon from its sheath, letting out a low groan of appreciation. The metal of the blade was as glossy and dark as the hilt. A strange sword, and rare by the looks of it.

149

Booth weighed it in his meaty hands. It would fetch a pretty penny. A *very* pretty penny. Only in the right places, of course. Couldn't be thought stolen, of course. Finders keepers ... finders sellers, that is, and such, of course.

Funny thing, though.

His fingertips, where they curled around the hilt, had started to prickle. *That is a bit peculiar*, he thought, in that calm and distant way that comes with thorough intoxication. He wasn't worried, not at first. But then he tried to loosen his hold on the weapon and couldn't. He told his fingers to let go, but they remained firmly around the sword's gleaming black hilt.

Booth shook his hand, first slowly, then vigorously, but couldn't seem to free his fingers from the weapon. And then, quite suddenly, the prickle became a jolt, hot and cold and foreign at once, a very *unpleasant* feeling. It spread up his arm, beneath his skin, and when he stumbled back a step, toward the light at the mouth of the alley, he saw that the veins on the back of his hand, over his wrist and up his forearm, were turning *black*.

He shook his hand harder and nearly lost his balance, but still, he couldn't seem to release the sword. It wouldn't let him.

"Let go," he grumbled, unsure of whether he was speaking to his own hand or the weapon locked within it.

In response, the hand holding the sword—which did not seem to belong to him anymore at all—tightened on the hilt. Booth gasped as his fingers turned the blade slowly back toward his own stomach. "What the devil," he swore, grappling with himself, his free hand fighting to hold the other at bay. But it wasn't enough—the thing taking hold was stronger than the rest—and with a single clean thrust, Booth's hand, the one with the sword, drove it into his gut and buried it to the hilt.

He doubled over in the alley with a groan, hand still fixed to the grip. The black sword glowed with a dark internal light, and then began to *dissolve*. The gleaming weapon melted, not down, but in. Through the wound, and into Booth's body. Into his blood. His heartbeat faltered and then redoubled, steady and strong in his veins as the magic spread. His body shuddered, then stilled.

For a long moment, Booth—what remained of him—crouched there on the alley floor, motionless, hands to his stomach, where the blade had driven in, and where now, only an inky black stain, like melted wax, remained in its wake. And then, slowly, his arms slipped to his sides, the veins running over them now a true black. The color of true magic. His head drifted up, and he blinked two black eyes and looked around, then down at himself, considering his form. He flexed his fingers, carefully, testing.

And then, slowly, steadily, he got to his feet.

VII

THE
FOLLOWER

⚭ I ⚭

Lila could have simply gone down into the belly of the Stone's Throw, but she owed Barron enough already—he wouldn't take her coin, either because he thought she needed it or because it wasn't hers to begin with—and she needed the fresh air to clear her head.

Other Londons.

Men walking through magical doors.

Stones that made something out of nothing.

It was all the stuff of stories.

Of *adventures*.

All of it at her fingertips. And then gone. And Lila left feeling empty, hungry, and hollow in a new and terrifying way. Or maybe it was the same kind of hunger she'd always felt, and now the missing thing had a name: *magic*. She wasn't sure. All she knew was that, holding the stone, she'd felt something. And looking into Kell's ruined eye, she'd felt something. And when the magic spun the wood of the wall around her wrist, she'd felt something. Again the questions surged, and again she shoved them down, and took in the night air—thick with soot and heavy with impending rain—and trudged through the web of streets, and across Westminster to the Barren Tide.

The Barren Tide sat near just north of the bridge on the

southern side, tucked between Belvedere and York in a crevice of a street called Mariner's Walk, and she'd taken to stopping in on some of her more successful nights before heading back to Powell (the way she'd seen it, it left one less coin for him to skim). She liked the pub because it was full of dark wood and fogging glass, rough edges and rougher fare. Not a smart place to pick pockets, but a fine place to blend in, to disappear. She had little fear of being recognized, either as a girl (the light was always kept low, and her hood kept up) or as a wanted thief (most of the patrons were wanted for *something*).

Her weapons were in easy reach, but she didn't think she'd need them. At the Barren Tide, people tended to mind their own business. On the not-so-rare occasion that a fight broke out, the regulars were more concerned for the safety of their drinks (they'd sooner save a pitcher from a shaking table than step in to help the man whose falling body shook it), and Lila imagined someone could cry for help in the middle of the room and earn little more than a tip of the cup and a raised brow.

Not a place for all nights, to be sure. But a place for tonight.

It wasn't until Lila was firmly stationed at the bar, fingers curled around a pint, that she let the questions take her mind and run free—the *why*s and *how*s and most of all *what now*s, because she knew she couldn't simply go back to not knowing and not seeing and not wondering—and she was so wrapped up in them, she didn't notice that a man had sat down beside her. Not until he spoke.

"Are you frightened?"

His voice was deep and smooth and foreign, and Lila looked up. "Excuse me?" she said, almost forgetting to keep her voice low.

"You're clutching your drink," explained the man, pointing at the fingers wrapped knuckles-white around her glass. Lila relaxed, but only a little.

"Long night," she said, bringing the warm beer to her lips.

"And yet still young," mused the man, taking a sip from

his tumbler. Even in the Barren Tide, whose belly filled each night with a motley crew, the man seemed out of place. In the low light of the pub, he looked strangely . . . faded. His clothes were dark grey, and he wore a simple short cloak held by a silver clasp. His skin was pale, made paler by the dark wood bar beneath his hands, his hair a strange, colorless shade just shy of black. When he spoke, his voice was steady without being sweet, empty in a way that gave her chills, and his accent had gravel in it.

"Not from around here, are you?" she asked.

The corner of his mouth tugged up at that. "No." He ran a finger absently around the rim of his glass. Except it didn't feel absent. None of his motions did. He moved with a slow precision that made Lila nervous.

There was something about him, odd and jarringly familiar at the same time. She couldn't see it, but she *felt* it. And then it struck her. That feeling. It was the same one she had looking into Kell's black eye, holding the stone, bound to the wall. A shiver. A tingle. A whisper.

Magic.

Lila tensed, and hoped it didn't show as she lifted the pint to her lips.

"I suppose we should be introduced," said the stranger, turning in his seat so she could see his face. Lila nearly choked on her drink. There was nothing amiss in the angle of his jaw or the set of his nose or the line of his lips. But his *eyes.* One was greyish green. The other was pitch-black. "My name is Holland."

A chill ran through her. He was the same as Kell, and yet entirely different. Looking into Kell's eye had been like looking through a window into a new world. Strange and confusing, but not frightening. Looking into Holland's eye made her skin crawl. Dark things swirled just beneath the smooth black depths. One word whispered through her mind. *Run.*

She didn't trust herself to lift her glass again, in case her

157

hands shook, so she nudged it away and casually dug a shilling from her pocket.

"Bard," she said, by way of introduction and farewell.

She was about to push away from the counter when the man caught her wrist, pinning it to the weathered wood between them. A shiver ran up her arm at his touch, and the fingers of her free hand twitched, tempted toward the dagger under her cloak, but she resisted. "And your first name, miss?"

She tried to pull free, but his grip was made of stone. He didn't even appear to be trying. "Delilah," she growled. "Lila, if you like. Now let me go unless you want to lose your fingers."

Again his lips tugged into something that wasn't quite a smile.

"Where is he, Lila?"

Her heart lurched. "Who?"

Holland's grip tightened in warning. Lila winced.

"Do not lie. I can smell his magic on you."

Lila held his gaze. "Perhaps because he used it to cuff me to a wall after I robbed him blind and tied him to a bed. If you're looking for your friend, don't look at me. We met on bad terms and parted on worse."

Holland's grip loosened, and Lila let out an inward sigh of relief. But it died an instant later when Holland was suddenly on his feet. He took her roughly by the arm and dragged her toward the door.

"What in bloody hell are you doing?" she snapped, boots scraping against the worn floor as she tried and failed to gain purchase. "I told you, we are not friends."

"We'll see," said Holland, driving her forward.

The patrons of the Barren Tide never even looked up from their drinks. *Bastards*, thought Lila as she was shoved roughly out into the street.

The moment the pub door closed behind them, Lila went for the revolver at her belt, but for someone whose movements seemed so slow, Holland was fast—*impossibly* fast—and by

158

the time she pulled the trigger, she'd fired into nothing but air. Before the shot even finished sounding, Holland reappeared, this time at her back. She felt him there, felt the air shift the barest moment before one of his hands closed around her throat, pinning her shoulders against his chest. The other hand wrapped around the fingers on her pistol and brought the barrel to rest against her temple. The whole thing had taken less than a breath.

"Divest yourself of weapons," he instructed. "Or I will do it for you."

His grip wasn't crushing; if anything, his hold was casual, confident, and Lila had been around cutthroats long enough to know that the ones you truly had to fear were the ones who gripped their guns loosely, like they'd been born holding them. Lila used her free hand to dig the knife out of her belt and drop it to the ground. She freed a second from her back. A third she usually kept in her boot, but it was sitting on her bed, ruined. Holland's hand slid from her throat to her shoulder, but he cocked the pistol in warning.

"What, no cannons?" he asked drily.

"You're mad," growled Lila. "Your friend Kell, he's long gone."

"Do you think?" asked Holland. "Let's find out."

The air around them began to crackle with energy. With *magic*. And Holland was right: she could *smell* it. Not flowers, as with Kell (flowers and something else, something grassy and clean). Instead, Holland's power smelled metallic, like heated steel. It singed the air.

She wondered if Kell would be able to smell it, too. If that's what Holland wanted.

There was something else in that magic—not a smell, but a sense all the same—something sharp, like anger, like hate. A fierceness that didn't show in the lines of Holland's face. No, his face was startlingly calm. Terrifyingly calm.

"Scream," he said.

Lila frowned. "What do you—"

The question was cut off by pain. A bolt of energy, like bottled lightning, shot up her arm where he gripped it, dancing over her skin and electrifying her nerves, and she cried out before she could stop herself. And then, almost as quickly as the pain came, it vanished, leaving Lila breathless and shaking.

"You . . . bastard," she snarled.

"Call his name," instructed Holland.

"I can assure you . . . he's not . . . going to come," she said, stumbling over the words. "Certainly not . . . for *me*. We—"

Another wave of pain, this one brighter, sharper, and Lila clenched her jaw against the scream and waited for the pain to pass, but this time it didn't; it only worsened, and through it she could hear Holland say calmly, "Perhaps I should start breaking bones?"

She tried to say no, but when she opened her mouth to answer, all she heard was a cry, and then, as if encouraged, the pain worsened. She called Kell's name then, for all the good it would do her. He wouldn't come. Maybe if she tried, this madman would realize that and let her go. Find another form of bait. The pain finally petered out, and Lila realized she was on her knees, one hand gripping the cold stone street, the other wrenched up behind her, still in Holland's grip. She thought she was going to be sick.

"Better," said Holland.

"Go to hell," she spat.

He jerked her up to her feet and back against him, and brought the gun beneath her chin. "I've never used a revolver," he said in her ear. "But I know how they work. Six shots, yes? You've fired one. That leaves five more, if the gun was full. Do you think I could fire the rest without killing you? Humans die so easily, but I bet, if I'm clever . . ." He let the gun slide down her body, pausing at her shoulder, her elbow, before trailing down her side to her thigh and coming to rest against her knee. "The sooner he comes, the sooner I will let you go. *Call his name.*"

"He won't come," she whispered bitterly. "Why do you refuse to believe—"

"Because I know our friend," said Holland. He lifted his gun-wielding hand—Lila shuddered with relief as the kiss of metal left her skin—and wrapped his arm casually around her shoulders. "He is near. I can hear his boots on the street stones. Close your eyes. Can you hear him?"

Lila squeezed her eyes shut, but all she could hear was the thud of her heart and the thought racing through her mind. *I don't want to die. Not here. Not now. Not like this.*

"Bring him to me," whispered Holland. The air began to hum again.

"Don't—" Lila's bones lit up with pain. It shot from her skull to her weathered boots and back, and she screamed. And then, suddenly, the agony stopped and the sound died on her lips and Holland let go. She crumpled forward to the cobbled street, the stones scraping against her knees and palms as she caught herself.

Through the pounding in her head, she heard Holland's voice say, "There you are."

She dragged her head up and saw Kell standing in the road, the strange magical boy in his black coat, looking breathless and angry.

Lila couldn't believe it.

He'd come back.

But *why* had he come back?

Before she could ask, he looked straight at her—one eye black and one blue and both wide—and said a single word.

"Run."

⤜ II ⤛

Kell had been standing on the bridge, leaning against the rail and trying to make sense of how and why he'd been set up—the false letter, the humble plea, the compelled cutthroats—when he caught the scent of magic on the air. Not a faint tendril, either, but a flare. A beacon of light in a darkened city. And a signature he would know anywhere. Heated steel and ash.

Holland.

Kell's feet carried him toward it; it wasn't until he stepped off the south edge of the bridge that he heard the first scream. He should have stopped right then, should have thought things through. It was a blunt and obvious trap—the only reason Holland would send up a flare of power was if he wanted to be noticed, and the only person in Grey London who would notice him was Kell—but he still broke into a sprint.

Were you followed? Lila had asked him.

No. They can't follow me here.

But Kell had been wrong. No one in the worlds could follow him . . . except for Holland. He was the only one who could, and had, which meant that he was after the stone. It also meant that Kell should be running *away* from the signature and the scream, not toward them.

The voice cried out again, and this time he was near

enough to recognize the source of the cry being raked across the heavy air.

Lila.

Why would Holland go after *her*?

But Kell knew the answer. It sat like a weight in his chest. Holland would go after Lila because of *him*. Because in a world with so little magic, every trace stood out. And Lila would have traces—both his magic, and the stone's—written all over her. Kell knew how to cover his. Lila couldn't possibly. She'd be like a torch.

It's her own fault, thought Kell, even as he ran toward the scream. *Her own damn fault.*

He raced down the street, ignoring the burn across his ribs and the voice in his head that told him to leave her, to get away while he still could.

A blunt and obvious trap.

He cut down along the river, through an alley, around a bend, and came to a staggering halt on a narrow street just in time to hear Lila's scream cut off, to see her body sagging forward to the cobblestones. Holland stood over her, but his eyes were trained on Kell.

"There you are," he said, as if he were happy to see the other *Antari*.

Kell's mind spun. Lila looked up.

"Run," he told her, but she just kept staring at him. "Lila, *go*."

Her eyes focused then, and she staggered to her feet, but Holland caught her by the shoulder and pressed a pistol to the base of her neck.

"No, Lila," he said in his calm, infuriating way. "Stay."

Kell's hands curled into fists. "What is this about, Holland?"

"You know quite well. You have something that isn't yours."

The stone hung heavy in his pocket. No, it wasn't his. But it wasn't Holland's, either. And it certainly didn't belong to the White throne. Had the power-hungry Danes possessed the talisman, they never would have relinquished it, let alone sent it away. But who *would*? Who *did*?

With its power, Astrid and Athos would be nearly invincible, yes, but a commoner could use the stone's magic to become a king. In a world starving for power, why would anyone go to such lengths to be rid of it?

Fear, thought Kell. Fear of the magic, and fear of what would happen if it fell into the twins' hands. Astrid and Athos must have learned of the stone and its escape, and sent Holland to retrieve it.

"Give me the stone, Kell."

His mind spun. "I don't know what you're talking about."

Holland gave him a withering look. His fingers tightened almost imperceptibly around Lila, and power crackled across her skin. She bit back a scream and fought to stay on her feet.

"*Stop,*" demanded Kell. Holland did.

"Will you make me repeat myself?" he asked.

"Just let her go," said Kell.

"The stone first," said Holland.

Kell swallowed as he drew the talisman from his coat. It sang through his fingertips, wanting to be used. "You can try and take it from me," he said, "as soon as you let her go." Even as the words left Kell's lips, he regretted them.

The corner of Holland's mouth curled grimly up. He withdrew his hand, one finger at a time, from Lila's arm. She staggered forward and spun on him.

"Fly away, little bird," he said, his gaze still trained on Kell.

"Go," snapped Kell.

He could feel Lila's eyes hanging on him, but he wasn't foolish enough to let his own stray from Holland—not now— and he let out a small breath when he finally heard her boots echoing on the street stones. *Good,* he thought. *Good.*

"That was foolish," said Holland, tossing the revolver aside as if it were beneath him. "Tell me, are you are as arrogant as you seem, or only as naïve?"

"Holland, please—"

The *Antari's* gaze darkened. "You look at me, Kell, and think we are alike. That we are the same, even, one person on two divergent paths. Perhaps you think our power bonds us. Allow me to correct your misapprehension. We may share an ability, you and I, but that does not make us equals."

He flexed his fingers, and Kell had the sneaking suspicion that this was going to end badly. Holland had fought against the Danes. Holland had spilled blood and life and magic. Holland had nearly claimed the White throne as his own.

Kell must seem like a spoiled child to the other *Antari*.

But Kell still had the stone. It was bad magic, forbidden magic, but it was something. It called to him, and he tightened his grip, the jagged side digging into his palm. Its power pressed at his edges, wanting to be let in, and he resisted, keeping a wall between the talisman's energy and his own. He didn't need much. He only needed to summon something inanimate—something that would stop Holland without turning on them both.

A cage, he thought. And then commanded. *A cage.*

The stone hummed in his hand, and black smoke began to pour between his fingers, and—

But Holland didn't wait.

A gust of wind ripped through the air and slammed Kell forcefully into the door of a shop behind him. The stone tumbled from his grip, the wisps of black smoke dissolving back into nothing as the talisman hit the street. Before Kell could lunge for it, the metal nails of another door shuddered free and sang through the air, driving into his coat and pinning him to the wood. Most of the nails found fabric, but one of them found flesh, and Kell gasped in pain as the spike drove through his arm and into the door behind him.

"Hesitation is the death of advantage," mused Holland as Kell fought in vain against the metal pinnings. He willed them to move, but Holland willed them to stay, and Holland's will proved stronger.

"What are you doing here?" asked Kell through gritted teeth.

Holland sighed. "I thought it would be obvious," he said, stepping toward the stone. "I'm cleaning up a mess."

As Holland made his way toward the talisman, Kell fought to focus on the metal pinning him. The nails began to tremble as his will pushed against the other *Antari*'s. They slid free an inch—Kell clenched his jaw as the one in his arm shifted— Holland's attention wavering as he knelt to fetch the stone from the ground.

"Don't," warned Kell.

But Holland ignored him. He took up the talisman and straightened, weighing it in his palm. His will and attention were both centered on the stone now, and this time when Kell focused, the nails holding him shuddered and slid free. They drew themselves out of the wall—and out of his coat and his flesh—and clattered to the ground just as Holland held the stone up to the nearest lamplight.

"Drop it," ordered Kell, clutching his wounded arm.

Holland didn't.

Instead, he cocked his head and considered the small black stone. "Have you figured out yet how it works?" And then, as Kell lunged forward, Holland's thin fingers folded over it. Such a small gesture, slow, casual, but the moment his fist closed, black smoke poured between his fingers and swept around Kell. It happened so fast. One moment he was surging forward, and the next his legs froze mid-step. When he looked down, he saw shadows swirling around his boots.

"Stay," commanded Holland as the smoke turned to steel, heavy black chains that grew straight out of the street and clanged as they locked around Kell's ankles, bolting him in place. When he reached for them, they burned his hands, and he pulled back, hissing in pain.

"Conviction is key," observed Holland, running his thumb over the stone's surface. "*You* believe that magic is an equal. A companion. A friend. But it is not. The stone is proof. You are either magic's master, or its slave."

"Put it down," said Kell. "No good will come of it."

"You're right," said Holland, still clutching the stone. "But I have my orders."

More smoke poured forth from the talisman, and Kell braced himself, but the magic didn't settle, didn't take shape. It swirled and curled around them, as if Holland hadn't yet decided what to do with it. Kell summoned a gust of air, hoping to dispel it, but the wind passed straight through, billowing Holland's cloak but leaving the dark magic untouched.

"Strange," said Holland as much to himself as to Kell. "How one small rock can do so much." His fingers tightened around the stone then, and the smoke coiled around Kell. Suddenly it was everywhere, Blotting out his vision and forcing its way into his nose and mouth, down his throat, choking him, smothering him.

And then it was gone.

Kell coughed and gasped for breath, and looked down at himself, unhurt.

For an instant, he thought the magic had failed.

And then he tasted blood.

Kell brought his fingers toward his lips, but stopped when he saw that his entire palm was wet with red. His wrists and arms felt damp, too.

"What . . . ," he started, but couldn't finish. His mouth filled with copper and salt. He doubled over and retched before losing his balance and collapsing to his hands and knees in the street.

"Some people say magic lives in the mind, others the heart," said Holland quietly, "but you and I both know it lives in the blood."

Kell coughed again, and fresh red dotted the ground. It dripped from his nose and mouth. It poured from his palms and wrists. Kell's head spun and his heart raced as he bled out onto the street. He wasn't bleeding from a wound. He was just *bleeding.* The cobblestones beneath him were quickly turning slick. He couldn't stop it. He couldn't even get to his feet. The only person who could break the spell was staring down at him with a resignation that bordered on disinterest.

"Holland . . . listen to me," pleaded Kell. "You can . . ." he fought to focus. "The stone . . . it can make . . ."

"Save your breath."

Kell swallowed and forced the words out. "You can use the stone . . . to *break your seal.*"

The White *Antari* raised a charcoal brow, and then shook his head. "This *thing,*" he said, tapping the silver circle at his shoulder, "is not what's binding me." He knelt before Kell, careful to avoid the spreading blood. "It's only the iron." He pulled aside his collar to reveal the mark scorched into the skin over his heart. "*This* is the brand." The skin was silvery, the mark strangely fresh, and even though Kell couldn't see Holland's back, he knew the symbol went all the way through. *A soul seal.* A spell burned not only into one's body, but into one's life.

Unbreakable.

"It never fades," said Holland, "but Athos still reapplies the mark now and then. When he thinks I'm wavering." He looked down at the stone in his hand. "Or when he's bored." His fingers tightened around it, and Kell coughed up more blood.

Desperately, he reached for the coin pendants around his neck, but Holland got there first. He dug them out from under Kell's collar and snapped the cords with a swift tug, tossing the tokens away down the alley. Kell's heart sank as he heard the sound of them bouncing into the dark. His mind spun over the blood commands, but he couldn't seem to hold the words in his head, let alone shape them. Every time one rose up, it fell apart, broken by the thing killing him from the inside. Every time he tried to make a word, more blood filled his mouth. He coughed and clutched at syllables, only to choke on them.

"*As . . . An . . .*" he stammered, but the magic forced blood up his throat, blocking the word.

Holland clucked his tongue. "My will against yours, Kell. You will never win."

"Please," Kell gasped, breath ragged. The dark stain beneath him was spreading too fast. "Don't . . . do this."

Holland gave him a pitying look. "You know I don't have a choice."

"Make one." The metallic smell of blood filled Kell's mouth and nose. His vision faltered again. One arm buckled beneath him.

"Are you afraid of dying?" asked Holland, as if genuinely curious. "Don't worry. It's really quite hard to kill *Antari*. But I can't have—"

He was cut off by a glint of metal in the air and the ringing sound of it striking bone as it connected with his skull. Holland went down hard, the stone tumbling from his grip and skittering several feet into the dark. Kell managed to focus his eyes enough to see Lila standing there, clutching an iron bar with both hands.

"Am I late?"

Kell let out a small dazed laugh that quickly dissolved into wracking coughs. Fresh blood stained his lips. The spell hadn't broken. The chains around his ankles began to tighten, and he gasped. Holland wasn't attacking him, but the magic still was.

He tried desperately to tell Lila, but he couldn't find the air. And thankfully, he didn't need it. She was ahead of him. She snatched up the stone, swiped it across the bloody ground, and then held it out in front of her like a light.

"Stop," she ordered. Nothing.

"Go away." The magic faltered.

Kell pressed his hands flat into the pool of blood beneath him. *"As Anasae,"* he said, and coughed, the command finally passing his lips without Holland's will to force it down.

And this time, the magic listened.

The spells broke. The chains dissolved to nothing around his legs, and Kell's lungs filled with air. Power flooded through what little blood was left in his veins. It felt like there was nearly none.

"Can you stand?" asked Lila. She helped him to his feet, and the whole world swayed, his sight plunging into black for several horrible seconds. He felt her grip on him tighten.

"Keep it together," she said.

"Holland . . ." he murmured, his voice sounding strange and faraway in his own ears. Lila looked back at the man sprawled on the ground. Her hand closed over the stone, and smoke poured out.

"Wait . . ." said Kell shakily, but the chains were already taking shape, first in smoke and then in the same dark metal he'd only just escaped. They seemed to grow straight out of the street and coil around Holland's body, his waist and wrists and ankles, pinning him to the damp ground as he had pinned Kell. It wouldn't hold him long, but it was better than nothing. At first, Kell marveled that Lila could summon something so specific. Then he remembered she didn't need to have power. She needed only to *want* a thing. The stone did the rest.

"No more magic," he warned as she shoved the stone into her pocket, the strain showing on her face. Her grip had vanished for a moment, and when he took a step forward, he nearly collapsed, but Lila was there again to catch him.

"Steady now," she said, pulling his arm around her narrow shoulders. "I had to find my gun. Stay with me."

Kell clung to consciousness as long as he could. But the world was dangerously quiet, the distance between his thoughts and his body growing further apart. He couldn't feel the pain in his arm where the nail had struck—couldn't feel much of anything, which scared him more than the pressing dark. Kell had fought before, but never like this, never for his life. He'd gotten into his fair share of scrapes (most of them Rhy's fault) and had had his fair share of bruises, but he'd always walked away intact. He'd never been seriously hurt, never struggled to keep his own heart beating. Now he feared that if he stopped fighting, if he stopped forcing his feet forward and his eyes open, that he might actually die. He didn't want to die. Rhy would never forgive him if he died.

"Stay with me," echoed Lila.

Kell tried to focus on the ground beneath his boots. On the rain that had started to fall. On Lila's voice. The words themselves began to blur together, but he held on to the sound as he fought to keep the darkness at bay. He held on as she helped him over the bridge that seemed to go on and on forever, and through the streets that wound and tipped around them. He held on as hands—Lila's and then another's—dragged him through a doorway and up a flight of old stairs and into a room, stripping off his blood-soaked clothes.

He held on until he felt a cot beneath him and Lila's voice stopped and the thread was gone.

And then he finally, gratefully, plummeted down into black.

❧ III ❧

Lila was soaked to the bone.

Halfway across the bridge, the sky had finally opened up—not a drizzle, as London often seemed to favor, but a downpour. Within moments, they had been soaked through. It certainly didn't make dragging the half-conscious Kell any easier. Lila's arms ached from holding him up—she nearly fumbled him twice—and by the time she reached the back door of the Stone's Throw, Kell was barely conscious and Lila was shivering and all she could think was that she should have kept running.

She hadn't lived this long and stayed this free by stopping to help every fool who got himself into trouble. It was all she could do to keep herself *out* of trouble, and whatever else Holland was, he was clearly trouble.

But Kell had come back.

He didn't have to—didn't have any reason to—but he had, all the same, and the weight of it clung to her when she fled, slowing her down before finally dragging her boots to a stop. Even as she turned around, raced back, a small part of her had hoped that she'd be too late. Hoped they'd already be gone. But the rest of her wanted get there in time, if only to know *why*.

Why had he come back?

Lila asked him that very question as she was dragging him to his feet. But Kell didn't answer. His head lolled against her collar. What the hell had happened? What had Holland done to him?

Lila couldn't even tell if Kell was still bleeding—she didn't see an obvious wound—but he was covered in blood and it made her wish she'd struck Holland a second time for good measure. Kell made a soft sound, between a gasp and a groan, and Lila started talking, worried that he might die on her and it would somehow be her fault, even though she'd come back.

"Stay with me," she'd said, wrapping his arm around her shoulders. With his body so close to hers, all she could think of was the smell. Not of blood—that didn't bother her—but of the *other* scents, the ones that clung to Kell, and to Holland. Flowers and earth and metal and ash.

I can smell his magic on you.

Is that what it was? The scent of magic? She had noticed Kell's in a passing way, when she first dragged his body across her bedroom floor. Now, with his arm draped around her, the scent was overpowering. The trace of Holland's burning steel lingered in the air. And even though the stone was safely in her pocket, she could smell it, too, its scent washing over the alley. Like sea and wood smoke. Salt and darkness. She felt a moment of pride for the strength of her senses until she remembered that she hadn't smelled Kell's flowers or the stone's smoke on herself as she made her way to the Barren Tide, or as she sat at the counter, and Holland had tracked her there by both.

But the rain fell heavy and steady, and soon she could smell nothing but water on stones. Maybe her nose wasn't strong enough. Maybe the scent of magic was still there, beneath the rain—she didn't know if it *could* be expunged, or at least dampened—but she hoped the storm would help cover their trail.

She was halfway up the stairs, Kell's boots leaving red-

173

tinged water in their wake, when a voice stopped her.

"What in *God's name* are you doing?"

Lila twisted around to see Barron, and Kell nearly slipped from her grasp. She caught him round the middle at the last instant, narrowly saving him from a tumble down the steps. "Long story. Heavy body."

Barron cast a backward glance at the tavern, shouted something to the barmaid, and charged up the steps, a rag thrown over his shoulder. Together they hoisted Kell's soaking body up the remaining stairs and into the little room at the top.

Barron held his tongue as they stripped away Kell's wet coat and stained shirt, and laid him down on Lila's bed. He didn't ask her where she'd found this stranger, or why there was no wound to explain the bloody trail he'd left on the tavern's stairs (though the gash across his ribs was still quite angry). When Lila scoured the room for something to burn (in case the rain had not been enough to hide their scent, in case it still lingered here from earlier that night) and came up empty, Barron didn't ask, only went to fetch some herbs from the kitchen below.

He watched silently as she held a bowl of them over a candle and let the room fill with an earthy smell that had nothing to do with Kell or Holland or magic. He stayed as she dug through the pockets of Kell's coat (which turned out to be several coats somehow folded into one) in search of something—anything—that might help mend him (he was a magician, after all, and it stood to reason that magicians carried around magic). And Barron said nothing when at last she dug the black stone from her pocket and dropped it in a small wooden box, setting a handful of warm herbs inside before shoving the lot into the bottom drawer of her chest.

It wasn't until Lila slumped down into the chair at the foot of the bed and began to clean her pistol that Barron finally spoke.

"What are you doing with this man?" His eyes were dark and narrow.

Lila looked up from her gun. "You know him?"

"In a way," said Barron archly.

"You know what he is then?" she asked.

"Do *you*?" challenged Barron.

"In a way," she retorted. "First I took him for a mark."

Barron ran a hand through his hair, and Lila realized for the first time that it was thinning. "Christ, Lila," he muttered. "What did you take?"

Her gaze flicked to the bottom drawer of the chest, then drifted back to Kell. He looked deathly pale against the dark blanket on her bed, and he wasn't moving, save for the faint rise and fall of his chest.

She took him in, the magical young man in her bed, first so guarded, now exposed. Vulnerable. Her eyes trailed up the lines of his stomach, over his wounded ribs, across his throat. They wandered down his arms, bare but for the knife strapped to his forearm. She hadn't touched it this time.

"What happened?" asked Barron.

Lila wasn't entirely sure how to answer that. It had been a very strange night.

"I stole something, and he came looking for it," she said quietly, unable to draw her eyes from Kell's face. He looked younger asleep. "Took it back. I thought that was the end of that. But someone else came looking for him. Found me instead . . ." She trailed off, then picked up. "He saved my life," she said, half to herself, brow crinkling. "I don't know why."

"So you brought him here."

"I'm sorry," said Lila, turning toward Barron. "I didn't have anywhere else to go." The words stung even as she said them. "As soon as he wakes—"

Barron was shaking his head. "I'd rather you here than dead. The person who did this"—he waved a hand at Kell's body—"are *they* dead?"

Lila shook her head.

Barron frowned. "Best tell me what they look like, so I know not to let them in."

Lila described Holland as best she could. His faded appearance. His two-toned eyes. "He feels like Kell," she added. "If that makes sense. Like—"

"Magic," said Barron matter-of-factly.

Lila's eyes widened. "How do you . . . ?"

"Running a tavern, you meet all kinds. Running *this* tavern, you meet all kinds, and then some."

Lila realized she was shivering, and Barron went in search of another tunic for Kell while she changed. He came back with an extra towel, a small pile of clothes, and a steaming bowl of soup. Lila felt ill and grateful at the same time. Barron's kindness was like a curse, because she knew she had done nothing to deserve it. It wasn't fair. Barron did not owe her anything. Yet she owed him so much. Too much. It drove her mad.

Still, her hunger had finally caught up with her fatigue, and the cold in her skin was quickly becoming the cold in her bones, so she took the soup and mumbled a thank-you and added the cost to the coin she already owed, as if this kind of debt could ever be paid.

Barron left them and went below. Outside, the night wore on. The rain wore on, too.

She didn't remember sitting down, but she woke up an hour or so later in her wooden chair with a blanket tossed over her shoulders. She was stiff, and Kell was still asleep.

Lila rolled her neck and sat forward.

"Why did you come back?" she asked again, as if Kell might answer in his sleep.

But he didn't. Didn't mumble. Didn't toss or turn. He just lay there, so pale and so still that now and then Lila would hold a piece of glass to his lips to make sure he hadn't died. His bare chest rose and fell, and she noticed that, present injuries aside, he had so few scars. A faint line at his shoulder. A much fresher one across his palm. A ghosted mark in the crook of his elbow.

Lila had too many scars to count, but she could count Kell's. And she did. Several times.

The tavern below had quieted, and Lila got to her feet and burned a few more herbs. She turned her silver watch and waited for Kell to wake. Sleep dragged at her bones, but every time she thought of rest, she imagined Holland stepping through her wall, the way Kell had. Pain echoed through her arm where he'd gripped her, a small jagged burn the only relic, and her fingers went to the Flintlock at her hip.

If she had another shot, she wouldn't miss.

VIII

AN ARRANGEMENT

✑ I ✑

Kell woke up in Lila's bed for the second time that night.

Though at least this time, he discovered, there were no ropes. His hands rested at his sides, bound by nothing but the rough blanket that had been cast over him. It took him a moment to remember that it was Lila's room, Lila's bed, to piece together the memory of Holland and the alley and the blood, and afterward, Lila's grip and her voice, as steady as the rain. The rain had stopped falling now, and low morning light was creeping into the sky, and for a moment all Kell wanted was to be home. Not in the shoddy room in the Ruby Fields, but at the palace. He closed his eyes and could almost hear Rhy pounding on his door, telling him to get dressed because the carriages were waiting, and so were the people.

"Get ready or be left behind," Rhy would say, bursting into the room.

"Then leave me," Kell would groan.

"Not a chance," Rhy would answer, wearing his best prince's grin. "Not today."

A cart clattered past outside, and Kell blinked, Rhy fading back into nothing.

Were they worried about him yet, the royal family? Did they have any idea what was happening? How could they?

Even Kell did not know. He knew only that he had the stone, and that he needed to be rid of it.

He tried to sit up, but his body cried out, and he had to bite his tongue to keep from voicing it. His skin, his muscle, his very bones . . . everything ached in a steady, horrible way, as if he were nothing but a bruise. Even the beat of his heart in his chest and the pulse of his blood through his veins felt sore, strained. He felt like death. It was as close as he had ever come, and closer than he ever wished to be. When the pain—or at least the novelty of it—lessened, he forced himself upright, bracing a hand against the headboard.

He fought to focus his vision, and when he managed, he found himself looking squarely into Lila's eyes. She was sitting in that same chair at the foot of the bed, her pistol in her lap.

"Why did you do it?" she asked, the question primed on her tongue, as if she'd been waiting.

Kell squinted. "Do what?"

"Come back," she said, the words low. "Why did you come back?" Two words hung in the air, unsaid but understood. *For me.*

Kell fought to drag his thoughts together, but even they were as stiff and sore as the rest of him. "I don't know."

Lila seemed unimpressed by the answer, but she only sighed and returned her weapon to the holster at her waist. "How are you feeling?"

Like hell, thought Kell. But then he looked down at himself and realized that, despite his aching body, the wound at his arm, where the nail had driven through, as well as the one across his stomach from the cutthroat's stolen sword, were nearly healed. "How long was I asleep?"

"A few hours," said Lila.

Kell ran a hand gingerly over his ribs. That didn't make sense. Cuts this deep took days to mend, not hours. Not unless he had a—

"I used this," said Lila, tossing a circular tin his way. Kell plucked it out of the air, wincing a little as he did. The container was unmarked, but he recognized it at once. The small metal tin contained a healing salve. Not just any healing salve, but one of his own, the royal emblem of the chalice and rising sun embossed on its lid. He'd misplaced it weeks ago.

"Where did you get this?" he asked.

"In a pocket in your coat," said Lila, stretching. "By the way, did you *know* that your coat is more than one coat? I'm pretty sure I went through five or six to find that."

Kell stared at her, slack-jawed.

"What?" she asked.

"How did you know what it was for?"

Lila shrugged. "I didn't."

"What if it had been *poison*?" he snapped.

"There's really no winning with you," she snapped back. "It smelled fine. It seemed fine." Kell groaned. "And obviously I tested it on myself first."

"You did *what*?"

Lila crossed her arms. "I'm not repeating myself just so you can gape and glare." Kell shook his head, cursing under his breath as she nodded at a pile of clothes at the foot of the bed. "Barron brought those for you."

Kell frowned (saints, even his brow hurt when it furrowed). He and Barron had a *business* agreement. He was pretty sure it didn't cover shelter and personal necessities. He would owe him for the trouble—and it *was* trouble. Both of them knew it.

Kell could feel Lila's eyes hanging on him as he reached for the clean tunic and shrugged it gingerly over his shoulders. "What is it?" he asked.

"You said no one would follow you."

"I said no one *could*," corrected Kell. "Because no one can, except for Holland." Kell looked at his hands and frowned. "I just never thought—"

"One is not the same thing as none, Kell," said Lila. And then she let out a breath and ran a hand through her cropped dark hair. "But I suppose you didn't exactly have all your wits about you." Kell looked up in surprise. Was she actually excusing him? "And I did hit you with a book."

"What?"

"Nothing," said Lila, waving her hand. "So this Holland. He's like you?"

Kell swallowed, remembering Holland's words in the alley—*We may share an ability, you and I, but that does not make us equals*—and the dark, almost disdainful look that crossed his face when he said it. He thought of the brand burned into the other *Antari*'s skin, and the patchwork of scars on his arms, and the White king's smug smile as Holland pressed the knife into his skin. No, Holland was nothing like Kell, and Kell was nothing like Holland.

"He can also move between worlds," explained Kell. "In that way, we are alike."

"And the eye?" questioned Lila.

"A mark of our magic," said Kell. "*Antari.* That is what we are called. Blood magicians."

Lila chewed her lip. "Are there any others I should know about?" she asked, and Kell thought he saw a sliver of something—fear?—cross her features, buried almost instantly behind the stubborn set of her jaw.

Kell shook his head slowly. "No," he said, "We are the only two."

He expected her to look relieved, but her expression only grew graver. "Is that why he didn't kill you?"

"What do you mean?"

Lila sat forward in her chair. "Well, if he'd wanted to kill you, he could have. Why bleed you dry? For the fun of it? He didn't seem to be enjoying himself."

She was right. Holland could have slit his throat. But he hadn't.

It's really quite hard to kill Antari. Holland's words echoed in Kell's head. *But I can't have—*

Can't have what? wondered Kell. Ending an *Antari*'s life might be hard, but it wasn't impossible. Had Holland been fighting against his orders, or following them?

"Kell?" pressed Lila.

"Holland never enjoys himself," he said under his breath. And then he looked up sharply. "Where is the stone now?"

Lila gave him a long weighing look and then said, "I have it."

"Then give it back," demanded Kell, surprising himself with his own urgency. He told himself it would be safest on his person, but in truth, he wanted to *hold* it, couldn't shake the sense that if he did, his aching muscles would be soothed and his weak blood strengthened.

She rolled her eyes. "Not this again."

"Lila, listen to me. You've no idea what—"

"Actually," she cut in, getting to her feet, "I'm starting to get a decent idea of what it can do. If you want it back, tell me the rest."

"You wouldn't understand," said Kell automatically.

"Try me," she challenged.

Kell squinted at her, this strange girl. Lila Bard did seem to have a way of figuring things out. She was still alive. That said something. *And* she'd come back for him. He didn't know why—cutthroats and thieves weren't usually known for their moral compasses—but he did know that without her, he would be in a far worse state.

"Very well," said Kell, swinging his legs off the bed. "The stone is from a place known as Black London."

"You mentioned other Londons," she said, as if the concept were curious, but not entirely impossible. She didn't faze easily. "How many are there?"

Kell ran a hand through his auburn hair. It stuck up at odd angles from rain and sleep. "There are four worlds," he said. "Think of them as different houses built on the same foundation. They have little in common, save for their geography, and the fact that each has a version of this city straddling this river on this island country, and in each, that city is called London."

"That must be confusing."

"It isn't, really, when you live in only one of them and never need think of the others. But as someone who moves between, I use color to keep them straight. Grey London, which is yours. Red London, which is mine. White London, which is Holland's. And Black London, which is no one's."

"And why's that?"

"Because it fell," said Kell, rubbing the back of his neck where the pendant cords had snapped. "Lost to darkness. The first thing about magic that you have to understand, Lila, is that it is not inanimate. It is alive. Alive in a different way than you or I, but still very much alive."

"Is that why it got angry?" she asked. "When I tried to get rid of it?"

Kell frowned. He'd never seen magic *that* alive.

"Nearly three centuries ago," he said slowly, working out the math (it seemed further away, the effect of being so long referred to as simply "the past"), "the four worlds were twined together; magic and those who wielded it able to move between them with relative ease through any one of the many sources."

"Sources?"

"Pools of immense natural power," explained Kell. "Some small, discreet—a copse of trees in the Far East, a ravine on the Continent—others vast, like your Thames."

"The Thames?" said Lila with a derisive snort. "A source of magic?"

"Perhaps the greatest source in the world," said Kell. "Not that you'd know it here, but if you could see it as it is in *my* London . . ." Kell trailed off. "As I was saying, the doors between the worlds were open, and the four cities of London intermingled. But even with constant transference, they were not entirely equal in their power. If true magic were a fire, then Black London sat closest to the heat." By this logic, White

London stood second in strength, and Kell knew it must have, though he could not imagine it now. "It was believed that the power there not only ran strong in the blood, but pulsed like a second soul through everything. And at some point, it grew too strong and overthrew its host.

"The world sits in balance," said Kell, "humanity in one hand, magic in the other. The two exist in every living thing, and in a perfect world, they maintain a kind of harmony, neither exceeding the other. But most worlds are not perfect. In Grey London—your London—humanity grew strong and magic weak. But in Black London, it was the other way around. The people there not only held magic in their bodies, they let magic into their minds, and it took them as its own, burning up their lives to fuel its power. They became vessels, conduits, for its will, and through them, it twisted whim into reality, blurring the lines, breaking them down, creating and destroying and corrupting everything."

Lila said nothing, only listened and paced.

"It spread like a plague," continued Kell, "and the other three remaining worlds retreated into themselves and locked their doors to prevent the spread of sickness." He did not say that it had been *Red* London's retreat, its sealing off of itself, that forced the other cities to follow, and left White London pinned between their closed doors and Black London's seething magic. He did not say that the world caught between was forced to fight the darkness back alone. "With the sources restricted, and the doors locked, the remaining three cities were isolated and began to diverge, each becoming as they are now. But what became of Black London and the rest of its world, we can only guess. Magic requires a living host— it can thrive only where life does, too—so most assume that the plague burned through its hosts and eventually ran out of kindling, leaving only charred remains. None know for sure. Over time, Black London became a ghost story. A fairy tale. Told so many times that some don't even think it real."

"But the stone . . . ?" said Lila, still pacing.

"The stone shouldn't exist," said Kell. "Once the doors were sealed, every relic from Black London was tracked down and destroyed as a precaution."

"Obviously not *every* relic," observed Lila.

Kell shook his head. "White London supposedly undertook the task with even more fervor than we did. You must understand, they feared the doors would not hold, feared the magic would break through and consume them. In their cleanse, they did not stop at objects and artifacts. They slit the throats of everyone they even suspected of possessing— of having come in contact with—Black London's corrupted magic." Kell brought his fingers to his blackened eye. "It is said that some mistook *Antari's* marks for such corruption and dragged them from their houses in the night. An entire generation slaughtered before they realized that, without the doors, such magicians would be their only way of reaching out." Kell's hand fell away. "But no, obviously not *every* relic was destroyed." He wondered if that was how it had been broken, if they'd tried, and failed and buried it, wondered if someone new had dug it up. "The stone shouldn't exist and it can't be allowed to exist. It's—"

Lila stopped pacing. "Evil?"

Kell shook his head. "No," he said. "It is *Vitari*. In a way, I suppose it is pure. But it is pure potential, pure power, pure *magic*."

"And no humanity," said Lila. "No harmony."

Kell nodded. "Purity without balance is its own corruption. The damage this talisman could manage in the wrong hands . . ." *In* anyone's *hands*, he thought. "The stone's magic is the magic of a ruined world. It cannot stay here."

"Well," said Lila, "what do you intend to do?"

Kell closed his eyes. He didn't know who had come across the stone, or how, but he understood their fear. The memory of it in Holland's hands—and the thought of it in Athos's or Astrid's—turned his stomach. His own skin sang for the talisman, thirsted for it, and that scared him more than anything. Black London fell because of magic like this. What horror would it bring to the Londons that remained? To the starving White, or the ripened Red, or the defenseless Grey?

No, the stone had to be destroyed.

But how? It wasn't like other relics. It wasn't a thing to be tossed in a fire or crushed beneath an ax. It looked as though someone had tried, but the broken edge did not seem to diminish its function, which meant that even if he did succeed in shattering it, it might only make more pieces, rendering every shard its own weapon. It was no mere token; the stone had a life—and a will—of its own, and had shown so more than once. Only strong magic would be able to unmake such a thing, but as the talisman was magic itself, he doubted that magic could ever be made to destroy it.

Kell's head ached with the realization that it could not be ruined—it had to be disposed of. Sent away, somewhere it could do no damage. And there was only one place it would be safe, and everyone safe from it.

Kell knew what he had to do. Some part of him had known since the moment the stone had passed into his hands.

"It belongs in Black London," he said. "I have to take it back."

Lila cocked her head. "But how can you? You don't know what's left of it, and even if you did, you said the world was sealed off."

"I don't know what's left of it, no, but *Antari* magic was originally used to make the doors between the worlds. And *Antari* magic would have been used to seal them shut. And so it stands to reason that *Antari* magic could open them again. Or at least create a crack."

"Then why haven't you?" challenged Lila, a glint in her eye. "Why hasn't anyone? I know you're a rare breed, but you cannot tell me that in the centuries since you locked yourselves out, no *Antari* has been curious enough to try and get back in."

Kell considered her defiant smile, and was grateful, for humanity's sake, that she lacked the magic to try. As for Kell, of course he'd been curious. Growing up, a small part of him never believed Black London was *real*, or that it had ever been—the doors had been sealed for so long. What child didn't wish to know if his bedtime stories were the stuff of fiction or of truth? But even if he'd *wanted* to break the seal— and he didn't, not enough to risk the darkness on the other side—he'd never had a way.

"Maybe some were curious enough," said Kell. "But an *Antari* needs *two* things to make a door: the first is blood, the second is a token from the place they want to go. And as I told you, the tokens were all destroyed."

Lila's eyes widened. "But the stone is a token."

"The stone is a token," echoed Kell.

Lila gestured to the wall where Kell had first come in. "So you open a door to Black London, and what? Throw the stone in? What on earth have you been waiting for?"

Kell shook his head. "I can't make a door from here to there."

Lila let out an exasperated noise. "But you just said—"

"The other Londons sit between," he explained. A small book rested on the table by the bed. He brushed his thumb over the pages. "The worlds are like pieces of paper," he said, "stacked one on top of the other." That's how he'd always thought of it. "You have to move in order." He pinched a few pages between his fingers. "Grey London," he said, letting one fall back to the stack. "Red London." He let go of a second. "White London." The third page fluttered as it fell. "And Black." He let the rest of the pages fall back to the book.

"So you'll have to go *through*," said Lila.

It sounded so simple when she put it like that. But it wouldn't be. No doubt the crown was searching for him in Red London, and saints only knew who else (had Holland compelled others there? Were they searching, too?), and without his pendants, he'd have to hunt down a new trinket to get from there to White London. And once he made it that far—*if* he made it that far—and assuming the Danes weren't on him in an instant, *and* assuming he was able to overcome the seal and open a door to Black London, the stone couldn't simply be thrown in. Doors didn't work that way. Kell would have to go with it. He tried not to think about that.

"So," said Lila, eyes glittering. "When do we go?"

Kell looked up. "*We* don't."

Lila was leaning back against the wall, just beside the place he'd cuffed her to the wood—the board was ripped and ruined where she'd hacked herself free—as if reminding him, both of his actions, and of hers.

"I want to come," she insisted. "I won't tell you where the stone is. Not until you agree to let me."

Kell's hands curled into fist. "Those binds you summoned up for Holland won't hold. *Antari* magic is strong enough to dispel them, and once he wakes, it won't take him long to realize that and free himself and start hunting us down again. Which means I don't have time for games."

"It's not a game," she said simply.

"Then what is it?"

"A chance." She pushed off the wall. "A way out." Her calm shifted, and for a moment Kell glimpsed the things beneath. The want, the fear, the desperation.

"You want out," he said, "but you have no idea what you're getting *into*."

"I don't care," she said. "I want to come."

"You can't," he said, pushing to his feet. A shallow wave of dizziness hit him, and he braced himself against the bed, waiting for it to pass.

She gave a mocking laugh. "You're in no shape to go alone."

"You *can't* come, Lila," he said again. "Only *Antari* can move between the worlds."

"That rock of mine—"

"It's not yours."

"It is right now. And you said yourself, it's pure magic. It *makes* magic. It will let me through." She said it as if she were certain.

"What if it won't?" he challenged. "What if it isn't all-powerful? What if it's only a trinket to conjure up small spells?" But she didn't seem to believe him. He wasn't sure he believed himself. He had held the stone. He had felt its power, and it felt limitless. But he did not wish for Lila to test it. "You cannot know for sure."

"That's my risk to take, not yours."

Kell stared at her. "Why?" he asked.

Lila shrugged. "I'm a wanted man."

"You're not a man."

Lila flashed a hollow smile. "The authorities don't know that yet. Probably why I'm still wanted instead of hanged."

Kell refused to let it go. "Why do you really want to do this?"

"Because I'm a fool."

"*Lila—*"

"Because I can't stay here," she snapped, the smile gone from her face. "Because I want to see the world, even if it's not mine. And because I will save your life."

Madness, thought Kell. Absolute madness. She wouldn't make it through the door. And even if the stone worked, even if she somehow did, what then? Transference was treason, and Kell was fairly certain that law extended to people, particularly fugitives. Smuggling a music box was one thing, but smuggling a thief was quite another. *And smuggling a relic of Black London?* chided a voice in Kell's head. He rubbed his eyes. He could feel hers fixed on him. Treason aside, the fact remained that she was a Grey-worlder; she didn't belong in his London. It was too dangerous. It was mad, and he'd be mad to let her try . . . but Lila was right about one thing. Kell did not feel strong enough to do this alone. And worse, he did not want to. He was afraid—more afraid than he wanted to admit—about the task ahead of him, and the fate that waited at its end. And someone would need to tell the Red throne—tell his mother and father and Rhy—what had happened. He could not bring this danger to their doorstep, but he could leave Lila there to tell them of it.

"You don't know anything about these worlds," he said, but the fight was bleeding out of his voice.

"Sure I do," countered Lila cheerfully. "There's Dull London, Kell London, Creepy London, and Dead London," she recited, ticking them off on her fingers. "See? I'm a fast learner."

You're also human, thought Kell. A strange, stubborn, cutthroat human, but human all the same. Light, thin and watered down by rain, was beginning to creep into the sky. He couldn't afford to stand here, waiting her out.

"Give me the stone," he said, "and I'll let you come."

Lila bit back a sharp laugh. "I think I'll hold on to it until we're through."

"And if you don't survive?" challenged Kell.

"Then you can raid my corpse," she said drily. "I doubt I'll care."

Kell stared at her, at a loss. Was her bravado a front, or did she truly have so little to lose? But she had a life, and a life was a thing that could always be lost. How could she fear nothing, even death?

Are you afraid of dying? Holland had asked him in the alley. And Kell was. Had always been, ever since he could remember. He feared *not living*, feared ceasing to exist. Lila's world may believe in Heaven and Hell, but his believed in dust. He was taught early that magic reclaimed magic, and earth reclaimed earth, the two dividing when the body died, the person they had combined to be simply forfeit, lost. Nothing lasted. Nothing remained.

Growing up, he had nightmares in which he suddenly broke apart, one minute running through the courtyard or standing on the palace steps, the next scattered into air and ash. He'd wake sweat-soaked and gasping, Rhy shaking his shoulder.

"Aren't you afraid of dying?" he asked Lila now.

She looked at him as if it were a strange question. And then she shook her head. "Death comes for everyone," she said simply. "I'm not afraid of dying. But I am afraid of dying *here*." She swept her hand over the room, the tavern, the city. "I'd rather die on an adventure than live standing still."

Kell considered her for a long moment. And then he said, "Very well."

Lila's brow crinkled distrustfully. "What do you mean, 'very well'?"

"You can come," clarified Kell.

Lila broke into a grin. It lit up her face in a whole new way, made her look young. Her eyes went to the window. "The sun is almost up," she said. "And Holland's likely looking for us by now. Are you well enough to go?" she asked.

It's really quite hard to kill Antari.

Kell nodded as Lila pulled the cloak around her shoulders and holstered her weapons, moving with brisk, efficient motions, as if afraid that if she took too long, he would revoke the offer. He only stood there, marveling.

"Don't you want to say good-bye?" he asked, gesturing at the floorboards and somewhere beneath them, Barron.

Lila hesitated, considering her boots and the world below them. "No," she said softly, her voice uncertain for the first time since they'd met.

He didn't know how Lila's and Barron's threads were tangled, but he let the issue lie. He did not blame her. After all, he had no plans to detour to the palace, to see his brother one last time. He told himself that it was too dangerous, or that Rhy would not let him go, but it was as much the truth that Kell could not bring himself to say good-bye.

Kell's coat was hanging on the chair, and he crossed to it and turned it inside out from left to right, exchanging the worn black for ruby red.

Interest flickered like a light behind Lila's eyes but never truly showed, and he supposed she'd seen the trick herself when she went searching through his pockets in the night.

"How many coats do you suppose there are inside that one?" she asked casually, as if inquiring about the weather, and not a complex enchantment.

"I'm not exactly sure," said Kell, digging in a gold-embroidered pocket and sighing inwardly with relief as his fingers skimmed a spare coin. "Every now and then I think I've found them all, and then I stumble on a new one. And sometimes, old ones get lost. A couple of years ago I came across a short coat, an ugly green thing with patched elbows. But I haven't seen it since." He drew the Red London lin from the coat and kissed it. Coins made perfect door keys. In theory, anything from a world would do—most of what Kell wore came from Red London—but coins were simple, solid, specific, and guaranteed to work. He couldn't afford to muddy this up, not when a second life was on his hands (and it was, no matter what she claimed).

While he'd been searching for the token, Lila had emptied the money from her own pockets—a rather eclectic assortment of shillings, pennies, and farthings—and piled them on the dresser by her bed. Kell reached out and plucked a halfpenny off its stack to replace the Grey token he'd lost, while Lila chewed her lip and stared down at the coins a moment, hands thrust into the inner pockets of her cloak. She was fiddling with something there, and a few moments later she pulled out an elegant silver watch and set it beside the pile of coins.

"I'm ready," she said, tearing her eyes from the timepiece.

I'm not, thought Kell, shrugging on his coat and crossing to the door. Another, smaller wave of dizziness hit, but it passed sooner than the last as he opened the door.

"Wait," said Lila. "I thought we'd go the way you came. By the wall."

"Walls aren't always where they ought to be," answered

Kell. In truth, the Stone's Throw was one of the only places where the walls *didn't* change, but that made it no safer. The Setting Sun might have sat on the same foundation in Red London, but it was also the place where Kell did business, and one of the first places someone might come looking for him.

"Besides, we don't know what—or who—" he amended, remembering the attackers under their compulsion, "is waiting on the other side. Better get closer to where we're going before we go there. Understand?"

Lila looked as though she didn't, but nodded all the same.

The two crept down the stairs, past a small landing that branched off down a narrow hall studded with rooms. Lila paused beside the nearest door and listened. A low rumbling snore came through the wood. Barron. She touched the door briefly, then pushed past Kell and down the remaining stairs without looking back. She slid the bolt on the back entrance and hurried into the alley. Kell followed her out, stopping long enough to raise his hand and will the metal lock back into place behind them. He listened to the *shhk* of metal sliding home, then turned to find Lila waiting, her back purposely to the tavern, as if her present were already her past.

❧ II ❧

The rain had ended and left the streets dreary and damp, but despite the wet ground and the October chill, London was beginning to drag itself awake. The sound of rickety carts filled the air, met with the smell of fresh bread and new fires, and merchants and buyers began the slow revival of work, pinning back the doors and shutters of shops and readying their businesses for the day. Kell and Lila made their way through the rousing city, moving briskly in the thin dawn light.

"You're sure you have the stone?" pressed Kell.

"Yes," said Lila, lips quirking. "And if you're thinking of stealing it back, I would advise against it, as you'd have to search me, and magic or no, I'm willing to bet my knife could find your heart before your hand could find the rock." She said it with such casual confidence that Kell suspected she might be right, but he had no desire to find out. Instead, he turned his attention to the streets around them, trying to picture them as if they were a world away. "We're nearly there."

"Where's there?" she asked.

"Whitbury Street," he said.

He'd crossed through at Whitbury before (it put him near his rooms at the Ruby Fields, which meant that he could drop any newly acquired items before reporting to the palace). But more important, the row of shops on Whitbury did not sit *directly* on top of the Ruby Fields, but sat a short two blocks shy. He'd learned long ago never to walk into a world exactly where you wanted to be. If trouble were waiting, you'd land right on top of it.

"There's an inn in Red London," he explained, trying not to think about the last time he was there. About the tracing spell and the attack and the corpses of the men in the alley beyond. Corpses *he'd* made. "I keep a room there," he went on. "It will have what I need to make a door to White London." Lila didn't pick up on his use of *I* instead of *we*, or if she did, she didn't bother to correct him. In fact, she seemed lost in her own thoughts as they wove through the network of back streets. Kell kept his chin up, his senses tuned.

"I'm not going to run into myself, am I?" asked Lila, breaking the silence.

Kell glanced her way. "What are you talking about?"

She kicked a loose stone. "Well, I mean, it's another world, isn't it? Another version of London? Is there another version of me?"

Kell frowned. "I've never met *anyone* like you."

He hadn't meant it as a compliment, but Lila took it that way, flashing him a grin. "What can I say," she said, "I'm one of a kind."

Kell managed an echo of her smile, and she gasped. "What's that on your face?"

The smile vanished. "What?"

"Never mind," she said, laughing. "It's gone." Kell only shook his head—he didn't grasp the joke—but whatever it was, it seemed to delight Lila, and she chuckled to herself all the way to Whitbury.

As they turned onto the pleasant little lane, Kell came to a stop on the curb between two shop fronts. One belonged to a dentist and the other a barber (in Red London, it was an herbalist and stonesmith), and if Kell squinted he could still see traces of his blood on the brick wall in front of him, the surface sheltered by a narrow overhang. Lila was staring intently at the wall. "Is this where they are? Your rooms?"

"No," he said, "but this is where we go through."

Lila's fists clenched and unclenched at her side. He thought she must be frightened, but when she glanced his way, her eyes were bright, the edge of a smile on her lips.

Kell swallowed and stepped up to the wall, and Lila joined him. He hesitated.

"What are we waiting for?"

"Nothing," said Kell. "It's just . . ." He slipped out of his coat and wrapped it around her shoulders, as if the magic could be so easily deceived. As if it wouldn't know the difference between human and *Antari*. He doubted his coat would make a difference—either the stone would let her through or it wouldn't—but he still relinquished it.

In response, Lila fetched her kerchief—the one she'd given him when she picked his pocket and reclaimed when he passed out on her floor—and tucked it into his back pocket.

"What are you doing?" he asked.

"Seems right somehow," she said. "You gave me something of yours. I give you something of mine. Now we're linked."

"It doesn't work that way," he said.

Lila shrugged. "Can't hurt."

Kell supposed she was right. He slid his knife free and drew the blade across his palm, a thin line of blood welling up. He dabbed it with his fingers and made a mark on the wall.

"Take out the stone," he said.

Lila eyed him distrustfully.

"You'll *need* it," he pressed.

She sighed and pulled her broad-brim hat from a fold in her coat. It was crumpled, but with a flick of her wrist it unfolded, and she reached into the hat's bowl like a magician and drew out the black rock. Something in Kell twisted at the sight of it, an ache in his blood, and it took all his strength not to reach for the talisman. He bit back the urge and thought for the first time that perhaps it was better if he didn't hold it.

Lila closed her fingers around the stone, and Kell closed his fingers around Lila's, and as it was he could *feel* the talisman humming through the flesh and bone of her hand. He tried not to think about the way it sang to him.

"Are you sure?" he asked one last time.

"It will work," said Lila. Her voice sounded less certain now than it had been, less like she believed and more like she *wanted* to, so Kell nodded. "You said yourself," she added, "that everyone has a mix of humanity and magic in them. That means I do, too." She turned her gaze up to his. "What happens now?"

"I don't know," he said truthfully.

Lila drew closer, so close their ribs were touching and he could feel her heart racing through them. She was so good at hiding it, her fear. It didn't show in her eyes, or the lines of her face, but her pulse betrayed her. And then Lila's lips tugged into a grin, and Kell wondered if it was fear she felt after all, or something else entirely.

"I'm not going to die," she said. "Not till I've seen it."

"Seen what?"

Her smile widened. "Everything."

Kell smiled back. And then Lila brought her free hand to his jaw and tugged his mouth toward hers. The kiss was there and then gone, like one of her smiles.

"What was that for?" he asked, dazed.

"For luck," she said, squaring her shoulders to the wall. "Not that I need it."

Kell stared at her a moment and then forced himself to turn toward the bloodstained bricks. He tightened his hand over hers, and he brought his fingers to the mark.

"*As Travars*," he said.

The wall gave way, and the traveler and the thief stepped forward and through.

✦ III ✧

Barron woke to a noise.

It was the second time that morning.

Noise was a fairly common thing in a tavern; the volume of it ebbed and flowed depending on the hour, at some times thunderous, at others murmuring, but it was always there, in some measure. Even when the pub was closed, the Stone's Throw was never truly silent. But Barron knew every kind of noise his tavern made, from the creak of the floorboards to the groan of the doors to the wind through the hundreds of cracks in the old walls.

He knew them all.

And this one was different.

Barron had owned the tavern at the seam—for that was how he thought of the aching old building—for a very long time. Long enough to understand the strange that drifted past and in like debris. Long enough for the strange to seem normal. And while he was not a part of that strange, having no interest or affinity for the practicing of that strangeness others called magic, he had come to develop a sense of sorts, where the strange was concerned.

And he listened to it.

Just as he listened now to the noise above his head. It

wasn't loud, not at all, but it was out of place and brought with it a feeling, under his skin and in his bones. A feeling of wrongness. Of danger. The hair on his arm prickled, and his heart, always steady, began to beat faster in warning.

The noise came again, and he recognized the groan of footsteps on the old wooden floor. He sat up in his bed. Lila's room sat directly over his own. But the footsteps did not belong to Lila.

When someone spends enough time under your roof (as Lila had beneath his), you come to know the kind of noise they make—not only their voices but the way they move through a space—and Barron knew the sound of Lila's tread when she wanted to be heard, and the sound of her tread when she didn't, and this was neither. And besides, he had first woken to the sound of Lila and Kell leaving not long before (he had not stopped her, had long since learned that it was futile to try, and had long since resolved to be instead an anchor, there and ready when she wandered back, which she invariably did).

But if Lila was not moving about her room, who was?

Barron got to his feet, the shivery feeling of wrong worsening as he tugged the suspenders from his waist up onto his broad shoulders and pulled on his boots.

A shotgun hung on the wall by the door, half rusted from disuse (on the occasion trouble brewed downstairs, Barron's hulking form was usually enough to quash it). Now he took hold of the gun by the barrel and pulled it down from its mount. He drew open the door, cringing as it groaned, and set off up the stairs to Lila's room.

Stealth, he knew, was useless. Barron had never been a small man, and the steps creaked loudly under his boots as he climbed. When he reached the short green door at the top of the stairs, he hesitated and pressed his ear to the wood. He heard nothing, and for a brief moment, he doubted himself. Thought he'd slept too lightly after Lila's departure and simply dreamt the threat out of concern. His grip, which had been knuckles white on the shotgun, began to loosen, and he let out a breath and thought of going back to bed. But then he heard the metallic sound of coins tumbling, and the doubt gutted like a candle. He threw open the door, shotgun raised.

Lila and Kell were both gone, but the room was not empty: a man stood beside the open window, weighing Lila's silver pocket watch in the palm of his hand. The lantern on the table burned with an odd pale light that made the man look strangely colorless, from his charcoal hair to his pale skin to his faded grey clothes. When his gaze drifted up casually from the timepiece and settled on Barron—he seemed entirely unfazed by the gun—the tavern owner saw that one of his eyes was green. The other was pitch black.

Lila had described the man to him and given him a name. *Holland.*

Barron did not hesitate. He pulled the trigger, and the shotgun blasted through the room with a deafening sound that left his ears ringing. But when the plume of smoke cleared, the colorless intruder stood exactly where he'd been before the blast, unharmed. Barron stared in disbelief. The air in front of Holland glittered faintly, and it took Barron a moment to grasp that it was full of shot pellets. The tiny metal beads hung suspended in front of Holland's chest. And then they fell, clattering to the floor like hail.

Before Barron could squeeze off the second shot, Holland's fingers twitched, and the weapon went flying out of Barron's hands and across the narrow room, crashing against the wall. He lunged for it, or at least he meant to, but his body refused, remaining firmly rooted to the spot, not out by fear, but something stronger. *Magic.* He willed his limbs to move, but the impossible force willed them still.

"Where are they?" asked Holland. His voice was low and cold and hollow.

A bead of sweat rolled down Barron's cheek as he fought the magic, but it was no use. "Gone," he said, his voice a low rumble.

Holland frowned, disappointed. He drew a curved knife from his belt. "I noticed that." He crossed the room with even, echoing steps, and brought the blade up slowly to Barron's throat. It was very cold, and very sharp. "Where have they gone?"

Up close, Kell smelled of lilies and grass. Holland smelled of ash and blood and metal.

Barron met the magician's eyes. They were so like Kell's. And so different. Looking into them, he saw anger and hatred and pain, things that never spread, never touched the rest of his face. "Well?" he pressed.

"No idea," growled Barron. It was the truth. He could only hope they were far away.

Holland's mouth turned down. "Wrong answer."

He drew the blade across, and Barron felt a searing heat at his throat, and then nothing.

IX

FESTIVAL
&
FIRE

∽ I ∾

Red London welcomed Kell home as if nothing were wrong. It had not rained here, and the sky was streaked with wisps of cloud and crimson light, as if a reflection of the Isle. Carriages rolled in rumbling fashion over street stones on their well-worn paths, and the air was filled with the sweet steam of spice and tea and, farther off, the sounds of building celebration.

Had it really been only a matter of hours since Kell had fled, wounded and confused, away from this world and into another? The simple, assuring calm, the rightness of this place, set him off-balance and made him doubt, if only for a moment, that anything could be amiss. But he knew the peace was superficial—somewhere in the palace that bridged the river, his presence had surely been missed; somewhere in the city, two men lay dead, and more with empty eyes were likely looking for him and his prize—but here, on what had been Whitbury and was now Ves Anash, the light of the river spilling in from one side and the morning sun from the other, Red London seemed oblivious to the danger it was in, the danger he was dragging through it.

A small black stone capable of creating anything and razing everything. He shuddered at the thought and tightened his grip on Lila's hand, only to realize it was not there.

He spun, hoping to find her standing next to him, hoping they'd been pulled apart only a step or two in the course of their passage. But he was alone. The echo of *Antari* magic glowed faintly on the wall, marking the way he'd come with Lila.

But Lila was gone.

And with her, the stone.

Kell slammed his hand against the wall, splitting open the cut that had just begun to close. Blood trickled down his wrist, and Kell swore and went to search for a cloth in his coat, forgetting that he'd draped it over Lila's shoulders. He was halfway through swearing again when he remembered Lila's kerchief. The one she'd given him in exchange, tucked into his back pocket.

Seems right somehow, she'd said. *You gave me something of yours. I give you something of mine. Now we're linked.*

Linked, thought Kell. His mind spun as he dragged the square of fabric free. Would it work? Not if she'd somehow been torn apart or trapped between the worlds (there were stories, of non-*Antari* who tried to open doors and got stuck). But if she'd never come through, or if she was here somewhere—alive or dead—it might.

He brought the bloodstained kerchief to the wall and pressed his hand flat against the echo of his recent mark.

"*As Enose,*" he commanded the magic. "*As Enose* Delilah Bard.*"

Lila opened her eyes and saw red.

Not a bold red, splashed like paint over the buildings, but a subtle, pervasive tint, like she was looking through a pane of colored glass. Lila tried to blink away the color, but it lingered. When Kell called his city *Red* London, she assumed he'd picked the color for some arbitrary—or at least ordinary—reason. Now she could see that he meant it literally. She drew a breath and tasted flowers on the air. Lilies and marigolds and stargazers. The scent was overpowering, verging on sickly sweet, like perfume—no wonder it clung to Kell. After a few moments, it calmed a little (so did the tint), as her senses adjusted to her new surroundings, but when she drew too deep a breath, it assaulted her again.

Lila coughed and lay still. She was on her back in an alley, in front of a rather pretty red door (painted, not tinted). A loose street stone dug into her spine through the coat. Kell's coat. It was spread beneath her on the ground, billowing out like wings.

But Kell was not there.

She tightened her fingers to make sure she could move them, and felt the black stone nested in her palm, still humming. *It worked*, she thought, letting out an amazed exhale as she sat up. It had actually *worked*.

Not perfectly—if it had worked perfectly, she and Kell would be standing in the same place—but she was here, which was to say *there*. Somewhere *new*.

She'd done it.

Delilah Bard had finally escaped, sailed away. Not with a ship, but with a stone.

As for where she was *exactly*, she hadn't the faintest idea. She got to her feet and realized that the red tint wasn't coming from the sky, but from the ground. The world to her right was considerably redder than the world to her left. And, she realized, senses tuning, considerably louder. Not just the usual noise of peddlers and carts, for the Londons seemed to have that in common, but the din of a growing crowd, all cheers and shouts and celebration. Part of her knew she should stay still and wait for Kell to find her, but the other part was already moving toward the swell of light and color and sound.

Kell had found her once, she reasoned. He could do it again.

She tucked the black stone into the hidden pocket of her worn cloak (the dizziness upon letting go was brief and shallow) then scooped up Kell's coat, dusted it off, and pulled it on over the top. She expected it to be bulky, if not outright unruly, but to her surprise, the coat fit perfectly, its silver buttons lying smooth and even on the rich black fabric.

Strange, thought Lila, shoving her hands into its pockets. Not the strangest thing by far, but still strange.

She wove through the streets, which were like her London in their narrow, twisting fashion and yet so different. Instead of rough stone and soot-stained glass, the shops were built of dark wood and smooth rock, colored glass, and shining metal. They looked strong and strangely delicate at once, and running through them all, through *everything*, was an energy (she could think of no other word). She walked in the direction of the crowd, marveling at the change wrought in the world, a world whose bones were shared with hers, but whose body was a new, glorious thing.

And then she turned a corner and saw the source of the commotion. Scores of people had gathered along a major road, bustling in anticipation. They had the air of commoners, and yet their dress was so much finer than Lila had ever seen on the commoners at home. Their style itself was not so foreign— the men wore elegant coats with high collars, the woman waist-cinched dresses under capes—but the materials flowed on them like melted metal, and threads of gold ran through hair and hat and cuff.

Lila pulled Kell's silver-buttoned coat close around her, thankful she could hide the threadbare cloak beneath. In the cracks between the jostling crowd, she could make out the red river beyond, right where the Thames should have been, its strange light washing over the banks.

The Thames? A source of magic?

Perhaps the greatest source in the world. Not that you'd know it here, but if you could see it as it is in my *London . . .*

It was indeed magnificent. And yet, Lila was drawn less to the water and more to the ships blanketing it. Vessels of all shapes and sizes, from brigs and galleys to schooners and frigates, bobbed on the red waves, their sails billowing. Dozens of emblems marked the fabric on their masts and flanks, but over them all, red and gold banners had been hung. They glittered, taunting her. *Come aboard*, they seemed to say. *I can be yours.* Had Lila been a man, and the ships fair maidens guiding up their skirts, she could not have wanted them more. *Hang the fine dresses*, she thought. *I'll take a ship*.

But though the mismatched fleet was enough to draw a gasp of approval from *Lila's* lips, it was neither the gorgeous ships nor the impossible red river that held the crowd's attention.

A procession was marching down the avenue.

Lila reached the edge of the crowd as a row of men paraded past clothed in swaths of dark fabric that wound around their bodies as if their limbs were spools. The men held fire in their palms, and when they danced and spun, the fire arced around them, tracing their paths and lingering in the air behind them. Their lips moved as they did, the words buried under the sounds of the parade, and Lila found herself pressing forward into the crush to get a better view. Too soon the men were gone, but in their wake a line of women came into view. Dressed in flowing gowns, they executed a more fluid version of the same dance, but with water. Lila watched, wide-eyed; it behaved like ribbon in their hands, twisting and curling through the air, as if by magic.

Of course, thought Lila, *it is by magic*.

The water dancers gave way to earth, and then metal and finally, wind, the last made visible by colored dust blown from palms into the air.

Every dancer was dressed in their own way, but all had ribbons of red and gold tied off along their arms and legs, trailing behind them like comet tails as they moved through the city.

Music rose in the dancers' wake, strong as drums but sweet as strings, drawing notes Lila had never heard from instruments she had never seen. The musicians continued on, but the music lingered in the air, hanging over the crowd like a tent ceiling, as

211

if sound itself could be made physical. It was hypnotic.

And then came the knights atop their mounts, armor shining in the sun and red cloaks billowing behind them. The horses themselves were glorious beasts, not speckled but solid whites and greys and glossy blacks *almost as beautiful*, thought Lila, *as the ships.* Their eyes were like polished stones, some brown, others blue, or green. Their glistening manes ran black or silver or gold, and they moved with a grace that didn't match their size or pace.

The knights all held banners like jousting poles, a golden sun rising against a red sky.

Just then a huddle of young boys cut in front of Lila on their way past, trailing ribbons from their arms and legs, and she hooked one around the collar.

"What's all this about?" she asked the squirming child.

The child's eyes went wide, and he spit out a string of words in a tongue she did not recognize. It certainly wasn't English.

"Can you understand me?" she asked, drawing out the words, but the boy only shook his head, wriggled in her grip, and spat out foreign words until she let him go.

Another, louder cheer rippled through the gathered crowd, and she looked up to see an open carriage approaching. It was pulled by a set of white horses and flanked by an armored guard. The carriage ran banners that were more ornate and more elaborate: here the sun she'd seen on so many flags rose over a chalice, as if the contents of the cup were morning light. The cup itself was marked by an ornate *M*, all of it woven in shades of gold thread against red silk.

In the carriage stood a man and a woman, holding hands, crimson cloaks pouring from their shoulders and pooling on the polished carriage floor. They were tan, both of them, with sun-kissed skin and black hair that showed off the gleaming gold crowns nested there. (*Royalty,* thought Lila. Of course. It was a different world. A different king and queen. But there was *always* royalty.)

And there between the king and queen, one boot up on the seat like a conqueror, stood a young man, a thin crown glinting in his dark, tousled locks, a cloak of pure gold spilling over his broad shoulders. A prince. He raised his hand in a wave to the crowd, and they devoured the gesture.

"Vares Rhy!" A shout went up from the other side of the parade, quickly taken up and carried on by a dozen other voices. *"Vares Rhy! Vares Rhy!"*

The prince flashed a dazzling smile and, several feet to Lila's left, a young woman actually swooned. Lila scoffed at the girl's silliness, but when she turned back to the parade, she caught the prince looking at *her*. Intensely. Lila felt her face go hot. He didn't smile, didn't wink, only held her gaze for a long, long moment, brow crinkling faintly as if he knew she didn't belong, as if he looked at her and saw something else. Lila knew she should probably bow, or at least avert her eyes, but she stared stubbornly back. And then the moment passed. The prince broke into a fresh smile and turned back toward his subjects, and the carriage continued on, leaving ribbons and dancers and excited citizens in its wake.

Lila dragged herself back to her senses. She didn't realize how far she'd pressed forward with the rest of the crowd until she heard the cluster of girls chattering at her elbow.

"Where was he?" murmured one of them. Lila started, relieved to hear *someone* speaking her language.

"Ser asina gose," said another, then, in heavily accented English, "You sound good."

"Rensa tav," said the first. "I'm practicing for tonight. You should as well, if you want a dance." She rose up onto her toes to wave at the disappearing prince.

"Your partner in dance," said a third in broken English, "is appears to be missing."

The first girl frowned. "He is always in the procession. I do hope he is well."

"Mas aven," said the second, rolling her eyes. "Elissa is in

213

love with the black-eyed prince."

Lila frowned. Black-eyed prince?

"You cannot deny he is dashing. In a haunted kind of way."

"*Anesh*. In a *frightening* kind of way."

"*Tac*. He is nothing compared to Rhy."

"Excuse me," cut in Lila. The trio of girls twisted toward her. "What is all this?" she asked, waving her hand at the parade. "What's it for?"

The one who spoke in broken English let out an amazed laugh, as though Lila must be joking.

"*Mas aven*," said the second. "Where are you from that you do not know? It is Prince Rhy's birthday, of course."

"Of course," echoed Lila.

"Your accent is remarkable," said the one who'd been searching for her black-eyed prince. Elissa. "Who is your tutor?"

Now it was Lila's turn to laugh. The girls only stared at her. But then trumpets—at least they sounded roughly like trumpets—began to sound from the direction the royals and the rest of the festival had come, and the crowd, now in the procession's wake, moved toward the music, taking the cluster of girls with it. Lila stepped out of the throng and brought her hand to her pocket, checking to make sure the black rock was still there. It was. It hummed, wanting to be held, but she resisted the urge. It may be clever, but so was she.

Without the procession blocking her view, Lila could fully see the glittering river on the other side of the road. It shone with an impossible red light, as if lit from beneath. A *source*, Kell had called the river, and Lila could see why. It *vibrated* with power, and the royal procession must have crossed a bridge, for now it trailed down the opposite bank to far-off chants and cheers. Lila's eyes trailed along the water until they reached a massive, vaulting structure that could only be the palace. It sat not on the banks of the river, like parliament, but *over* the river itself, spanning the water like a bridge. It seemed carved out of glass, or crystal, its joints fused with copper and stone.

Lila took in the structure with hungry eyes. The palace looked like a jewel. No, a crown of jewels, better sized to a *mountain* than a head.

The trumpets were issuing from the steps, where servants in red and gold half-cloaks were pouring out, carrying trays of food and drink for the masses.

The scent on the air—of strange food and drink and magic—was utterly intoxicating. Lila felt her head swimming with it as she stepped into the street.

The crowds were thinning, and between the emptying road and the red river, a market had blossomed like a hedge of roses. A portion of the masses had gone with the royal parade, but the rest had taken to the market, and Lila followed.

"*Crysac!*" called a woman, holding up fiery red gems. "*Nissa lin.*"

"*Tessane!*" urged another, with what looked like a steaming metal teapot. "*Cas tessane.*" He waved two fingers in the air. "*Sessa lin.*"

Everywhere merchants announced their wares in their strange tongue. Lila tried to pick up terms here and there, to pair the shouted words with the items held aloft—*cas* seemed to mean hot, and *lin,* she guessed, was a kind of coin—but everything was bright and colorful and humming with power, and she could hardly focus long enough to keep track of anything.

She pulled Kell's coat tighter about her shoulders and wandered the booths and stalls with hungry eyes. She had no money, but she had quick fingers. She passed a stall marked ESSENIR, and saw within a table piled high with polished stones of every color—not simple reds or blues, but perfect imitations of nature: fire yellow, summer grass green, night blue. The merchant's back was to her, and she couldn't help herself.

Lila reached for the nearest charm, a lovely blue-green stone the color of the open sea—at least, the color she imagined it must be, the color she'd seen it painted—with small white marks, like breaking waves. But when her fingers curled around it, a hot pain seared across her skin.

She gasped, more from the shock of being burned than the heat itself, and pulled back sharply, hand singing. Before she could retreat, the merchant caught her by the wrist.

"Kers la?" he demanded. When she didn't answer— couldn't answer—he started shouting faster and louder, the words blurring together in her ears.

"Unhand me," she demanded.

The merchant's brow furrowed at the sound of her voice. "What you think?" he said, in guttural English. "You get free by speaking fancy?"

"I haven't the faintest idea what you're talking about," snapped Lila. "Now let *go.*"

"Speak *Arnesian.* Speak English. Doesn't matter. Still *gast.* Still thief."

"I am not a *gast,*" growled Lila.

"Viris gast. Fool thief. Tries to steal from enchanted tent."

"I didn't know it was enchanted," countered Lila, reaching for the dagger at her waist.

"Pilse," growled the merchant, and Lila had a feeling she'd just been insulted. And then the merchant raised his voice. *"Strast!"* he shouted, and Lila twisted in his grip to see armored guards at the edge of the market. *"Strast!"* he called again, and one of the men cocked his head and turned toward them.

Shit, thought Lila, wrenching free of the merchant's grip, only to stumble back into another set of hands. They tightened on her shoulders and she was about to draw her knife when the merchant went pale.

"Mas aven," he said, hunching forward into a bow.

The hands holding Lila vanished, and she spun to find Kell standing there, frowning his usual frown and staring past her at the merchant.

"What is the meaning of this?" he asked, and Lila didn't know which surprised her more: his sudden appearance, the way he spoke to the merchant—his voice cool, dismissive—or the way the merchant looked at him, with a mixture of awe and fear.

Kell's auburn hair was pushed back, his black eye on display in the red morning light.

"*Aven vares.* If I knew she was with y-you . . ." stammered the merchant before lapsing back into Arnesian, or whatever the language was called. Lila was surprised to hear the tongue pour out of Kell's mouth in response as he tried to calm the merchant. And then she caught that word again, *gast,* on the merchant's tongue and lunged for him. Kell hauled her back.

"Enough," Kell snarled in her ear. "*Solase,*" he said to the merchant, apologetically. "She's a *foreigner*. Uncivilized, but harmless."

Lila shot him a dark look.

"*Anesh, mas vares,*" said the merchant, bowing even lower. "Harmful enough to steal . . ." With his head down, the merchant didn't see Kell look back over his shoulder at the guard weaving through the market toward them. He didn't see the way Kell stiffened. But Lila did.

"I will buy whatever she tried to take," said Kell hastily, digging a hand in the pocket of his coat, unconcerned by the fact Lila was still wearing it.

The merchant straightened and started shaking his head. "*An. An.* I cannot be taking money from you."

The guard was getting closer, and Kell clearly didn't want to be there when he arrived, because he fetched a coin from the coat and set it on the table with a snap.

"For your trouble," he said, turning Lila away. "*Vas ir.*"

He didn't wait for the merchant's answer, only shoved Lila through the crowd, away from the stall and the guard about to reach it.

"*Uncivilized?*" growled Lila as Kell clasped her shoulder and guided her out of the market.

"Five minutes!" said Kell, sliding his coat from her

shoulders and back onto his own, flicking up the collar. "You can't keep your hands to yourself for five minutes! Tell me you haven't already gone and sold off the stone."

Lila let out an exasperated noise. "Unbelievable," she snapped as he led her out of the throngs and away from the river, toward one of the narrower streets. "I'm so glad you're all right, Lila," she parroted. "Thank God using the stone didn't rip you into a thousand thieving pieces."

Kell's hand loosened on her shoulder. "I can't believe it worked."

"Don't sound so excited," shot Lila drily.

Kell came to a stop and turned her toward him. "I'm not," he said. His blue eye looked troubled, his black unreadable. "I'm glad you're unhurt, Lila, but the doors between worlds are meant to be locked to all but *Antari*, and the fact that the stone granted you passage only proves how dangerous it is. And every moment it's here, in *my* world, I'm terrified."

Lila found her eyes going to the ground. "Well, then," she said. "Let's get it out of here."

A small grateful smile crossed Kell's lips. And then Lila dug the stone out of her pocket and held it up, and Kell let out a dismayed sound and swallowed her hand with his, hiding the stone from sight. Something flickered through his eyes when he touched her, but she didn't think it was *her* touch that moved him. The stone gave a strange little shudder in her hand, as if it felt Kell and wanted to be with him. Lila felt vaguely insulted.

"*Sanct!*" he swore at her. "Just hold it up for all to see, why don't you."

"I thought you wanted it back!" she shot back, exasperated. "There's no winning with you."

"Just keep it," he hissed. "And for king's sake, keep it out of sight."

Lila shoved it back into her cloak and said a very many unkind things under her breath.

"And on the topic of language," said Kell, "you cannot speak so freely here. English is not a common tongue."

"I noticed that. Thanks for the warning."

"I told you the worlds would be different. But you're right, I should have warned you. Here English is a tongue used by the elite, and those who wish to mingle with them. Your very use of it will cause you to stand out."

Lila's eyes narrowed. "What would you have me do? *Not* speak?"

"The thought had crossed my mind," said Kell. Lila scowled. "But as I doubt that's possible for you, I'd ask that you simply keep your voice down." He smiled, and Lila smiled back, resisting the urge to break his nose.

"Now that that's settled . . ." He turned to go.

"Pilse," she grumbled, hoping it meant something foul indeed as she fell into step behind him.

❦ II ❧

Aldus Fletcher was not an honest man.

He ran a pawnshop in an alley by the docks, and each day, men came off the boats, some with things they wanted, others with things they wanted to be rid of. Fletcher provided for both. And for the locals, too. It was a truth widely known in the darker corners of Red London that Fletcher's shop was the place for anything you shouldn't have.

Now and again *honest* folk wandered in, of course, wanting to find or dispose of smoking pipes and instruments, scrying boards and rune stones and candlesticks, and Fletcher didn't mind padding the shop with their wares as well, in case the royal guard came to inspect. But his true trade lay in risk and rarity.

A smooth stone panel hung on the wall beside the counter, big as a window but black as pitch. On its surface, white smoke shifted and shimmered and spread itself like chalk, announcing the full itinerary of the prince's birthday celebrations. An echo of Rhy's smiling face ghosted itself on the scrying board above the notice. He beamed and winked as beneath his throat the message hovered:

> *The king and queen invite*
> *you to celebrate the prince's*

twentieth year on the palace steps
following the annual parade.

After a few seconds, the message and the prince's face both dissolved and, for a moment, the scrying board went dark, then came back to life and began to cycle through a handful of other announcements.

"*Erase es ferase?*" rumbled Fletcher in his deep voice. *Coming or going?*

The question was lobbed at a boy—and he *was* a boy, the stumble of his first beard growing patchily in—who stood considering a table of trinkets by the door. *Coming* meant a buyer, *going* meant a seller.

"Neither," murmured the boy. Fletcher kept an eye on the youth's wandering hands, but he wasn't too worried; the shop was warded against thieving. It was a slow day, and Fletcher almost wished the boy would try. He could use a little entertainment. "Just looking," he added nervously.

Fletcher's shop didn't usually get lookers. People came with a purpose. And they had to make that purpose known. Whatever the boy was after, he didn't want it badly enough to say.

"You let me know," said Fletcher, "if you can't find what it is you're looking for."

The boy nodded, but kept cheating glances at Fletcher. Or rather, at Fletcher's arms, which were resting on the counter. The air outside was heavy for a morning so late in the harvest season (one might have thought that, given his clientele, the shop would run thieves' hours, dusk till dawn, but Fletcher had found that the best crooks knew how to play off crime as casual), and Fletcher had his sleeves rolled up to the elbows, exposing a variety of marks and scars on his sun-browned forearms. Fletcher's skin was a map of his life. And a hard-lived life at that.

"S'true what they say?" the boy finally asked.

221

"About what?" said Fletcher, raising a thick brow.

" 'Bout you." The boy's gaze went to the markings around Fletcher's wrists. The limiters circled both his hands like cuffs, scarred into flesh and something deeper. "Can I see them?"

"Ah, these?" asked Fletcher, holding up his hands.

The markings were a punishment, given only to those who defied the golden rule of magic.

"Thou shalt not use thy power to control another," he recited, flashing a cold and crooked grin. For such a crime, the crown showed little mercy. The guilty were *bound*, branded with limiters designed to tourniquet their power.

But Fletcher's were broken. The marks on the inside of his wrists were marred, obscured, like fractured links in a metal chain. He had gone to the ends of the world to break those binds, had traded blood and soul and years of life, but here he was. Free again. Of a sort. He was still bound to the shop and the illusion of impotence—an illusion he maintained lest the guards learn of his recovery and return to claim more than his magic. It helped, of course, that he'd bought favor with a few of them. Everyone—even the rich and the proud and the royal—wanted things they shouldn't have. And those things were Fletcher's specialty.

The boy was still staring at the marks, wide-eyed and pale. *"Tac."* Fletcher brought his arms back to rest on the counter. "Time for looking's over. You going to buy something or not?"

The boy scurried out, empty-handed, and Fletcher sighed and tugged a pipe from his back pocket. He snapped his fingers, and a small blue flame danced on the end of his thumb, which he used to light the leaves pressed into the bowl. And then he drew something from his shirt pocket and set it on the wooden counter.

It was a chess piece. A small, white rook to be exact. A marker of a debt he'd yet to pay but would.

The rook had once belonged to the young *Antari* whelp, Kell, but it had come to Fletcher's shop several years before as part of the pot in a round of Sanct.

Sanct was the kind of game that grew. A mix of strategy and luck and a fair bit of cheating, it could be over in minutes or last for hours. And the final hand of the night had been going on for nearly two. They were the last players, Fletcher and Kell, and as the night had grown, so had the pot. They weren't playing for coins, of course. The table was piled high with tokens and trinkets and rare magic. A vial of hope sand. A water blade. A coat that concealed an infinite number of sides.

Fletcher had played every card but three: a pair of kings with a saint among them. He was sure he'd won. And then Kell played three saints. The problem was, there were only three saints in the whole deck, and Fletcher had one in his hand. But as Kell laid out his hand, the card in Fletcher's shimmered and changed from a saint to a servant, the lowest card in the deck.

Fletcher turned red as he watched it. The royal brat had slipped an enchanted card into the set and played Fletcher as well as the game. And that was the best and worst thing about Sanct. Nothing was off-limits. You didn't have to win fair. You only had to win.

Fletcher had no choice but to lay out his ruined hand, and the room broke into raucous comments and jeers. Kell only smiled and shrugged and got to his feet. He plucked a trinket from the top of the pile—a chess piece from another London—and tossed it to Fletcher.

"No hard feelings," he said with a wink before he took the lot and left.

No hard feelings.

Fletcher's fingers tightened on the small stone statue. The bell at the front of the shop rang as another customer stepped in, a tall, thin man with a greying beard and a hungry glint in his eye. Fletcher pocketed the rook and managed a grim smile.

"Erase es ferase?" he asked.

Coming or going?

⌒ III ⌒

Kell could *feel* the stone in Lila's pocket as they walked.

There had been a moment when his fingers closed over hers and his skin had brushed the talisman, when all he wanted was to take it from her. It felt like everything would be all right if he could simply hold it. Which was an absurd notion. Nothing would be all right so long as the stone existed. Still, it pulled at his senses, and he shivered and tried not to think about it as he led Lila through Red London, away from the noise and toward the Ruby Fields.

Rhy's celebrations would last all day, drawing the majority of the city—its people and its guard—to the banks of the river and the red palace.

Guilt rolled through him. He should have been a part of the procession, should have ridden in the open carriage with the royal family, should have been there to tease and chide his brother for the way he relished the attention.

Kell was sure that Rhy would sulk for weeks about his absence. And then he remembered that he'd never have the chance to apologize. The thought cut like a knife, even though he told himself it had to be this way, that when the time came, Lila would explain. And Rhy? Rhy would forgive him.

Kell kept his collar up and his head down, but he still

felt eyes on him as they moved through the streets. He kept looking over his shoulder, unable to shake the feeling of being followed. Which he was, of course, by Lila, who looked at him with increasing scrutiny as they wove through the streets.

Something was clearly bothering her, but she held her tongue, and for a while Kell wondered if she was biding his order or simply biding her time. And then, when the appearance of a pair of royal guards, helmets tucked casually under their arms, sent Kell—and by necessity Lila—retreating hastily into a recessed doorway, she finally broke her silence.

"Tell me something, Kell," she said as they stepped back onto the curb when the men were gone. "The commoners treat you like a noble yet you hide from the guards like a thief. Which is it?"

"Neither," he answered, silently willing her to let the matter go.

But Lila wouldn't. "Are you some kind of valiant criminal?" she pressed. "A Robin Hood, all hero to the people and outlaw to the crown?"

"No."

"Are you wanted for something?"

"Not exactly."

"In my experience," observed Lila, "a person is either wanted or they're not. Why would you hide from the guards if you're not?"

"Because I thought they might be looking for me."

"And why would they be doing that?"

"Because I'm missing."

He heard Lila's steps slow. "Why would they care?" she asked, coming to a stop. "Who are you?"

Kell turned to face her. "I told you—"

"No," she said, eyes narrowing. "Who are you *here*? Who are you to *them*?"

Kell hesitated. All he wanted was to cross through his city as quickly as possible, retrieve a White London token from his rooms, and get the wretched black stone out of this world. But Lila didn't look like she planned on moving until he answered her. "I belong to the royal family," he said.

In the matter of hours he'd known Lila, he'd learned that she didn't surprise easily, but at this claim, her eyes finally went wide with disbelief. "You're a *prince*?"

"No," he said firmly.

"Like the pretty fellow in the carriage? Is he your brother?"

"His name is Rhy, and no." Kell cringed when he said it. "Well . . . not exactly."

"So *you're* the black-eyed prince. I have to admit, I never took you for a—"

"I'm not a prince, Lila."

"I suppose I can see it, you are rather arrogant and—"

"I'm *not a*—"

"But what's a member of the royal family doing—"

Kell pushed her back against the brick wall of the alley. "I'm not a *member* of the royal family," he snapped. "I *belong* to them."

Lila's forehead crinkled. "What do you mean?"

"They own me," he said, cringing at the words. "I'm a possession. A trinket. So you see, I grew up in the palace, but it is not my home. I was raised by the royals, but they are not my family, not by blood. I have worth to them and so they keep me, but that is not the same as belonging."

The words burned when he spoke them. He knew he wasn't being fair to the king and queen, who treated him with warmth if not love, or to Rhy, who had always looked on him as a brother. But it was true, wasn't it? As much as it pained him. For all his caring, and for theirs, the fact remained he was a weapon, a shield, a tool to be used. He was not a prince. He was not a son.

"You poor thing," said Lila coldly, pushing him away. "What do you want? Pity? You won't find it from me."

Kell clenched his jaw. "I didn't—"

"You have a house if not a home," she spat. "You have people who care for you if not about you. You may not have everything you want, but I'd wager you have everything you could ever *need*, and you have the audacity to claim it all forfeit because it is not love."

"I—"

"Love doesn't keep us from freezing to death, Kell," she continued, "or starving, or being knifed for the coins in our pocket. Love doesn't buy us anything, so be glad for what you have and who you have because you may want for things but you *need* for nothing."

She was breathless by the time she finished, her eyes bright and her cheeks flushed.

And for the first time, Kell saw Lila. Not as she wanted to be, but as she was. A frightened, albeit clever, girl trying desperately to stay alive. One who had likely frozen and starved and fought—and almost certainly killed—to hold on to some semblance of a life, guarding it like a candle in a harsh wind.

"Say something," she challenged.

Kell swallowed, clenched his hands into fists at his sides, and looked at her hard. "You're right," he said.

The admission left him strangely gutted, and in that moment, he just wanted to go home (and it was a home, far more of one than Lila probably had). To let the queen touch his cheek, and the king his shoulder. To swing his arm around Rhy's neck and toast to his birthday and listen to him ramble and laugh.

It ached, how badly he wanted it.

But he couldn't.

He had made a mistake. He had put them all in danger, and he had to make it right.

Because it was his duty to protect them.

And because he loved them.

Lila was still staring, waiting for the catch in his words, but there was none.

"You're right," he said again. "I'm sorry. Compared to your life, mine must seem a jewel—"

"Don't you dare pity me, magic boy," growled Lila, a knife in her hand. And just like that, the scared street rat was gone, and the cutthroat was back. Kell smiled thinly. There was no winning these battles with Lila, but he was relieved to see her back in threatening form. He broke her gaze and looked up at the sky, the red of the Isle reflecting off the low clouds. A storm was coming. Rhy would sulk at that, too, spiteful of anything that might dampen the splendor of his day.

"Come on," said Kell, "we're almost there."

Lila sheathed her blade and followed, this time with fewer daggers in her eyes.

"This place we're headed," she said. "Does it have a name?"

"Is Kir Ayes," said Kell. "The Ruby Fields." He had not told Lila yet that her journey would end here. That it had to. For his peace of mind and for her safety.

"What are you hoping to find there?"

"A token," said Kell. "Something that will grant us passage to White London." He parsed through the shelves and drawers in his mind, the various trinkets from the various cities glittering behind his eyes. "The inn itself," he went on, "is run by a woman named Fauna. You two should get along splendidly."

"Why's that?"

"Because you're both—"

He was about to say *hard as tacks*, but then he rounded the corner and came to a sharp stop, the words dying on his tongue.

"Is that the Ruby Fields?" asked Lila at his shoulder.

"It is," said Kell quietly. "Or, it was."

There was nothing left but ash and smoke.

The inn, and everything in it, had been burned to the ground.

～ IV ～

It had been no ordinary fire.

Ordinary fires didn't consume metal as well as wood. And ordinary fires spread. This one hadn't. It had traced the edges of the building and burned in a near-perfect inn-shaped blaze, only a few tendrils scorching the street stones that circled the building.

No, this was spellwork.

And it was fresh. Warmth still wafted off the ruins as Kell and Lila waded through them, searching for something—*anything*—that might have survived. But nothing had.

Kell felt sick.

This kind of fire burned hot and fast, and the edges suggested a binding circle. It wouldn't simply have contained the flames. It would have contained everything. Everyone. How many people had been trapped inside? How many corpses now in the wreckage, reduced to bone, or merely ash?

And then Kell thought, selfishly, of his room.

Years of collecting—music boxes and lockets, instruments and ornaments, the precious and the simple and the strange—all gone.

Rhy's warning—*give up this foolishness before you're caught*—echoed in his head, and for an instant, Kell was glad that he'd been robbed of the bounty before it could be discovered. And then the weight of it sank in. Whoever did this, they hadn't *robbed* him—at least, that hadn't been the point. But they'd stripped him of his loot to cut him off. An *Antari* could not travel without tokens. They were trying to corner him, to make sure that if he managed to flee back into Red London, he would have nothing at his disposal.

It was a measure of thoroughness that reeked of Holland's own hand. The same hand that had ripped the London coins from Kell's throat and cast them away into the dark.

Lila toed the melted remains of a kettle. "What now?"

"There's nothing here," said Kell, letting a handful of ash slide through his fingers. "We'll have to find another token." He brushed the soot from his hands, thinking. He wasn't the only person in Red London with a trinket, but the list was short, as he'd been far more willing to trade in artifacts from the novel, harmless Grey than the warped and violent White. The king himself had a token, passed down over the years. Fauna had one, a trinket as part of their deal (though Fauna, he feared, was now buried somewhere in the rubble).

And Fletcher had one.

Kell cringed inwardly.

"I know a man," he said, which wasn't the half of it, but was certainly simpler than explaining that Fletcher was a petty criminal who'd lost a bounty to him in a game of Sanct when Kell was several years younger and several shades more arrogant, and Kell had gifted him the White London trinket as either a peace offering (if he felt like lying to himself) or a jab (if he was being honest). "Fletcher. He keeps a shop by the docks. He'll have a token."

"Yes, well, let's hope they haven't burned *his* shop down as well."

"I'd like to see them tr—" The words died in Kell's throat. Someone was coming. Someone who smelled of dried blood and burning metal. Kell lunged for Lila, and she got out half a word of protest before he clamped one hand over her mouth and shoved the other into her pocket. His fingers found the stone and folded over it, and power surged through his body, coursed through his blood. Kell caught his breath as a shudder ran through him, but there was no time to dwell on the sensation—at once thrilling and terrifying—and no time to hesitate. *Conviction*, Holland had said, *conviction is key*, so Kell did not waffle, did not waver.

"*Conceal us,*" he ordered the talisman.

And the stone obliged. It sang to life, its power ringing through him as—between one heartbeat and the next—black smoke enveloped Kell and Lila both. It settled over them like a shadow, a veil; when he brought his fingers to it, they met something that was more than air and less than cloth. When Kell looked down at Lila, he could see her, and when she looked up, she could clearly see him, and the world around them was still perfectly visible, albeit tinted by the spell. Kell held his breath and hoped the stone had done its task. He didn't have a choice. There was no time to run.

Just then Holland appeared at the mouth of the side street.

Kell and Lila both tensed at the sight of him. He looked slightly crumpled from his time on the alley floor. His wrists were red and raw beneath his wrinkled half-cloak. His silver clasp was tarnished, his collar flecked with mud, and his expression as close to anger as Kell had ever seen it. A small crease between his brows. A tightness in his jaw.

Kell could feel the stone shudder in his hand, and he wondered if Holland was drawn to it, or if it was drawn to Holland.

The other *Antari* was holding something—a flattened crystal, the size and shape of a playing card—up to his lips, and speaking into it in his low even way.

"*Öva sö taro,*" he said in his native tongue. *He is in the city.*

Kell couldn't hear the other person's answer, but after a pause, Holland answered, "*Kösa*"—*I'm sure*—and slipped the crystal back into his pocket. The *Antari* tipped his shoulder against the wall and studied the charred ruins of the inn. He stood there, as if lost in thought.

Or waiting.

The steadiness of his gaze made Lila fidget ever so slightly against Kell, and he tightened his grip over her mouth.

Holland squinted. Perhaps in thought. Perhaps at them. And then he spoke.

"They screamed while the building was burning," he said in English, his voice too loud to be meant only for himself. "All of them screamed by the end. Even the old woman."

Kell gritted his teeth.

"I know you're here, Kell," continued Holland. "Even the burned remains cannot hide your scent. And even the stone's magic cannot hide the stone. Not from me. It calls to me the way it does to you. I would find you anywhere, so end this foolishness and face me."

Kell and Lila stood frozen in front of him, only a few short strides separating them.

"I'm in no mood for games," warned Holland, his usual calm now flecked by annoyance. When neither Kell nor Lila moved, he sighed and drew a silver pocket watch from his cloak. Kell recognized it as the one Lila had left behind for Barron. He felt her stiffen against him as Holland tossed the timepiece in their direction; it bounced along the blackened street, skidding to a stop at the edge of the inn's charred remains. From here Kell could see that it was stained with blood.

"He died because of you," said Holland, addressing Lila. "Because you ran. You were a coward. Are you still?"

Lila struggled to get free of Kell's arms, but he held her there with all his strength, pinning her against his chest. He felt tears slide over his hand at her mouth, but he didn't let go. "No," he said breathlessly into her ear. "Not here. Not like this."

Holland sighed. "You will die a coward's death, Delilah Bard." He drew a curved blade from beneath his cloak. "When this is over," he said, "you will both wish you had come out."

He lifted his empty hand, and a wind caught up the ashes of the ruined inn, whipping them into the air overhead. Kell looked up at the cloud of it above them and said a prayer under his breath.

"Last chance," said Holland.

When he was met by silence, he lowered his hand, and the ash began to fall. And Kell saw what would happen. It would drift down, and settle on the veil, exposing them, and Holland would be upon them both in an instant. Kell's mind spun as his grip tightened on the stone, and he was about to summon its power again when the ash met their veil . . . and passed through.

It sank straight through the impossible cloth, and then through them, as though they were not there. As though they were not real. The crease between Holland's two-toned eyes deepened as the last of the ash settled back to the ruins, and Kell took a (very small) measure of comfort from the *Antari*'s frustration. He may be able to *sense* them, but he could not *see* them.

Finally, when the wind was gone and the ground lay still, and Kell and Lila remained concealed by the power of the stone, Holland's certainty faltered. He sheathed the curved blade and took a step back, turned, and strode away, cloak billowing behind him.

The moment he was gone, Kell's grip on Lila loosened, and she wrenched free of him and the spell and shot forward to the silver watch on the street.

"Lila," he called.

She didn't seem to hear him, and he didn't know if it was because she'd abandoned their protective shroud or because her world had narrowed to the size and shape of a small bloodied watch. He watched her sink to one knee and take up the timepiece with shaking fingers.

He went to Lila's side and brought his hand to her shoulder, or tried, but it went straight through. So he was right. The veil didn't simply make them invisible. It made them incorporeal.

"Reveal me," he ordered the stone. Energy rippled through him, and a moment later, the veil dissolved. Kell marveled a moment at how easy it had been as he knelt beside her—the magic had come effortlessly—but this was the first time it had willingly undone itself. They could not afford to stay there, exposed, so Kell took her arm and silently summoned the magic to conceal them once more. It obeyed, the shadow veil settling again over them both.

Lila shook under his touch, and he wanted to tell her it was all right, that Holland might have taken the timepiece and left Barron's life, but he did not want to lie. Holland was many things—most of them well hidden—but he was not sentimental. If he had ever been compassionate, or at least merciful, Athos had bled it out of him long ago, carved it out along with his soul.

No, Holland was ruthless.

And Barron was dead.

"Lila," said Kell gently. "I'm sorry."

Her fingers curled tightly around the timepiece as she rose to her feet. Kell rose with her, and even though she would not look him in the eye, he could see the anger and pain written in the lines of her face.

"When this is over," she said, tucking the watch into a fold of her cloak. "I want to be the one to slit his throat." And then she straightened and let out a small, shuddering breath. "Now," she said, "which way to Fletcher?"

X

ONE WHITE ROOK

ᥫ I ᥬ

Booth was beginning to fall apart.

In this grim grey London, the drunkard's body hadn't lasted long at all—much to the displeasure of the thing burning its way through him. It wasn't the magic's fault; there was so little to hold on to here, so little to feed on. The people had only a candle's light of life inside them, not the fire to which the darkness was accustomed. So little heat, so easily extinguished. The moment he got inside, he burned them up to nothing, blood and bone to husk and ash in no time at all.

Booth's black eyes drifted down to his charred fingers. With such poor kindling, he couldn't seem to spread, couldn't last long in any body.

Not for lack of trying. After all, he'd left a trail of discarded shells along the docks.

Burned through the place they all called Southwark in a mere hour.

But his current body—the one he'd taken in the tavern alley—was now coming undone. The black stain across his shirtfront pulsed, trying to keep the last of the life from bleeding out. Perhaps he shouldn't have stabbed the drunkard first, but it seemed the fastest way in.

But the failing shell and the lack of prospects had left him with a predicament. He appeared to be rotting.

Bits of skin flaked off with every step. The people in the street looked at him and moved away, out of reach, as if whatever was eating him was contagious. Which, of course, it was. Magic was a truly beautiful disease. But only when the hosts were strong enough. Pure enough. The people here were not.

He walked on through the city—shuffled, hobbled, really, at this point—the power in this shell only embers now, and quickly cooling.

And in his desperation, he found himself drawn on—drawn *back*—to the place where he had started: the Stone's Throw. He wondered at the pull of the odd little tavern. It was a flicker of warmth in the cold, dead city. A glimmer of light, of life, of magic.

If he could get there, he might find a fire yet.

He was so consumed by the need to reach the tavern that he did not notice the man standing by its door, nor the carriage fast approaching as he stepped off the curb and into the street.

Edward Archibald Tuttle stood outside the Stone's Throw, frowning at the time.

It should be open by now, but the bolts were still thrown, the windows shuttered, and everything within seemed strangely still. He checked his pocket watch. It was after noon. How odd. *Suspicious*, he thought. *Nefarious, even.* His mind spun over the possibilities, all of them dark.

His family insisted that he had too vivid an imagination, but he held that the rest of the world simply lacked the sight, the sense for magic, which he, obviously, possessed. Or at least endeavored to possess. Or, truly, had begun to fear he would never possess, had begun to think (though he would not admit it) did not exist.

Until he found the traveler. The renowned magician known only as Kell.

That single—and singular—meeting had rekindled his belief, stoked the fires hotter than they had ever been.

And so Edward had done as he was told, and returned to the Stone's Throw in hopes of finding the magician a second time and receiving his promised bag of earth. To that end, he had come yesterday, and to that end, he would come again tomorrow, and the next, until the illustrious figure returned.

While he waited, Ned—for that was what his friends and family called him—spun stories in his head, trying to imagine how the eventual meeting would take shape, how it would unfold. The details changed, but the end remained the same: in every version, the magician Kell would tip his head and consider Ned with his black eye.

"Edward Archibald Tuttle," he'd say, "May I call you Ned?"

"All my friends do."

"Well, Ned, I see something special in you. . . ."

He'd then insist upon being Ned's mentor, or even better, his partner. After that, the fantasy usually devolved into praise.

Ned had been playing out yet another of these daydreams while he stood on the steps of the Stone's Throw, waiting. His pockets were weighed with trinkets and coins, anything the magician might want in exchange for his prize. But the magician had not come, and the tavern was all locked up, and Ned—after whispering something that was equal parts spell and prayer and nonsense and trying unsuccessfully to will the bolt from its place—was about to pause his pursuit for the moment and go pass a few hours in an open establishment, when he heard a crash behind him in the street.

Horses whinnied and wheels clattered to a halt. Several crates of apples tumbling out of a cart as the driver pulled back sharply on the reins. He looked more frightened than his horses.

"What's the matter?" asked Ned, striding over.

"Bloody hell," the driver was saying. "I've hit him. I've hit someone."

Ned looked around. "I don't think you've hit anything."

"Is he under the cart?" went on the driver. "Oh God. I didn't see him."

But when he knelt to inspect the space beneath the carriage, the spokes of its wheels, Ned saw nothing but a stretch of soot—it was, strangely enough, vaguely person-shaped—across the stones, already blowing away. One small mound seemed to move, but then it crumbled inward and was gone. *Strange*, he thought with a frown. *Ominous.* He held his breath and reached out toward the smear of charcoal dust, expecting it to spring to life. His fingers met the ash and . . . nothing happened. He rubbed the soot between his thumb and forefinger, disappointed.

"Nothing there, sir," he said, getting to his feet.

"I swear," said the driver. "There was someone here. Right here."

"Must have been mistaken."

The driver shook his head, mumbling, then climbed down from the cart and reloaded the crates, looking under the cart a few more times, just in case.

Ned held his fingers up to the light, wondering at the soot. He had felt something—or *thought* he had—a prickle of warmth, but the feeling had quickly faded to nothing. He sniffed the soot once and sneezed roundly, then wiped the ash on his pant leg and wandered off down the street.

∞ II ∞

Kell and Lila made their way to the docks, invisible to passersby. But not only invisible. *Intangible.* Just as the ash had passed through them at the ruined inn, and Kell's hand through Lila's shoulder, so did the people on the street. They could neither feel nor hear them. It was as if, beneath the veil, Kell and Lila were not part of the world around them. As if they existed outside of it. And just as the world could not touch them, they could not touch the world. When Lila absently tried to pocket an apple from a cart, her hand went through the fruit as sure as the fruit went through her hand. They were as ghosts in the bustling city.

This was strong magic, even in a London rich with power. The stone's energy thrummed through Kell, twining with his own like a second pulse. A voice in the back of his head warned him against the thing coursing through his body, but he pushed the voice away. For the first time since he'd been wounded, Kell didn't feel dizzy and weak, and he clung to the strength as much as to the stone itself as he led Lila toward the docks.

She'd been quiet since they left the remains of the inn, holding on to Kell with one hand and the timepiece with the other. When she finally spoke, her voice was low and sharp.

"Before you go thinking Barron and I were blood, we weren't," she said as they walked side by side. "He wasn't my family. Not really." The words rang stiff and hollow, and the way she clenched her jaw and rubbed her eyes (when she thought he wasn't looking) told another story. But Kell let Lila keep her lie.

"Do you have any?" he asked, remembering her biting remarks about his situation with the crown. "Family, that is?"

Lila shook her head. "Mum's been dead since I was ten."

"No father?"

Lila gave a small humorless laugh. "My *father*." She said it like it was a bad word. "The last time I saw *him*, he tried to sell my flesh to pay his tab."

"I'm sorry," said Kell.

"Don't be," said Lila, managing the sharp edge of a smile. "I cut the man's throat before he could get his belt off." Kell tensed. "I was fifteen," she went on casually. "I remember wondering at the amount of blood, the way it kept spilling out of him. . . ."

"First time you killed someone?" asked Kell.

"Indeed," she said, her smile turning rueful. "But I suppose the nice thing about killing is that it gets easier."

Kell's brow furrowed. "It shouldn't."

Lila's eyes flicked up to his. "Have *you* ever killed anyone?" she asked.

Kell's frown deepened. "Yes."

"And?"

"And what?" he challenged. He expected her to ask who or where or when or how. But she didn't. She asked why.

"Because I had no choice," he said.

"Did you enjoy it?" she asked.

"Of course not."

"I did." There was a streak of bitterness woven through the admission. "I mean, I didn't enjoy the blood, or the gurgling sound he made as he died, or the way the body looked when

242

it was over. Empty. But the moment I decided to do it, and the moment after that when the knife bit in and I knew that I'd done it, I felt"—Lila searched for the words—"powerful." She considered Kell then. "Is that what magic feels like?" she asked honestly.

Maybe in White London, thought Kell, where power was held like a knife, a weapon to be used against those in your way.

"No," he said. "That's not magic, Lila. That's just murder. Magic is . . ." But he trailed off, distracted by the nearest scrying board, which had suddenly gone dark.

Up and down the streets, the black notice boards affixed to lampposts and storefronts went blank. Kell slowed. All morning they had been running notices of Rhy's celebrations, a cycling itinerary of the day's—and week's—parades and public feasts, festivals and private dances. When the boards first went dark, Kell assumed that they were simply changing over stories. But then they all began to flash the same alarming message. A single word:

MISSING

The letters flashed, bold and white, at the top of every board, and beneath it, a picture of *Kell*. Red hair and black eye and silver-buttoned coat. The image moved faintly, but didn't smile, only stared out at the world. A second word wrote itself beneath the portrait:

REWARD

Sanct.

Kell slammed to a stop, and Lila, who'd been half a step behind, ran into him.

"What's the matter?" she asked, pushing off his arm. And then she saw it, too. "Oh . . ."

An old man stopped a few feet away to read the board,

oblivious to the fact that the missing man stood just behind his shoulder. Beneath the wavering image of Kell's face, an empty circle drew itself in chalk. The instructions beside it read:

If seen, touch here.

Kell swore under his breath. Being hunted by Holland was bad enough, but now the whole city would be on alert. And they couldn't stay invisible forever. He wouldn't be able to lift a token, let alone use it, as long as they were under the veil.

"Come on." He picked up his pace, dragging Lila with him until they reached the docks. All around, his face stared back at them, frowning slightly.

When they reached Fletcher's shop, the door was shut and locked, a small sign hanging on its front that read RENACHE. *Away*.

"Do we wait?" asked Lila.

"Not out here," said Kell. The door was bolted three ways, and likely charmed as well, but they didn't need to be let in. They passed straight through the wood, the way they had half a dozen people on the street.

Only once they were safe within the shop did Kell will the magic to release the veil. Again it listened and obeyed without protest, the magic thinning and then dissolving entirely. *Conviction*, he mused as the spell slid from his shoulders, the room coming into sharper focus around him. Holland had been right. It was about staying in control. And Kell had.

Lila let go of his hand and turned back to face him. She froze.

"Kell," she said carefully.

"What is it?" he asked.

"Put down the stone."

He frowned, looked down at the talisman in his grip, and caught his breath. The veins on the back of his hand were dark, so dark that they stood out like ink against his flesh, the lines tracing up toward his elbow. The power he'd felt pulsing through him was *actually* pulsing through him, turning his blood black. He had been so focused on his renewed strength, and on the spell itself, on staying hidden, that he had not felt— had not wanted to feel—the warmth of the magic spreading up his arm like poison. But he should have noticed, should have known—that was the thing. Kell *knew* better. He knew how dangerous the stone was, and yet, even now, staring down at his darkened veins, that danger felt strangely faraway. A persistent calm pressed through him stride for stride with the stone's magic, telling him that everything would be all right, so long as he kept holding—

A knife buried itself in the post beside his head, and the room snapped back into focus.

"Have you gone deaf?" growled Lila, freeing another blade. "I said *put it down.*"

Before the calm could close over him again, Kell willed himself to release the stone. At first, his fingers stayed clasped around the talisman as warmth—and in its wake, a kind of numbness—seeped through him. He brought his free, untainted hand to his darkening wrist and gripped hard, willing his resisting fingers to uncurl, to release the stone.

And finally, reluctantly, they did.

The stone tumbled from his grip, and Kell's knee instantly buckled beneath him. He caught himself on a table's edge, gasping for breath as his vision swam and the room tilted. He hadn't felt the stone leeching his energy, but now that it was gone, it was like someone had doused his fire. Everything went cold.

The talisman glinted on the wooden floor, a streak of blood against the jagged edge where Kell had gripped too hard. Even in its wake, it took all Kell's will not to take it up again. Shaking and chilled, he still longed to hold it. There were men who lurked in dens and in the dark corners of London, chasing highs like this, but Kell had never been one of them, never craved the raw power. Never needed to. Magic wasn't something he lusted for; it was something he simply *had*. But now his veins felt starved of it, and starving *for* it.

Before he could lose battle for control, Lila knelt beside the stone. "Clever little thing," she said, reaching for it.

"Don't—" started Kell, but she'd already used her handkerchief to sweep it up.

"Someone's got to hold on to it," she said, slipping the talisman into her pocket. "And I'd wager I'm the better choice right now."

Kell clutched the table as the magic withdrew, the veins in his arm lightening little by little.

"Still with us?" asked Lila.

Kell swallowed and nodded. The stone was a poison, and they had to be rid of it. He steadied himself. "I'm all right."

Lila raised a brow. "Yes. You are the very image of health."

Kell sighed and slumped into a chair. On the docks outside, the celebrations were in full swing. Fireworks punctuated the music and cheers, the noise dulled, but not much, by the walls of the shop.

"What's he like?" asked Lila, looking in a cabinet. "The prince."

"Rhy?" Kell ran a hand through his hair. "He's . . . charming and spoiled, generous and fickle and hedonistic. He would flirt with a nicely upholstered chair, and he never takes anything seriously."

"Does he get into as much trouble as you do?"

Kell cracked a smile. "Oh, much more. Believe it or not, I'm the responsible one."

"But you two are close."

Kell's smile fell, and he nodded once. "Yes. The king and queen may not be my parents, but Rhy is my brother. I would die for him. I would kill for him. And I have."

"Oh?" asked Lila, admiring a hat. "Do tell."

"It's not a pleasant story," said Kell, sitting forward.

"Now I want to hear it even more," said Lila.

Kell considered her and sighed, looking down at his hands. "When Rhy was thirteen, he was abducted. We were playing some stupid game in the palace courtyard when he was taken. Though, knowing Rhy, he might have gone willingly at first. Growing up, he was always too trusting."

Lila set the hat aside. "What happened?"

"Red London is a good place," insisted Kell. "The royals here are kind, and just, and most of the subjects are happy. But," he continued, "I have been to all three Londons, and I can say this: there is no version that does not suffer in one way or another."

He thought of the opulence, the glittering wealth, and what it must look like to those without. Those who had been stripped of power for crimes, and those never blessed with much to begin with. Kell could not help wondering, What would have become of Rhy Maresh if he were not a royal? Where would he be? But of course, Rhy could survive on his charm and his smile. He would always get by.

"My world is a world made of magic," he said. "The gifted reap the blessings, and the royal family wants to believe that those who are not gifted do as well. That their generosity and their care extend to every citizen." He found Lila's eyes. "But I have seen the darker parts of this city. In your world, magic is a rarity. In mine, the lack of it is just as strange. And those without gifts are often looked down upon as unworthy of them, and treated as less for it. The people here believe that magic chooses its path. That it judges, and so can they. *Aven essen*, they call it. *Divine balance*."

But by that logic, the magic had *chosen* Kell, and he did not believe that. Someone else could just have easily woken or been born with the *Antari* mark, and been brought into the lush red folds of the palace in his stead.

"We live brightly," said Kell. "For better or worse, our city burns with life. With light. And where there's light . . . well. Several years ago, a group began to form. They called themselves the Shadows. Half a dozen men and women—some with power, some without—who believed the city burned its power too brightly and with too little care, squandering it. To them, Rhy was not a boy, but a symbol of everything wrong. And so they took him. I later learned they meant to hang his body from the palace doors. Saints be thanked, they never got the chance.

"I was fourteen when it happened, a year Rhy's senior and still coming into my power. When the king and queen learned of their son's abduction, they sent the royal guard across the city. Every scrying board in every public square and private home burned with the urgent message to find the stolen prince. And I knew they would not find him. I knew it in my bones and in my blood.

"I went to Rhy's rooms—I remember how empty the palace was, with all the guards out searching—and found the first thing I knew was truly his, a small wooden horse he'd carved, no bigger than a palm. I had made doors using tokens before, but never one like this, never to a person instead of a place. But there is an *Antari* word for *find,* and so I thought it would work. It had to. And it did. The wall of his room gave way to the bottom of a boat. Rhy was lying on the floor. And he wasn't breathing."

Air hissed between Lila's teeth, but she didn't interrupt.

"I had learned the blood commands for many things," said Kell. "*As Athera.* To grow. *As Pyrata.* To burn. *As Illumae.* To light. *As Travars.* To Travel. *As Orense.* To open. *As Anasae.* To dispel. *As Hasari.* To heal. So I tried to heal him. I cut my hand and pressed it to his chest and said the words. And it didn't work." Kell would never shake the image of Rhy lying on the damp deck floor, pale and still. It was one of the only times in his life that he looked small.

"I didn't know what to do," continued Kell. "I thought maybe I hadn't used enough blood. So I cut my wrists."

He could feel Lila's unwavering stare as he looked down at

his hands now, palms up, considering the ghosted scars.

"I remember kneeling over him, the dull ache spreading up my arms as I pressed my palms against him and said the words over and over and over. *As Hasari. As Hasari. As Hasari.* What I didn't realize then was that a healing spell—even a blood command—takes time. It was already working, had been since the first invocation. A few moments later, Rhy woke up." Kell broke into a sad smile. "He looked up and saw me crouching over him, bleeding, and the first thing he said wasn't 'What happened?' or 'Where are we?' He touched the blood on his chest and said, 'Is it yours? Is it all yours?' and when I nodded, he burst into tears, and I took him home."

When he found Lila's gaze, her dark eyes were wide.

"But what happened to the Shadows?" she asked, when it was clear that he was done. "The ones who took him? Were they in the boat? Did you go back for them? Did you send the guards?"

"Indeed," said Kell. "The king and queen tracked down every member of the Shadows. And Rhy pardoned them all."

"What?" gasped Lila. "After they tried to kill him?"

"That's the thing about my brother. He's headstrong and thinks with every part of his body but his brain most days, but he's a *good* prince. He possesses something many lack: *empathy.* He forgave his captors. He understood why they did it, and he felt their suffering. And he was convinced that if he showed them mercy, they wouldn't try to harm him again." Kell's eyes went to the floor. "And I made sure they couldn't."

Lila's brow crinkled as she realized what he was saying. "I thought you said—"

"I said *Rhy* forgave them." Kell pushed to his feet. "I never said I did."

Lila stared at him, not with shock or horror, but a measure of respect. Kell rolled his shoulders and smoothed his coat. "I guess we better start looking."

She blinked once, twice, obviously wanting to say more, but

Kell made it as clear as he could that this particular discussion was over. "What are we looking for?" she finally asked.

Kell surveyed the packed shelves, the overflowing cabinets and cupboards.

"A white rook."

ℭ III ℭ

For all the digging he'd done through the ruins of the Ruby Fields, Kell had failed to notice the alley where he'd been attacked—and where he'd left two bodies behind—only hours before. If he'd ventured there, he would have seen that one of those bodies—the cutthroat previously encased in stone—was missing.

That same cutthroat now made his way down the curb, humming faintly as he relished the warmth of the sun and the far-off sounds of celebration.

His body wasn't doing very well. Better than the other shell, of course, the drunkard in the duller London; that one hadn't lasted long at all. This one had fared better, much better, but now it was all burnt up inside and beginning to blacken without, the darkness spreading through its veins and over its skin like a stain. He looked less like a man now, and more like a charred piece of wood.

But that was to be expected. After all, he had been busy.

The night before, the lights of the pleasure house had burned bright and luring in the dark, and a woman stood waiting for him in the doorway with a painted smile and hair the color of fire, of life.

"*Avan, res nastar,*" she purred in the smooth Arnesian

tongue. She drew up her skirts as she said it, flashing a glimpse of knee. "Won't you come in?"

And he had, the cutthroat's coins jingling in his pocket.

She'd led him down a hall—it was dark, much darker than it had been outside—and he'd let her lead, enjoying the feel of her hand—or in truth, her pulse—in his. She never looked him in the eyes, or she might have seen that they were darker than the hall around them. Instead, she focused on his lips, his collar, his belt.

He was still learning the nuances of his new body, but he managed to press his cracking lips to the woman's soft mouth. Something passed between them—the ember of a pure black flame—and the woman shivered.

"*As Besara,*" he whispered in her ear. *Take.*

He slid the dress from her shoulders and kissed her deeper, his darkness passing over her tongue and through her head, intoxicating. Power. Everybody wanted it, wanted to be closer to magic, to its source. And she welcomed it. Welcomed *him.* Nerves tingled as the magic took them, feasting on the current of life, the blood, the body. He'd taken the drunkard, Booth, by force, but a willing host was always better. Or at least, they tended to last longer.

"*As Herena,*" he cooed, pressing the woman's body back onto the bed. *Give.*

"*As Athera,*" he moaned as he took her, and she took him in. *Grow.*

They moved together like a perfect pulse, one bleeding into the other, and when it was over, and the woman's eyes floated open, they reflected his, both a glossy black. The thing inside her skin pulled her rouged lips into a crooked smile.

"*As Athera,*" she echoed, sliding up from the bed. He rose and followed, and they set out—one mind in two bodies— first through the pleasure house, and then through the night.

Yes, he had been busy.

He could feel himself spreading through the city as he

made his way toward the waiting red river, the pulse of magic and life laid out like a promised feast.

⚬ IV ⚭

Fletcher's shop was built like a maze, arranged in a way that only the snake himself would understand. Kell had spent the last ten minutes turning through drawers and had uncovered a variety of weapons and charms, and a fairly innocuous parasol, but no white rook. He groaned and tossed the parasol aside.

"Can't you just find the damned thing using magic?" asked Lila.

"The whole place is warded," answered Kell. "Against locator spells. And against thieving, so put that back."

Lila dropped the trinket she was about to palm back on the counter. "So," she said, considering the contents of a glass case, "you and Fletcher are friends?"

Kell pictured Fletcher's face the night he'd lost the pot. "Not exactly."

Lila raised a brow. "Good," she said. "More fun to steal from enemies."

Enemies was a fair word. The strange thing was, they could have been partners.

"A smuggler and a fence," he'd said. "We'd make a perfect team."

"I'll pass," said Kell. But when the game of Sanct had been

in its last hand, and he'd known that he had won, he'd baited Fletcher with the one thing he wouldn't refuse. *"Anesh,"* he'd conceded. "If you win, I'll work for you."

Fletcher had smiled his greedy smile and drawn his last card.

And Kell had smiled back and played his hand and won everything, leaving Fletcher with nothing more than a bruised ego and a small white rook.

No hard feelings.

Now Kell turned over half the store, searching for the token and glancing every few moments at the door while his own face watched them from the scrying board on the wall.

MISSING

Meanwhile, Lila had stopped searching and was staring at a framed map. She squinted and tilted her head, frowning as if something were amiss.

"What is it?" asked Kell.

"Where's Paris?" she asked, pointing to the place on the continent where it should be.

"There is no Paris," said Kell, rummaging through a cupboard. "No France. No England, either."

"But how can there be a London without an England?"

"I told you, the city's a linguistic oddity. Here London is the capital of Arnes."

"So Arnes is simply your name for England."

Kell laughed. "No," he said, shaking his head as he crossed to her side. "Arnes covers more than half of your Europe. The island—your England—is called the *raska*. The *crown*. But it's only the tip of the empire." He traced the territory lines with his fingertip. "Beyond our country lies Vesk, to the north, and Faro, to the south."

"And beyond them?"

Kell shrugged. "More countries. Some grand, some small. It's a whole world, after all."

Her gaze trailed over the map, eyes bright. A small private smile crossed her lips. "Yes, it is."

She pulled away and wandered into another room. And then moments later, she called, "Aha!"

Kell started. "Did you find it?" he called back.

She reappeared, holding up her prize, but it wasn't the rook. It was a knife. Kell's spirits sank.

"No," she said, "but isn't this clever?" She held it up for Kell to see. The hilt of the dagger wasn't simply a grip; the metal curved around over the knuckles in a wavering loop before rejoining the stock.

"For hitting," explained Lila, as if Kell couldn't grasp the meaning of the metal knuckles. "You can stab them, or you can knock their teeth out. Or you can do both." She touched the tip of the blade with her finger. "Not at the same time, of course."

"Of course," echoed Kell, shutting a cabinet. "You're very fond of weapons."

Lila stared at him blankly. "Who isn't?"

"And you already have a knife," he pointed out.

"So?" asked Lila, admiring the grip. "No such thing as too many knives."

"You're a violent sort."

She wagged the blade. "We can't all turn blood and whispers into weapons."

Kell bristled. "I don't whisper. And we're not here to loot."

"I thought that's *exactly* why we're here."

Kell sighed and continued to look around the shop. He'd turned over the whole thing, including Fletcher's cramped little room at the back, and come up empty. Fletcher wouldn't have sold it . . . or would he? Kell closed his eyes, letting his senses wander, as if maybe he could feel the foreign magic. But the space was practically humming with power, overlapping tones that made it impossible to parse the foreign and forbidden from the merely forbidden.

"I've got a question," said Lila, her pockets jingling suspiciously.

"Of course you do." Kell sighed, opening his eyes. "And I thought I said no thieving."

She chewed her lip and dug a few stones and a metal contraption even Kell didn't recognize the use of out of her pocket, setting them on a chest. "You said the worlds were cut off. So how does this man—Fletcher—have a piece of White London?"

Kell sifted through a desk he swore he'd searched, then felt under the lip for hidden drawers. "Because I gave it to him."

"Well, what were *you* doing with it?" Her eyes narrowed. "Did you steal it?"

Kell frowned. He had. "No."

"Liar."

"I didn't take it for myself," said Kell. "Few people in your world know about mine. Those that do—Collectors and Enthusiasts—are willing to pay a precious sum for a piece of it. A trinket. A token. In my world, most know about yours—a few people are as intrigued by your mundaneness as you are by our magic—but everyone knows about the *other* London. White London. And for a piece of *that* world, some would pay dearly."

A wry smile cut across Lila's mouth. "You're a smuggler."

"Says the pickpocket," snapped Kell defensively.

"I know I'm a thief," said Lila, lifting a red lin from the top of the chest and rolling it over her knuckles. "I've accepted that. It's not my fault that you haven't." The coin vanished. Kell opened his mouth to protest, but the lin reappeared an instant later in her other palm. "I don't understand, though. If you're a royal—"

"I'm *not*—"

Lila gave him a withering look. "If you *live* with royals and you *dine* with them and you *belong* to them, surely you don't want for money. Why risk it?"

Kell clenched his jaw, thinking of Rhy's plea to stop his

foolish games. "You wouldn't understand."

Lila quirked a brow. "Crime isn't that complicated," she said. "People steal because taking something gives them something. If they're not in it for the money, they're in it for control. The act of taking, of breaking the rules, makes them feel powerful. They're in it for the sheer defiance." She turned away. "Some people steal to stay alive, and some steal to feel alive. Simple as that."

"And which are you?" asked Kell.

"I steal for freedom," said Lila. "I suppose that's a bit of both." She wandered into a short hallway between two rooms. "So that's how you came across the black rock?" she called back. "You made a deal for it?"

"No," said Kell. "I made a mistake. One I intend to fix, if I can find the damned thing." He slammed a drawer shut in frustration.

"Careful," said a gruff voice in Arnesian. "You might break something."

Kell spun to find the shop's owner standing there, shoulder tipped against a wardrobe, looking vaguely bemused.

"Fletcher," said Kell.

"How did you get in?" asked Fletcher.

Kell forced himself to shrug as he shot a glance toward Lila, who'd had the good sense to stay in the hallway and out of sight. "I guess your wards are wearing thin."

Fletcher crossed his arms. "I doubt that."

Kell stole a second glance toward Lila, but she was no longer in the hall. A spike of panic ran through him, one that worsened a moment later when she reappeared behind Fletcher. She moved with silent steps, a knife glittering in one hand.

"*Tac*," said Fletcher, lifting his hand beside his head. "Your friend is very rude." As he said it, Lila froze mid-stride. The strain showed in her face as she tried to fight the invisible force holding her in place, but it was no use. Fletcher had the rare and dangerous ability to control *bones*, and therefore *bodies*. It was an ability that had earned him the binding scars he was so proud of breaking.

Lila, for one, seemed unimpressed. She muttered some very violent things, and Fletcher splayed his fingers. Kell heard a sound like cracking ice, and Lila let out a stifled cry, the knife tumbling from her fingers.

"I thought you preferred to work alone," said Fletcher conversationally.

"Let her go," ordered Kell.

"Are you going to make me, *Antari*?"

Kell's fingers curled into fists—the shop was warded a dozen ways, against intruders and thieves and, with Kell's luck, anyone who meant Fletcher harm—but the shop owner himself gave a low chuckle and dropped his hand, and Lila went stumbling to her hands and knees, clutching her wrist and swearing vehemently.

"*Anesh*," he said casually. "What brings you back to my humble shop?"

"I gave you something once," said Kell. "I'd like to borrow it."

Fletcher gave a derisive snort. "I am not in the business of borrowers."

"I'll buy it then."

"And if it's not for sale?"

Kell forced himself to smile. "You of all people know," he said, "that *everything* is for sale."

Fletcher parroted the smile, cold and dry. "I won't sell it to you, but I might sell it to her"—his gaze glanced to Lila, who had gotten to her feet and retreated to the nearest wall to lurk and curse—"for the right price."

"She doesn't speak Arnesian," said Kell. "She hasn't the faintest idea what you're saying."

"Oh?" Fletcher grabbed his crotch. "I bet I can make her understand," he said, shaking himself in her direction.

Lila's eyes narrowed. "Burn in hell, you fu—"

"I wouldn't bother with her," cut in Kell. "She bites."

Fletcher sighed and shook his head. "What kind of trouble are you in, *Master Kell*?"

"None."

"You must be in some, to come here. And besides," said Fletcher, smile sharpening. "They don't put your face up on the boards for nothing."

Kell's eyes flicked to the scrying board on the wall, the one that had been painted with his face for the last hour. And then he paled. The circle at the bottom, the one that said *If seen touch here* was pulsing bright green.

"What have you done?" growled Kell.

Fletcher only smiled.

"No hard feelings," he said darkly, right before the shop doors burst open, and the royal guard poured in.

V

Kell had only an instant to arrange his features, to force panic into composure, before the guards were there, five in all, filling up the room with movement and noise.

He couldn't run—there was nowhere to run *to*—and he didn't want to hurt them, and Lila . . . Well, he had no idea where Lila was. One moment she'd been right there against the wall, and the next she'd vanished (though Kell had seen her fingers go into the pocket of her coat the instant before she disappeared, and he could feel the subtle hum of the stone's magic in the air, the way Holland must have felt it at the Ruby Fields).

Kell forced himself to stay still, to feign calm, even though his heart was racing in his chest. He tried to remind himself that he wasn't a criminal, that the royals were likely only worried by his disappearance. He hadn't done anything wrong, not in the eyes of the *crown*. Not that they *knew* of. Unless, in his absence, Rhy had told the king and queen of his transgressions. He wouldn't—Kell *hoped* he wouldn't—but even if he had, Kell was *Antari*, a member of the royal family, someone to be respected, even feared. He coated himself in that knowledge as he leaned back lazily, almost arrogantly, against the table behind him.

When the members of the royal guard saw him standing

261

there, alive and unconcerned, confusion spread across their features. Had they expected a body? A brawl? Half went to kneel, and half brought hands to rest on the hilts of their swords, and one stood there, frowning, in the middle.

"Ellis," said Kell, nodding at the head of the royal guard.

"Master Kell," said Ellis, stepping forward. "Are you well?"

"Of course."

Ellis fidgeted. "We've been worried about you. The whole palace has been."

"I didn't mean to worry anyone," he said, considering the guard around him. "As you can see, I'm perfectly all right."

Ellis looked around, then back at Kell. "It's just . . . sir . . . when you did not return from your errand abroad . . ."

"I was delayed," said Kell, hoping that would quell the questions.

Ellis frowned. "Did you not see the signs? They're posted everywhere."

"I only just returned."

"Then, forgive me," countered Ellis, gesturing to the shop. "But what are you doing *here*?"

Fletcher frowned. Though he spoke only Arnesian, he clearly understood the royal tongue well enough to know he was being insulted.

Kell forced a thin smile. "Shopping for Rhy's present."

A nervous laugh passed through the guard.

"You'll come with us, then?" asked Ellis, and Kell understood the words that went unsaid. *Without a fight.*

"Of course," said Kell, rising to his full height and smoothing his jacket.

The guards looked relieved. Kell's mind spun as he turned to Fletcher and thanked him for his help.

"*Mas marist,*" answered the shop's owner darkly. *My pleasure.* "Just doing my civic duty."

"I'll be back," said Kell in English (which garnered a raised brow from the royal guard), "as soon as I am through. To find what I was looking for." The words were directed at Lila. He could still feel her in the room, feel the stone even as it hid her. It whispered to him.

"Sir," said Ellis, gesturing to the door. "After you."

Kell nodded and followed him out.

The moment she heard the guards burst in, Lila had the good sense to close her hand over the stone and say *"Conceal me."*

And the stone had obeyed once more.

She'd felt a flutter up her arm, just beneath her skin, a lovely sensation—had it felt that nice the last time she'd used the talisman?—and then the veil had settled over her again and she was gone. Just as before, she could see herself, but no one else could see her. Not the guards, not Fletcher, not even Kell, whose two-toned eyes leveled on her but seemed to make out only the place she'd been, and not the place she was.

But though he could not see her, she could see him, and in his face she read a flicker of worry, disguised by his voice but not his posture, and under it a warning, threaded through the false calm of his words.

Stay, it seemed to urge, even before he said the words, lobbed at the room but clearly meant for her. So she stayed and waited and watched as Kell and four of the five members of the guard poured out into the street. Watched as a single guard hung back, his face hidden beneath the lowered visor of his helmet.

Fletcher was saying something to him, gesturing at his palm in the universal sign for payment. The guard nodded, and his hand went to his belt as Fletcher turned to watch Kell through the window.

Lila saw it coming.

Fletcher never did.

Instead of reaching for a purse, the guard went for a blade. The metal glinted once in the shop's low light, and then it

263

was under Fletcher's chin, drawing a silent red line across his throat.

A closed carriage, pulled by royal white horses, gold and red ribbons still woven through their manes from the earlier parade, was waiting for Kell in front of the shop.

As Kell made his way to it, he shrugged out of his coat and turned it left to right, sliding his arms back into the now-red sleeves of his royal attire. His thoughts spun over what to tell the king and queen—not the truth, of course. But the king himself had a White London token, an ornament that sat on a shelf in his private chamber, and if Kell could get it, and get back to Lila and the stone . . . Lila and the stone loose in the city—it was a troubling thought. But hopefully she would stay put, just a little while. Stay out of trouble.

Ellis walked a half step behind Kell, three more guards trailing in his wake. The last had stayed behind to talk to Fletcher, and most likely settle the matter of the reward (though Kell was fairly sure Fletcher hated him enough to turn him in even without the added prospect of money).

Down the river toward the palace, the day's celebrations were dying down—no, not dying, *shifting*—to make way for the evening's festivities. The music had softened, and the crowds along the docks and up the market stretch had thinned, migrating to the city's various pubs and inns to continue toasting Rhy's name.

"Come, sir," said Ellis, holding the carriage door open for him. Instead of seats that faced each other, this carriage had two sets of benches both facing forward; two of the guards took the seat behind, and one went up to sit with the driver, while Ellis slid onto the front bench beside Kell and pulled the carriage door closed. "Let's get you home."

Kell's chest ached at the thought of it. He had tried not to let himself think of home, of how badly he wanted to be there, not since the stone—and the grim task of its disposal—had fallen to him. Now all he wanted was to see Rhy, to embrace him one last time, and he was secretly glad of the chance.

He let out a shaky breath and sank back onto the bench as Ellis drew the carriage curtains.

"I'm sorry about this, sir," he said, and Kell was about to ask what for when a hand clamped a cloth over his mouth, and his lungs filled with something bitter and sweet. He tried to wrench free, but armored gloves closed over his wrists and held him back against the bench, and within moments, everything went dark.

Lila sucked in a breath, unheard beneath the veil, as the guard let go of Fletcher's shoulder and he fell forward, thudding in a lifeless mass against the worn floorboards of the shop.

The guard stood there, unfazed by the murder and seemingly oblivious to the fact he was now splattered with someone else's blood. He surveyed the room, his gaze drifting past her, but through the slot in his helmet, Lila thought she saw an odd shimmer in his eyes. Something like magic. Satisfied that there was no one else to dispose of, the guard returned his blade to its sheath, turned on his heel, and left the shop. A dull bell followed him out, and a few moments later, Lila heard a carriage shudder to life and rumble away down the street.

Fletcher's body lay sprawled on the floor of his shop, blood soaking through his wiry blond hair and staining the boards beneath his chest. His smug expression was gone, replaced by surprise, the emotion preserved by death like an insect in amber. His eyes were open and empty, but something pale had tumbled from his shirt pocket and was now caught between his body and the floor.

Something that looked very much like a white rook.

Lila looked around to make sure she was alone, then

did away with the concealment spell. It was easy enough, undoing the magic, but letting go of the stone itself proved considerably more difficult; it took her a long moment, and when she finally managed to pull free and drop the talisman back into her pocket, the whole room tilted. A shudder passed through her, stealing warmth and something more. In the magic's wake, she felt . . . *empty*. Lila was used to hunger, but the stone left her feeling starved in a bone-deep way. Hollow.

Bloody rock, she thought, tucking the toe of her boot under Fletcher's dead shoulder and turning him over, his blank stare now directed up at the ceiling, and at her.

She knelt, careful to avoid the spreading red slick as she picked up the blood-flecked chess piece.

Lila swore with relief and straightened, weighing it appraisingly. At first glance, it looked rather ordinary, and yet, when she curled her fingers around the stone—or bone, or whatever it was carved out of—she could almost feel the difference between its energy and that of the London around her. It was subtle, and perhaps she was imagining it, but the rook felt like a draft in a warm room. Just cold enough to seem out of place.

She shrugged off the sensation and tucked the chess piece into her boot (she didn't know how magic worked, but it didn't seem a wise idea to keep the two talismans close together, not until they were needed, and she wasn't touching the thieving little rock again unless she absolutely had to). She wiped Fletcher's blood off on her pants.

All things considered, Lila was feeling rather accomplished. After all, she had the Black London stone *and* the White London token. Now all she needed was Kell.

Lila turned toward the door and hesitated. He'd told her to stay put, but as she looked down at Fletcher's fresh corpse, she feared he'd walked into trouble of his own. She'd been in Red London only a day, but it didn't seem like the place where royal guards went around slitting people's throats.

Maybe Kell would be fine. But if he wasn't?

Her gut said to go, and years of stealing to survive had taught her to listen when it spoke. Besides, she reasoned, no one in the city was looking for *her*.

Lila made for the door, and she was almost to it when she saw the knife again, the one she'd been so keen on, sitting on top of the chest where she'd left it. Kell had warned her against thieving in the shop, but the owner was dead and it was just sitting there, unappreciated. She took it up and ran a finger gingerly along the blade. It really was a lovely knife. She eyed the door, wondering if the wards protecting the shop from thieves had died with their maker. Might as well test it. Carefully, she opened the door, set the weapon on the floor, and used the toe of her boot to kick the knife over the threshold. She cringed, waiting for the backlash—a current of energy, a wave of pain, or even the knife's stubborn return shop-side—but none came.

Lila smiled greedily and stepped out onto the street. She fetched up the knife and slid it into her belt and went to find— and most likely *rescue*—Kell from whatever mess he'd gotten himself into now.

✿ VI ✿

Parrish and Gen milled around the festival, helmets in one hand and mugs of wine in the other. Parrish had won back his coin—really, between the constant cards and the odd gambles, the two seemed to trade the pocket money back and forth without much gain or loss—and, being the better of the two sports, offered to buy Gen a drink.

It was, after all, a celebration.

Prince Rhy had been kind enough to give the two closest members of his private guard a few hours off, to enjoy the festivities with the masses gathered along the Isle. Parrish, prone to worry, had hesitated, but Gen had reasoned that on this day of all days, Rhy would be suitably well attended without them. At least for a little while. And so the two had wandered into the fray of the festival.

The celebration hugged the river, the market triple its usual size, its banks overflowing with patrons and cheer, music and magic. Every year, the festivities seemed to grow grander, once a simple hour or two of merriment, now a full day of revelry (followed by several more days of recovery, the excitement tapering off slowly until life returned to normal). But on this, the main day, the morning parade gave way to an afternoon of food and drink and good spirits, and finally, an evening ball.

This year it was to be a masquerade.

The great steps of the palace were already being cleared, the flowers gathered up and taken in to line the entry hall. Orbs of crisp light were being hung like low stars both outside the palace and within, and dark blue carpets unrolled, so that for the evening, the royal grounds would seem to float not on the river as a rising sun, but far above, a moon surrounded by the dazzling night sky. All over London, the young and beautiful and elite were climbing into their carriages, practicing their Royal under their breath as they rode to the palace in their masks and dresses and capes. And once there, they would worship the prince as though he were divine, and he would drink in their adoration as he always did, with relish and good cheer.

The masquerade within the palace walls was an invitation-only affair, but out on the riverbanks, the party was open to all and would go on in its own fashion until after midnight before finally dying down, the remnants wandering home with the merry revelers.

Parrish and Gen would soon be recalled to the prince's side, but for now they were leaning against a tent pole in the market, watching the crowds and enjoying themselves immensely. Now and then, Parrish would knock Gen's shoulder, a silent nudge to keep a sharp eye on the crowd. Even though they weren't officially on duty, they (or at least, Parrish) took enough pride in their jobs to wear their royal armor (though it didn't hurt that ladies seemed to enjoy a man in arms) and watch for signs of trouble. Most of the afternoon, trouble had come in the form of someone celebrating Rhy's day with a little too much enthusiasm, but now and then a fight broke out, and a weapon or a flash of magic was cause for intervention.

Gen appeared to be having a perfectly pleasant time, but Parrish was getting restless. His partner insisted that it was because Parrish had stopped at one drink, but he didn't think that was it. There was an energy in the air, and even though he knew the buzz was most likely coming from the festival itself, it still made him nervous. It wasn't just that there was *more* power than usual. It felt *different*. He rolled his empty cup between his hands and tried to set his mind at ease.

A troupe of fire workers was putting on a show nearby, twisting flames into dragons and horses and birds, and as Parrish watched them, the light from their enchanted fire blurred his vision. As it came back into focus, he caught the gaze of a woman just beyond, a lovely one with red lips and golden hair and a voluptuous, only half-concealed bosom. He dragged his gaze from her chest up to her eyes, and then frowned. They weren't blue or green or brown.

They were black.

Black as a starless sky or a scrying board.

Black as Master Kell's right eye.

He squinted to make sure, then called to Gen. When his compatriot didn't answer, he turned and saw the guard watching a young man—no, a *girl* in men's clothes, and strange dull clothes at that—weaving through the crowd toward the palace.

Gen was frowning at her faintly, as if she looked odd, out of place, and she did, but not as odd as the woman with black eyes. Parrish grabbed Gen's arm and dragged his attention forcefully away.

"Kers?" growled Gen, nearly spilling his wine. *What?*

"That woman there in blue," said Parrish, turning back to the crowd. "Her eyes . . ." But he trailed off. The black-eyed woman was gone.

"Smitten, are you?"

"It's not that. I swear her eyes—they were *black*."

Gen raised a brow and took a sip from his cup.

"Perhaps you've done a little too much celebrating after all," he said, clapping the other guard on the arm. Over his shoulder, Parrish watched the girl in boy's clothes disappear into a tent before Gen frowned and added, "Looks like you're not the only one."

Parrish followed his gaze and saw a man, his back to them, embracing a woman in the middle of the market. The man's hands were wandering a bit too much, even for a celebration day, and the woman didn't seem to be enjoying herself. She brought her hands to the man's chest, as if to push away, but he responded by kissing her deeper. Gen and Parrish abandoned their post and made their way toward the couple. And then, abruptly, the woman stopped struggling. Her hands fell to her sides and her head lolled, and when the man released her a moment later, she swayed on her feet and slumped into a seat. The man, meanwhile, simply turned and walked away, half walking, half stumbling through the crowd.

Parrish and Gen both followed, closing the gap in a slow, steady way so as not to cause alarm. The man appeared and disappeared through the crowd before finally cutting between tents toward the riverbank. The guards picked up their pace and reached the gap right after the man vanished through.

"You there," called Gen, taking the lead. He always did. "Stop."

The man heading for the Isle now slowed to a halt.

"Turn around," ordered Gen when he was nearly to him, one hand on his sword.

The man did. Parrish's eyes widened as they snagged on the stranger's face. Two pools, shining and black as river stones at night, sat where eyes should be, the skin around them veined with black. When the man tugged his mouth into a smile, flecks drifted off like ash.

"*Asan narana,*" he said in a language that wasn't Arnesian. He held out his hand, and Parrish recoiled when he saw that it was entirely black, the fingertips tapering into charred bone points.

"What in king's name—" started Gen, but he didn't have a chance to finish because the man smiled and thrust his blackened hand through the armor and into the guard's chest.

"Dark heart," he said, this time in Royal.

Parrish stood frozen with shock and horror as the man,

or whatever he was, withdrew his hand, what was left of his fingers wet with blood. Gen crumpled to the ground, and Parrish's shock shattered into motion. He charged forward, drawing his royal short sword, and thrust the blade into the stomach of the black-eyed monster.

For an instant, the creature looked amused. And then Parrish's sword began to glow as the spellwork on the enchanted blade took effect and severed the man from his magic. His eyes went wide, the black retreating from them, and from his veins, until he looked more or less like an ordinary man again (albeit a dying one). He drew in a rattling breath and gripped Parrish's armor—he bore an X, the mark of cutthroats, on the back of his hand—and then he crumbled to ash around Parrish's blade.

"*Sanct,*" he swore, staring at the mound of soot as it began to blow away.

And then, out of nowhere, pain blossomed in his back, white-hot, and he looked down to see the tip of a sword protruding from his chest. It slid out with a horrible, wet sound, and Parrish's knees buckled as his attacker rounded him.

He took a shuddering breath, his lungs filling with blood, and looked up to see Gen looming over him, the blood-slicked blade hanging at his side.

"Why?" whispered Parrish.

Gen gazed down at him with two black eyes and a grim smile. "*Asan harana,*" he said. "Noble heart."

And then he raised the sword above his head and swung it down.

XI

MASQUERADE

~ I ~

The palace rose like a second sun over the Isle as the day's light sank low behind it, haloing its edges with gold. Lila made her way toward the glowing structure, weaving through the crowded market—it had become a rather raucous festival as the day and drink wore on—her mind spinning over the matter of how to get *into* the palace once she'd reached it. The stone pulsed in her pocket, luring her with its easy answer, but she'd made a decision not to use the magic again, not unless she had no other choice. It took too much, and did so with the quiet cunning of a thief. No, if there were another way in, she'd find it.

And then, as the palace neared and the front steps came into sight, Lila saw her opportunity.

The main doors were flung open, silky blue carpet spilling like night water down the stairs, and on them ascended a steady stream of partygoers. They appeared to be attending a ball.

Not just a ball, she realized, watching the river of guests.

A *masquerade*.

Every man and woman wore a disguise. Some masks were simple stained leather, some far more ornate, adorned by horns or feathers or jewels, some fell only across the eyes, and others revealed nothing at all. Lila broke into a wicked grin. She wouldn't need to be a member of society to get in. She need never show her face.

But there was another thing that every guest appeared to have: an *invitation*. That, she feared, would be harder to obtain. But just then, as if by a stroke of luck, or providence, Lila heard the high sweet sound of laughter, and turned to see three girls no older than she being helped out of a carriage, their dresses full and their smiles wide as they chattered and chirped and settled themselves on the street. Lila recognized them instantly from the morning parade, the girls who had been swooning over Rhy and the "black-eyed prince," whom Lila now knew to be Kell. The girls who had been practicing their English. Of *course*. Because English was the language of the royals, and those who mingled with them. Lila's smiled widened. Perhaps Kell was right: in any other setting, her accent would cause her to stand out. But here, here it would help her blend in, help her *belong*.

One of the girls—the one who'd prided herself on her English—produced a gold-trimmed invitation, and the three pored over it for several moments before she tucked it beneath her arm. Lila approached.

"Excuse me," she said, bringing a hand to rest at the girl's elbow. "What time does the masquerade begin?"

The girl didn't seem to remember her. She gave Lila a slow appraising look—the kind that made her want to free a few teeth from the girl's head—before smiling tightly. "It's starting now."

Lila parroted the smile. "Of course," she said as the girl pulled free, oblivious to the fact she was now short an invitation.

The girls set off toward the palace steps, and Lila considered her prize. She ran a thumb over the paper's gilded edges and ornate Arnesian script. Her eyes drifted up again, taking in the procession to the palace doors, but she didn't join it. The men and women ascending the stairs practically glittered in their jewel-tone gowns and dark, elegant suits. Lush cloaks spilled over their shoulders and threads of precious metal shone in their hair. Lila looked down at herself, her threadbare cloak and worn brown boots, and felt shabbier than ever. She tugged her own mask—nothing but a crumpled strip of black fabric—from her pocket. Even with an invitation and a healthy grasp of the English language, she'd never be let in, not looking like this.

She shoved the mask back in her cloak pocket and looked around at the market stalls that stood nearby. Farther down the booths were filled with food and drink, but here, at the edge nearest the palace, the stalls sold other wares. Charms, yes, but also canes and shoes and other fineries. Fabric and light spilled out of the mouth of the nearest tent, and Lila straightened and stepped inside.

A hundred faces greeted her from the far wall, the surface of which was covered in masks. From the austere to the intricate, the beautiful to the grotesque, the faces squinted and scowled and welcomed her in turn. Lila crossed to them and reached out to free one from its hook. A black half-mask with two horns spiraling up from the temples.

"A tes fera, kes ile?"

Lila jumped, and saw a woman standing at her side. She was small and round, with half a dozen braids coiled like snakes around her head, a mask nested in them like a hairpin.

"I'm sorry," said Lila slowly. "I don't speak Arnesian."

The woman only smiled and laced her hands in front of her broad stomach. "Ah, but your English is superb."

Lila sighed with relief. "As is yours," she said.

The woman blushed. It was obviously a point of pride. "I am a servant of the ball," she replied. "It is only fitting." She then gestured to the mask in Lila's hands. "A little dark, don't you think?"

Lila looked the mask in the eyes. "No," she said. "I think it's perfect."

And then Lila turned the mask over and saw a string of numbers that must have been the price. It wasn't written in shillings or pounds, but Lila was sure that, regardless of the kind of coin, she couldn't afford it. Reluctantly, she returned the mask to its hook.

"Why set it back, if it is perfect?" pressed the woman.

Lila sighed. She would have stolen it had the merchant not been standing there. "I don't have any money," she said, thrusting a hand into her pocket. She felt the silver of the watch and swallowed. "But I do have this. . . ." She pulled the timepiece from her pocket and held it out, hoping the woman wouldn't notice the blood (she'd tried to wipe most of it off).

But the woman only shook her head. *"An, an,"* she said, folding Lila's fingers back over the watch. "I cannot take your payment. No matter its shape."

Lila's brow furrowed. "I don't understand—"

"I saw you this morning. In the market." Lila's thoughts turned back to the scene, to her almost being arrested for stealing. But the woman wasn't speaking of the theft. "You and Master Kell, you are . . . friends, yes?"

"Of a sort," said Lila, blushing when that drew a secretive smile from the woman. "No," she amended, "No, I don't mean . . ." But the woman simply patted her hand.

"Ise av eran," she said lightly. "It's not my place to"—she paused, searching for a word—"pry. But Master Kell is *aven—blessed*—a jewel in our city's crown. And if you are his, or he is yours, my shop is yours as well."

Lila cringed. She hated charity. Even when people thought they were giving something freely, it always came with a chain, a weight that set everything off-balance. Lila would rather steal a thing outright than be indebted to kindness. But she needed the clothes.

The woman seemed to read the hesitation in her eyes. "You are not from here, so you do not know. Arnesians pay their debts in many ways. Not all of them with coin. I need nothing from you now, so you will pay me back another time, and in your own way. Yes?"

Lila hesitated. And then bells began to ring in the palace, loud enough to echo through her, and she nodded. "Very well," she said.

The merchant smiled. *"Ir chas,"* she said. "Now, let us find you something fitting."

"Hmm." The merchant woman—who called herself Calla—chewed her lip. "Are you certain you wouldn't prefer something with a corset? Or a train?"

Calla had tried to lead Lila to a rack of dresses, but her eyes had gone straight to the men's coats. Glorious things, with strong shoulders and high collars and gleaming buttons.

"No," said Lila, lifting one from the rack. "This is *exactly* what I want."

The merchant looked at her with strange fascination, but little—or, at the very least, well-concealed—judgment, and said, *"Anesh.* If you're set on that direction, I will find you some boots."

A few minutes later, Lila found herself in a curtained corner of the tent, holding the nicest clothes she'd ever touched, let alone owned. *Borrowed,* she corrected herself. Borrowed until paid for.

Lila pulled the artifacts from her various pockets—the black stone, the white rook, the bloodstained silver watch, the invitation—and set them on the floor before tugging off her boots and shrugging out of her old worn cloak. Calla had given her a new black tunic—it fit so well that she wondered if there was some kind of tailoring spell on it—and a pair of close-fitting pants that still hung a little loosely on her bony frame. She'd insisted on keeping her belt, and Calla had the decency not to gawk at the number of weapons threaded through it as she handed her the boots.

Every pirate needed a good pair of boots, and these were gorgeous things, sculpted out of black leather and lined with something softer than loose cotton, and Lila let out a rare gleeful sound as she pulled them on. And then there was the coat. It was an absolute dream, high-collared and lovely and black—*true* black, velvety and rich—with a fitted waist and a built-in half-cloak that gathered at glassy red clasps on either side of her throat and spilled over her shoulders and down her back. Lila ran her fingers admiringly over the glossy jet-black buttons that cascaded down its front. She'd never been one for baubles and fineries, never wanted anything more than salt air and a solid boat and an empty map, but now that she was standing in a foreign stall in a faraway land, clothed in rich fabrics, she was beginning to see the appeal.

At last, she lifted up the waiting mask. So many of the faces that hung around the stall were lovely, delicate things made of feather and lace and garnished with glass. But this one was beautiful in a different way, an opposite way. It reminded Lila less of dresses and finery, and more of sharpened knives and ships on the seas at night. It looked *dangerous*. She brought it to rest against her face and smiled.

There was a silver-tinted looking glass propped in the corner, and she admired her reflection in it. She looked little like the shadow of a thief on the WANTED posters back home, and nothing like the scrawny girl hoarding coppers to escape a dingy life. Her polished boots glistened from knee to toe, lengthening her legs. Her coat broadened her shoulders and hugged her waist. And her mask tapered down her cheeks, the black horns curling up over her head in a way that was at once elegant and monstrous. She gave herself a long, appraising look, the way the girl had in the street, but there was nothing to scoff at now.

Delilah Bard looked like a king.

No, she thought, straightening. She looked like a *conqueror*.

"Lila?" came the merchant woman's voice beyond the curtain. She pronounced the name as though it were full of *e*'s. "Does it fit?" Lila slid the trinkets into the new silk-lined pockets of her coat and emerged. The heels of her boots clicked proudly on the stone ground—and yet, she had tested the tread and knew that if she moved on the balls of her feet, the steps would be silent—and Calla smiled, a mischievous twinkle in her eyes, even as she *tsk*ed.

"*Mas aven,*" she said. "You look more ready to storm a city than seduce a man."

"Kell will love it," assured Lila, and the way she said his name, infusing it with a subtle softness, an intimacy, made the merchant woman ruffle cheerfully. And then the bells chimed again through the city, and Lila swore to herself. "I must go," she said. "Thank you again."

"You'll pay me back," said Calla simply.

Lila nodded. "I will."

She was to the mouth of the tent when the merchant woman added, "Look after him."

Lila smiled grimly and tugged up the collar of her coat. "I will," she said again before vanishing into the street.

~ II ~

Colors blossomed over Kell's head, blurs of red and gold and rich dark blue. At first they were nothing more than broad streaks, but as his vision came into focus, he recognized them as palace draperies, the kind that hung from the ceilings in each of the royal bedrooms, drawing sky-like patterns out of cloth.

Squinting up, Kell realized he must be in Rhy's room.

He knew this because the ceiling in his own was decorated like midnight, billows of near-black fabric studded with silver thread, and the queen's ceiling was like noon, cloudless and blue, and the king's was like dusk with its bands of yellow and orange. Only Rhy's was draped like this. Like dawn. Kell's head spun, and he closed his eyes and took a deep breath as he tried to piece his thoughts together.

He was lying on a couch, his body sinking into the soft cushions beneath him. Music played beyond the walls of the room, an orchestra, and woven through it, the sounds of laughter and revelry. Of course. Rhy's birthday ball. Just then, someone cleared his throat, and Kell dragged his eyes back open and turned his head to see Rhy himself sitting across from him.

The prince was draped in a chair, one ankle across his knee, sipping tea and looking thoroughly annoyed.

"Brother," said Rhy, tipping his cup. He was dressed in all black, his coat and pants and boots adorned with dozens of gold buttons. A mask—a gaudy thing, decorated with thousands of tiny sparkling gold scales—rested on top of his head in place of his usual crown.

Kell went to push the hair out of his eyes and quickly discovered that he could not. His hands were cuffed behind his back.

"You've got to be joking . . ." He shuffled himself up into a sitting position. "Rhy, why in king's name am I wearing these?" The cuffs weren't like those ordinary manacles found in Grey London, made of metal links. Nor were they like the binds in White, which caused blinding pain upon resistance. No, these were sculpted out of a solid piece of iron and carved with spellwork designed to dampen magic. Not as severe as the royal swords, to be sure, but effective.

Rhy set his teacup on an ornate side table. "I couldn't very well have you running away again."

Kell sighed and tipped his head back against the couch. "This is preposterous. I suppose that's why you had me drugged, too? Honestly, Rhy."

Rhy crossed his arms. He was clearly sulking. Kell dragged his head up and looked around, noticing that there were two members of the royal guard in the room with them, still dressed in formal armor, their helmets on, their visors down. But Kell knew Rhy's personal guard well enough to recognize them, armor or none, and these were not them.

"Where are Gen and Parrish?" asked Kell.

Rhy shrugged lazily. "Having a little too much fun, I imagine."

Kell shifted on the couch, trying to free himself from the cuffs. They were too tight. "Don't you think you're blowing this a little out of proportion?"

"Where have you been, brother?"

"Rhy," said Kell sternly. "Take these off."

Rhy's boot slid from his knee and came to rest firmly on the ground. He straightened in his seat, squaring himself to Kell. "Is it true?"

Kell's brow furrowed. "Is what true?"

"That you have a piece of Black London?"

Kell stiffened. "What are you talking about?"

"Is it true?" persisted the prince.

"Rhy," said Kell slowly. "Who told you that?" No one knew, none except those who wanted the stone gone and those who wanted it reclaimed.

Rhy shook his head sadly. "What have you brought into our city, Kell? What have you brought upon it?"

"Rhy, I—"

"I warned you this would happen. I told you that if you carried on with your deals, you would be caught and that even I could not protect you then."

Kell's blood ran cold.

"Do the king and queen know?"

Rhy's eyes narrowed. "No. Not yet."

Kell let out a small sigh of relief. "They don't need to. I'm doing what I have to do. I'm taking it back, Rhy. All the way back to the fallen city."

Rhy's brow crinkled. "I can't let you do that."

"Why not?" demanded Kell. "It is the only place the talisman belongs."

"Where is it now?"

"Safe," said Kell, hoping that was true.

"Kell, I can't help you if you won't let me."

"I'm taking care of it, Rhy. I promise you I am."

The prince was shaking his head. "Promises are not enough," he said. "Not anymore. Tell me where the stone is."

Kell froze. "I never told you it was a stone."

Heavy silence fell between them. Rhy held his gaze. And then, finally, his lips drew into a small, dark smile, twisting his face in a way that made it look like someone else's.

"Oh, Kell," he said. He leaned forward, resting his elbows

on his knees, and Kell caught sight of something under the collar of his shirt and stiffened. It was a pendant. A glass necklace with blood-red edges. He knew it, had seen it before only days earlier.

On Astrid Dane.

Kell lunged to his feet, but the guards were upon him, holding him back. Their motions were too even, their grip too crushing. Compelled. Of course. No wonder their visors were down. Compulsion showed in the eyes.

"Hello, flower boy." The words came from Rhy's mouth in a voice that was, and wasn't, his.

"Astrid," hissed Kell. "Have you compelled everyone in this palace?"

A low chuckle escaped Rhy's lips. "Not yet, but I'm working on it."

"What have you done with my brother?"

"I've only borrowed him." Rhy's fingers curled under his shirt collar and drew out the pendant. There was only one thing it could be: a possession charm. "*Antari* blood," she said proudly. "Allows the spell to exist in both worlds."

"You will pay for this," growled Kell. "I will—"

"You will what? Hurt me? And risk hurting your dear prince? I doubt it." Again, that cold smile, so foreign to Rhy's face, spread across his lips. "Where is the stone, Kell?"

"What are you doing here?"

"Isn't it obvious?" Rhy's hand swept across the room. "I'm branching out."

Kell pulled against his binds, the metal digging into his wrists. The dampening cuffs were strong enough to mute elemental abilities and prevent spellwork, but they couldn't prevent *Antari* magic. If he could only—

"Tell me where you've hidden the stone."

"Tell me why you are wearing my brother's body," he shot back, trying to buy time.

Astrid sighed from within the prince's shell. "You know so

little of war. Battles may be fought from the outside in, but wars are won from the inside out." She gestured down at Rhy's body. "Kingdoms and crowns are taken from within. The strongest fortress can withstand any attack from *beyond* its walls, and yet even it is not fortified against an attack from behind them. Had I marched upon your palace from the steps, would I have made it this far? But now, now no one will see me coming. Not the king, nor the queen, nor the people. I am their beloved prince, and will be so until the moment I choose not to be."

"I know," said Kell. "I know what and who you are. What will you do, Astrid? Kill me?"

Rhy's face lit up with a strange kind of glee. "No"—the word slid over his tongue—"but I'm sure you'll wish I had. Now"—Rhy's hand lifted Kell's chin—"where is my stone?"

Kell looked into his brother's amber eyes, and beyond them, to the thing lurking in his brother's body. He wanted to beg Rhy, to plead with him to fight against the spell. But it wouldn't work. As long as *she* was in there, he wasn't.

"I don't know where it is," said Kell.

Rhy's smile spread, wolfish and sharp. "You know. . . ." Rhy's mouth formed the words, and Rhy held up his hand, considering his long fingers, the knuckles adorned with glittering rings. Those same hands began twisting the rings so that their jeweled settings were on the inside. "A little piece of me was hoping you would say that."

And then Rhy's fingers curled into a fist and connected with Kell's jaw.

Kell's head cracked to the side, and he nearly stumbled, but the guards tightened their grips and held him on his feet. Kell tasted blood, but Rhy just smiled that horrible smile and rubbed his knuckles. "This is going to be fun."

⟨ III ⟩

Lila ascended the palace stairs, the half-cloak of her new coat billowing behind her. The shimmering midnight carpet rippled faintly with every upward step, as though it were truly water. Other guests climbed the stairs in pairs or small groups, but Lila did her best to mimic their lofty arrogance—shoulders back, head high—as she ascended alone. She might not be of money, but she'd stolen enough from those who were to copy their manners and their mannerisms.

At the top, she presented the invitation to a man in black and gold who bowed and stepped aside, allowing her into a foyer blanketed in flowers. More flowers than Lila had ever seen. Roses and lilies and peonies, daffodils and azaleas, and scores more she could not recognize by sight. Clusters of tiny white blossoms like snowflakes, and massive stems that resembled sunflowers if sunflowers were sky blue. The room filled with the fragrance of them all, and yet it did not overwhelm her. Perhaps she was simply getting used to it.

Music poured through a second, curtained doorway, and the mystery of what lay beyond drew Lila forward through the gallery of flowers. And then, just as she reached out to pull the curtain aside, a second servant appeared from the other side and barred her path. Lila tensed, worried that somehow her disguise and invitation were not enough, that she would be discovered as an impostor, an outsider. Her fingers twitched toward the knife under her coat.

And then the man smiled and said in stiff English, "I am presenting whom?"

"Excuse me?" asked Lila, keeping her voice low, gruff.

The attendant's brow crinkled. "What title and name should I announce you under, sir?"

"Oh." Relief swept over her, and her hand slid back to her side. A smile spread across her lips. "Captain Bard," she said, "of the *Sea King*." The attendant looked uncertain, but turned away and said the words without protest.

Her name echoed and was swallowed by the room before she'd even stepped inside.

When she did, her mouth fell open.

The vivid glamour of the world outside paled in comparison to the world within. It was a palace of vaulting glass and shimmering tapestry and, woven through it all like light, *magic*. The air was alive with it. Not the secret, seductive magic of the stone, but a loud, bright, encompassing thing. Kell had told Lila that magic was like an extra sense, layered on top of sight and smell and taste, and now she understood. It was everywhere. In everything. And it was intoxicating. She could not tell if the energy was coming from the hundreds of bodies in the room, or from the room itself, which certainly reflected it. *Amplified* it like sound in an echoing chamber.

And it was strangely—*impossibly*—familiar.

Beneath the magic, or perhaps because of it, the space itself was alive with color and light. She'd never set foot inside St. James, but it couldn't possibly have compared to the splendor of this. Nothing in her London could. Her world felt truly grey by comparison, bleak and empty in a way that made Lila want to kiss the stone for freeing her from it, for bringing her here, to this glittering jewel of a place. Everywhere she looked, she saw wealth. Her fingers itched, and she resisted the urge to start picking pockets, reminding herself that the cargo in her own was too precious to risk being caught.

The curtained doorway led onto a landing, a set of stairs sloping down and away onto the hall's polished floor, the stone itself lost beneath boots and twirling skirts.

At the base of the stairs stood the king and queen, greeting each of their guests. Standing there, dressed in gold, they looked unbearably elegant. Lila had never been so near to royalty—she didn't count Kell—and knew she should slip away as soon as possible, but she couldn't resist the urge to flaunt her disguise. And besides, it would be rude not to greet her hosts. *Reckless,* growled a voice in her head, but Lila only smiled and descended the stairs.

"Welcome, Captain," said the king, his grip firm around Lila's hand.

"Your Majesty," she said, struggling to keep her voice from drifting up. She nodded her mask toward him, careful not to jab him with her horns.

"Welcome," echoed the queen as Lila kissed her outstretched hand. But as she pulled away, the queen added, "We have not met before."

"I am a friend of Kell's," said Lila as casually as possible, her gaze still on the floor.

"Ah," said the queen. "Then welcome."

"Actually," Lila went on, "Your Highness, I am looking for him. Do you know where he might be?"

The queen considered her blankly and said, "He is not here." Lila frowned, and the queen added, "But I am not worried." Her tone was strangely steady, as if she were reciting a line that wasn't hers. The bad feeling in Lila's chest grew worse.

"I'm sure he'll turn up," said Lila, sliding her hand free of the queen's.

"Everything will be okay," said the king, his voice similarly hollow.

"It will," added the queen.

Lila frowned. Something was wrong. She lifted her gaze, risking impertinence to look the queen in the eye, and saw there a subtle gleam. The same shimmer she'd seen in the eyes of the guard after he'd slit Fletcher's throat. Some kind of *spell*. Had no one else noticed? Or had no one else been brazen enough to stare so baldly at the crown?

The next guest cleared his throat at Lila's back, and she broke the queen's gaze. "I'm sorry to have kept you," she said quickly, shifting past the royal hosts and into the ballroom. She skirted the crowd of dancers and drinkers, looking for signs of the prince, but judging by the eagerness in the air, the way eyes constantly darted toward doors and sets of stairs, he'd yet to make an appearance.

She slipped away, through a pair of doors at the edge of the ballroom, and found herself in a corridor. It was empty, save for a guard and a young woman wrapped in a rather amorous embrace and too occupied to notice as Lila slid past and vanished through another set of doors. And then another. Navigating the streets of London had taught her a fair amount about the mazelike flow of places, the way wealth gathers in the heart and tapers to the corners. She moved from hall to hall, winding around the palace's beating heart without straying too far. Everywhere she went, she found guests and guards and servants, but no sign of Kell or the prince or any break in the maze. Until, finally, she came upon a set of spiral stairs. They were elegant but narrow, clearly not meant for public use. She cast a last glance back in the direction of the ball and then ascended the steps.

The floor above was quiet in a private way, and she knew she must be getting close, not only because of that silence, but also because the stone in her pocket was beginning to hum. As if it could *feel* Kell near and wished to be nearer. Again, Lila tried not to be offended.

She found herself in a new set of halls, the first of which was empty, the second of which was not. Lila rounded the corner and caught her breath. She pressed herself back into a shadowed nook, narrowly missing the eyes of a guard. He was standing in front of a set of ornate doors, and he was not alone. In fact, while every other door in the hall stood unmanned, the one at the end was guarded by no fewer than three armed and armored men.

Lila swallowed and slid her newest knife from her belt. She hesitated. For the second time in as many days, she found herself one against three. It had yet to end well. Her grip tightened on the knife as she scrounged for a plan that wasn't sure to end in a grave. The stone took up its murmuring rhythm again, and she was reluctantly about to draw it from her coat when she stopped and noticed something.

The hall was studded with doors, and while the farthest one was guarded, the nearest one stood ajar. It led onto a luxurious bedroom, and at the back of it, a balcony, curtains fluttering in the evening air.

Lila smiled and returned the knife to her belt.

She had an idea.

⌒ IV ⌒

Kell spat blood onto Rhy's lovely inlaid floor, marring the intricate pattern. If Rhy himself were here, he would not be happy. But Rhy wasn't here.

"The stone, my rose." Astrid's sultry tone poured between Rhy's lips. "Where is it?"

Kell struggled to get to his knees with his arms still pinned behind his back. "What do you want with it?" he growled as the two guards dragged him to his feet.

"To take the throne, of course."

"You already have a throne," observed Kell.

"In a dying London. And do you know why it dies? Because of you. Because of this city and its cowardly retreat. It made of us a shield, and now it thrives while we perish. It seems only just that I should take it, as reparation. Retribution."

"So you would, what?" asked Kell. "Abandon your brother to the decaying corpse of your world so you can enjoy the splendors of this one?"

A cold, dry laugh escaped Rhy's throat. "Not at all. That would make me a very poor sister. Athos and I will rule together. Side by side."

Kell's eyes narrowed. "What do you mean?"

"We are going to restore balance to the worlds. Reopen the

doors. Or rather, tear them down, create one that stays open, so that anyone—*everyone*—can move between. A merger, if you will, of our two illustrious Londons."

Kell paled. Even when the doors had been unlocked, they had been *doors*. And they were kept closed. An open door between the worlds wouldn't only be dangerous. It would be *unstable*.

"The stone is not strong enough to do that," he said, trying to sound sure. But he wasn't. The stone had made a door for Lila. But making a pinprick in a piece of cloth was very different from tearing the fabric in half.

"Are you certain?" teased Astrid. "Perhaps you are right. Perhaps your half of the stone is not enough."

Kell's blood went cold. "My half?"

Rhy's mouth curled into a smile. "Haven't you noticed that it is broken?"

Kell reeled. "The jagged edge."

"Athos found it like that, in two pieces. He likes to find treasure, you see. Always has. Growing up, we used to scavenge the rocks along the coast, searching for anything of value. A habit he never lost. His searching merely became a bit more sophisticated. A bit more pointed. Of course, we knew of the Black London purge, of the eradication of artifacts, but he was so sure there must be something—*anything*—to help save our dying world."

"And he found it," said Kell, digging his wrists into the metal cuff. The edges were smooth, not sharp, and dull pain spread up his arm, but the skin refused to break. He stared down at the blood from his lip on Rhy's floor, but the guards were holding him up, their grip unyielding.

"He scoured," continued Astrid in Rhy's tongue. "Found a few useless things secreted away—a notebook, a piece of cloth—and then, lo and behold, he found the stone. Broken in two, yes, but, as I'm sure you've noticed, its state has not stopped it from working. It is magic, after all. It may divide, but it does not weaken. The two halves remain connected, even when they are apart. Each half is strong enough on its own, strong enough to change the world. But they want each other, you see. They are drawn together through the wall. If a drop of your blood is enough to make a door, think what two halves of the stone could do."

It could tear down the wall itself, thought Kell. Tear reality apart.

Rhy's fingers rapped along the back of a chair. "It was my idea, I confess, giving you the stone, allowing you to carry it across the line."

Kell grimaced as he twisted his wrists against the iron binding them. "Why not use Holland?" he asked, trying to buy more time. "To smuggle the stone here? He obviously delivered that necklace to Rhy."

Astrid drew Rhy's lips into a smile and ran a finger lightly over Kell's cheek. "I wanted you." Rhy's hand continued up and tangled in Kell's hair as Astrid leaned in, pressed her stolen cheek to Kell's bloody one, and whispered in his ear, "I told you once, that I would own your life." Kell wrenched back, and Rhy's hand fell away.

"Besides," she said with a sigh. "It made sense. If things went wrong, and Holland was caught, the guilt would lie on our crown, and we would not have another chance. If things went wrong and *you* were caught, the guilt would lie on your head. I know of your hobbies, Kell. You think the Scorched Bone keeps secrets? *Nothing* goes unnoticed in my city." Rhy's tongue clicked. "A royal servant with a bad habit of smuggling things across borders. Not so hard to believe. And if things went *right*, and I succeeded in taking this castle, this kingdom, I couldn't have you out there, unaccounted for, fighting against me. I wanted you here, where you belong. At my feet."

Dark energy began to crackle in Rhy's palm, and Kell braced himself, but Astrid couldn't seem to control it, not with Rhy's crude skills. The lightning shot to the left, striking the metal post of the prince's bed.

Kell forced himself to chuckle thinly. "You should have picked a better body," he said. "My brother has never had a gift for magic."

Astrid rolled Rhy's wrist, considering his fingers. "No matter," she said. "I have an entire family to choose from."

Kell had an idea. "Why don't you try on someone a little stronger?" he goaded.

"Like you?" asked Astrid coolly. "Would you like me to take *your* body for a spin?"

"I'd like to see you try," said Kell. If he could get her to take off the necklace, to put it on him instead . . .

"I could," she whispered. "But possession doesn't work on *Antari*," she added drily. Kell's heart sank. "I know that, and so do you. Nice try, though." Kell watched as his brother turned and lifted a knife from a nearby table. "Now, *compulsion*," he said—she said—admiring the glinting edge. "That's another matter."

Rhy's fingers tightened on the blade, and Kell pulled back, but there was nowhere to go. The guards gripped him, vise-tight, as the prince strode over lazily and raised the knife, slicing the buttons off Kell's shirt and pushing the collar aside to reveal the smooth, fair flesh over his heart.

"So few scars . . ." Rhy's fingers brought the knifepoint to Kell's skin. "We'll fix that."

"Stop right there," came a voice at the balcony.

Kell twisted, and saw Lila. She was dressed differently, in a black coat and a horned mask, and she was standing atop the banister, bracing herself in the balcony's doorframe and pointing her pistol at the prince's chest.

"This is a family matter," warned Astrid with Rhy's voice.

"I've heard enough to know you're not really family." Lila cocked the gun and leveled it on Rhy. "Now step away from Kell."

Rhy's mouth made a grim smile. And then his hand flew out. This time the lightning found its mark, striking Lila square in the chest. She gasped and lost her grip on the doorframe, her boots slipping off the banister rail as she stumbled back and plunged into the dark.

"Lila!" shouted Kell as she disappeared over the rail. He jerked free of the guards, the cuff finally cutting into his wrist enough to draw blood. In an instant, he had curled his fingers around the metal and spat out the command to unlock the cuff.

"As Orense." Open.

His shackles fell away, and the rest of Kell's power flooded back. The guards lunged at him, but his hands came up and the men went flying backward, one into the wall and the other into the metal frame of Rhy's bed. Kell freed his dagger and spun on the prince, ready for a fight.

But Rhy only gazed at him, amused. "What do you plan to do now, Kell? You won't hurt me, not as long as I'm wearing your brother."

"But I will." It was Lila's voice again, followed instantly by the sound of a gun. Pain and surprise both flashed across Rhy's face, and then one of his legs crumpled beneath him, blood darkening the fabric around his calf. Lila was standing outside, not on the banister as she'd been before, but in the air above it, feet resting on a plume of black smoke. Relief poured over Kell, followed instantly by horror. She hadn't just walked into danger. She'd brought the stone with her.

"You'll have to try harder than that to kill me," she said, hopping down from the smoke platform and onto the balcony. She strode into the chamber.

Rhy got to his feet. "Is that a challenge?" The guards were recovering, too, one moving behind Lila, the other hovering behind Kell.

"Run," he said to Lila.

"Nice to see you, too," she snapped, shoving the talisman back in her pocket. He saw the weakness sweep over her in the magic's wake, but only in her eyes and jaw. She was good at hiding it.

"You shouldn't have come here," growled Kell.

"No," echoed Rhy. "You shouldn't have. But you're here now. And you've brought me a gift." Lila's hand pressed against her coat, and Rhy's mouth curled into that horrible smile. Kell readied himself for an attack, but instead, Rhy's hand brought the blade to his own chest and rested the tip between his ribs, just under his heart. Kell stiffened. "Give me the stone, or I will kill the prince."

Lila frowned, eyes flicking between Rhy and Kell, uncertain.

"You wouldn't kill him," challenged Kell.

Rhy raised a dark brow. "Do you really believe that, flower boy, or do you only hope it's true?"

"You chose his body because he's part of your plan. You won't—"

"Never presume to know your enemy." Rhy's hand pressed down on the knife, the tip sinking between his ribs. "I have a closetful of kings."

"Stop," demanded Kell as blood spread out from the knife's tip. He tried commanding the bones in Rhy's arm to still, but Astrid's own powerful will inside the prince's body made Kell's grip tenuous.

"How long can you stay my hand?" challenged Astrid. "What happens when your focus starts to slip?" Rhy's amber eyes went to Lila. "He doesn't want me to hurt his brother. You best give me the stone before I do."

Lila hesitated, and Rhy's free hand curled around the possession charm and drew it over his head, holding it loosely in his palm. "The stone, Lila."

"Don't do this," said Kell, and he didn't know if he meant the words for Astrid or Lila or both.

"The *stone*."

"Astrid, please," whispered Kell, his voice wavering.

At that, Rhy's mouth twisted into a triumphant smile. "You are mine, Kell, and I will break you. Starting with your heart."

"Astrid."

But it was too late. Rhy's body twisted toward Lila, and a single word left his mouth—*catch*—before he cast the pendant into the air and drove the knife into his chest.

∽ V ∾

It happened so fast, the pendant moving at the same time as the blade. Kell saw Lila lunge out of the charm's reach, and he twisted back in time to see Rhy burying the knife between his ribs.

"No!" screamed Kell, surging forward.

The necklace skidded along the floor and fetched up against a guard's boot, and Rhy crumpled forward, the blade driven in to the hilt as Kell scrambled to his side and pulled the knife free.

Rhy—and it *was* Rhy now—let out a choked sound, and Kell pressed his blood-streaked fingers to his brother's chest. Rhy's shirtfront was already wet, and he shuddered under Kell's touch. Kell had just began to speak, to command the magic to heal the prince, when a guard slammed into him from the side and they both went down on the inlaid floor.

Several feet away Lila was grappling with the other guard while Kell's attacker clutched the talisman in one hand and tried to wrap the other around Kell's throat. Kell kicked and fought and dragged himself free, and when the guard (and Astrid within) charged forward, he threw up his hand. The metal armor—and the body inside—went flying backward, not into the wall, but into the banister at the balcony, which crumbled under the force and sent the guard's body over and down. It landed with a crash on the courtyard stones below, the sound followed instantly by screams, and Kell ran to the patio to see a dozen of the ball's dancers circling the body. One of them, a woman in a lovely green gown, reached out curiously for the pendant, now discarded on the courtyard stones.

"Stop!" called Kell, but it was too late. The moment the woman's fingers curled around it, he could see her change, the possession rippling through her in a single drawn-out shiver before her head flicked up at him, mouth drawing into a cold grim smile. She turned on her heel and plunged into the palace.

"Kell!" called Lila, and he spun, taking in the room for the first time as it was, in disarray. The remaining guard lay motionless on the floor, a dagger driven through the visor of his helmet, and Lila crouched over Rhy, her mask lifted and her tangled hands pressing against the prince's chest. She was covered in blood, but it wasn't hers. Rhy's shirt was soaked through.

"*Rhy,*" said Kell, the word a sob, a shuddering breath as he knelt over his brother. He drew his dagger and slashed his hand, cutting deep. "Hold on, Rhy." He pressed his wounded palm to the prince's chest—it was rising and falling in staccato breaths—and said, "*As Hasari.*"

Heal.

Rhy coughed up blood.

The courtyard below had exploded into activity, voices pouring up through the broken balcony. Footsteps were sounding through the halls, fists banging on the chamber doors, which Kell now saw were scrawled with spellwork. Locking charms.

"We have to go," said Lila.

"*As Hasari,*" said Kell again, putting pressure on the wound. There was so much blood. Too much.

"I'm sorry," murmured Rhy.

"Shut up, Rhy," said Kell.

300

"Kell," ordered Lila.

"I'm not leaving him," he said simply.

"So take him with us." Kell hesitated. "You said the magic needs time to work. We can't wait. Bring him with us if you will, but we need to *go*."

Kell swallowed. "I'm sorry," he said, just before forcing himself—and Rhy—to his feet. The prince gasped in pain. "I'm sorry."

They couldn't go by the door. Couldn't parade the wounded prince in front of a palace full of people there to celebrate his birthday. And, somewhere among them, Astrid Dane. But there was a private hall between Rhy's room and Kell's, one they'd used since they were boys, and now he half dragged, half carried his brother toward a concealed door, and then through it. He led the prince and Lila down the narrow corridor, the walls of which were covered with an assortment of odd marks—bets and challenges and personal scores kept by tallies, the tasks themselves long forgotten. A trail through their strange and sheltered youth.

Now they left a trail of blood.

"Stay with me," said Kell. "Stay with me. Rhy. Listen to my voice."

"Such a nice voice," said Rhy quietly, his head lolling forward.

"Rhy."

Kell heard armored bodies break into the prince's room as they reached his own, and he shut the door to the hall and pressed his bloodied hand to the wood and said, *"As Staro." Seal.*

As the word left his lips, metalwork spread out from his fingers, tracing back and forth over the door and binding it shut.

"We can't keep running from bedroom to bedroom," snapped Lila. "We have to get out of this palace!"

Kell knew that. Knew they had to get away. He led them to the private study at the far edge of his room, the one with the blood markings on the back of the door. Shortcuts to half a dozen places in the city. The one that led to the Ruby Fields was useless now, but the others would work. He scanned the options until he found the one—the only one—he knew would be safe.

"Will this work?" asked Lila.

Kell wasn't sure. Doors *within* worlds were harder to make but easier to use; they could only be created by *Antari*, but others could—*hypothetically*—pass through. Indeed, Kell had led Rhy through a portal once before—the day he found him on the boat—but there had been only two of them then, and now there were three.

"Don't let go," said Kell. He drew fresh blood over the mark and held Rhy and Lila as closely as he could, hoping the door—and the magic—would be strong enough to lead them all to sanctuary.

XII

SANCTUARY & SACRIFICE

❦ I ❧

The London Sanctuary sat at a bend in the river near the edge of the city, a stone structure with the simple elegance of a temple and an air just as reverent. It was a place where men and women came to study magic as much as worship it. Scholars and masters here spent their lives striving to comprehend—and connect with—the essence of power, the origin, the source. To understand the element of magic. The entity in all, and yet of none.

As a child, Kell had spent as much time in the sanctuary as he had in the palace, studying under—and being studied by— his tutor, Master Tieren, but though he visited now and then, he had not been back to stay in years (not since Rhy began to throw tantrums at Kell's every absence, insisting that the latter be not only a fixture, but also a family member). Still, Tieren insisted that he would always have a room there, and so Kell had kept the door drawn on his wall, marked by a simple circle of blood with an X drawn through.

The symbol of sanctuary.

Now he and Lila—with a bloody Rhy between them— stumbled through, out of the grandeur and current chaos of the palace and into a simple stone room.

Candlelight flickered against the smooth rock walls, and the chamber itself was narrow and high-ceilinged and sparsely furnished. The sanctuary scorned distraction, the private chambers supplied with only the essential. Kell may have been *aven*—blessed—but Tieren insisted on treating him as he would any other student (a fact for which Kell was grateful). As such, his room held neither more nor less than any other: a wooden desk along one wall and a low cot along another, with a small table beside it. On the table, burning, as it always burned, sat an infinite candle. The room had no windows and only one door, and the air held the coolness of underground places, of crypts.

A circle was etched into the floor, symbols scrawled around the edges. An enhancing sphere meant for meditation. Rhy's blood trailed a path across it as Kell and Lila dragged him to the cot and laid him down as gently as possible.

"Stay with me," Kell kept saying, but Rhy's quiet "sure" and "all right" and "as you wish" had given way to silence and shallow breaths.

How many *As Hasari*s had Kell said? The words had once more become a low chant on his lips, in his head, in his heartbeat, but Rhy was not healing. How long until the magic worked? It had to work. Fear clawed its way up Kell's throat. He should have looked at Astrid's weapon. Should have paid attention to the metal and the markings on it. Had she done something to block his magic? *Why wasn't it working?*

"Stay with me," he murmured. Rhy had stopped moving. His eyes were closed, and the strain had gone out of his jaw.

"Kell," Lila said softly. "I think it's too late."

"No," he said, gripping the cot. "It's not. The magic just needs time. You don't understand how it works."

"Kell."

"It just needs time." Kell pressed both hands to his brother's chest and stifled a cry. It neither rose nor fell. He couldn't feel a heartbeat underneath the ribs. "I can't . . ." he said, gasping as if he, too, were starved of air. "I can't . . ." Kell's voice wavered

as his fingers tangled in his brother's bloody shirt. "I can't give up."

"It's over," said Lila. "There's nothing you can do."

But that wasn't true. There was still something. All the warmth went out of Kell's body. But so did the hesitation, and the confusion, and the fear. He knew what to do. Knew what he *had* to do. "Give me the stone," he said.

"No."

"Lila, give me the bloody stone before it's too late."

"It's *already* too late. He's—"

"He's not dead!" snapped Kell. He held out a stained and shaking hand. "Give it to me."

Lila's hand went to her pocket and hovered there. "There's a reason I'm holding it, Kell," she said.

"Dammit, Lila. *Please.*"

She let out a shaky breath and withdrew the stone. He ripped it from her fingers, ignoring the pulse of power up his arm as he turned back to Rhy's body.

"You told me yourself, nothing good comes out of this," said Lila as Kell set the stone over Rhy's unbeating heart and pressed his palm down on top of it. "I know you're upset, but you can't think that this . . ."

But he couldn't hear her. Her voice dissolved, along with everything else, as Kell focused on the magic coursing in his veins.

Save him, he ordered the stone.

Power sang through his blood, and smoke poured out from under his fingers. It snaked up his arm and around Rhy's ribs, turning to blackened rope as it tangled around them. Tying them together. Binding them. But Rhy still lay there, unmoving.

My life is his life, thought Kell. *His life is mine. Bind it to mine and bring him back.*

He could feel the magic, hungry and wanting, pushing against him, trying to tap in to his body, his power, his life force. And this time, he let it in.

As soon as he did, the black rope tightened, and Kell's heart lurched in his chest. It skipped a beat, and Rhy's heart caught it, thudding once beneath Kell's touch. For an instant, all he felt was relief, joy.

Then, *pain*.

Like being torn apart, one nerve at a time. Kell screamed as he doubled forward over the prince, but he didn't let go. Rhy's back arched under his hand, the dark coils of magic cinching around them. The pain only worsened, carved itself in burning strokes over Kell's skin, his heart, his life.

"Kell!" Lila's voice broke through the fog, and he saw her rushing forward a step and then two, already reaching out to stop him, to pull him free of the spell. *Stop,* he thought. He didn't say it, didn't raise a finger, but the magic was in his head and it heard his will. It rushed through him and the smoke rushed out and slammed Lila backward. She hit the stone wall hard and crumpled to the floor.

Something in Kell stirred, distant and hushed. *Wrong,* it whispered. *This is . . .* But then another wave of pain sent him reeling. Power pounded through his veins, and his head came to rest against his brother's ribs as the pain tore through him, skin and muscle, bone and soul.

Rhy gasped, and so did Kell, his heart skipping once more in his chest.

And then it stopped.

⌒ II ⌒

The room went deathly still.

Kell's hand slipped from Rhy's ribs, and his body tumbled from the cot to the stone floor with a sickening thud. Lila's ears were still ringing from the force of her head meeting the wall as she pushed herself to her hands and knees, and then to her feet.

Kell wasn't moving. Wasn't breathing.

And then, after a moment that seemed to last hours, he drew a deep, shuddering breath. And so did Rhy.

Lila swore with relief as she knelt over Kell. His shirt was open, his stomach and chest streaked with blood, but under that, a black symbol, made up of concentric circles, was branded into his skin, directly over his heart. Lila looked up at the cot. The same mark was scrawled over Rhy's bloody chest.

"What have you done?" she whispered. She didn't know that much about magic, but she was fairly certain that bringing someone back from the dead was solidly in the *bad* column. If all magic came at a price, what had this cost Kell?

As if in answer, his eyes floated open. Lila was relieved to see that one of them was still blue. There had been an instant, during the spell, when both had gone solid black.

"Welcome back," she said.

Kell groaned, and Lila helped him up into a sitting position on the cold stone floor. His attention went to the bed, where Rhy's chest rose and fell in a slow but steady motion. His eyes went from the mark on the prince's skin to the mirrored mark on his own, which he touched, wincing faintly.

"What did you do?" asked Lila.

"I bound Rhy's life to mine," he said hoarsely. "As long as I survive, so will he."

"That seems like a dangerous spell."

"It's not a spell," he said softly. She didn't know if he lacked the strength to speak louder or was afraid of waking his brother. "It's called a soul seal. Spells can be broken. A soul seal cannot. It's a piece of permanent magic. But *this*," he added, grazing the mark, "this is . . ."

"Forbidden?" ventured Lila.

"Impossible," said Kell. "This kind of magic, it doesn't exist."

He seemed dazed and distant as he got to his feet, and Lila tensed when she saw that he was still gripping the stone. Black veins traced up his arm. "You need to let go of that now."

Kell looked down, as if he'd forgotten he was holding it. But when he managed to unclench his fingers, the talisman didn't fall out. Threads of black spun out from the rock, winding down his fingers and up his wrist. He stared down at the stone for several long moments. "It appears I can't," he said at last.

"Isn't that bad?" pressed Lila.

"Yes," he said, and his calm worried her more than anything. "But I didn't have a choice. . . . I had to . . ." He trailed off, turning toward Rhy.

"Kell, are you all right?" It seemed an absurd question, given the circumstances, and Kell gave her a look that said as much, so Lila added, "When you were doing that spell, you weren't *you*."

"Well, I am now."

"Are you sure about that?" she asked, gesturing at his hand.

310

"Because that's new." Kell frowned. "That rock is bad magic; you said it yourself. It feeds on energy. On people. And now it's strapped itself to you. You can't tell me that doesn't worry you."

"Lila," he said darkly. "I couldn't let him die."

"But what you've done instead—"

"I did what I had to do," he said. "I suppose it doesn't matter. I am already lost."

Lila scowled. "What do you mean by that?"

Kell's eyes softened a little. "Someone has to return the stone to Black London, Lila. It's not just a matter of opening a door and casting the object through. I have to *take it there*. I have to walk through with it." Kell looked down at the stone binding itself to his hand. "I never expected to make it back."

"Christ, Kell," growled Lila. "If you're not going to bother staying alive, then what's the damn point? Why tether Rhy's life to yours if you're just going to throw it away?"

Kell cringed. "So long as I live, so will he. And I didn't say I planned on dying."

"But you just said—"

"I said I'm not coming *back*. The seals on Black London were designed less to keep anyone from going in, and more to keep anyone from getting out. I can't strip the spells. And even if I could, I wouldn't. And with the spells intact, even if I manage to make a door *into* Black London, the seals will never let me back *out*."

"And you weren't going to mention *any* of this. You were just going to let me follow you on a one-way trip to—"

"You said you wanted an adventure," snapped Kell, "and no, I never intended to let you—"

Just then the door swung open. Kell and Lila fell silent, their argument echoing on the walls of the narrow stone chamber.

An old man was standing in the doorway wearing a black robe, one hand against the doorframe, the other holding up a sphere of pale white light. He wasn't old in a withered way. In fact, he stood straight and broad-shouldered, his age belied only by his white hair and the deep creases on his face, made deeper by the shadows cast from the light in his palm. Kell pulled his coat around himself and buried his damaged hand in his pocket.

"Master Tieren," he said casually, as if the informality of his voice could cover up the fact that he and Lila were streaked with blood and standing in front of the body of a nearly dead prince.

"Kell," said the man, frowning deeply. *"Kers la? Ir vanesh mer. . . ."* And then he trailed off and looked at Lila. His eyes were pale and startlingly blue; they seemed to go straight through her. His brow furrowed, and then he began speaking again, this time in English. As if he could tell, with a single glance, that she did not understand, did not belong. "What brings you here?" he asked, addressing both of them.

"You said I would always have a room," answered Kell wearily. "I'm afraid I had need of it."

He stepped aside so that Master Tieren could see the wounded prince.

The man's eyes went wide, and he touched his fingers to his lips in a small prayer-like gesture. "Is he . . . ?"

"He's alive," said Kell, hand drifting to his collar to hide the mark. "But the palace is under attack. I cannot explain everything, not now, but you must believe me, Tieren. It has been taken by traitors. They are using forbidden magic, possessing the bodies and minds of those around them. No one is safe—*nowhere* is safe—and no one is to be trusted." He was breathless by the time he finished.

Tieren crossed to Kell in a handful of slow strides. He took Kell's face in his hands, the gesture strangely intimate, and looked into his eyes as he had Lila's, as if he could see past them. "What have you done to yourself?"

Kell's voice caught in his throat. "Only what I had to." His coat had fallen open, and the man's gaze drifted down to the blackened mark over Kell's heart. "Please," he said, sounding

312

frightened. "I would not have brought danger into these halls, but I had no choice."

The man's hands fell away. "The sanctuary is warded against darkness. The prince will be safe within these walls."

Relief swept across Kell's features. Tieren turned to consider Lila a second time.

"You are not from here," he said by way of introduction.

Lila held out her hand. "Delilah Bard."

The man took it, and something like a shiver, but warmer, passed beneath her skin, a calm spreading through her in its wake. "My name is Master Tieren," he said. "I am the *onase aven*—that is to say, the head priest—of the London Sanctuary. And a healer," he added, as if to explain the sensation. Their hands fell apart, and Tieren went to the prince's side and brought his bony fingers to rest feather-light on top of Rhy's chest. "His injuries are severe."

"I know," said Kell shakily. "I can feel them as if they were my own."

Lila tensed, and Tieren's expression darkened. "Then I will do what I can to ease his pain, and yours."

Kell nodded gratefully. "It's my fault," he said. "But I will set things right." Tieren opened his mouth to speak, but Kell stopped him. "I cannot tell you," he said. "I must ask for your trust as well as your discretion."

Tieren's mouth became a thin line. "I will lead you to the tunnels," he said. "From there you will be able to find your way. Whichever way you need."

Kell had been silent since leaving the small room. He hadn't been able to look at his brother, hadn't been able to say good-bye, had only swallowed and nodded and turned away, following Master Tieren out. Lila trailed behind, picking Rhy's dried blood from the cuffs of her new coat (she supposed she would have had to get her hands—and sleeves—dirty sooner or later). As they made their way through the bowels of the sanctuary, she watched Kell and the way his gaze hung on Tieren, as if willing the priest to say something. But the priest kept his mouth shut and his eyes ahead, and eventually Kell's step began to trail, until he and Lila were side by side in the head priest's wake.

"The clothing suits you," he said quietly. "Do I want to know how you came by it?"

Lila tilted her head. "I didn't steal it, if that's what you're asking. I bought it from a woman in the market named Calla."

Kell smiled faintly at the name. "And how did you pay for it?"

"I haven't yet," retorted Lila. "But that doesn't mean I won't." Her gaze dropped away. "Though I don't know when I'll have the chance . . ."

"You will," said Kell. "Because you're staying here."

"Like hell I am," shot Lila.

"The sanctuary will keep you safe."

"I will not be left behind."

Kell shook his head. "You were never meant to go farther. When I said yes, I did so with the intent to leave you here, in my city, to deliver word of my fate to the king and queen." Lila drew a breath, but he held up his uninjured hand. "And to keep you safe. White London is no place for a Grey-worlder. It's no place for *anyone*."

"I'll be the judge of that," she said. "I'm going with you."

"Lila, this isn't some *game*. Enough people have died, and I—"

"You're right, it's not a game," pressed Lila. "It's *strategy*. I heard what the queen said about the stone being broken in two. You need to dispose of *both* pieces, and as of right now, you only have one. The White king has the other, right? Which means we have our work cut out for us. And it is *we*, Kell. Two of them means there should be two of us as well. You can take the king, and I'll handle the queen."

"You're no match for Astrid Dane."

314

"Tell me, do you underestimate everyone, or just me? Is it because I'm a girl?"

"It's because you're a *human*," he snapped. "Because you may be the bravest, boldest soul I've ever met, but you're still too much flesh and blood and too little power. Astrid Dane is made of magic and malice."

"Yes, well, that's all well and good for her, but she's not even *in* her body, is she? She's here, having a grand time in Red London. Which means she should make an easy target." Lila gave him the sharpest edge of a grin. "And I may be human, but I've made it this far."

Kell frowned deeply.

It is amazing, thought Lila, *that he doesn't have more wrinkles.*

"You have," he said. "But no farther."

"The girl has power in her," offered Tieren without looking back.

Lila brightened. "See?" she preened. "I've been telling you that all along."

"What *kind* of power?" asked Kell, raising a brow.

"Don't sound so skeptical," Lila shot back.

"Unnurtured," said Tieren. "Untended. Unawakened."

"Well, come on then, *onase aven*," she said, holding out her hands. "Wake it up."

Tieren glanced back and offered her a ghost of a smile. "It shall awake on its own, Delilah Bard. And if you nurture it, it will grow."

"She comes from the other London," said Kell. Tieren showed no surprise. "The one without magic."

"No London is truly without magic," observed the priest.

"And human or not," added Lila sharply, "I'd like to remind you that you're still alive because of me. *I'm* the reason that White queen's not wearing you like a coat. *And* I've got something you need."

"What's that?"

Lila pulled the white rook from her pocket. "The key."

Kell's eyes widened a fraction in surprise, and then narrowed. "Do you honestly think you could keep it from me, if I wished to take it?"

In an instant, Lila had the rook in one hand and her knife in the other. The brass knuckles of the handle glinted in the candlelight while the stone hummed low and steady, as if whispering to Kell.

"Try it," she sneered.

Kell stopped walking and looked at her. "What is *wrong* with you?" he asked, sounding honestly baffled. "Do you care so little about your life that you would throw it all away for a few hours of adventure and a violent death?"

Lila frowned. She'd admit that, in the beginning, all she wanted was an adventure, but that wasn't why she was insisting now. The truth was, she'd seen the change in Kell, seen the shadow sweep across his eyes when he summoned that clever cursed magic, seen how hard it was for him to return to his senses after. Every time he used the stone, he seemed to lose a bigger piece of himself. So no, Lila wasn't going with him just to satisfy some thirst for danger. And she wasn't going with him just to keep him company. She was going because they'd come this far, and because she feared he wouldn't succeed, not alone.

"My life is mine to spend," she said. "And I will not spend it here, no matter how nice your city is, or how much safer it might be. We had a deal, Kell. And you now have Tieren to guard your story and heal your brother. I'm of no use to him. Let me be of use to you."

Kell looked her in the eyes. "You will be trapped there," he said. "When it is over."

Lila shivered. "Perhaps," she said, "or perhaps I will go with you to the end of the world. After all, you've made me curious."

"Lila—" His eyes were dark with pain and worry, but she only smiled.

"One adventure at a time," she said.

They reached the edge of the tunnel, and Tieren pushed open a pair of metal gates. The red river glowed up at them from below. They were standing on its northern bank, the palace shimmering in the distance, still surrounded by starry light, as if nothing were amiss.

Tieren brought his hand to Kell's shoulder and murmured something in Arnesian before adding in English, "May the saints and source of all be with you both."

Kell nodded and gripped the priest's hand with his unwounded one before stepping out into the evening. But as Lila went to follow, Tieren caught her arm. He squinted at her as if searching for a secret.

"What?" asked Lila.

"How did you lose it?" he asked.

Lila frowned. "Lose what?"

His weathered fingers drifted up beneath her chin. "Your eye."

Lila pulled her face from his grip, her hand going to the darker of her two brown eyes. The one made of glass. Few people ever noticed. Her hair cut a sharp line across her face, and even when she did look someone in the eye, they rarely held the gaze for long enough to mark the difference. "I don't remember," she said. It wasn't a lie. "I was a child, and it was an accident, I'm told."

"Hm," said Tieren pensively. "Does Kell know?"

Her frown deepened. "Does it matter?"

After a long moment, the old man tilted his head. "I suppose not," he said.

Kell was looking back at Lila, waiting for her.

"If the darkness takes him," said Tieren under his breath, "you must end his life." He looked at her. Through her. "Do you think you can?"

Lila didn't know whether he wanted to know if she had the strength, or the will.

"If he dies," she said, "so will Rhy."

Tieren sighed. "Then the world will be as it should," he said, sadly. "Instead of as it is."

Lila swallowed, and nodded, and went to join Kell.

"To White London, then?" she asked when she reached him, holding out the rook. Kell did not move. He was staring out at the river and the palace arching over it. She thought he might be taking in his London, his home, saying his good-byes, but then he spoke.

"The bones are the same in every world," he said, gesturing to the city, "but the rest of it will be different. As different as this world is from yours." He pointed across the river, and toward the center of London. "Where we're going, the castle is there. Athos and Astrid will be there, too. Once we cross through, stay close. Do not leave my side. It is night here, which means it is night in White London, too, and the city is full of shadows." Kell looked at Lila. "You can still change your mind."

Lila straightened and tugged up the collar of her coat. She smiled. "Not a chance."

❦ III ❧

The palace was in a state of upheaval.

Guests were spilling, confused and concerned, down the great stairs, ushered out by the royal guards. Rumors spread like fire through the crowd, rumors of violence and death and wounded royalty. Words like *treason* and *coup* and *assassin* filled the air, only feeding the frenzy.

Someone claimed that a guard had been murdered. Another claimed to have seen that guard fall from the prince's balcony to the courtyard below. Another still said that a woman in a green gown had stolen a necklace from the gruesome scene and rushed into the palace. Another insisted he'd seen her thrust the pendant into the hands of another guard and then collapse at his feet. The guard had not even called for help. He'd simply stormed away toward the royal chambers.

There the king and queen had withdrawn, their strange calm only adding to the guests' confusion. The guard had vanished into their room, and a moment later, the king had apparently burst forth, his steadiness cast off as he shouted about treason. He claimed that the prince had been stabbed and that Kell was to blame, demanding the *Antari*'s arrest. And just like that, the confusion shattered into to panic, chaos billowing like smoke through the night.

By the time Gen's boots approached the palace, the stairs were crowded with worried guests. The thing inside Gen's armor turned its black eyes up at the dancing lights and jostling bodies. It wasn't the mayhem that drew him there. It was the scent. Someone had used strong magic, beautiful magic, and he meant to find out who.

He set off up the stairs, pressing past the flustered guests. No one seemed to notice that his armor was rent, peeled back over the heart, a stain like black wax across his front. Nor did they notice the blood—Parrish's blood—splashed across the metal.

When he reached the top of the stairs, he drew a deep breath and smiled; the night hung heavy with panic and power, the energy filling his lungs, stoking him like coals. He could smell the magic now. He could *taste* it.

And he was hungry.

He'd chosen his latest shell quite well; the guards, in their commotion, let him pass. It wasn't until he was inside, through the flower-lined antechamber and striding across the emptied ballroom, that a helmeted figure stopped him.

"Gen," demanded the guard, "where have you . . ." But the words died in the guard's throat when he saw the man's eyes. *"Mas aven—"*

The oath was cut off by Gen's sword, sliding through armor and between ribs. The guard dragged in a single, shuddering breath and tried to cry out, but the sword cut sideways and up, and the air died in his throat. Easing the body down, the thing wearing Gen's skin resheathed his weapon and removed the guard's helmet, sliding it over his own head. When he pulled the visor down, his black eyes were nothing but a glint through the metal slit.

Footsteps sounded through the palace, and shouted orders echoed overhead. He straightened. The air was full of blood and magic, and he went to find its source.

* * *

320

The stone still sang in Kell's hand, but not quite the way it had before. Now the melody, the thrum of power, seemed to be singing *in* his bones instead of over them. Every moment, he felt it in his heartbeat and in his head. With it came a strange quiet, a calm, one he trusted even less than the initial surge of power. The calm told him everything would be well. It cooed and soothed and steadied his heart and made Kell forget that anything was wrong, made him forget that he was holding the stone at all. That was the worst part. It was bound to his hand, and yet it hung at the outside of his senses; he had to fight to remember it was there with him. *Inside* of him. Every time he remembered, it was like waking from a dream, full of panic and fear, only to be dragged down into sleep again. In those brief moments of clarity, he wanted to claw free, break or tear or cut the stone from his skin. But he didn't, because competing with that urge to cast it off was the equal, opposite desire to hold it close, to cling to its warmth as if he were dying of cold. He *needed* its strength. Now more than ever.

Kell didn't want Lila to see how scared he was, but he thought she saw it anyway.

They had woven back toward the city center, the streets mostly deserted on this side of the river, but had yet to cross any of the bridges that arced back and forth over the Isle. It was too dangerous, too exposed. Especially since, halfway there, Kell's face had reappeared on the scrying boards that lined the streets.

Only this time, instead of saying:

MISSING

It now said:

WANTED

For *treason, murder,* and *abduction*.

Kell's chest tightened at the accusations, and he held fast to the fact that Rhy was safe—as safe as he could possibly be. His fingers went to the brand over his heart; if he focused, he could feel the echo of Rhy's heartbeat, the pulse a fraction of time after his own.

He looked around, trying to picture the streets not only as they were here, but as they would be in White London, superimposing the images in his mind.

"This will have to do," he said.

Where they stood now, at the mouth of an alley across from a string of ships—Lila had surveyed them with an appraising eye—they would stand before a bridge in the next city. A bridge that led to a street that ended at the walls of the White Castle. As they'd walked, Kell had described to Lila the dangers of the other London, from its twin rulers to its starving, power-hungry populace. And then he had described the castle and the bones of his plan, because bones were all he had right now.

Bones and hope. Hope that they would make it, that he would be able to hold on to himself long enough to beat Athos and retrieve the second half of the stone and then—

Kell closed his eyes and took a low, steadying breath. *One adventure at a time.* Lila's words echoed in his mind.

"What are we waiting for?"

Lila was leaning against the wall. She tapped the bricks. "Come on, Kell. Door time." And her casual air, her defiant energy, the way, even now, she didn't seem concerned or afraid, only *excited* him, gave him strength.

The gash across his palm, though now partially obscured by the black stone, was still fresh. He touched the cut with his finger and drew a mark on the brick wall in front of them. Lila took his hand, palm to palm with the stone singing between them, and offered him the white rook, and he brought it to the blood on the wall, swallowing his nerves.

"*As Travars,*" he commanded, and the world softened and

darkened around them as they stepped forward and through the newly hewn doorway.

Or at least, that's how it should have happened.

But halfway through the stride, a force jarred Kell backward, tearing Lila's hand from his as it ripped him out of the place between worlds and back onto the hard stone street of Red London. Kell blinked up at the night, dazed, and then realized he was not alone. Someone was standing over him. At first, the figure was no more than a shadow, rolling up his sleeves. And then Kell saw the silver circle glittering at his collar.

Holland looked down at him and frowned.

"Leaving so soon?"

ᑕ IV ᑐ

Lila's black boots landed on the pale street. Her head spun a little from the sudden change, and she steadied herself against the wall. She heard the sound of Kell's steps behind her.

"Well, that's an improvement," she said, turning. "At least we're in the same place this—"

But he wasn't there.

She was standing on the curb in front of a bridge, the White Castle rising in the distance across the river, which was neither grey nor red, but a pearly, half-frozen stretch of water, shining dully in the thickening night. Lanterns along the river burned with a pale blue fire that cast the world in a strange, colorless way, and Lila, in her crisp black clothes, stood out as much a light in the dark.

Something shone near her feet, and she looked down to find the white rook on the ground, its pale surface still dotted with Kell's blood. But no Kell. She picked up the token and pocketed it, trying to swallow her rising nerves.

Nearby, a starved dog was watching her with empty eyes.

And then, quickly, Lila became aware of other eyes. In windows and doorways, and in the shadows between pools of sickly light. Her hand went to the knife with the metal knuckles.

"Kell?" she called out under her breath, but there was no

answer. Maybe it was like last time. Maybe they'd simply been separated, and he was making his way toward her now. Maybe, but Lila had felt the strange pull as they stepped through, had felt his hand vanish from hers too soon.

Footsteps echoed, and she turned in a slow circle but saw no one.

Kell had warned her of this world—he'd called it *dangerous*—but so much of Lila's own world had fit that term, so she hadn't given it much stock. After all, he'd grown up in a palace and she'd grown up on the streets, and Lila thought she knew a good bit more about bad alleys and worse men than Kell. Now, standing here, alone, Lila was beginning to think she hadn't given him enough credit. Anyone—even a highborn—could see the danger here. Could smell it. Death and ash and winter air.

She shivered. Not only from cold, but from fear. A simple bone-deep sense of *wrong*. It was like looking into Holland's black eye. For the first time, Lila wished she had more than knives and the Flintlock.

"*Övos norevjk*," came a voice to her right, and she spun to see a man, bald, every inch of exposed skin, from the crown of his head down to his fingers, covered in tattoos. Whatever he was speaking, it didn't sound like Arnesian. It was gruff and guttural, and even though she didn't know the words, she could grasp the tone, and she didn't like it.

"*Tovach ös mostevna*," said another, appearing to her left, his skin like parchment.

The first man chuckled. The second *tsk*ed.

Lila pulled the knife free. "Stay back," she ordered, hoping her gesture would make up for any language barrier.

The men exchanged a look and then withdrew their own jagged weapons.

A cold breeze cut through, and Lila fought down a shiver. The men broke into rotting grins. She lowered her knife. And then, in one smooth move, she drew the pistol from her belt, raised it, and shot the first man between the eyes. He went down like a sack of stones, and Lila smiled before she realized how loud the gunshot sounded. She hadn't noticed how quiet the city was until the shot rang out, the blast carrying down the streets. All around them, doors began to open. Shadows moved. Whispers and murmurs came from corners of the street—first one, then two, then half a dozen.

The second man, the one with papery skin, looked at the dead one, and then at Lila. He started talking again in a low threatening growl, and Lila was glad she didn't speak his tongue. She didn't want to know what he was saying.

Slivers of dark energy crackled through the air around the man's blade. She could feel people moving behind her, the shadows taking shape into people, gaunt and grey.

Come on, Kell, she thought as she raised the gun again. *Where are you?*

ᴄ V ᴐ

"Let me pass," said Kell.

Holland only raised a brow.

"Please," said Kell. "I can end this."

"Can you?" challenged Holland. "I do not think you have it in you." His gaze went to Kell's hand, the dark magic twining around it. "I warned you, magic is not about balance. It is about dominance. You control it, or it controls you."

"I am still in control," said Kell through gritted teeth.

"No," said Holland. "You're not. Once you let the magic in, you've already lost."

Kell's chest tightened. "I don't want to fight you, Holland."

"You do not have a choice." Holland wore a sharpened ring on one hand and used it now to cut a line across his palm. Blood dripped to the street. *"As Isera,"* he said softly. *Freeze.*

The dark drops hit the ground and turned to black ice, shooting forward across the street. Kell tried to step back, but the ice moved too fast, and within seconds he was standing on top of it, fighting for balance.

"Do you know what makes you weak?" said Holland. "You've never had to be strong. You've never had to try. You've never had to fight. And you've certainly never had to fight for your *life*. But tonight that changes, Kell. Tonight, if you do not fight, you *will* die. And if you—"

Kell didn't wait for him to finish. A sudden gust of wind whipped forward, nearly knocking Kell off-balance as it cycloned toward Holland. It surrounded the *Antari,* swallowing him from sight. The wind whistled, but through it Kell could hear a low, haunting sound. And then he realized it was a laugh.

Holland was laughing.

A moment later, Holland's blood-streaked hand appeared, parting the cyclone wall, and then the rest of him stepped through, the column of wind crumbling around him. "Air cannot be made sharp," he chided. "Cannot hurt. Cannot kill. You should choose your elements with more care. Watch."

Holland moved with such smooth swiftness, it was hard to follow his motions, let alone keep up. In a single fluid move, he dropped to a knee and touched the ground and said *"As Steno."*
Break.

The paving stone beneath his palm shattered into a dozen sharpened shards, and as he stood, the shards came with him, hovering in the air the way the nails had done in the alley. He flicked his wrist, and the shards shot forward through the air toward Kell. The stone against his palm sang with warning, and he barely had time to throw up his hand, the talisman shining in it, and say, "Stop."

The smoke poured forth and caught the slivers in their path, crushing them to dust. Power shot through Kell with the command, followed instantly by something darker, colder. He gasped at the sensation. He could feel the magic climbing over his skin, and under it, and he willed it to stop, pushed back with all his strength as the smoke dissolved.

Holland was shaking his head. "Go ahead, Kell. Use the stone. It will consume you faster, but you might just win."

Kell swore under breath and summoned another cyclone, this one in front of him. He snapped the fingers of the hand without the stone. A flame appeared in his palm, and when he touched it to the twisting air, it took it, engulfing the wind in fire. The burning cyclone scorched across the ground, melting the ice as it charged toward Holland, who threw out his hand and summoned the ground up into a shield, and then, the instant the flame was gone, sent the stone wall surging toward Kell. He threw up his hands, fighting for control over the rocks, and realized too late that they were only a distraction for the arcing wave of water that struck him from behind.

The surge from the river slammed Kell to his hands and knees, but before he could recover, it swept him up and coiled around him. In moments, Kell was trapped by the swell, gasping for air before it swallowed him entirely. He fought, pinned by the force of the water.

"Astrid wanted you alive," said Holland, drawing the curved blade from beneath his cloak. "She insisted upon it." His free hand curled into a fist, and the water tightened, crushing the air from Kell's lungs. "But I'm sure she will understand if I have no choice but to kill you in order to retrieve the stone."

Holland strode toward him with measured steps over the icy ground, the curved blade hanging at his side, and Kell twisted and thrashed, scouring for something, anything he could use. He reached for the knife in Holland's grip, but the metal was warded, and it didn't even quiver. Kell was running out of air, and Holland was nearly to him. And then through the wall of water he saw the rippling image of the ship supplies, the pile of boards and poles and the dark metal of chains coiled on posts by the bridge.

Kell's fingers twitched, and the nearest set of chains flew forward, wrapping around Holland's wrist, jarring his focus. The water lost its shape and fell apart, and Kell stumbled forward to the ground, soaking wet and gasping for breath. Holland was still trying to free himself, and Kell knew he couldn't afford to hesitate. Another set of chains, from another post, snaked around the *Antari*'s leg and up his waist. Holland moved to throw the curved blade, but a third set of chains caught his arm and drew taut. It wouldn't hold, not for long. Kell willed a metal pole up from the dock floor and through the air, the bar hovering a foot or so behind Holland.

"I can't let you win," said Kell.

"Then you'd better kill me," growled Holland. "If you don't, it will never end."

Kell drew the knife from his forearm and lifted it as if to strike.

"You're going to have to try harder than that," said Holland as Kell's hand froze, the bones held still by the other *Antari's* will. It was exactly what Kell was hoping for. The moment Holland's focus was on the knife, Kell attacked, not from the front, but from behind, willing the metal bar forward with all his strength.

It soared through the air and found its mark, striking Holland in the back with enough force to pierce through cloak and skin and bone. It protruded from Holland's chest, the metal and blood obscuring the seal scarred over his heart. The silver circle clasp broke and tumbled away, the half-cloak sliding off Holland's shoulders as his knees folded.

Kell staggered to his feet as Holland collapsed onto the damp street. A horrible sadness rolled through him as he crossed to the *Antari's* body. They had been two of a kind, a dying breed. Now he was the only one. And soon, there would be none. Perhaps that was how it should be. How it *needed* to be.

Kell wrapped his fingers around the bloody metal bar and pulled it free of Holland's chest. He tossed the pole aside, the dull sound of it clanging down the road like a faltering heartbeat. Kell knelt beside Holland's body as blood began to pool beneath it. When he felt for a pulse, he found one there. But it was shallow, fading.

"I'm sorry," he said. It felt stupid and useless to say, but the sharpness had gone out of his anger, and his sadness, his fear, his loss—they had all dulled into a steady ache, one he felt he might never shake as he reached under the *Antari*'s collar and found a White London token on a cord around his neck.

Holland *knew*. He'd seen the attack coming, and he hadn't stopped it. The instant before the metal struck him from behind, Holland had stopped fighting. It was only a second, a fraction of a breath, but it had been enough to give Kell the edge, the opening. And in the sliver of time after the metal pierced his body, and before he fell, it wasn't anger or pain that crossed his face. It was relief.

Kell snapped the cord and straightened, but couldn't bring himself to leave the *Antari* there, in the street. He looked from the token to the waiting wall and then dragged Holland's body to its feet.

↶ VI ↷

The first thing Kell saw when he stepped into White London was Lila brandishing two knives, both of them bloody. She'd managed to cut a path through several men—their bodies littered the street—but four or five were circling her, and more hung back and watched with hungry eyes and whispered in their guttural tongue.

"Pretty red blood."

"Smells like magic."

"Open her up."

"See what's inside."

Kell lowered Holland's body to the ground, and stepped forward.

"Vös rensk torejk!" he boomed, rumbling the ground for good measure. *Back away from her.*

A ripple went through the crowd when they saw him—some fled, but others, too curious, took only a step or two back. The moment Lila saw him, her eyes narrowed.

"You are *very, very* late," she growled. Her usual calm had cracked, and underneath she looked tense with fear. "And why are you wet?" Kell looked down at his dripping clothes. He ran his hands along them, willing the water out, and a moment later, he stood, dry except for the puddle at his boots.

"I hit a snag," he said, gesturing back toward Holland. But several dark-eyed citizens were already beginning to investigate the body. One pulled out a knife and pressed it to the dying *Antari*'s wrist.

"Stop," ordered Kell, slamming the assailants backward with a gust of wind. He hauled the *Antari* up over his shoulder.

"Leave him," spat Lila. "Let them pick his bones clean."

But Kell shook his head.

"If you don't," she said. "They'll pick *ours*."

Kell turned and saw the men and women closing in around them.

The people of White London knew the orders, knew the Danes would take the head of any who touched their guest from afar, but it was night, and the lure of fresh magic and Holland's defenseless state—"Let me make a crown from him," murmured one; "I bet there's still blood left," said another—seemed to tip them off their senses. Lila and Kell moved backward until their heels met the bridge.

"Lila?" said Kell as they backed onto it.

"Yeah?" she said, her voice low and tight.

"Run."

She didn't hesitate, but turned and took off sprinting across the bridge. Kell's hand shot up, and with it, a wall of stone, a barricade to buy them time. And then he, too, was running. As fast as he could, with Holland's body over his narrow shoulder and the black magic surging in his veins.

Kell was halfway across the bridge—and Lila nearly to the other side—when the commoners finally tore down the wall and surged after them onto the structure. The moment he reached the opposite bank, Kell sank to the ground and touched his bloody hand to the floor of the bridge.

"As Steno," he commanded, just as Holland had, and instantly, the bridge began to crumble, plunging stone and bodies down into the icy Sijlt. Kell fought for breath, his pulse thudding his ears. Lila was standing over him, glaring at Holland's body.

"Is he dead?"

"Close enough," said Kell, getting to his feet, hauling the *Antari*'s body with him.

"I hope you made him suffer," she spat, turning toward the looming castle.

No, thought Kell as they set off. *He suffered long enough.*

He could feel the people watching as they moved through the streets, but no one came out of their houses. They were too near the castle now, and the castle had eyes. Soon, it loomed before them, the stone citadel behind its high wall, the archway like a gaping mouth, leading onto the darkened courtyard and its statues.

The stone hummed against Kell's palm, and he realized it wasn't calling only to him now. It was calling to its other half. Beside him, Lila drew yet another blade from beneath her coat. But this one wasn't an ordinary knife. It was a royal half-sword from Red London.

Kell's mouth fell open. "Where did you get that?" he asked.

"Nicked it off the guard who tried to kill me," she said, admiring the weapon. He could see the markings scrawled across the blade. Metal that disabled magic. "Like I said, you can never have too many knives."

Kell held out his hand. "Can you spare it?"

Lila considered him a moment, then shrugged and handed it over. Kell fingered the grip as she drew out her pistol and began to reload it.

"Are you ready?" she asked, spinning the chamber.

Kell gazed through the gate at the waiting castle. "No."

At that, she offered him the sharpest edge of a grin. "Good," she said. "The ones who think they're ready always end up dead."

Kell managed a ghost of a smile. "Thank you, Lila."

"For what?"

But Kell didn't answer, only stepped forward into the waiting dark.

XIII

THE
WAITING
KING

❧ I ❧

A cloud of black smoke hung in the air of the white throne room, a patch of night against the pale backdrop. Its edges frayed and curled and faded, but its center was smooth and glossy, like the fragment of stone in Athos's hand, or the surface of a scrying board, which was exactly what the king had summoned with it.

Athos Dane sat on his throne, his sister's body in her own chair beside him, and turned the stone over in his hand as he watched the shifting image of Kell and his companion pass into the courtyard of his castle.

Where the stone's other half had gone, so had its gaze.

The farthest London had been little more than a blur, but as Kell and his companion traveled nearer, the image in the surface had grown crisp and clear. Athos had watched the events unfold across the various cities—Kell's flight, the girl's cunning, his servant's failure, and his sister's foolishness, the wounded prince, and the slaughtered *Antari*.

His fingers tightened on the talisman.

Athos had watched it all unfold with a mixture of amusement and annoyance and, admittedly, excitement. He bristled at the loss of Holland, but a spike of pleasure ran through him at the thought of killing Kell.

Astrid would be furious.

Athos rolled his head and considered his sister's body, propped up on its throne, the charm pulsing at her throat. A London away, she might still be wreaking havoc, but here she sat, still and pale as the sculpted stone beneath her. Her hands draped on the arms of the chair, and wisps of white hair ribboned over her closed eyes. Athos *tsk*ed at his sister.

"*Ös vosa nochten,*" he said. "You should have let me go to the masquerade instead. Now my plaything is dead, and yours has made an awful mess. What do you have to say for yourself?"

Of course, she did not answer.

Athos rapped his long fingers on the edge of his throne, thinking. If he broke the spell and woke her, she would only complicate things. No, he had given her the chance to deal with Kell in her own way, and she had failed. It was his turn now.

Athos smiled and rose to his feet. His fingers tightened on the stone, and the image of Kell dissolved into smoke and then into nothing. Power thrummed through the king, the magic hungry for more, but he held it in place, feeding it only what it needed. It was a thing to be controlled, and Athos had never been a lenient master.

"Do not worry yourself, Astrid," he said to the spellbound queen. "I will make things right."

And then he smoothed his hair, readjusted the collar of his white cloak, and went to greet his guests.

୶ II ୬

The White London fortress rose in a column of sharp light out of the shadowed stone courtyard. Lila slipped into the forest of statues to fulfill her part of the plan while Kell made his way toward the waiting steps. He laid Holland's body on a stone bench and ascended the stairs, one hand curled around the royal blade, the other around the Black London talisman.

Go ahead, Kell, Holland had goaded. *Use the stone. It will consume you faster, but you might just win.*

He wouldn't. He vowed not to. His recent use in battle had only spurred the darkness on. Black threads now coiled up past his elbow and toward his shoulder, and Kell couldn't afford to lose any more of himself. As it was, every heartbeat seemed to spread the poison more.

His pulse thudded in his ears as he climbed the steps. Kell wasn't foolish enough to think he could sneak up on Athos—not here. He had to know that Kell was coming, yet he let him approach his doors without assault. The ten empty-eyed guards that usually flanked the stairs were gone, the way cleared for Kell. The unhindered path was itself a challenge. An act of arrogance befitting White London's king.

Kell would rather have faced an army than the unmanned doors and whatever waited on the other side. Every forward step that went unchecked, unobstructed, only made him more nervous for the next. By the time he reached the landing at the top, his hands were trembling and his chest was tight.

He brought his shaking fingertips to the doors and forced a last breath of cold air into his lungs. And then he pushed. The castle doors opened under his touch, requiring neither force nor magic, and Kell's shadow spilled forward into the corridor. He took a step over the threshold, and the torches of the chamber lit with pale fire, trailing up against the vaulted ceilings and down the hall and revealing the faces of the dozen guards who lined it.

Kell sucked in a breath, bracing himself, but the soldiers did not move.

"They won't lay a hand on you," came a silvery voice. "Not unless you try to flee." Athos Dane stepped out of the shadows, dressed in his usual pristine white, his faded features rendered colorless by the torchlight. "The pleasure of killing you will be mine. And mine alone."

Athos held the other half of the black stone loosely in one hand, and a thrum of power spiked through Kell's body at the sight of it.

"Astrid will sulk, of course," continued Athos. "She wanted you as a pet, but I have always maintained that you were more trouble alive than dead. And I think recent events would serve as evidence of that."

"It's over, Athos," said Kell. "Your plan failed."

Athos smiled grimly. "You are like Holland," he said. "Do you know why he could not take the crown? He never relished war. He saw bloodshed and battle as means to an end. A destination. But *I* have always relished the journey. And I promise you, I'm going to savor this."

His fingers tightened over his half of the stone, and smoke poured forth. Kell didn't hesitate. He willed the armor—and the guards within—from their places against the wall and into a barricade between himself and the king. But it was not

340

enough. The smoke went over, and under, and through, and reached for Kell, trying to twine around his arms. He willed the wall of guards forward into Athos, and sliced at the smoke with the royal sword. But the king did not drop the stone, and the magic was clever and moved around Kell's blade, catching hold of his wrists and turning instantly into forged chains that ran not down to the floor but out to the walls on either side of the antechamber hall.

The metal pulled taut, forcing Kell's arms wide as Athos vaulted over the guards and landed smoothly, effortlessly in front of him. The chains cinched, cutting into Kell's already wounded wrists, and his stolen sword tumbled from his fingers as Athos produced a silver whip. It uncoiled from his hand, cascading to the floor, its forked tip licking the stone.

"Shall we see how well you suffer?"

As Athos went to raise the whip, Kell wrapped his fingers around the chains. The blood on his palm was nearly dry, but he grabbed the metal hard enough to reopen the gash.

"*As Orense,*" he said an instant before the whip cracked through the air, and the chains released Kell just in time for him to dodge the forked silver. He rolled, fetching up the discarded blade, and pressed his bleeding palm to the floor stones, remembering Holland's attack.

"*As Steno,*" he said. The floor stone cracked into a dozen sharp shards under his fingers. Kell rose, the jagged pieces rising with him, and when he cast his hand out, they shot forward toward the king. Athos casually held up his hand in response, the stone clutched within, and a shield took shape in front of him, the slivers of rock shattering uselessly against it.

Athos smiled darkly. "Oh, yes," he said, lowering the shield. "I'm going to enjoy this."

Lila wove through the forest of statues, their heads bowed in surrender, hands up in plea.

She circled the vaulting fortress—it looked like a cathedral, if a cathedral were built on stilts and had no stained glass, only steel and stone. Still, the fortress was long and narrow like a church with one main set of doors on the north side, and three smaller, albeit still impressive, entrances at the south, east, and west sides. Lila's heart hammered as she approached the south entrance, the path to the stairs lined by stone supplicants.

She would have preferred to scale the walls and go in by an upper window, something more discreet than marching up the stairs, but she had no rope and no hook, and even if she'd had the necessary outfittings for such a jaunt, Kell had warned her against it.

The Danes, he had told her, trusted no one, and the castle was as much trap as it was a king's seat. "The main doors face north," he'd said, "I'll go by those. You enter through the south doors."

"Isn't that dangerous?"

"In this place," he'd answered, "everything is dangerous. But if the doors deny you, at least the fall won't be as steep."

So Lila had agreed to go by the doors despite her nagging fear that they were traps. It was all a trap. She reached the south stairs and pulled her horned mask down over her eyes before scaling the steps. At the top, the doors gave way without resistance, and again Lila's gut told her to go, to run the other way, but for the first time in her life, she ignored the warning and stepped inside. The space beyond the doors was dark, but the moment she crossed the threshold, lanterns flared to light, and Lila froze. Dozens of guards lined the walls like living suits of armor. Their heads twisted toward the open door, toward her, and she steeled herself against the impending assault.

But it never came.

Kell had told her that White London was a throne taken—and held—by force, and that this type of ascension didn't usually inspire loyalty. The guards here were clearly bound by magic, trapped under some kind of control spell. But that was the problem with forcing people to do things they didn't want to do. You had to be so specific. They had no choice but to follow orders, but they probably weren't inclined to go above and beyond them.

A slow smile drew across her lips.

Whatever order King Athos had given his guards, it didn't seem to extend to her. Their empty eyes followed her as she moved down the hall as calmly as possible. As if she belonged there. As if she had not come to kill their queen. She wondered, as she moved past them, how many wanted her to succeed.

The halls in the red palace had been labyrinthine, but here there was a simple grid of lines and intersections, further proof that the castle had once been something like a church. One hall gave onto another before putting her out in front of the throne room, just as Kell had said it would.

But Kell had also said the hall would be empty.

And it was not.

A boy stood in front of the throne room door. He was younger than Lila, and thin in a wiry way, and unlike the guards with their empty eyes, his were dark and bruised and feverish. When he saw her coming, he drew his sword.

"*Vösk,*" he ordered.

Lila's brow furrowed.

"*Vösk,*" he said again. "*Ös reijkav vösk.*"

"Hey, you," she said curtly. "Move."

The boy started speaking low and urgently in his own language. Lila shook her head and drew the knife with the brass knuckles from its sheath. "Get out of my way."

Feeling she had made herself understood, Lila strode forward toward the door. But the boy lifted his sword, put himself squarely in her path, and said, "*Vösk.*"

"Look," she snapped. "I have no idea what you're saying. . . ."

The young guard looked around, exasperated.

"But I would strongly advise you to go and pretend this interaction never took place and—hey, what the bloody hell do you think you're doing?"

The boy had shaken his head and muttered something under his breath, and then he brought his sword to his own arm, and began to cut.

"*Hey,*" Lila said again as the boy gritted his teeth and drew a second line, and then a third. "*Stop that.*"

She went to catch his wrist, but he stopped cutting the pattern and looked her in the eyes, and said, "*Leave.*"

For a moment, Lila thought she'd heard him wrong. And then she realized he was speaking English. When she looked down, she saw that he'd carved some kind of symbol into his skin.

"Leave," he said again. "*Now.*"

"Get out of my way," countered Lila.

"I can't."

"Boy—" she warned.

"I can't," he said again. "I have to guard the door."

"Or what?" challenged Lila.

"There is no *or what.*" He pulled aside the collar of his shirt to show a mark, angry and black, scarred into his skin. "He ordered me to guard the door, so I must guard it."

Lila frowned. The mark was different from Kell's, but she understood what it must be: some kind of seal. "What happens if you step aside?" she asked.

"I can't."

"What happens if I cut you down?"

"I'll die."

He said both things with sad and equal certainty. *What a mad world,* thought Lila.

"What's your name?" she asked.

"Beloc."

"How old are you?"

"Old enough." There was a proud tilt to his jaw, and a fire in his eyes she recognized. A defiance. But he was still young. Too young for this.

"I don't want to hurt you, Beloc," she said. "Don't make me."

"I wish I didn't have to."

He squared himself to her, holding his sword with both hands, his knuckles white. "You'll have to go through me."

Lila growled and gripped her knife.

"Please," he added. "Please go through me."

Lila gave him a long hard look. "How?" she said at last.

His brows went up in question.

"How do you want to die?" she clarified.

The fire in his eyes wavered for an instant, and then he recovered, and said, "Quickly."

Lila nodded. She lifted her knife, and he lowered his sword just a fraction, just enough. And then he closed his eyes and began to whisper something to himself. Lila didn't hesitate. She knew how to use a knife, how to wound, and how to kill. She closed the gap between them and drove the blade between Beloc's ribs and up before he'd even finished his prayer. There were worse ways to go, but she still swore under her breath at Athos and Astrid and the whole forsaken city as she lowered the boy's body to the floor.

She wiped her blade on the hem of her shirt and sheathed the knife as she stepped up to the waiting doors of the throne room. A circle of symbols was etched into the wood, twelve marks in all. She brought her hand to the dial, remembering Kell's instructions.

"Think of it as a clockface," he'd said, drawing the motion in the air. "One, seven, three, nine." Now she drew it with her finger, touching the symbol at the first hour, then drawing her fingertip down and across the circle to the seventh, around and up to the three, and straight through the middle to the nine.

"Are you certain you've got it?" Kell had asked, and Lila had sighed and blown the hair out of her eyes.

"I told you, I'm a fast learner."

At first, nothing happened. And then something passed between her fingers and the wood, and a lock slid within.

"Told you," she murmured, pushing the door open.

⌒ III ⌒

Athos was laughing. It was a horrible sound.

The hall around them was in disarray, the hollow guards in a heap, the hangings torn, and the torches scattered on the ground, still burning. A bruise blossomed beneath Kell's eye, and Athos's white cloak was singed and flecked with blackish blood.

"Shall we go again?" said Athos. Before the words had even left his lips, a bolt of dark energy shot out like lightning from the front of the king's shield. Kell threw up his hand, and the floor shot up between them, but he wasn't fast enough. The electricity slammed into him and hurled him backward into the front doors of the castle hard enough to split the wood. He coughed, breathless and dizzy from the blow, but he had no chance to recover. The air crackled and came alive, and another bolt struck him so hard that the doors splintered and broke, and Kell went tumbling back into the night.

For an instant, everything went black, and then his vision came back, and he was falling.

The air sprang up to catch him, or at least muffle the fall, but he still hit the stone courtyard at the base of the stairs hard enough to crack bone. The royal blade went skittering away several feet. Blood dripped from Kell's nose to the stones.

"We both hold swords," chided Athos as he descended the

stairs, his white cloak billowing regally behind him. "Yet you choose to fight with a pin."

Kell struggled to his feet, cursing. The king seemed unaffected by the black stone's magic. His veins had always been dark, and his eyes remained their usual icy blue. He was clearly in control, and for the first time Kell wondered if Holland had been right. If there was no such thing as balance, only victors and victims. Had he already lost? The dark magic hummed through his body, begging to be used.

"You're going to die, Kell," said Athos when he reached the courtyard. "You might as well die trying."

Smoke poured from Athos's stone and shot forward, the tendrils of darkness turning to glossy black knifepoints as they surged toward Kell. He threw up his empty hand and tried to will the blades to stop, but they were made of magic, not metal, and they didn't yield, didn't slow. And then, the instant before wall of knives shredded Kell, his other hand— the one bound to the stone—flew up, as if on its own, and the order echoed through his mind.

Protect me.

No sooner had the thought formed than it became real. Shadow wrapped around him, colliding with the knife-tipped smoke. Power surged through Kell's body, fire and ice water and energy all at once, and he gasped as the darkness spread farther beneath his skin and over it, ribboning out from the stone, past his arm and across his chest as the wall of magic deflected the attack and turned it back on Athos.

The king dodged, striking the blades aside with a wave of his stone. Most rained down on the courtyard floor, but one found its mark and buried itself in Athos's leg. The king hissed and dug the knifepoint out. He cast it aside and smiled darkly as he straightened. "That's more like it."

Lila's steps echoed through the throne room. The space was

cavernous and circular and as white as snow, interrupted only by a ring of pillars around the edges and the two thrones on the platform in the middle, sitting side by side and carved out of a single piece of pale stone. One of the thrones sat empty.

The other one held Astrid Dane.

Her hair—so blond, it seemed colorless—was coiled like a crown around her head, wisps as fine as spider silk falling onto her face, which tipped forward as if she'd dozed off. Astrid was deathly pale and dressed in white, but not the soft whites of a fairytale queen, no velvet or lace. No, this queen's clothes wrapped around her like armor, tapering sharply along her collar and down her wrists, and where others would have worn dresses, Astrid Dane wore tightly fitted pants that ran into crisp white boots. Her long fingers curled around the arms of the throne, half the knuckles marked by rings, though the only true color on her came from the pendant hanging around her neck, the edges rimmed with blood.

Lila stared at the motionless queen. Her pendant looked exactly like the one Rhy had been wearing in Red London when he wasn't Rhy. A possession charm.

And by the looks of it, Astrid Dane was still under its spell.

Lila took a step forward, cringing as her boots echoed through the hollow room with unnatural clarity. *Clever*, thought Lila. The throne room's shape wasn't just an aesthetic decision. It was designed to carry sound. Perfect for a paranoid ruler. But despite the sound of Lila's steps, the queen never stirred. Lila continued forward, half expecting guards to burst forth from hidden corners—of which there were none—and rush to Astrid's aid.

But no one came.

Serves you right, thought Lila. Hundreds of guards, and the only one to raise a sword wanted to fall on it. Some queen.

The pendant glittered against Astrid's chest, pulsing faintly with light. Somewhere in another city, in another world, she had taken another body—maybe the king or queen or the captain of the guard—but here, she was defenseless.

Lila smiled grimly. She would have liked to take her time, make the queen pay—for Kell's sake—but she knew better than to test her luck. She slid her pistol from its holster. One shot. Quick and easy and over.

She raised the weapon, leveled it at the queen's head, and fired.

The shot rang out through the throne room, followed instantly by a ripple of light, a rumble like thunder, and a blinding pain in Lila's shoulder. It sent her staggering back, the gun tumbling from her hand. She gripped her arm with a gasp, cussing roundly as blood seeped through her shirt and coat. She'd been shot.

The bullet had clearly ricocheted, but off of what?

Lila squinted at Astrid on her throne and realized that the air around the woman in white wasn't as empty as it seemed; it rippled in the gunshot's wake, the direct assault revealing air that shivered and shone, flecked with glassy shards of light. With *magic*. Lila gritted her teeth as her hand fell from her wounded shoulder (and her torn coat) to her waist. She retrieved her knife, still flecked with Beloc's blood, and inched closer until she was standing squarely in front of the throne. Her breath bounced against the nearly invisible barrier and brushed back against her own cheeks.

She raised the knife slowly, bringing the tip of the blade forward until it met the edge of the spell. The air crackled around the knifepoint, glinting like frost, but did not give. Lila swore under her breath as her gaze shifted down through the air, over the queen's body, before landing on the floor at her feet. There, her eyes narrowed. On the stone at the base of the throne were symbols. She couldn't read them, of course, but the way they wove together, the way they wove around the entire throne and the queen made it clear they were important. Links in the chain of a spell.

And links could be broken.

Lila crouched and brought the blade to the nearest symbol's edge. She held her breath and dragged the knife along the ground, scratching away at the marking from her side until she'd erased a narrow band of ink or blood or whatever the spell had been written in (she didn't want to know).

The air around the throne lost its shimmer and dimmed, and as Lila stood, wincing, she knew that whatever enchantment had been protecting the queen was gone.

Lila's fingers shifted on her knife.

"Good-bye, Astrid," she said, plunging the blade forward toward the queen's chest.

But before the tip could tear the white tunic, a hand caught Lila's wrist. She looked down to see Astrid Dane's pale blue eyes staring up at her. Awake. The queen's mouth drew into a thin, sharp smile.

"Bad little thief," she whispered. And then Astrid's grip tightened, and searing pain tore up Lila's arm. She heard someone screaming, and it took her a moment to realize the sound was coming from her throat.

Blood streaked Athos's cheek.

Kell gasped for breath.

The king's white cloak was torn, and shallow gashes marred Kell's leg, his wrist, his stomach. Half the statues in the courtyard around them lay toppled and broken as the magic clashed, striking against itself like flint.

"I will take that black eye of yours," said Athos, "and wear it around my neck."

He lashed out again, and Kell countered, will to will, stone to stone. But Kell was fighting two fights, one with the king, and the other with himself. The darkness kept spreading, claiming more of him with every moment, every motion. He could not win; at this rate, he would either lose the fight or lose himself. Something had to give.

Athos's magic found a fissure in Kell's shadow-drawn shield and hit him hard, cracking his ribs. Kell coughed, tasting blood as he fought to focus his vision on the king. He had to do something, and he had to do it soon. The royal half-sword glittered on the ground nearby. Athos lifted the stone to strike again.

"Is that all you have?" Kell goaded through gritted teeth. "The same, tired tricks? You lack your sister's creativity."

Athos's eyes narrowed. And then he held out the stone and summoned something new.

Not a wall, or a blade, or a chain. No, the smoke coiled around him, shaping itself into a sinister curving shadow. A massive silver serpent with black eyes, its forked tongue flicking the air as it rose, taller than the king himself.

Kell forced himself to give a low, derisive laugh, even though it hurt his broken ribs. He fetched the royal half-sword from the ground. It was chipped and slick with dust and blood, but he could still make out the symbols running down its metal length. "I've been waiting for you to do that," he said. "Create something strong enough to kill me. Since you clearly cannot do it yourself."

Athos frowned. "What does it matter, the shape your death takes? It is still at my hand."

"You said you wanted to kill me yourself," countered Kell. "But I suppose this is as close as you can come. Go ahead and hide behind the stone's magic. Call it your own."

Athos let out a low growl. "You're right," he said. "Your death should—and will—be mine."

He tightened his fingers around the stone, clearly intending to dispel the serpent. The snake, which had been slithering around the king, now stopped its course, but it did not dissolve. Instead, it turned its glossy black eyes on Athos, the way Kell's mirror image had on Lila in her room. Athos glared up at the serpent, willing it away. When it did not obey his thought, he gave voice to the command.

"You submit to *me*," ordered Athos as the serpent flicked its tongue. "You are my creation, and I am your—"

He never had the chance to finish.

The serpent reared back and struck. Its fanged jaws closed over the stone in Athos's hand, and before the king could even scream, the snake had enveloped him. Its silver body coiled around his arms and chest, and then around his neck, snapping it with an audible crack.

Kell sucked in a breath as Athos Dane's head slumped forward, the terrifying king reduced to nothing but a rag doll corpse. The serpent uncoiled, and the king's body tumbled forward to the broken ground. And then the serpent turned its shining black eyes on Kell. It slithered toward him with frightening speed, but Kell was ready.

He drove the royal half-sword up into the serpent's belly. It pierced the snake's rough skin, the spellwork on the metal glowing for an instant before the creature's thrashing broke the blade in two. The snake shuddered and fell, dispelled to nothing but a shadow at Kell's feet.

A shadow, and in the midst of it, a broken piece of black stone.

ᴄᴜ IV ᴄᴏ

Lila's back hit the pillar hard.

She crumpled to the stone floor of the throne room, and blood ran into her false eye as she struggled to push herself to her hands and knees. Her shoulder cried out with pain, but so did the rest of her. She tried not to think about it. Astrid, meanwhile, seemed to be having a grand time. She was smiling lazily at Lila, like a cat with a kitchen mouse.

"I am going to cut that smile off your face," growled Lila as she staggered to her feet.

She had been in a lot of fights with a lot of people, but she'd never fought anyone like Astrid Dane. The woman moved with both jarring speed and awkward grace, one moment slow and smooth, the next striking so fast that it was all Lila could do to stay on her feet. Stay alive.

Lila knew she was going to lose.

Lila knew she was going to *die*.

But she'd be damned if it counted for nothing.

Judging by the rumbling of the castle grounds around them, Kell had his hands full. The least she could do was keep the number of Danes he had to fight to one. Buy him a little time.

Honestly, what had happened to her? The Lila Bard of south London looked out for herself. That Lila would never waste her life on someone else. She'd never choose right over wrong so long as wrong meant staying alive. She'd never have turned back to help the stranger who helped her. Lila spit a mouthful of blood and straightened. Perhaps she never should have stolen the damned stone, but even here, and now, facing death in the form of a pale queen, she didn't regret it. She'd wanted freedom. She'd wanted adventure. And she didn't think she minded dying for it. She only wished dying didn't hurt so much.

"You've gotten in the way long enough," said Astrid, raising her hands in front of her.

Lila's mouth quirked. "I do seem to have a talent for that."

Astrid began to speak in that guttural tongue Lila had heard in the streets. But in the queen's mouth, the words sounded different. Strange and harsh and beautiful, they poured from her lips, rustling like a breeze through rotting leaves. They reminded Lila of the music blanketing the crowd in Rhy's parade, sound made physical. *Powerful.*

And Lila wasn't foolish enough to stand there and listen to it. Her pistol, now empty, lay discarded several feet away, her newest knife at the foot of the throne. She still had one dagger at her back and she went for it, sliding the weapon free. But before the blade could leave her fingers, Astrid finished the incantation, and a wave of energy slammed into Lila, knocking the wind out of her lungs as she hit the floor and slid several feet.

She rolled up into a crouch, gasping for air. The queen was toying with her.

Astrid's fingers rose as she prepared to strike again, and Lila knew it was her only chance. Her fingers tightened on the dagger, and she threw it, hard and fast and straight, at the queen's heart. It flew right at Astrid, but instead of dodging, she simply reached out and plucked the metal out of the air. With her bare hand. Lila's heart sank as the queen snapped the blade in two and tossed the pieces aside, all without interrupting her spell.

Shit, thought Lila, right before the stone floor beneath her began to rumble and shake. She fought to keep her footing and very nearly missed the wave of broken stone cresting over her head. Pebbles rained from above, and she dove out of the way just as the whole thing came crashing down. She was fast, but not fast enough. Pain tore up her right side, her leg, from heel to knee, which was trapped beneath the rubble, pale stone flecked with fragments of whitened rock.

No, not whitened rock, realized Lila with horror.

Bones.

Lila scrambled to free her leg, but Astrid was there, wrenching her onto her back and kneeling on her chest. Astrid reached down and ripped the horned mask from Lila's facs, tossing it aside. She took hold of Lila's jaw and wrenched her face up to hers.

"Pretty little thing," said the queen. "Under all that blood."

"Burn in hell," spat Lila.

Astrid only smiled. And then the nails of her other hand sank into Lila's wounded shoulder. Lila bit back a scream and thrashed under the queen's grip, but it was no use.

"If you're going to kill me," she snapped, "just do it already."

"Oh, I will," said Astrid, withdrawing her fingers from Lila's throbbing shoulder. "But not yet. When I have finished with Kell, I shall come back for you, and I shall take my time divesting you of your life. And when I'm done, I'll add you to my floor." She held up her hand between them, showing Lila her fingertips, now stained with blood. It was such a vivid red against the queen's pale skin. "But first . . ." Astrid brought a bloody finger to the place between Lila's eyes, tracing a pattern there.

Lila fought as hard as she could to get free, but Astrid was an unmovable force on top of her, pinning her down as she drew a bloody mark on her own pale forehead.

Astrid began to speak, low and fast and in that other tongue. Lila struggled frantically now, and tried to scream, attempting to interrupt the spell, but the queen's long fingers clamped over her mouth, and Astrid's spell spilled out, taking shape in the air around them. A spike of ice shot through Lila, her skin prickling as the magic rippled over her. And above her, the queen's face began to *change*.

Her chin sharpened, and her cheeks warmed from porcelain to a healthier hue. Her lips reddened, and her eyes darkened from blue to brown—two different shades—and her hair, once as white as snow and wound about her head, now fell down onto her face, chestnut brown and chopped in a sharp line along her jaw. Even her clothes rippled and shifted and took on an all-too-familiar form. The queen smiled a knifelike grin, and Lila gazed up in horror not at Astrid Dane, but at the mirror image of herself.

When Astrid spoke, Lila's own voice poured out. "I better go," she said. "I'm sure Kell could use a hand."

Lila swung a last, desperate punch, but Astrid caught her wrist as if it were nothing more than a nuisance, and pinned it against the floor. She bent her head over Lila's, bringing her lips to her ear. "Don't worry," she whispered. "I'll give him your regards."

And then Astrid slammed Lila's head back against the ruined floor, and Lila's world went dark.

Kell stood in the stone courtyard, surrounded by broken statues, a dead king, and a jagged piece of black stone. He was bleeding, and broken, but he was still alive. He let the ruined royal sword slip through this fingers and clatter to the ground and drew a shuddering breath, the cold air burning his lungs and fogging in front of his bloody lips. Something was moving through him, warm and cool, lulling and dangerous. He wanted to stop fighting, wanted to give in, but he couldn't. It wasn't over yet.

Half of the stone pulsed against his palm. The other half glinted on the ground where the serpent had dropped it. It called to him, and Kell's body moved of its own accord toward the missing piece. The stone guided his fingers down to the splintered ground and closed them around the fragment of rock waiting there. The moment the two pieces met, Kell felt words form on his lips.

"*As Hasari,*" he said, the command spilling out on its own in a voice that was and wasn't his. In his hand, the two halves of the stone began to *heal*. The pieces fused back together, the cracks untracing themselves until the surface was a smooth, unblemished black, and in its wake an immense power—clear, beautiful, and sweet—poured through Kell's body, bringing with it a sense of right. A sense of *whole*. It filled him with calm. With quiet. The simple steady rhythm of magic pulled him down like sleep. All Kell wanted to do was to let go, to disappear into the power and darkness and peace.

Give in, said a voice in his head. His eyes drifted shut, and he swayed on his feet.

And then he heard Lila's voice calling his name.

The stillness rippled as Kell forced his eyes open, and he saw her descending the stairs. She seemed far away. Everything seemed far away.

"Kell," she said again as she reached him. Her eyes took in the scene—the ruined courtyard; Athos's corpse; his own, battered form—and the talisman, now whole.

"It's over," she said. "It's time to let it go."

He looked down at the talisman in his hand, at the way the black threads had thickened and become like rope, wrapping around his body.

"Please," said Lila. "I know you can do this. I know you can hear me." She held out her hand, eyes wide with worry. Kell frowned, power still coursing through him, distorting his vision, his thoughts.

"*Please,*" she said again.

"Lila," he said softly, desperately. He reached out and steadied himself on her shoulder.

"I'm here," she whispered. "Just give me the stone."

He considered the talisman. And then his fingers closed over it, and smoke whispered out. He didn't have to speak. The magic was in his head now, and it knew what he wanted. Between one instant and the next, the smoke became a knife. He stared down at the metal's glinting edge.

"Lila," he said again.

"Yes, Kell?"

His fingers tightened on it. "Catch."

And then he drove the blade into her stomach.

Lila let out a gasp of pain. And then her whole body shuddered, rippled, and became someone else's. It stretched into the form of Astrid Dane, dark blood blossoming against her white clothes.

"How . . ." she growled, but Kell willed her body still, her jaw shut. No words—no spell—would save her now. He wanted to kill Astrid Dane. But more than that, he wanted her to *suffer*. For his brother. His prince. Because in that moment, staring into her wide blue eyes, all he could see was Rhy.

Rhy wearing her talisman.

Rhy flashing a smile that was too cruel and too cold to be his own.

Rhy curling his fingers around Kell's throat and whispering in his ear with someone else's words.

Rhy thrusting a knife into his stomach.

Rhy—*his* Rhy—crumpling to the stone floor.

Rhy bleeding.

Rhy dying.

Kell wanted to *crush* her for what she'd done. And in his hands, the want became a will, and the darkness began to spread out from the knife buried in her stomach. It crawled over her clothes and under her skin, and turned everything it touched to pale white stone. Astrid tried to open her mouth, to speak or to scream, but before any sound could escape her clenched teeth, the stone had reached her chest, her throat, her faded red lips. It overtook her stomach, trailed down her legs and over her boots before running straight into the pitted ground. Kell stood there, staring at the statue of Astrid Dane, her eyes frozen wide with shock, lips drawn into a permanent snarl. She looked like the rest of the courtyard now.

But it wasn't enough.

As much as he wanted to leave her there in the broken garden with her brother's corpse, he couldn't. Magic, like everything, faded. Spells were broken. Astrid could be free again one day. And he couldn't let that happen.

Kell gripped her white stone shoulder. His fingers were bloody, like the rest of him, and the *Antari* magic came as easily as air. *"As Steno,"* he said.

Deep cracks formed across the queen's face, jagged fissures carving down her body, and when his fingers tightened, the stone statue of Astrid Dane shattered under his touch.

❦ V ❧

Kell shivered, the strange calm settling over him again.

It was heavier this time. And then someone called his name, just as they had moments earlier, and he looked up to see Lila clutching her shoulder as she half ran, half limped down the stairs, bruised and bloody, but alive. Her black mask hung from her bloody fingers.

"You all right?" she asked when she reached him.

"Never better," he said, even though it was taking every ounce of his strength to focus his eyes on her, his mind on her.

"How did you know?" she asked, looking down at the rubble of the queen. "How did you know she wasn't me?"

Kell managed an exhausted smile. "Because she said *please*."

Lila stared at him, aghast. "Is that a joke?"

Kell shrugged slightly. It took a lot of effort. "I just knew," he said.

"You just knew," she echoed.

Kell nodded. Lila took him in with careful eyes, and he wondered what he must look like in that moment.

"You look terrible," she said. "You better get rid of that rock."

Kell nodded.

"I could come with you."

Kell shook his head. "No. Please. I don't want you to." It

was the honest answer. He didn't know what waited on the other side, but whatever it was, he would face it alone.

"Fine," said Lila, swallowing. "I'll stay here."

"What will you do?" he asked.

Lila forced a shrug. "Saw some nice ships on the dock when we were running for our lives. One of them will do."

"Lila . . ."

"I'll be okay," she said tightly. "Now, hurry up before someone notices we've killed the monarchs."

Kell tried to laugh, and something shot through him, like pain but darker. He doubled over, his vision blurring.

"Kell?" Lila dropped to her knees beside him. "What is it? What's happening?"

No, he pleaded with his body. *No. Not now.* He was so close. So close. All he had to do was—

Another wave sent him to his hands and knees.

"Kell!" demanded Lila. "Talk to me."

He tried to answer, tried to say something, anything, but his jaw locked shut, his teeth grinding together. He fought the darkness, but the darkness fought back. And it was winning.

Lila's voice was getting further and further away. "Kell . . . can you hear me? Stay with me. Stay with me."

Stop fighting, said a voice in his head. *You've already lost.*

No, thought Kell. *No. Not yet.* He managed to bring his fingers to the shallow gash across his stomach, and began to draw a mark on the cracked stone. But before he could press his stone-bound hand against it, a force slammed him backward to the ground. The darkness twined around him and dragged him down. He fought against the magic, but it was already inside him, coursing through his veins. He tried to tear free of its hold, to push it away, but it was too late.

He took one last gasp of air, and then the magic dragged him under.

* * *

Kell couldn't move.

Shadows wove around his limbs and held like stone, pinning him still. The more he fought, the tighter they coiled, leeching the last of his strength. Lila's voice was far, far away and then gone, and Kell was left in a world filled with only darkness.

A darkness that was everywhere.

And then, somehow, it wasn't. It drew itself together, coiling in front of him, coalescing until it was first a shadow and then a man. He was shaped like Kell, from his height and his hair to his coat, but every inch of him was the smooth and glossy black of the recovered stone.

"Hello, Kell," said the darkness, the words not in English or Arnesian or Maktahn, but the native tongue of magic. And finally, Kell understood. This was *Vitari*. The thing that had been pulling at him, pushing to get in, making him stronger while weakening his will and feeding on his life.

"Where are we?" he asked, his voice hoarse.

"We are in you," said *Vitari*. "We are *becoming* you."

Kell struggled uselessly against the dark ropes. "Get out of my body," he growled.

Vitari smiled his shadowy black smile and took a step toward Kell.

"You've fought well," he said. "But the time for fighting is over." He closed the gap and brought a hand to Kell's chest. "You were made for me, *Antari*," he said. "A perfect vessel. I will wear your skin forever."

Kell twisted under his touch. He had to fight. He'd come so far. He couldn't give up now.

"It's too late," said *Vitari*. "I already have your heart." At that, his fingertips pressed down, and Kell gasped as *Vitari*'s hand passed *into* his chest. He felt *Vitari*'s fingers close around his beating heart, felt it lurch, darkness spilling across his tattered shirtfront like blood.

"It's over, Kell," said the magic. "You're mine."

* * *

362

Kell's body shuddered on the ground. Lila took his face in her hands. It was burning up. The veins on his throat and at his temple had darkened to black, and the strain showed in the lines of his jaw, but he wasn't moving, wouldn't open his eyes.

"Fight this!" she shouted as his body spasmed. "You've come all this way. You can't just *give up*."

His back arched against the ground, and Lila pushed open Kell's shirt and saw black spreading over his heart.

"Dammit," she swore, trying to pry the stone out of his hand. It wouldn't budge.

"If you die," she snapped, "what happens to Rhy?"

Kell's back hit the ground, and he let out a labored breath.

Lila had recovered her weapons, and now she freed her knife, weighing it in her palm. She didn't want to have to kill him. But she could. And she didn't want to cut off his hand, but she certainly would.

A groan escaped between his lips.

"Don't you fucking give up, Kell. Do you hear me?"

Kell's heart stuttered, skipping a beat.

"I asked so nicely," said *Vitari*, his hand still buried in Kell's chest. "I gave you the chance to give in. You made me use force."

Heat spread through Kell's limbs, leaving a strange cold in its wake. He heard Lila's voice. Far away and stretched so thin, the words, an echo of an echo, barely reached him. But he heard a name. *Rhy*.

If he died, so would Rhy. He couldn't stop fighting.

"I'm not going to kill you, Kell. Not exactly."

Kell squeezed his eyes shut, darkness folding over him.

"Isn't there a word for this?" Lila's voice echoed through his head. *"What is it? Come on, Kell. Say the blasted word."*

Kell forced himself to focus. Of course. Lila was right. There was a word. *Vitari* was pure magic. And all magic was bound by rules. By order. *Vitari* was a creation, but everything that could be created could also be destroyed. *Dispelled*.

"*As Anasae*," said Kell. He felt a glimmer of power. But nothing happened.

Vitari's free hand closed around his throat.

"Did you really think that would work?" sneered the magic in Kell's shape, but there was something in his voice and in the way he tensed. *Fear*. It could work. It would work. It had to.

But *Antari* magic was a verbal pact. He'd never been able to summon it with thought alone, and here, in his head, everything was thought. Kell had to *say* the word. He focused, reaching with his fading senses until he could feel his body, not as it was here in this illusion, this mental plane, but as it was in truth, stretched on the bitterly cold ground of the broken courtyard, Lila crouching over it. Over him. He clung to that chill, focusing on the way it pressed into his back. He struggled to feel his fingers, wrapped around the stone so hard that they ached. He focused on his mouth, clenched shut in pain, and forced it to unlock. Forced his lips to part.

To form the words. "*As An—*"

His heart faltered as *Vitari*'s fingers tightened around it.

"*No*," growled the magic, the fear bold now, twisting his impatience into anger. And Kell understood his fear. *Vitari* wasn't simply a spell. He was the *source* of all the stone's power. Dispelling him would dispel the talisman itself. It would all be over.

Kell fought to hold on to his body. To himself. He forced air into his lungs and out his mouth.

"*As Anas—*" he managed before Vitari's hand shifted from heart to lungs, crushing the air out of them.

"You can't," said the magic desperately. "I am the only thing keeping your brother alive."

Kell hesitated. He didn't know if that was true, if the bond he'd made with his brother *could* be broken. But he did know that Rhy would never forgive him for what he'd done, and it wouldn't even matter unless they both made it through.

Kell summoned the last of his strength and focused not on *Vitari* trying to crush his life, or on the darkness sweeping through him, but on Lila's voice and the cold ground and his aching fingers and his bloody lips as they formed the words.

"As Anasae."

℃ VI ℥

Across Red London, the bodies fell.

Men and women who'd been kissed or taken, wooed or forced, those who had let the magic in and those who had had it thrust upon them, all of them fell as the black flame inside them gutted and went out. Dispelled.

Everywhere, the magic left a trail of bodies.

In the streets, they staggered and collapsed. Some crumbled to ash, all burned up, and some were reduced to husks, empty inside, and a lucky few crumpled, gasping and weak but still alive.

In the palace, the magic dressed as Gen had just reached the royal chambers, his blackening hand on the door, when the darkness died and took him with it.

And in the sanctuary, far from the castle walls, on a bare cot in a candlelit room, the prince of Red London shivered and fell still.

XIV

THE FINAL
DOOR

I

Kell opened his eyes and saw stars.

They floated high above the castle walls, nothing but pricks of pale white light in the distance.

The stone slipped from his fingers, hitting the ground with a dull clink. There was nothing to it now, no hum, no urge, no promise. It was just a piece of rock.

Lila was saying something, and for once she didn't sound angry, not as angry as usual, but he couldn't hear her over the pounding of his heart as he brought one shaking hand to the collar of his shirt. He didn't really want to see. Didn't want to know. But he tugged his collar down anyway and looked at the skin over his heart, the place where the seal had bonded Rhy's life to his own.

The black tracery of the magic was gone.

But the scar of it wasn't. The seal itself was still intact. Which meant it hadn't only been tethered to *Vitari*. It had been tethered to *him*.

Kell let out a small sobbing sound of relief.

And finally, the world around him came back into focus. The cold stone of the courtyard and Athos's corpse and the shards of Astrid, and Lila, with her arms flung around his shoulders for an instant—and only an instant, gone before he could appreciate their presence.

"Miss me?" whispered Kell, his throat raw.

"Sure," she said, her eyes red. She toed the talisman with her boot. "Is it dead?" she asked.

Kell picked up the stone, feeling nothing but its weight.

"You can't kill magic," said Kell, getting slowly to his feet. "Only dispel it. But it's gone."

Lila chewed her lip. "Do you still have to send it back?"

Kell considered the hollow rock and nodded slowly. "To be safe," he said. But maybe, now that he was finally free of its grip, he didn't have to be the one to go with it. Kell scanned the courtyard until he saw Holland's body. In the fight the *Antari* had fallen from the stone bench, and now lay stretched on the ground, his blood-soaked cloak the only sign that Holland wasn't merely sleeping.

Kell got to his feet, every inch of him protesting, and went to Holland's side. He knelt and took one of the *Antari*'s hands in his. Holland's skin was going cold, the pulse at his wrist weak, and getting weaker, his heart dragging itself through the final beats. But he was still alive.

It's really quite hard to kill Antari, he had once said. It appeared he was right.

Kell felt Lila hovering behind him. He didn't know if this would work, if one *Antari* could command for another, but he pressed his fingers to the wound at Holland's chest and drew a single line on the ground beside his body. And then he touched the hollow stone to the blood and set it on the line, bringing Holland's hand to rest on top of it.

"Peace," he said softly, a parting word for a broken man. And then he pressed his hand on top of Holland's and said, "*As Travars.*"

The ground beneath the *Antari* gave way, bending into shadow. Kell pulled back as the darkness, and whatever lay beyond, swallowed Holland's body and the stone, leaving only blood-streaked ground behind.

Kell stared at the stained earth, unwilling to believe that it had actually worked. That he had been spared. That he was alive. That he could go *home.*

He swayed on his feet, and Lila caught him.

"Stay with me," she said.

Kell nodded, dizzy. The stone had masked the pain, but in its absence, his vision blurred with it. Rhy's wounds layered on top of his own, and when he tried to bite back a groan, he tasted blood.

"We have to go," said Kell. Now that the city was absent a ruler—or two—the fighting would start again. Someone would claw their bloody way to the throne. They always did.

"Let's get you home," said Lila. Relief poured over him in a wave before the hard reality caught up.

"Lila," he said, stiffening. "I don't know if I can take you with me." The stone had guaranteed her passage through the worlds, made a door for her where none should be. Without it, the chances of the world allowing her through . . .

Lila seemed to understand. She looked around and wrapped her arms around herself. She was bruised and bleeding. How long would she last here alone? Then again, it was Lila. She'd probably survive anything.

"Well," she said. "We can try."

Kell swallowed.

"What's the worst that could happen?" she added as they made their way to the courtyard wall. "I get pulled into a hundred little pieces between worlds?" She said it with a wry smile, but he could see the fear in her eyes. "I'm prepared to stay. But I want to try and leave."

"If it doesn't work—"

"Then I'll find my way," said Lila.

Kell nodded and led her to the courtyard wall. He made a mark on the pale stones and dug the Red London coin from his pocket. And then he pulled Lila close, wrapped his broken body around hers, and tipped his forehead against hers.

"Hey, Lila," he said softly into the space between them.

"Yeah?"

He pressed his mouth to hers for one brief moment, the warmth there and then gone. She frowned up at him, but did not pull away.

"What was that for?" she asked.

"For luck," he said. "Not that you need it."

And then he pressed his hand against the wall and thought of home.

❧ II ❧

Red London took shape around Kell, heavy with night. It smelled of earth and fire, of blooming flowers and spiced tea, and underneath it all, of home. Kell had never been so happy to be back. But his heart sank when he realized that his arms were empty.

Lila wasn't with him.

She hadn't made it back.

Kell swallowed and looked down at the token in his bloody hand. And then he threw it as hard as he could. He closed his eyes and took a deep breath, trying to steady himself.

And then he heard a voice. Her voice.

"Never thought I'd be so happy to smell the flowers."

Kell blinked and spun to see Lila standing there. Alive, and in one piece.

"It's not possible," he said.

The edge of her mouth quirked up. "It's nice to see you, too."

Kell threw his arms around her. And for a second, only a second, she didn't pull away, didn't threaten to stab him. For a second, and only a second, she hugged him back.

"What are you?" he asked, amazed.

Lila only shrugged. "Stubborn."

They stood there a moment, leaning on each other, one

keeping the other on their feet, though neither was sure which needed more supporting. Both knew only that they were happy to be here, to be alive.

And then he heard the sounds of boots and swords, and saw the flares of light.

"I think we're being attacked," whispered Lila into the collar of his coat.

Kell lifted his head from her shoulder to see a dozen members of the guard surrounding them, blades drawn. Through their helmets, their eyes looked at him with fear and rage. He could feel Lila tense against him, feel her itching to reach for a pistol or a knife.

"Don't fight," he whispered as he slid his arms slowly from her back. He took her hand and turned toward his family's men. "We surrender."

The guards forced Kell and Lila to their knees before the king and queen, and held them there despite Lila's muttered oaths. Their wrists were bound in metal behind them, the way Kell's had been earlier that night in Rhy's chambers. Had it really been only hours? They weighed on Kell like years.

"Leave us," ordered King Maxim.

"Sir," protested one of the royal guard, shooting a glance at Kell. "It is not safe to—"

"*I said get out,*" he boomed.

The guard withdrew, leaving only Kell and Lila on their knees in the emptied ballroom, the king and queen looming over them. King Maxim's eyes were feverish, his skin blotching with anger. At his side, Queen Emira looked deathly pale.

"What have you done?" demanded the king.

Kell cringed, but he told them the truth. Of Astrid's possession charm, and the Dane twins' plan, but also of the stone, and of the way he came by it (and of its preceding habit). He told them of its discovery, and of trying to return it to the only place it would be safe. And the king and queen listened, less with disbelief than with horror, the king growing redder and the queen growing paler with every explanation.

"The stone is gone now," finished Kell. "And the magic with it."

The king slammed his fist against a banister. "The Danes will pay for what they've—"

"The Danes are dead," said Kell. "I killed them myself."

Lila cleared her throat.

Kell rolled his eyes. "With Lila's help."

The king seemed to notice Lila for the first time. "Who are you? What madness have you added to these plots?"

"My name is Delilah Bard," she shot back. "We met, just earlier this evening. When I was trying to save your city, and you were standing there, all blank-eyed under some kind of spell."

"*Lila*," snapped Kell in horror.

"I'm half the reason your city is still standing."

"*Our* city?" questioned the queen. "You're not from here, then?"

Kell tensed. Lila opened her mouth, but before she could answer, he said, "No. She's from afar."

The king's brow furrowed. "How *far* afar?"

And before Kell could answer, Lila threw her shoulders back. "My ship docked a few days ago," she announced. "I came to London because I heard that your son's festivities were not to be missed, and because I had business with a merchant named Calla in the market on the river. Kell and I have crossed paths once or twice before, and when it was clear that he needed help, I gave it." Kell stared at Lila. She gave him a single raised a brow and added, "He promised me a reward, of course."

The king and queen stared at Lila, too, as if trying to decide which piece of her story sounded *least* plausible (it was either the fact that she owned a ship, or the fact that a foreigner spoke such flawless English), but at last the queen's composure faltered.

"Where is our *son*?" she pleaded. The way she said it, as if they had only one, made Kell flinch.

"Is Rhy alive?" demanded the king.

"Thanks to Kell," cut in Lila. "We've spent the last day trying to save your kingdom, and you don't even—"

"He's alive," said Kell, cutting her off. "And he will live," he added, holding the king's gaze. "As long as I do." There was a faint challenge in the line.

"What do you mean?"

"Sir," said Kell, breaking the gaze. "I did only what I had to do. If I could have given him my life, I would have. Instead, I could only share it." He twisted in his bonds, the edge of the scar visible under his collar. The queen drew in a breath. The king's face darkened.

"Where is he, Kell?" asked the king, his voice softening.

Kell's shoulders loosened, the weight sliding from them. "Release us," he said. "And I will bring him home."

✑ III ✑

"Come in."

Kell had never been so glad to hear his brother's voice. He opened the door and stepped into Rhy's room, trying not to picture the way it had been when he last left it, the prince's blood streaked across the floor.

It had been three days since that night, and all signs of the chaos had since been erased. The balcony had been repaired, the blood polished out of the inlaid wood, the furniture and fabrics made new.

Now Rhy lay propped up in his bed. There were circles under his eyes, but he looked more bored than ill, and that was progress. The healers had fixed him up as best they could (they'd fixed Kell and Lila, too), but the prince wasn't mending as quickly as he should have been. Kell knew why, of course. Rhy hadn't simply been wounded, as they had been told. He'd been *dead*.

Two attendants stood at a table nearby, and a guard sat in a chair beside the door, and all three watched Kell as he entered. Part of Rhy's dark mood came from the fact that the guard was neither Parrish nor Gen. Both had been found dead—one by sword, and the other by the black fever, as it was quickly named, that had raged through the city—a fact that troubled Rhy as much as his own condition.

The attendants and the guard watched Kell with new caution as he approached the prince's bed.

"They will not let me up, the bastards," grumbled Rhy, glaring at them. "If I cannot leave," he said to them, "then be so kind as to leave yourselves." The weight of loss and guilt, paired with the nuisance of injury and confinement, had put Rhy in a foul humor. "By all means," he added as his servants rose, "stand guard outside. Make me feel like more of a prisoner than I already do."

When they were gone, Rhy sighed and slumped back against the pillows.

"They mean only to help," said Kell.

"Perhaps it wouldn't be so bad," he said, "if they were prettier to look at." But the boyish jab rang strangely hollow. His eyes found Kell's, and his look darkened. "Tell me everything," he said. "But start with this." He touched the place over his heart, where he wore a scar that matched Kell's own. "What foolish thing have you done, my brother?"

Kell looked down at the rich red linens on the bed and pulled aside his collar to show the mirroring scar. "I did only what you would have done, if you were me."

Rhy frowned. "I love you, Kell, but I had no interest in matching tattoos."

Kell smiled sadly. "You were dying, Rhy. I saved your life."

He couldn't bring himself to tell Rhy the whole truth: that the stone hadn't only saved his life but had restored it.

"How?" demanded the prince. "At what cost?"

"One I paid," said Kell. "And would pay again."

"Answer me without circles!"

"I bound your life to mine," said Kell, "As long as I live, so shall you."

Rhy's eyes widened. "You did what?" he whispered, horrified. "I should get out of this bed and wring your neck."

"I wouldn't," advised Kell. "Your pain is mine and mine is yours."

Rhy's hands curled into fists. "How could you?" he said, and Kell worried that the prince was bitter about being tethered to him. Instead, Rhy said, "How could you carry that weight?"

"It is as it is, Rhy. It cannot be undone. So please, be grateful, and be done with it."

"How can I be done with it?" scorned Rhy, already slipping back into a more playful tone. "It is carved into my chest."

"Lovers like men with scars," said Kell, cracking a smile. "Or so I've heard."

Rhy sighed and tipped his head back, and the two fell into silence. At first, it was an easy quiet, but then it began to thicken, and just when Kell was about to break it, Rhy beat him to the act.

"What have I done?" he whispered, amber eyes cast up against the gossamer ceiling. "What have I done, Kell?" He rolled his head so he could see his brother. "Holland brought me that necklace. He said it was a gift, and I believed him. Said it was from this London, and I believed him."

"You made a mistake, Rhy. Everybody makes them. Even royal princes. I've made many. It's only fair that you make one."

"I should have known better. I *did* know better," he added, his voice cracking.

He tried to sit up, and winced. Kell urged him back down. "Why did you take it?" he asked when the prince was settled.

For once, Rhy would not meet his gaze. "Holland said it would bring me strength."

Kell's brow furrowed. "You are already strong."

"Not like you. That is, I know I'll never be like you. But I have no gift for magic, and it makes me feel weak. One day I'm going to be king. I wanted to be a strong king."

"Magic does not make people strong, Rhy. Trust me. And you have something better. You have the people's love."

"It's easy to be loved. I want to be respected, and I thought . . ." Rhy's voice was barely a whisper. "I took the necklace. All that matters is that I took it." Tears began to escape, running into his black curls. "And I could have ruined everything. I could have lost the crown before I ever wore it. I could have doomed my city to war or chaos or collapse."

"What sons our parents have," said Kell gently. "Between the two of us, we'll tear the whole world down."

Rhy let out a stifled sound between a laugh and a sob. "Will they ever forgive us?"

Kell mustered a smile. "I am no longer in chains. That speaks to progress."

The king and queen had sent word across the city, by guard and scrying board alike, that Kell was innocent of all charges. But the eyes in the street still hung on him, wariness and fear and suspicion woven through the reverence. Maybe when Rhy was well again and could speak to his people directly, they would believe he was all right and that Kell had had no hand in the darkness that had fallen over the palace that night. Maybe, but Kell doubted it would ever be as simple as it had been before.

"I meant to tell you," said Rhy. "Tieren came to visit. He brought some—"

He was interrupted by a knock at the door. Before either Rhy or Kell could answer, Lila stormed into the room. She was still wearing her new coat—patches sewn over the spots where it had been torn by bullet and blade and stone—but she'd been bathed at least, and a gold clasp held the hair out of her eyes. She still looked a bit like a starved bird, but she was clean and fed and mended.

"I don't like the way the guards are looking at me," she said before glancing up and seeing the prince's gold eyes on her. "I'm sorry," she added. "I didn't mean to intrude."

"Then what did you mean to do?" challenged Kell.

Rhy held up his hand. "You are surely not an intrusion," he said, pushing himself up in the bed. "Though I fear you've met me rather out of my usual state of grace. Do you have a name?"

"Delilah Bard," she said. "We've met before. And you looked worse."

Rhy laughed silently. "I apologize for anything I might have done. I was not myself."

"I apologize for shooting you in the leg," said Lila. "I was myself entirely."

Rhy broke into his perfect smile.

"I like this one," he said to Kell. "Can I borrow her?"

"You can try," said Lila, raising a brow. "But you'll be a prince without his fingers."

Kell grimaced, but Rhy only laughed. The laughter quickly dissolved into wincing, and Kell reached out to steady his brother, even as the pain echoed in his own chest.

"Save your flirting for when you're well," he said.

Kell pushed to his feet and began to usher Lila out.

"Will I see more of you, Delilah Bard?" called the prince.

"Perhaps our paths will cross again."

Rhy's smile went crooked. "If I have any say in it, they will."

Kell rolled his eyes but thought he caught Lila actually blushing as he guided her out and shut the door, leaving the prince to rest.

∽ IV ∾

"I could try and take you back," Kell was saying. "To your London."

He and Lila were walking along the river's edge, past the evening market—where people's eyes still hung too heavy and too long—and farther on toward the docks. The sun was sinking behind them, casting long shadows in front of them like paths.

Lila shook her head and pulled the silver watch from her pocket. "There's nothing for me there," she said, snapping the timepiece open and shut. "Not anymore."

"You don't belong here, either," he said simply.

She shrugged. "I'll find my way." And then she tipped her chip up and looked him in the eyes. "Will you?"

The scar over his heart twinged dully, a ghost of pain, and he rubbed his shoulder. "I'll try." He dug a hand in the pocket of his coat—the black one with the silver buttons—and withdrew a small parcel. "I got you something."

He handed it over and watched Lila undo the wrappings of the box, then slide the lid off. It fell open in her hand, revealing a small puzzle board and a handful of elements. "For practice," he said. "Tieren says you've got some magic in you. Better find it."

They paused on a bench, and he showed her how it worked,

and she chided him for showing off, and then she put the box away and said thank you. It seemed to be a hard phrase for her to say, but she managed. They got to their feet, neither willing to walk away just yet, and Kell looked down at Delilah Bard, a cutthroat and a thief, a valiant partner and a strange, terrifying girl.

He would see her again. He knew he would. Magic bent the world. Pulled it into shape. There were fixed points. Most of the time those points were places. But sometimes, rarely, they were people. For someone who never stood still, Lila still felt like a pin in Kell's world. One he was sure to snag on.

He didn't know what to say, so he simply said, "Stay out of trouble."

She flashed him a smile that said she wouldn't, of course.

And then she tugged up her collar, shoved her hands into her pockets, and strolled away.

Kell watched her go.

She never once looked back.

Delilah Bard was finally free.

She thought of the map back in London—Grey London, her London, old London—the parchment she'd left in the cramped little room at the top of the stairs in the Stone's Throw. The map to anywhere. Isn't that what she had now?

Her bones sang with the promise of it.

Tieren had said there was something in her. Something untended. She didn't know what shape it would take, but she was keen to find out. Whether it was the kind of magic that ran through Kell, or something different, something new, Lila knew one thing:

The world was hers.

The *worlds* were hers.

And she was going to take them all.

Her eyes wandered over the ships on the far side of the river, their gleaming sides and carved masts tall and sharp enough to pierce the low clouds. Flags and sails flapped in the breeze in reds and golds, but also greens and purples and blues.

Boats with royal banners, and boats without. Boats from other lands across other seas, from near and far, wide and away.

And there, tucked between them, she saw a proud, dark ship, with polished sides and a silver banner and sails the color of night, a black that hinted at blue when it caught the light just so.

That one, thought Lila with a smile.

That one'll do.

ACKNOWLEDGMENTS

We think of authors as solitary creatures hunched over work in cramped but empty rooms, and while it's true that writing is a pursuit most often done alone, a book is the result not of one mind, or pair of hands, but of many. To thank every soul would be impossible, but there are some I *cannot* forget to mention. They are as much responsible for this book as I am.

To my editor, Miriam, my partner in crime, for loving Kell and Lila and Rhy as much as I do, and for helping me pave the foundation of this series with blood, shadow, and stylish outfits. A great editor doesn't have all the answers, but they ask the right questions, and you are a *truly* great editor.

To my agent, Holly, for being such a wonderful advocate of this strange little fantasy, even when I pitched it as *pirates, thieves, sadist kings, and violent magic-y stuff*. And to my film agent, Jon, for matching Holly's passion stride for stride. No one could ask for better champions.

To my mother, for wandering the streets of London with me in Kell's footsteps, and to my father, for taking me seriously when I said I was writing a book about cross-dressing thieves and magical men in fabulous coats. In fact, to both of my parents, for never scoffing when I said I wanted to be a writer.

To Lady Hawkins, for traipsing with me through the streets

of Edinburgh, and to Edinburgh, for being its magical self. My bones belong to you.

To Patricia, for knowing this book as well as I do, and for always being willing and able eyes, no matter how rough the pages.

To Carla and Courtney, the best cheerleaders—and the best *friends*—a neurotic, caffeine-addicted author could ask for.

To the Nashville creative community—Ruta, David, Lauren, Sarah, Sharon, Rae Ann, Dawn, Paige, and so many others—who welcomed me home with love and charm and margaritas.

To Tor, and to Irene Gallo, Will Staehle, Leah Withers, Becky Yeager, Heather Saunders, and everyone else who has helped to make this book ready for the world.

And to my readers, both the loyal and the new, because without you, I'm just a girl talking to myself in public.

This is for you.

ABOUT THE AUTHOR

Victoria "V.E." Schwab is the product of a British mother, a Beverly Hills father, and a southern upbringing. Because of this, she has been known to say "tom-ah-toes", "like", and "y'all". She also suffers from a wicked case of wanderlust, made worse by the fact that wandering is a good way to stir up stories. When she's not haunting Paris streets or trudging up English hillsides, she's usually tucked in the corner of a coffee shop, dreaming up monsters. She is the author of several books for teens, including *The Near Witch*, about a village where the children begin to disappear, and The Archived series, about a library of the dead. Her first book for adults, *Vicious*, was named a Best Book of 2013 by both *Publisher's Weekly* and Amazon.

VICIOUS

V.E. SCHWAB

Victor and Eli started out as college roommates—
brilliant, arrogant, lonely boys who recognized the same
ambition in each other. A shared interest in adrenaline,
near- death experiences, and seemingly supernatural
events reveals an intriguing possibility: that under the
right conditions, someone could develop extraordinary
abilities. But when their thesis moves from the academic
to the experimental, things go horribly wrong.

Ten years later, Victor breaks out of prison, determined
to catch up to his old friend (now foe), aided by a
young girl with a stunning ability. Meanwhile, Eli is
on a mission to eradicate every other super-powered
person that he can find—aside from his sidekick, an
enigmatic woman with an unbreakable will. Armed with
terrible power on both sides, driven by the memory of
betrayal and loss, the arch-nemeses have set a course for
revenge—but who will be left alive at the end?

"Supremely plotted and incredibly well-written."

The Independent on Sunday

"Schwab's characters feel vital and real... [T]his is a rare superhero novel as epic and gripping as any classic comic. Schwab's tale of betrayal, self-hatred, and survival will resonate with superhero fans as well as readers who have never heard of Charles Xavier or Victor von Doom."

Publishers Weekly (starred review)

"Vicious is the superhero novel I've been waiting for: fresh, merciless, and yes, vicious."

Mira Grant, New York Times bestselling author

"Schwab writes with the fiendish ingenuity, sardonic wit, and twisted imagination of a true supervillian."

Greg Cox, New York Times bestselling author

"A dynamic and original twist on what it means to be a hero and a villain. A killer from page one... highly recommended!"

Jonathan Maberry, New York Times bestselling author

"Schwab gathers all the superhero/supervillain tropes and turns them on their sundry heads... I could not put it down."

F. Paul Wilson, New York Times bestselling author

"Vivid, highly original, Vicious is a masterclass in storytelling, a superlative left-field take on familiar superhero tropes that is, quite simply, unmissable."

Adam Christopher, author of Empire State

"An epic collision of super-powered nemeses. The writing and storycraft is Schwab's own superpower as this tale leaps off the page in all its dark, four-color comic-book glory."

Chuck Wendig, author of Blackbirds

TITANBOOKS.COM

AFTERPARTY

DARYL GREGORY

In the years after the smart drug revolution, any high school student with a chemjet can print drugs... or invent them. A teenaged girl finds God through a new brain-altering drug called Numinous, used as a sacrament by a Church that preys on the underclass. But she is arrested and put into detention, and without the drug, commits suicide.

Lyda Rose, another patient in the detention facility, has a dark secret: she was one of the original scientists who developed the drug, and is all too aware of what it can do; she has her own personal hallucinated angel to remind her. With the help of an ex-government agent and the imaginary, drug-induced Dr. Gloria, Lyda sets out to find the other three survivors of the five who made the Numinous to try and set things right...

"A great giggling psychedelic trip down the big pharma rabbit hole."

Paolo Bacigalupi,
Hugo and Nebula Award-winning author of *The Windup Girl*

ECKO RISING

DANIE WARE

Ecko is an unlikely saviour: a savage, gleefully cynical rebel/ assassin, he operates out of hi-tech London, making his own rules in a repressed and subdued society, When the biggest job of his life goes horribly wrong, Ecko awakes in a world he doesn't recognise: a world without tech, weapons, cams, cables – anything that makes sense to him. Can this be his own creation, or is it something much more?

If Ecko can win though, then he might just learn to care – or break the program and get home.

"Science-fiction with the safety catch off."

Adam Nevill, author of *Apartment 16*

"Strange, surprising, haunting and exceedingly well written. Not to be missed."

Lavie Tidhar, World Fantasy Award-winning author of *Osama*

Chosen as one of *The Independent on Sunday's* SF Books of the Year 2012 and the *Financial Times'* Best Books of 2012

PIRATE CINEMA

CORY DOCTOROW

Trent McCauley is obsessed with making movies. But when his illegal download habit causes his family's Internet to be cut off, he's forced to run away from Bradford to London. Squatting in an East End pub, Trent falls in with a band of activists who introduce him to dumpster diving, graveyard raves and the anarchist girl of his dreams. When a new bill threatens to criminalise Internet creativity, the future looks bleak, but the film industry fat cats—and the MPs they hold in their pocket—haven't reckoned with the power of a gripping movie to change people's minds...

"A counter-culture rabble rouser."

Booklist (starred review)

"Doctorow's books are just too enlightening to miss."

Wired

DEPTH

LEV AC ROSEN

Depth combines hardboiled mystery and dystopian science fiction in a future where the rising ocean levels have left New York twenty-one stories under water and cut off from the rest of the United States. But the city survives, and Simone Pierce is one of its best private investigators. Her latest case, running surveillance on a potentially unfaithful husband, was supposed to be easy. Then her target is murdered, and the search for his killer points Simone towards a secret from the past that can't possibly be real—but that won't stop the city's most powerful men and women from trying to acquire it for themselves, with Simone caught in the middle.

AVAILABLE JUNE 2015

TITANBOOKS.COM

NEW POMPEII

DANIEL GODFREY

Sometime in the near future, energy giant NovusCorp develops technology with an unexpected side-effect: it can transport objects and people from deep in the past to the present day.

For post-grad historian Nick Houghton, the controversy surrounding the programme matters less than the opportunity the company offers him. NovusCorp's executives reveal their biggest secret: they have saved most of the people from Pompeii, minutes before the volcanic eruption. Somewhere in central Asia, far from prying eyes, the company has built a replica of the city. In it are thousands of real Romans.

The Romans may be ignorant of modern technology – for now – but city boss Marcus Barbatus wasn't appointed by the emperor because he was soft. The Romans carved out the biggest empire the world had ever seen, thanks to the uncompromising leadership of men like Barbatus. The stage is set for the ultimate clash of cultures…

AVAILABLE AUGUST 2016

TITANBOOKS.COM

What did you think of this book?

We love to hear from our readers.
Please email us at readerfeedback@titanemail.com
or write to us at the above address.

To receive advance information, news, competitions,
and exclusive offers online, please sign up for the Titan
newsletter on our website:

www.titanbooks.com